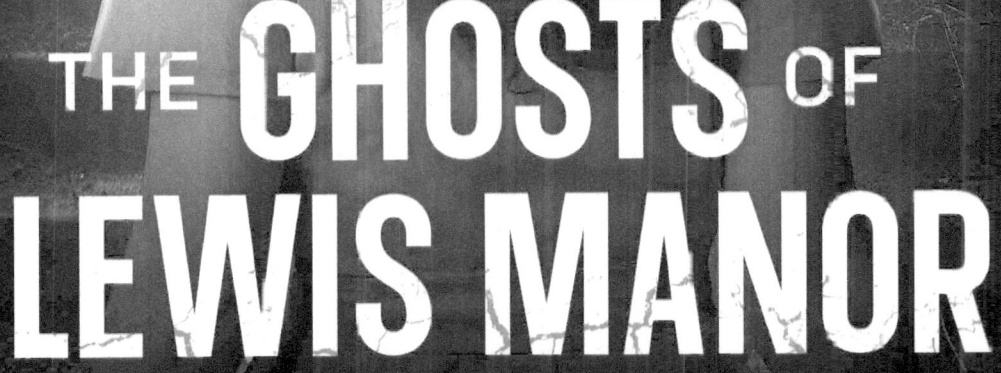

MARCIA ARMANDI

THE GHOSTS OF LEWIS MANOR

THE GHOSTS OF LEWIS MANOR

MARCIA ARMANDI

CITY OWL
PRESS

THE GHOSTS OF LEWIS MANOR
By Marcia Armandi

CITY OWL PRESS
www.cityowlpress.com

Cover Design by MiblArt. All stock photos licensed appropriately.

Edited by Lisa Green.

For information on subsidiary rights, please contact the publisher at info@cityowlpress.com.

Print Edition ISBN: 978-1-64898-230-9

Digital Edition ISBN: 978-1-64898-229-3

Printed in the United States of America

To my husband, Chad, and our children Zach, Brooke, and Conner, who are the greatest joy in my life.

PROLOGUE

Too soon, I was startled awake. My Yorkshire terrier's whining and scratching at the side of the bed finally registered. I came to, clutching my blanket. Almost immediately, the bomb sirens went off, followed by my parents shouting to get to the pavement. Mechanically, I bolted from bed, counting out loud. *One*, I put on my coat and shoes. *Two*, I snatched up Piper with one arm. *Three*, I grabbed the bag.

Next thing I knew, we were out of the house and into the night. Under the faint moon, the row houses looked like soldiers in formation, standing stalwart amid the unfolding chaos. Merging with the stampede of people, we rushed down the road toward the Underground, my heart thumping against my ribs as hard as Piper's. Though we had the routine established by now, fleeing for our lives was never easy. I pressed my hand tighter against Piper's chest to comfort her.

I felt for my little friend. This was much different from the peaceful evening strolls she had been accustomed to. The star-filled nights accompanied by a soft, calming breeze sweeping the streets of London were a thing of the past. Along with that, my job as an assistant teacher at the school had also gone. Last week a bomb had erased much of its south wing and its inner court, prompting its closure indefinitely.

Complicating matters, being unemployed destroyed my hopes of securing my own flat and becoming independent anytime soon. For irremediably, while I lived under my parents' roof, they would continue to regard me as a child. And at almost twenty years old, I was hardly one. Not surprisingly, they did not favor the idea of me living on my own, unless, of course, I left London altogether.

Calling me back to the escalating commotion, Father encouraged in a wheezy voice, "Almost there," as the rumbling of the airplanes filled the sky. At any moment, the bombers would start their brutal attack, lighting up the city in flames.

"There it is," Mother exclaimed as the staircase into the Underground materialized as if from a dream. It was strange to think that hell was above us, heaven in the ground below.

"Mum, where are you? Please don't leave me," a faint yet poignant voice pleaded.

Piper's ears pricked and pointed, and a soft growl grew in her throat. I came to a halt, searching for the owner of the voice.

"Mum, where are you? Please don't leave me. Please."

"Seraphina, what are you doing? Keep moving!" Father ordered.

"Do you hear that?"

"Hear what?"

"A child. There is a child."

My parents listened for a moment or two, and though the child cried again, I could tell from their blank looks they could hear nothing beyond the sound of the feet scrambling past us.

Mother shook her head. "Come on, we mustn't linger. It's not safe." As if fulfilling her words, the first blast sounded in the distance, followed by a successive wave of smaller explosions. The Nazis came in waves, dropping explosives over the city and then incendiary bombs on the already burning warehouses.

As my parents moved down the stairs, I lingered, still listening for the child. Piper began to kick, and before I could stop her, she leaped out of my arms to the ground, dashing toward the shops.

"Please don't leave me!" pleaded the voice again as I turned to rush after Piper.

Then I saw him—a boy huddled by the window of the chemist shop. The wretched appearance of the tiny creature made my heart ache. He was not more than five or six years old, and still in his pajamas and barefoot, he had not been prepared to leave his house. His fist was clenched between his teeth as he sobbed.

"Seraphina, come back here!" I heard my parents desperately calling behind me as I hurried to reach the boy.

"Have you lost your mum?" I asked, halting but a few feet from him.

His large teary eyes stared back at me, but he said nothing.

"Listen, it's all right. I can help you."

Piper emerged from behind a magazine kiosk and suddenly barked at the boy with a fury I hadn't seen from her.

"Piper, stop! You'll frighten him!"

The boy turned his head to look at her, and she pranced backward, retreating a considerable distance.

"Come on. Come with me," I invited, extending my hand to him.

"Will you help me find my mummy?" the child sobbed in a high, piercing voice that brought a chill to my body.

"Yes, I'll help you find her." Seeing his hesitation, I knelt to gather him, but he vanished. There was nothing in my grasp but air. He had not been a child but one of...*them*.

Rampant chills cut through my skin—I'd tried to embrace a ghost— and there was nothing but a frosty emptiness in its spot.

"Seraphina, what in the world are you doing?" Mother's voice rang in my ears, and I turned to face my parents, who had hustled after me. They stared at me in confusion, their eyes flitting to the empty spot upon which I knelt.

"I..." I stuttered but never found the words.

The bewilderment of the moment was interrupted by a bomber flying overhead. And almost instantly, the ground shook as a bomb lit the night sky, much too close to our street. Grabbing my wrist, Father said, "Enough," not giving me a chance to protest.

"Piper, come on—let's go," Mother called.

At her command, Piper, who had cowered under the awning of a shop at the explosion, joined us. I gathered her trembling body in my arms, aware that I wasn't fending much better.

While we marched back to the underground, my situation became clear; as I looked at their faces and could see the old debate was lost—after tonight, I would have no choice but to be sent away from London. Air raids were one thing, but my life was doubly vulnerable to the death and destruction they brought, for I could see the dead.

And, it appeared, they could now see me.

CHAPTER 1
NEWFOUND FREEDOM

Brockenhurst, the New Forest, England, 1942

As the train creaked into the station, my thoughts remained on the incident that had landed me here. I was not sure when I first became aware I could see the dead. In my nineteen years of life, they had hovered around the edges of my awareness like a faint melody heard from another room. When I was younger, they'd blended with the living well enough—the girl in an old-fashioned dress in the park who'd ignored my invitation to play, the old man with a blank look who'd stood on our porch one moment and was gone the next. The sightings were rare, and as an adult, I treated those old memories as dreams. That was, until the war started. The overwhelming number of disembodied spirits roaming the streets of the city could not be ignored.

Thankfully, most spirits—at least those *I'd* encountered—seemed oblivious to the world of the living, completely absorbed with whatever it was they did. They paid me no heed, and though seeing them had been slightly disconcerting, I considered them mostly benign. That was, until the boy called for my attention.

Being deceived to the point of endangering my family made me realize I might have to look more closely at this ability, for if I failed to comprehend what lay beyond the veil separating the living from the dead, I could find myself on the wrong side of it. The thought was grim. For if I were to ever understand the supernatural world, I would have to step farther in. But as I considered the possibility, goose bumps crawled up my arms, and fear of the unknown made me think better of it. I decided to brush away the uncomfortable thought as the train finally stopped, and I rose to gather my belongings. After all, I was here to escape the ghosts.

Alighting from the train, the first thing I noticed was the sky. Compared to the hellish brew of London, it was vast and endless—paradisal to behold. Yet dragging my suitcase across the platform, I felt the part of a vagabond, a refugee from the land of the dead. Piper sniffed the air, which had the refreshing scent of recent rain.

The other travelers brushed past me, impatiently trying to get on with their journeys. Feeling a little of that impatience myself, I readjusted Piper in my arms and took a fruitless lap around the station, avoiding the puddles as best I could. The groundskeepers of All Hallows, the Goswicks, were supposed to fetch me. But no one appeared to be looking for me.

Within minutes, I was the only person in sight except for the clerk behind the ticket window and a man wiping the water droplets off a black car in the parking lot. "Excuse me, sir," I said to the clerk. "Is there a way to call for a cab?"

His dark eyes rose to meet mine as he put down the pipe he had been smoking apparently nonstop, for he stood in a cloud of fumes. "How far are you going?"

"Burley. I understand it is a neighboring town?"

"That's correct, and Albert Craven"—he pointed at the man by the car—"offers local transportation." Looking at his wristwatch, he added, "You might want to speak to him right away. He usually leaves about now."

"I'm most obliged, sir."

Mr. Craven was a middle-aged man with a thick mustache and bushy eyebrows. Folding the cloth in his hand, he took a step back from his vehicle—an unmarked, older car I would have never guessed to be a cab —to make sure he hadn't missed any water spots. Piper growled as we approached, capturing his immediate attention.

"Good afternoon, sir. The clerk told me you are a cab driver. I'm in need of a lift to Burley."

"Indeed, I am." He extended his hand to me. "Craven, miss. Albert Craven."

"Seraphina Addington." I met his strong grip with my own.

"Burley, you said?"

"Yes."

"Not too far from here, about five miles. We can be there in a jiffy."

"Thank you." I was relieved, hoping that once I reached the Goswicks, I would regain a bit of that security which came from belonging somewhere.

After the incident in London, Father had contacted General John Lewis, an old comrade of his from the Great War, and accepted his previous offer to let me stay at his country house, away from the chaos of the conflict. Prior to becoming a general, John Lewis had been a familiar face, the image of an uncle in my mind. He was a wealthy and influential man but also acquainted with grief, having lost his wife at a young age and never remarried. Of course, we hadn't seen him since the war broke out.

"If you'll permit," the man said as he hefted my suitcase into the boot of the car. I settled into the back with Piper snuggled against the folds of my blue dress, which Mother insisted I wear, arguing that it matched my eyes and contrasted with my brown hair. I had acquiesced only to avoid an unnecessary confrontation on the day of my departure. Under any other circumstances, I would have worn slacks despite her disapproval. She was one of those who clung to the past, shunning twentieth-century styles.

The car left the station, making all sorts of racket and complaining of long-needed maintenance. The roads were lined with thatched-roof cottages that sat far back from the street, some with hydrangea hedges, others with evergreen shrubs. When we reached the end of the paved streets, Mr. Craven turned onto a rural road guarded by trees of every shape and sort. Through them, I caught glimpses of meadowland flowing through the ancient yews. It was breathtakingly green.

I was surprised to feel the unexpected beauty and calmness of my surroundings flood me, the contrast with what I had left behind startling. The war had taken so much from us, and we had quite rapidly adjusted to its ugliness—the sky dotted with black-and-red clouds of smoke as if heaven itself cried over the world; the explosions of the bombs followed by the shattering of windows; the mangled corpses; and for me, the spirits of the dead who walked aimlessly amid the rubble.

The New Forest, brimming with life, reminded me that our world was still beautiful, our people resilient. The war would end, and we would rise stronger and rebuild all that had been lost. Now that I was away from my family and needed a steadiness to allay my fears for them, I resolved to hold on to this belief more than ever.

Piper rearranged herself on the seat as we bumped along the muddy road. I ran my hand reassuringly through her fur, steadying my emotions at the same time. No doubt she would prefer the country to the air raids, which spared no one, tormenting humans and animals alike.

Apologetically, Mr. Craven explained, "The main road to Burley gets particularly nasty after a rainstorm. You must forgive me, but I'm taking a detour. A longer route through the forest. We don't want old Harvey getting stuck in the mud—no, surely not."

The car has a name. I smiled.

Up ahead, trotting gently along the roadside, a group of soldiers on horseback headed in our direction. Mr. Craven steered Harvey to the side of the road, if *road* was the proper name for this patch of mud in the woods.

"That's the Mounted Home Guard," he informed proudly. "They are volunteer soldiers operating out of Breamore. Great lads, they are. We also have both British and American troops stationed here, but thankfully, no bombs have fallen yet. Well, apart from Southampton, that is. The port is a target, but we've been spared farther inland."

"That's a mercy from heaven. Let us hope it remains like this." I had seen firsthand the erasure of history, brick and mortar, paper and binding. Hundreds of years destroyed in a matter of minutes.

"Where in Burley are you staying? Where should I let you out?"

"I'm not sure how to find it. I'm afraid I don't have an address."

"Don't fret, miss. In these parts, places have names. That's how we find them, not by numbers or anything like that."

"The name escapes me at the moment, but I'm a guest of General Lewis."

"Oh, I see. He is well known in the region—he owns the Burley mansion. The largest structure in the region." Just as he said that, a new thought seemed to startle him. "Wait, are you certain? The mansion currently serves as a military post—soldiers coming in and out all day. Not a good destination for a young lady, if you know what I mean."

The straightforward honesty of country folk was something I could get used to. "Agreed. No, I'm not going to the mansion. I understand the general owns a country house as well."

"You aren't speaking of All Hallows, are you?" His gaze found mine through the rearview mirror. For a split second, a shadow of disbelief crossed what I could see of his face.

"Yes, that sounds about right. I'll be staying there until things settle down in London."

He reached to loosen the collar of his shirt as if it suddenly strangled him. "That could be a long time...a long time indeed, to be in a house like that."

Was there something wrong with the house? Leaning forward, I asked, "Mr. Craven, what do you mean, 'in a house like that'?"

When he took longer than needed to respond, I knew he would not disclose the truth; however, I kept my gaze on him through the mirror until he did answer.

"It's one of the oldest houses in the region. Hundreds of years of history, you understand. I'm afraid All Hallows's fame will live forever. But it has been deserted since..."

"Since when?"

"An awfully long time...I didn't think it was habitable anymore."

"For my sake, I hope it is. But why is it famous? I imagine there are plenty of old houses around here competing for fame."

"Actually...since I've never been to the manor, I'm afraid my opinion wouldn't be an educated one." He cleared his throat, obviously unhappy with my questioning.

"I would still like to hear it."

"It's better that you wait to hear it from those familiar with the place." These last words he said with finality, putting an end to the subject.

His reason for not sharing was simply an excuse. Just as I considered pressing him further, the car slowed to almost an idling stage, but I couldn't see any reason for it. Piper lifted her head as high as she could, ears pointed, eyes wide open, in response to the unexpected change.

"Is anything the matter?"

"Miss, I thought you were going downtown. The manor is on the outskirts, and the roads are impossible during this weather. I'm afraid all I can do is let you out in town. Maybe you can spend the night there— rethink things?"

Rethink things? What did I have to rethink? Even if I wanted to stay in town, I had no money to spare. "Surely the roads can't be any worse than the ones we've traveled on."

In a faltering voice that betrayed his businesslike approach, he replied, "If the car gets stuck, it would be days before I could get any help. So, no, I can't drive you there." He glanced at the lowering sun. "No one would, at least not until tomorrow."

I said the first words that came to mind. "You must be having a laugh." I imagined Mother's response to such boldness, but after all, I had not come this far just to come this far. "There must be another way. Tell me there is."

He thought for a moment or two. By the way he fidgeted in his seat, I could tell he fought whatever idea he considered. At last, he let it out. "There is, but I don't recommend it. The forest is not safe for a woman to go about alone."

"It involves walking, then?"

He moved his head in assent.

I turned his words in my mind. There were areas in London where women felt unsafe to travel alone, daylight or not. I'd had to traverse them a time or two. This couldn't be any worse. *I should have brought*

Mother's frying pan. I had seen her chase away several solicitors with it. It worked wonders.

"Walking Piper and I can handle. We just need directions."

He frowned as if saying, *"The foolishness of this woman will get her in trouble,"* but aloud, he said, "I can drop you off at the edge of Oker field. The manor is not far from there." He paused and then suggested yet again, "But I must insist that staying in town is a wise choice." The assertion made me want to successfully brave the trail to All Hallows all the more.

"I'll take my chances."

With a severe expression of disapproval, Mr. Craven pressed his foot on the gas pedal. Harvey picked up speed, and at length, we came to a lane free of trees on one side. I leaned against the window to observe wild ponies roaming freely in the fields. If ponies were the type of threat my driver was worried about, my biggest challenge would be to keep Piper's excitement under control. She did not like anything, apart from her own kind, that had four legs, and she made sure they knew it.

The more I focused on the scenery, the more ponies I saw. "Oh my. There are so many of them."

"They belong to the commoners," Mr. Craven informed. "They have the right to graze their animals in the forest. A good thing too. The ponies and the cattle help maintain the landscape."

The vehicle made its way deeper into the woods, and soon the ponies were but a distant image. I was about to ask Mr. Craven how much longer we had when Harvey produced a jerking sound and came to a halt in the middle of nowhere. There were no houses in sight, just a welded wire fence guarding the meadow. Beyond that was a thickly wooded area. It was so still it didn't seem real.

I noticed Mr. Craven's hand tremble as he looked at his wristwatch. But the hour appeared to calm his nerves, for he said, "Oh, good." I imagined he meant that the remaining daylight was good enough for me to make the journey on foot. I certainly hoped that was the case, for time could be treacherous when moving against it.

With unexpected agility, he sprang from the car as though a fire burned unattended somewhere and opened the back door for me to follow suit. I stepped out and immediately felt my shoes—my nicest pair, meant to accompany the dress—sink into the wet ground. Piper jumped down after me.

"Remember, cross the field and go straight south through those trees. You'll see the manor soon enough." He flipped the boot open and quickly set my bag on the grass. Piper barked at the rushed handling of our property. "May I suggest you waste no time."

Civility, though I wasn't feeling it at the moment, called for me to say thank you. I handed him a few bills to cover the ride. He stashed them in his pocket without counting them.

"It's not too far. You'll be all right," he said, as if willing it to be true. Without further ado, he was back in his car. Harvey made a sharp turn, and with surprising speed, Mr. Craven drove away.

CHAPTER 2
CAPTAIN ROSS STEWART

My gaze swept over the meadow. Its terrain, covered by dense wild grass, challenged my ability to drag the suitcase toward the fence. I sighed at how circumstances had modified my perspective, for yesterday I had wished to own a bigger bag. Now, I was conscious that I had brought too much.

I looked down at my dress. I should have worn slacks. Now and forever, comfort was more sensible than protocol. Why society had for so long confined women to disadvantageous clothing was beyond my understanding. Fuming at the inconvenience of my attire and the unfavorable conditions of nature, I pressed on, the bag's weight already slowing me down.

"Come on, girl. We must beat dusk," I encouraged the poor wretch behind me as she scampered from one muddy patch to the next. "What a little coward you are." I nearly laughed. She looked the sight of a mouse set loose from its cage—very small and shabby in the grass. Yet as we emerged onto higher ground, she soon discovered the joy of unprecedented freedom. She had always been a house dog, but here in the vast tranquility of the open space, she was a free spirit.

A sudden kinship with her new attitude struck me. My entire existence, I had also been a house pet, confined by the restrictions of my parents and their constant hovering—a hovering that had intensified in the past months. Whilst I had always resisted their old-fashioned views, lately it seemed futile to fight over insignificant things —like my choice of clothing—when at any given moment one of us could be taken by the war. Of course, I tried to get away with what I could, but it wasn't much.

I had concluded that my being their only child was the main reason for their overzealous care. And that, along with the war and my ability to see the dead, had them at the end of their tethers. Hence, sending me away must have been extremely difficult for them. They'd had to consider it an absolute necessity for my well-being, especially since they couldn't accompany me.

Father, being at the head of the Royal Mail in east London, was needed more than ever. And Mother couldn't fathom the idea of abandoning her husband amid the chaos.

"The country air will do wonders for you," my mother had said. "It will heal your troubled soul." And here I was, alone for the first time in my life, hoping to have left behind more than just physical danger. What I hadn't thought of was that I now had to face freedom on my own. All I could hope for was to handle it without regrets.

But just now, I had a different problem to tackle. I studied the fence and the wrought-iron gate obstructing my path. Faint tracks on the ground revealed that at some point in time, a road had gone through here, but precautions had been taken to shut it down. I rested the suitcase against the gate, not believing my eyes. There was a thick chain at the center with a lock in place. The lock was somewhat newer and used a combination of numbers instead of a key.

Piper slipped through the bars without difficulty, but my size and the rusted conditions of the metal made me hesitant to try the same route. I fidgeted with the lock, trying all sorts of numbers, hoping that if it didn't open, it would somehow break. I wrestled with it until my fingers hurt. Right combination or not, it wouldn't budge.

Dreading the solution at hand, I strategically squeezed through the two center bars. *I suppose food rationing offers the occasional advantage.* Once on the other side, marveling that I hadn't gotten stuck, I looked down at my clothing. The oxidation had left long streaks on my dress.

Well, I look more like a convict than a lady. I wish Mother could see me now.

Reaching my arms back through the gate, I tugged my bag toward me. Too thick, it clashed against the metal. With a sigh of exasperation, I unzipped it and pulled out clothing until I could force it through. After repacking it, I started across the field, easing the growing pain in my arms by alternating hands to drag the bag. It hadn't occurred to me to ask Mr. Craven how many miles he spoke of when he said "not too far." It had sounded like a walk in the park, but in reality, it was more like crossing the Sahara Desert. And I wondered if the trees were a mirage, for the closer I got, the farther they seemed.

Nonetheless, the fading day urged me to pick up my speed, only to find that the grass became taller, making it difficult to see where and on what my feet landed. My arms were burning now, and if it weren't that I most definitely needed my belongings, I would have gladly given up on them.

Piper barked from a distance, her voice echoing through the field. As soon as my eyes found her in the dense chickweed, she vanished into the woods with great enthusiasm. Under other circumstances, her optimism would be contagious, but all I wanted now was to reach my destination in one piece and set down this blasted bag.

One step at a time, I went on, and I was almost overjoyed when at last I reached the edge of the forest. Giving my arms a break, I stopped to assess the imposing trees that shot up in magnificent height, like guardians of the somber woods. In a trice, an oversized rook dove to the ground from a high branch. I gave a startled jump at its sudden drop.

The bird looked at me with surreal intelligence, as if trying to speak to me. I took a half step forward, and the rook smacked his beak on the forest floor's debris. I took another step, and his claws stabbed the ground, scattering leaves and twigs from the spot.

Was he warning me of something? Or was he just overzealous of his territory?

Go around him. Matching the speed of my thought, the bird's gaze pierced mine. I felt chills crawl up my spine, like when I had tried to embrace the ghost of the child. *No, not here, not now.*

While fighting the growing uneasiness, my peripheral vision caught movement along the tree line to my right. An obscure form moved slowly in my direction, and instinctively, my gaze fixed upon it, fearing to lose sight of it. Almost imperceptibly, it formed into a man.

Could this be Mr. Goswick? Had he heard of my arrival and come looking for me? My supposition proved vain when, through squinted eyes, I saw him through the pale twilight mist. The man wore a helmet, tall boots, and a rifle over his shoulder. *A soldier.*

With a petrifying shriek, the rook took flight. And simultaneously something brushed against my foot. *A snake?* I hated snakes. My gaze found the perpetrator, and relieved that it wasn't anything slithery, I exclaimed, "Piper! You silly dog. Where have you been?" Like a leaf flying in the wind, she made a few frenzied laps around me.

When I looked up again, the soldier was gone. At that moment, Piper let out an explosive howl whilst the hackles along her neck went up. I attempted to grab her, but she would have none of it. Her behavior was concerning, for she had done this in London when the ghosts were near. And at this point, I could use a break from the war as well as the disembodied spirits.

Perhaps prompted by Piper's rackety, a fleet of rooks catapulted from the treetops, cawing with a nerve-racking pitch. As they flew overhead and formed a black wall, the daylight seemed to diminish, and for that instant, the universe stood still. Only the birds moved.

When they were quite a ways across the meadow, Piper broke out barking again. "Piper, stop!" Raising her snout as far as she could without her front paws leaving the ground, she emitted another long cry that made my skin crawl. "Stop it—right now!"

Ignoring my reprimands, she bolted into the trees, producing howls mixed with short barks that did nothing but disrupt the forest. I plunged after her. Since the ground here wasn't as moist as that of the field, I was able to travel faster. As Piper's voice faded away, silence surrounded me, and I became acutely aware that I had lost too much time. *I need to reach the Goswicks.* With renewed resolution, I marched on, tackling one yard at a time until quite a few had been left behind.

Then, of course, I realized I might have lost all sense of direction.

South. Am I still going south? Under the thick canopy of trees and the lateness of the hour, it was impossible to tell. Though my orientation was disrupted, my hearing sharpened at a fast-approaching sound. This forest was proving to be anything but peaceful. The now thundering noise seemed vaguely familiar, but I couldn't place it, even when it grew near. With the hairs on the back of my neck raised, just like Piper's moments ago, I backed up against the security of a redwood tree.

From behind a hedge of shrubs emerged a horse. Jet black and sturdy, it neighed at the sight of me. Its rider beheld me with a startled look. He had not expected to find me here. Piper was happily seated in front of the young soldier, his arm around her.

I supposed I bore the same disconcerted expression as I regarded him and Piper. What had I anticipated? A monster? A demon? Thank heaven, it was none of that. And seeing Piper's wagging tail, relief washed over me, along with a sense of chagrin at my overactive imagination.

The soldier spoke. "Who are you? What are you doing out here?" His strong American accent made me question if I'd misunderstood him, but his displeased and suspicious expression clarified things. I had not misheard. He'd spoken in a casual, if not disrespectful, manner.

Bothered by the way he'd addressed me, I responded with another question, "What are you doing with my dog?"

"This disturber of the peace is yours, then?"

"I'm afraid so."

He visually scouted the area before dismounting and handing Piper to me. Naturally, I made a quick assessment: he was taller than most men. I had to look up to meet his gaze, and I was not short for my gender. He had dark-brown hair and eyes, a tanned face, and distinct features.

"He could benefit from a leash, you know."

"She. Piper is a she."

"Well, that explains it."

"Explains what?" I averted my gaze and gave Piper a few pats on the head.

"Her temper. She doesn't know she's a small breed. She acts like a Great Dane."

He was so quaintly American I was forced to laugh. "Good things come in small packages, Mr....?"

"Captain Ross Stewart, United States Air Force." While we shook hands, I noticed his uniform somewhat resembled that of the soldier I had seen, though there had been something unique about the other. I tried to force the details of the recollection, but they remained elusive. Then again, it could have been the same man. "But call me Ross," he added, pulling me from my thoughts.

"Seraphina Addington." Retrieving my hand, I took a step backward as his eyes bored into mine. I could only imagine how disheveled I looked after the long walk and my colorful encounter with the gate. "But call me Miss Addington."

He produced a short laugh. "Not a chance." Evidently, he did not like being told what to do. How did he manage being in the military? He proceeded to look me up and down. "Having a rough day, Seraphina?"

"I suppose you could say that, *Captain* Stewart."

"Ross. My name is Ross, remember?"

I sighed. Americans and their manners. "Very well, Ross."

"What are you doing out here? This is not a place for a woman to take a Sunday walk."

Rather than be put in my place, I decided to match his overly familiar and confident style for the duration of our exchange. "Thank goodness it's not Sunday, then," I retorted. "And I've been warned about the forest already."

"Yeah, and you obviously heeded the advice." He produced a smile that would have disarmed any other girl, but not me. I had never been one to fall easily for roguish charm.

Intrigued again if he had been the elusive soldier I'd seen earlier, I fished for the truth. "If I shouldn't be here, then why didn't you stop me when you saw me in the field?"

"I didn't see you in the field." He looked at me, puzzled.

"Hmm. There was a soldier on foot not ten yards from the clearing."

"A few of us patrol these woods. But there is never more than one in each sector at a time," Ross said. "My watch goes until midnight, so no one else should be out here."

There was no reason to disbelieve him. Nevertheless, there *had* been someone else in uniform out here. More to myself than to him, I reflected, "If it wasn't you, who did I see?"

"Are you sure it was a soldier?"

"Quite sure."

"Can you describe him?"

"No, he was too far away for me to see his features."

"What made you think he was a soldier?"

"He wore a helmet and carried a rifle," I responded with total assurance. "That's all I can tell you, but there is no doubt in my mind that he was one of yours."

"Okay...did you see which way he went?"

"No. I'm afraid Piper distracted me, and when I looked back, he was gone."

"How...unfortunate." I had the clear impression his words said more than I'd heard. He seemed truly intrigued with the possibility of this other soldier. However, he gently changed the topic. "Well, you haven't told me where *you* are going."

"All Hallows, but I'm not sure I'm headed in the right direction."

Piper yawned, rested her head on my arm, and closed her eyes. The poor thing had had enough of our adventure already. All I could hope was that the worst was behind us.

"Are you talking about the old house on the southwest side?" Ross inquired.

Was I? I didn't know, but I wasn't about to say so. He probably thought me a sufficient fool already. On the other hand, I understood All Hallows was quite isolated, so the odds were in my favor.

"That's the one."

"What in the world are you going there for? It's deserted, isn't it? And yes, you are off track."

"It's not deserted. The Goswicks live there. I'm staying with them."

"The Goswicks?" he said with an edge in his voice.

"Do you know them?"

"I see them now and then but don't really know them." A light flickered in his eyes. "Wait, General Lewis owns that house. Are you his guest?"

To hear the name General Lewis—something familiar—was reassuring.

"He's an old comrade of my father from the Great War."

"Oh yeah?" Ross chuckled. "You should have started there. I wouldn't want to cross the general by mistreating his guest. I'm stationed at the Burley mansion. I work under his supervision."

Why hadn't it occurred to me? Mr. Craven had mentioned the mansion's function as a military station. "That's good to know." Finally, I could relax a little. Accountability to his superior officer played in my favor, or so I hoped.

Ross's gaze fell on the inert bag beside me, and he blurted out, "Holy smokes! Is that monstrosity yours?"

I was divided between annoyance and amusement. It wasn't hard to guess what had crossed his mind—I looked too feeble for the task. True, I was slim, but I wasn't weak. Regaining some ground, I answered, "Of course it's mine. Who else's would it be? A cab dropped us off somewhere on the other side, and we cut through Oker field. And believe it or not, I carried the *monstrosity* all this way. See for yourself." I kicked the suitcase onto its side to display the mud-covered leather. He looked swiftly at the bag, then at me, and then at the former again.

"Why didn't the driver just take you to the manor?"

"He said the roads were too muddy."

Ross shook his head in disbelief. "The people around here never stop surprising me," he said, and as if he remembered something, he scanned our surroundings with intensity. "But we better get moving. You still have a ways to go."

I made the pathetic effort to lift the bag. Truth be told, I didn't think I could move it any farther, but I wasn't about to show it. "All right, if you would, please point me in the right direction."

He chuckled, seeing through my bravado. "You British are always protecting your pride." I was utterly lost, tired, and in need of his help, but I wouldn't admit it.

"Come with me. I'll get you there," he added.

To say anything besides "Thank you" would humiliate me further, so that's exactly what I did.

Before I realized what he was doing, he took hold of my waist. I held on to Piper as he sat me sidesaddle on the horse as easily as if I were a feather. Then he lifted the suitcase and placed it sideways in front of me. "You seriously should consider traveling lighter."

"I shall remember that." Hopefully, I would never have to carry the blessed bag through the forest again.

"You hold on to the Great Dane and the bag. I'll walk beside and lead Popeye."

"Popeye? What kind of name is that?"

"You've never heard of Popeye?"

"Should I have?"

"Maybe. Popeye is a comic-book character."

"Never heard of it."

"He is an American sailor, a regular guy, you know, built much like me—when he eats right, of course." A smile formed at the edges of his lips, though I wasn't sure why. Giving the bag a tap, he went on to say, "Whatever you do, don't drop this on me. I haven't had my spinach today."

Spinach? What an interesting fellow he is. "I shall do my best." Ross raised an eyebrow. Was he not convinced my best was enough?

Again, he looked around in all directions before taking the reins and guiding the horse through the thicket as the night continued to gather strength. In the ensuing absence of words, I became aware of a symphony of crickets, cicadas, and whatever else croaked in the woods, rapidly engulfing our journey. It was beautiful and soul-soothing.

Cutting through the evening concerto, Ross informed, "Your dog was in a fit of rage when I found her. I think she was after something."

"After what?"

"A demon."

When I didn't reply, he gave a short laugh. "I'm joking. You don't believe in those things, do you?"

If he only knew. "Of course not."

"Good, because if you did, you would go crazy out here. Burley is the cradle of ghosts and witches. It's a bunch of baloney, but the rumors keep the imagination active. I wouldn't be surprised if that's why the driver didn't take you all the way. There are plenty of stories about people being spooked at dusk on the final stretch to the house."

Crazy? Too late for that. If Mother had known, she would have kept me in London. And out of all the places under heaven, this is where I end up. So much for peace of mind.

Purposely redirecting the conversation, I reminded him, "You haven't truthfully answered my question. What do you think Piper was after?"

He shrugged. "Probably one of the ponies. They are everywhere in the woods."

"That's what the cab driver said." Knowing Piper, she could very well have been wreaking havoc with the ponies. Still, why did I have the feeling this fellow kept something from me?

"We're almost through the trees." His strides lengthened. Lightly tugging on the reins, he encouraged Popeye to keep up with him.

"I didn't imagine the New Forest to be this vast."

"Where are you from?"

"London."

"Are you escaping a lover? Pretty ugly guy, I imagine."

It was my turn to laugh. If only he were correct. But the war had taken even the ugly fellows. I told him a half-truth. "After forty consecutive air raids, my parents sent me away."

"That's war for you."

"Is that what you do?"

"What?"

"Drop bombs on cities. You said you're with the United States Air Force."

"Yep. That's what I do. You know, when you say it like that, it sounds as if we are the bad guys. We didn't start this, but we will end it. Otherwise, the whole world will be enslaved by the Nazis."

"You must forgive me. I did not mean to offend."

"None taken."

An extended silence settled between us, broken only by the plodding of the horse and the stridulation of the insects. I felt a twinge of guilt—

though the offense was unintended—for the implication in my words. Ross was irrefutably correct. The conflict had fallen upon us unsolicited. It had started in Germany with a disregard for human life and been carefully taught and nursed until out of control. And the Nazis were determined to force this conflict upon others by invading their countries.

We all knew this fight to protect our borders, to protect human life, was worth the sacrifice, though my generation had no idea what that meant until the bombs hit our city, the terror brought to our front door. Indisputably, the entrance of the Americans had given the world a renewed hope of ending the nightmare. I really had misspoken, I realized miserably.

Breaching the awkwardness, I asked, "Where in the United States do you hail from?"

"California."

"People say it's beautiful there."

"It is," he said guardedly. Perhaps he had indeed been bothered by my comments.

Gently, I reflected, "It must be difficult to be away from your family— your parents, your siblings."

"Not really, though I miss the beach and the girls."

I didn't respond. Through the failing light, I saw his white teeth flash a smile. Whatever his past, Ross brimmed with confidence. *I definitely should have brought my mother's frying pan.*

We traversed a few more yards, and he exclaimed, "Finally," when up ahead, a clearing, or "road," materialized. Taking a short break, he extracted a few pieces of apple from his pocket and rewarded Popeye. "Good boy." The horse ate them eagerly, then snorted and nudged Ross's chest. "That's all you get. Come on, now. Let's keep moving."

Popeye pressed into the new terrain, and my body became less tense. Here the path was smoother and gentler on my aching bones. I beheld the dark sky and quickly discovered a few feeble stars making their appearance. Their mere presence warmed my heart. I had not seen their faces since the air strikes began, and just that fast, I'd forgotten how pretty they were. They shone down on us like magnificent diamonds caressed by the moonlight. *War has taken so much from us.*

"See that dim light up ahead?" Ross asked.

"I think so. It's dim, all right."

"That's where the Goswicks live."

As we approached, the light grew brighter, and I could see a cottage.

"They don't live in the manor?"

"No." Pointing to another spot, he added, "But there's All Hallows."

Behind the cottage, I could just make out the shape of an enormous house hunched in the darkness, waiting. An imposing structure that felt like an entity of its own—a living entity. I thought about Mr. Craven's refusal to come this far and his carefully chosen words—words that revealed nothing—about the manor. The warmth in my heart was abruptly replaced by a biting coldness that made me shudder.

CHAPTER 3
THE GOSWICKS

Ross took my suitcase and set it on the ground, then reached for Piper. She gave a whimper of protest, not happy with the exchange. I slid off the horse before the soldier could reach for me. Not up to finishing the walk in the dark, my legs wobbled a little as they hit the ground.

"Are you okay?"

"It's been a while since I last rode a horse." An understatement. I had been twelve at the time, and it had been a short enterprise for which I had been prepared. Riding sideways while holding Piper and the suitcase had been nothing less than a strenuous, conscious effort.

"You'll be fine once your blood gets going."

"Right." I would be sore for days.

"Here, you take the Great Dane." Ross handed Piper to me. "I'll carry the bag."

"Aren't you going to tie Popeye up?"

"Nope. He won't go too far."

It was dark but for the glowworms that flitted about us, their color like lanterns on a foggy night. It made me think of the men I'd seen in the streets of London carrying lamps to find their way through the obscurity. As the thought crossed my mind, it took a sinister shape. Had those men been dead or alive?

At the cottage, I rapped firmly on the wooden door.

"Do you mind if I stick around for a bit?"

Piper perked up her ears at his words. Did I mind? No, I did not mind. He provided a sense of security amid the unknown. "Not at all."

The door swung inward, and a large, older man with white hair and of an apparently despondent disposition faced us. Piper produced an unfriendly sound before she hid her snout under my arm.

"Good evening, sir," I greeted. "I'm Seraphina Addington."

"Miss Addington?" Concern and confusion crossed the man's countenance. "We weren't expecting you today." His gaze fell upon my companion and lingered there with a trace of something unclear but intriguing.

Ross was quick to return the man's scrutiny and even quicker to interject, "Well, she's here. You are Mr. Goswick, right?"

Before the man could respond, a short, gray-haired woman with an air of competence about her surfaced from behind him. "Yes, yes," she replied, "we are the Goswicks. Samuel and Agatha Goswick, groundskeeper and housekeeper of All Hallows."

Samuel retreated to the shadows in the corner of the room, seeming content to let his wife take over.

"Miss Addington, welcome. Please, come in. Do forgive the untidiness." Her gaze swept over my dress, surely recognizing that being arranged neatly wasn't at the forefront of my day either. "We weren't expecting company."

We stepped inside a well-sized room furnished with a table, four chairs, and an old sofa propped to the side. Two lanterns hanging on the walls were the only source of light. The first thing that drew my attention was a pungent smell. The second, the bountiful vegetables lying atop the table.

"Please, do sit." With a gesture toward the kitchen, which could be seen through a small archway, she explained, "I'm making cabbage soup." In a matter of seconds, her well-trained hands had cleared the table.

I took a chair by the dining table with Piper on my lap. Agatha Goswick sat across from me. Ross remained on his feet as if he didn't trust the confines of these close quarters.

Observing her distress over our unexpected presence, I said, "Mrs. Goswick, I'm sorry about the lateness of the hour. I'm afraid I got lost in the woods. Captain Stewart"—I signaled toward him—"was kind enough to show me the way."

"Thank goodness for that." A brief smile crossed the housekeeper's round face.

"You can say that again. The forest isn't safe these days," Samuel stated, still standing in the shadows, arms folded squarely across his chest.

"General Lewis said he would inform us of your arrival. We should have met you at the station," the housekeeper observed.

"My father sent a telegram. It didn't arrive, I presume."

"Apparently not, although the general is a busy man, and things occasionally slip through the cracks."

With a little steam in his voice, Ross explained, "She was left at the east side of the woods with no clue where to go—not a good situation, if you know what I mean."

I gave him a sideways glance. Whatever he alluded to caused a sudden tension in the room. And no clue where to go? His straightforwardness was a painful reminder of my stubbornness to get to All Hallows at all costs.

Smoothing over the moment, Mrs. Goswick affirmed, "Well, well the important thing is that Miss Addington is now safe and sound." She smiled sweetly, but behind the smile, I sensed a darker comprehension.

"I would like to keep it that way," Ross said.

Piper's body stiffened in my arms, and her ears pricked in alertness. "What is it, girl?" I lowered my head to soothe her, but she produced an angry growl from deep in her throat. A moment later, the back door flung open like a small explosion and a large-framed man entered the house. When he saw us, he halted.

Piper grew frantic. Placing my hand over her eyes, I brought her to rest against my chest, and for that instant, she settled down, though she continued to sound her disapproval.

"Come meet our guests, son," invited Samuel.

The son didn't move an inch. His mother approached him

reassuringly. "Come, now." Pulling him by the arm, she coaxed him from the penumbras of the kitchen and into the dining room. A man in a black trench coat down to his ankles and who appeared to be in his early forties—much older than I anticipated by the way his mother had spoken to him—emerged. From under a head full of dark, messy, shoulder-length hair, he stared at the space past my shoulder as if I weren't there. His right fist repeatedly opened and closed, giving me the impression that he did not want to be in company.

"Name's Julius," he grunted.

Piper let out a piercing bark, and I pressed my arms around her tighter. "Shh. Hush now." Doing my best to sound confident, I greeted in a solid voice, "A pleasure to make your acquaintance, Julius. Seraphina Addington."

Piper managed another disapproving growl, though softer this time. Julius threw a cold look at her, and I noticed several scars, faded but present, on his face. Some of the cicatrices appeared to be thin and shallow, others wide and deep.

"Been out for a walk, Julius?" Ross asked. It wasn't hard to spot the mud on Julius's boots and coat hem.

"Yes, long walk it was," he responded, a glazed look in his eyes.

"We also have a daughter, Caroline," Mrs. Goswick interjected. "She's away visiting family for the week."

"If you'll excuse us, we'd better fetch some firewood for the night. Come, now, Julius, give me a hand," said Samuel as if anxious to remove his son from the meeting.

With a grunt, Julius acknowledged his father's request.

"Do bring Miss Addington's luggage to the manor," the housekeeper requisitioned.

The two large men left the cottage, Julius with my bag in tow.

"Do put the dog down, dear. Let her stretch her legs," Mrs. Goswick suggested. "Both of you must be famished. Would you like some soup?"

My answer came out a bit hastily. "No, thank you." The smell of the cabbage had extinguished most of my appetite.

Mrs. Goswick looked at Ross, and as if she had momentarily

forgotten his presence, she exclaimed, "For goodness' sake, Captain, do sit down. You'll get indigestion from all that standing."

Perhaps it was due to her firm tone, but Ross obediently settled into the chair closest to mine.

She addressed him again. "Would you like some soup?"

"Thank you, I'll pass."

She looked at me, then at him, and then back at me. "I must apologize for not having much to offer. Had I known, I would have prepared a proper meal."

"Please, there is no need for apologies," I assured her.

"May I offer tea?"

"Tea sounds lovely," I said

"Wonderful." She smiled. "That will allow old Goswick enough time to light the fireplaces at the manor. It's an icebox otherwise."

"That's considerate," observed Ross.

"Just doing our duty," Mrs. Goswick said, withdrawing, and soon she could be heard bustling about the kitchen.

Ross gazed around the room, inspecting the place with a soldier's thoroughness, while I reflected on my initial impressions of my host, especially Julius. I gave a silent sigh at my previous anticipation of a family atmosphere as I knew it. For as it was, I couldn't imagine either the Goswicks as my parents or Julius as my brother. And presently, I fought the urge to inquire about him.

The housekeeper called out from the kitchen, "Come on, little puppy. Come have your supper." Recognizing the sound of a metal bowl scraping the floor, Piper dashed for the food. I wondered if Mrs. Goswick had sacrificed one of her mixing bowls to feed the dog—a generous gesture.

The desire to know won me over, and I asked Ross, "You know Julius?"

"I see him in the woods now and then. He likes to hunt."

I lowered my voice. "Does he suffer from some kind of...impairment?"

"I don't think so," he whispered back. "His social skills are lacking, but don't underestimate him. He is a man of great cunning."

"I would never have guessed that."

"Looks can be deceiving. He is a brutal hunter, so most people steer clear of him."

"What do you mean?"

"I mean that he hunts anything and everything. No prey escapes him."

Anything and everything? His words unsettled me, but I kept it to myself. "He does seem intimidating. Yet you don't seem fazed by him."

"If I didn't have a gun, I might be." He gave me a crooked smile. "The guy is double my size."

"The scars on his face..."

"What about them?"

"How did he get them?"

Ross shrugged. "I'm not sure. From animals, perhaps."

Definitely from something that wanted to escape from him.

A few minutes later, Piper came back into the room, made two laps around the table and jumped into Ross's arms. Amazingly, Mrs. Goswick had given her a quick wash. I could only imagine that Piper's mud-drenched coat didn't sit well with the housekeeper.

"Hey, your fur is soft now," Ross said to Piper, running his hand down her back.

"And she is in a much better mood," I noted. My little friend wasn't exactly fond of water, so I suspected that treats might have been involved.

In excitement, Piper stood on her hind legs and tried to lick Ross's face.

"I think she likes you," I teased.

"Most girls do," he mumbled, dodging Piper's determined show of affection.

Mrs. Goswick returned wearing a colorful apron, wet in spots. Piper might not have behaved so well after all. "Here we are." She placed the food tray on the table and handed us our cups. Piper's attention instantly migrated from Ross to the tray, and he put her down to protect the food.

I took a swift sip of the tea, doing my best not to burn my tongue. "This is exceptionally good."

"Most of the herbs are harvested locally. Please, help yourself to a scone." Mrs. Goswick settled on the chair opposite me and Ross.

I reached for a biscuit-like cake and, from the corner of my eye, noticed Ross contemplating his drink. Of course, he probably preferred coffee.

"You have a beautiful home," I said. "That painting there. It's magnificent."

The housekeeper turned to acknowledge a painting of the sea and a man and woman standing before sunset-colored waves. It hung on the right side of the archway.

"Ah yes. That was painted by Rose Lewis a long time ago."

"Rose Lewis?" Ross inquired with a raised eyebrow.

"Yes."

Intrigued by their conversation, I inquired, "Is Rose Lewis the daughter of General Lewis?"

"Oh no. The general doesn't have children. Rose's father, Richard Lewis, was the general's cousin and owner of All Hallows," Mrs. Goswick explained. "Richard passed away, and when Rose left, the general took responsibility for the manor—taxes, maintenance, all of that, you know."

"Where did she go?" Ross asked.

The answer came in an edgy response. "No one knows. She vanished into thin air." Mrs. Goswick shifted uncomfortably on her seat. "At any rate, that was two decades ago."

"Mmm...I was under the impression Miss Lewis was murdered," he remarked in a careful manner.

I almost choked on the last bit of the lemon scone.

"I see, you have heard the rumors," she said. "But let's not forget that hearsay is nothing but the wild imagination of folks who have too much time on their hands. And *murder* is a dreadful word, young man. No trace of her was ever found; hence, as far as I'm concerned, she may still be alive." Mrs. Goswick's face clouded with emotion.

"How old was Rose?" I asked.

"Twenty years old," the housekeeper answered.

About my age.

"If she's alive, why disappear the way she did? It doesn't make sense that a young, wealthy woman would disappear into thin air, does it?" Like a hound on a scent, Ross was undeterred.

Mrs. Goswick looked down at her cup of tea. I wondered what memories had invaded her. The aging housekeeper must have cared for Rose very much, for it was evident Rose's memory brought her a great measure of sadness.

My stomach turned when Ross's inquisitiveness continued. "I mean, if she were alive, someone would have seen her or heard something about her through the years."

"Perhaps, Captain, perhaps." Mrs. Goswick collected the dishes from the table. "Now, Miss Addington—"

"Please, call me Seraphina."

"I'd rather call you Miss Addington to keep things in their proper place. I think old Goswick has had ample time to ready the house. I'll put these things away, and what do you say—shall we get going?"

"Very well." I smiled, pleased at how skillfully she had dismissed Ross's persistence. For even when the discussion was intriguing, the subject seemed to upset Mrs. Goswick.

The housekeeper went to the kitchen. Ross strode to the window and, pulling the curtains aside, peered through the glass. I joined him. Compared to London, the thick night of the country was a shock.

"Are you sure you want to stay at the manor?"

"I wouldn't have traveled so far if I wasn't." I sounded exactly the opposite of how I felt. The image of the large manor looming in the darkness came to mind. "Besides, where else would I stay?"

Facing me, Ross opened his mouth to speak but must have thought better of it, for he closed it again. His sudden forbearance seemed out of character.

"Don't worry about me. Piper and I will take care of each other." We both glanced at the little dog snuggled up by the couch.

Though Ross's expression softened, I feared my words had done nothing to alleviate his concern. Whatever notion he entertained was not pleasant. I would have pressed him had Mrs. Goswick not reappeared, a set of bulky keys in one hand, a brown basket in the other.

Proudly, she informed, "This is my favorite basket. Caroline made it out of willow branches. I've packed some food in case you get hungry later. Tomorrow, I'll stock the larder, which has been depleted for a while. But I'll make sure you have plenty of food while you are here."

Plenty of food was a luxury most did not enjoy. The memory of Mother coming home from the market with a look of utter helplessness suddenly struck me. Guilt and gratitude ran through me in equal measure. *Guilt* that I would not suffer due to my parents' sacrifice to send me here, even though they—and others in areas hit by the war where food was scarce—still would. *Gratitude* that the rural parts of England were still producing enough to feed their people and apparently with some to spare.

"That's very kind, Mrs. Goswick."

"Well then, shall we?"

"After you," Ross encouraged.

The three of us moved outside to the porch. There were no stars visible now, the clear night having been replaced by an overcast sky. The housekeeper secured the door without locking it.

"Good luck to you, Seraphina. I better get going," Ross said.

"Thank you, Captain," I said, feeling out of place calling him by his first name in front of the housekeeper, who liked to keep things proper.

"Don't mention it." With that exchange, he whistled for his horse and, in a matter of seconds, disappeared from view.

Piper, who stood beside me, let out a sharp bark, drawing my attention to the door behind us. Having believed that no one remained in the house, I was startled when the door opened and Julius's large frame materialized in the doorway—and even more startled when he said, "I'll come with you."

"Is all in order?" Mrs. Goswick asked him as he harshly shut the door behind him.

"Yes," Julius responded curtly. "I forgot my bag." He turned a bit to show his mother. It was a green satchel with a long strap over his left shoulder.

"Tools." She pointed to her son's knapsack and quickly led the way.

Once we started down the hill and into the hollow, a dense fog enveloped us on all sides. It did not seem to bother my companions. Piper took off into the darkened hollow, ignoring my call for her to return. Julius followed suit, brushing past me without a word. His bulky frame merged with the smog and soon faded away.

"Don't mind him," excused his mother. "He does things of his own accord."

That was an understatement. I wasn't at all sure what to make of his unusual behavior, but hopefully, I would not have to associate much with him.

As we neared the manor, a soft breeze blew, sweeping away some of the haze. Lanterns on each side of the door faintly beckoned to us. It wasn't until now that I noticed the many windows that, like dark eyes, seemed to watch our approach with disdain. A sense of foreboding possessed me, as if nothing good awaited me within All Hallows's walls.

CHAPTER 4
ALL HALLOWS

I had nearly paused at the disturbing thought, but Mrs. Goswick seemed undeterred, so I took a steadying breath and marched on, putting my trust in her kind efficiency. With a little effort, she pushed open the massive front door, which swung inward with the sound of splintering, rending wood.

We came into the grand hall or, more commonly, the foyer. It was spacious, with high ceilings, but poorly lit. Though it was unquestionably a mercy from heaven that the manor had electricity, it had fallen into a great state of disrepair. The housekeeper went straight to a sconce that flickered on the wall. She fidgeted with the lightbulb, the glass casing, and everything else she could touch to make it work properly. I wondered how many times she had done this.

My gaze fell on the staircase directly ahead of us. Judging by the iron handrail and ancient wood, it was better suited for a medieval castle than a country manor. It rose proudly to the second floor, where the landing split between the east and west sides of the structure.

I stepped farther in and saw that I was surrounded by ghosts. The humorous thought made me smile and loosened the tension in my chest, for the sitting room lay deep in slumber, white sheets concealing the grand piano, sofas, and armchairs. The only thing alive was the gray stone fireplace. I was comforted by the notion that in the morning, the windows would entertain a great deal of light, even though they did nothing but gather darkness at nighttime.

I was spared further rumination on this uncomfortable thought when Mrs. Goswick finally managed to stabilize the light. Now she pointed to the white sheets. "We'll have all this dealt with in the morning. Should you need anything, I shall be quite close at hand. Old Goswick and I are staying in the room adjacent to the kitchen—in the back of the house, just around the staircase."

"And Julius?"

"Julius will sleep at the cottage to keep watch over the animals."

I felt a wave of relief. Though I knew my hesitation toward him was unfounded, I couldn't fathom the idea of sleeping under the same roof.

With quick, short steps, the housekeeper traversed the sitting room to check on the fireplace. "I imagine you'd prefer to see the rest of the house during daylight?" I recognized from interactions with my mother that this wasn't a question but rather a firm suggestion.

"That would be best." As I said those words, my vision was drawn to the staircase. Something had moved down the stairs so rapidly I could have imagined it.

My stomach dropped as my gaze jumped to the foot of the steps. A nebulous shape, like a dark mass of air, dashed across the hall. It formed into the hem of a black dress and then quickly vanished through the front door. My chest was impossibly tight, my breathing constricted. I glanced at the housekeeper. If she had perceived any abnormality, she didn't show it.

Was that a ghost? I had never seen a ghost inside my own house, so this was a drastic change. My house had been a place of refuge, where I didn't have to worry about running into one of them when I least expected it. As it was, it drained me emotionally to observe them on the streets, always wondering about their capabilities and purposes. The prospect of dealing with them on a more intimate level made me quiver.

"You are trembling, dear," the housekeeper observed. "Come closer to the fire."

Nearing the hearth, I made a conscious effort to get ahold of my emotions, telling myself that whatever I had seen was a product of my overactive imagination, frenzied by the journey through the woods and the foreboding house. It momentarily worked to calm my breathing, but beneath my facade, I knew whatever I had seen carried a malevolent aura.

I extended my hands toward the crackling flames, feeling the pleasant heat caress my body. And it was then that Piper's furious barking from the lawn sounded loud and clear, like she fought a fierce enemy.

"The little fur ball has returned," the housekeeper stated, moving swiftly to open the door. "She must have seen a rabbit. There are quite a few around here."

But I knew that desperate bark all too well. Piper must have encountered whatever had exited the house. I was glad when she didn't hesitate to heed the call of the housekeeper and came right inside. I released the breath caught in my throat when the door closed again, as if ghosts couldn't enter the house otherwise. Even if that were true in other houses, All Hallows had just proved it wasn't the case here.

How in the world am I going to live here with them?

Somewhat mercifully, bringing me from the supernatural to the technical issues of the house, the same sconce started to flicker, deepening the shadows of the foyer.

"Oh, dear, the connection is so old I'm afraid it will go out anytime."

Or start a fire.

At last, it blinked into obscurity with a buzzing sound, and I froze as a figure emerged near the staircase. When the sconce came back to life, Julius stood there with my suitcase. I pressed a hand to my poor heart. It had had enough for one day.

"Here," he announced. I wasn't sure if he meant that he was here, that my bag was here, or that both had arrived. His eyes snapped to me, and try as I might, I couldn't pull my gaze from his. It was as if he had locked it in place.

Mrs. Goswick's firm voice broke the connection. "What are you still doing with Miss Addington's luggage? Do take it up to her bedroom at once."

"Yes, ma'am."

Julius tramped up the steps as if he carried nothing more than a pillow. My gaze followed him, trailing his shadow until he was out of view. I was aghast. In stark comparison to my former presumptions, I had seen in Julius's eyes a man of great awareness, a clever fierceness I had seldom encountered. And there was pain, too, framed by the scars on his cheeks.

Looking at me with an expression of pity on her face, Mrs. Goswick asked, "Ready for a good night of rest?"

"Most definitely." The last twelve hours had felt like months—too many new things, too soon, too strange. Perhaps the exhaustion would rescue me from my hyperactive imagination and sleep would find me—after all, there were no bombs falling, no need to flee the house for my life in the middle of the night.

"Let's get you settled in the blue room. You'll feel like new in the morning."

I followed the housekeeper up the steps. Piper dashed ahead, sniffing the floor as if knowing where to go. The east corridor was deep and narrow, scarcely lit by wall sconces that flickered each time our feet hit the floorboards. The dimness of the light enhanced the shadows of the doors lining the hallway, and I found myself shying away from the portraits on either side. Each person seemed to watch me as I passed. There was a mixture of young and old, male and female. Their clothing revealed lives lived centuries ago. The lack of smiles portrayed gloomy, troubled dispositions. However, their most poignant features were their eyes. They penetrated mine with unnatural vitality, giving me the impression they were very much alive despite the new age.

The door at the end of the hall stood wide open. I entered the bedroom behind the housekeeper and was instantly welcomed by the heat coming from the hearth. The fire burned in all splendor, filling the room with a coziness.

"It's beautiful." Pleasantly taken aback, I calculated that half the first floor of my London home would fit in here with ease. An ancient, dark wood, four-poster bed displaying a flowery blue coverlet sat on a gigantic navy Persian rug in the center of the space.

Mrs. Goswick neared her son, who was engaged in fixing a panel of drapes that had fallen off its rail. The fabric matched the color of the coverlet and contrasted the cream-and-cyan wallpaper dressing the walls most beautifully.

"Sorry about the curtains," she said. "The rods are old and don't slide as easily anymore." I assumed this was the reason Julius had gone back for his tool bag earlier.

My attention shifted to Piper, who jumped up on the bed and situated herself comfortably between the pillows. Her contentment brought a smile to my lips and a much-needed peace to my heart. My little friend gave out a small sound of approval at her accommodations. "You silly girl, don't get any ideas. Your place is on the rug by the fire." My eyes took in the beauty of the room once again. "I see why it's called the blue room," I reflected mostly to myself.

"Oh yes, you can find just about any shade of blue in here," the housekeeper observed.

"Rose loved blue," Julius stated.

"Was this Rose's room?"

Mrs. Goswick threw a look of disapproval at her son. It was clear she hadn't wanted me to know.

"It was," Julius answered.

The crystal chandelier above the bed produced a few consecutive sparks, briefly denying us of its light—not that it provided much in the first place, but it was something.

"You'll find a torch in the top drawer of the nightstand. It might come in handy," the housekeeper informed me. Then, motioning to a door near the massive chest of drawers, she continued. "Through there is a small dressing room. Nothing too fancy, but it does have a proper washbasin."

"Your luggage is already in there," Julius added over his shoulder as he retrieved a torque wrench and a screwdriver from the floor and deposited them in his bag.

"The lavatory is the third door to your right down the hall. In the morning, I'll bring tea and fresh rolls. How does eight o'clock sound?" Mrs. Goswick offered.

"Wonderful, but I will be happy to come down for breakfast."

"Nonsense. I'll bring it up."

Turning from the drapes, Julius announced, "All done." He pulled softly on the fabric, demonstrating that they would hold.

"Just in time," Mrs. Goswick said to her son, and then to me, "Good night, dear. If you need anything, you know where to find me."

Though Piper was uncharacteristically determined to sleep with me, I finally convinced her to stay on the rug after several attempts. Thankfully, once she closed her eyes, she was out for the night. I wasn't so lucky. I tossed and turned, unable to shake the notion that the ghosts had not remained in London.

Time dragged on, and in the vulnerability of the night, my mind worked overtime, defending itself from the unknown. It created doubt to soothe my fears. Had the nebulous shape on the stairs been real? It had seemed very real. Furthermore, the hem of a dress could only mean one thing: the ghost of a woman haunted the house. And judging by the dreadful sensation I had felt, I had no idea what to expect from such a being. Worse yet, I had never had to deal with one in living quarters.

I took a deep, cleansing breath. My contemplation wasn't an exciting bedtime story. The last thing I wanted was to fall asleep fearing that instead of the bomb sirens, I would be awoken by spirits roaming my room. Forcing the distress away, I focused on better days. Days long gone. Days before the war, when I took Sunday strolls in Hyde Park with my parents and Father bought fish and chips for us to eat before returning home. The memory warmed my heart. I missed them.

At last, I drifted in and out of a light sleep. Mixed feelings and images filled my obliviousness. I dreamed of my parents in London, the bombs falling on the city, and the red sky refusing to let the stars shine through. And next, Captain Stewart, with his lively eyes and upbeat voice, made his way into my dreams.

I felt myself sinking into a more profound rest as he spoke about safety and how important it was that I stay away from the woods.

.   .   .

In spite of Captain Stewart's warning, I have strayed deep into the trees. They obstruct my path at every turn. I am filled with the notion that they harbor a dark secret they wish to tell me. The soldier I first saw at the edge of the forest appears. He stands in my path and refuses to let me through. I can't see his face, but at once, I recognize what is different about him—his clothing. His uniform, his helmet, his rifle, all of it is from another war, not the current one.

"Will you help me?" he asks, and his voice fades, replaced by the sound of Piper's growling, warning me—

I bolted upright, my head still reeling. Where were we? Had the sirens gone off? Why hadn't Mother shouted at me to drop to the pavement?

All about me was unfamiliar, the vast space disorienting. Piper let out a sharp bark, and I searched the shadows. Her warning wasn't part of my dreams. I found a feeble gleam coming from the ashes of the hearth, and at once I remembered I was at All Hallows.

I slipped out of the bed. Piper stood on the floor, hackles raised, her attention directed at the closed door. I scooped her shivering body into my arms, and, holding my breath, moved to the door. Piper squirmed, trying to break free, but when I didn't allow her, she hid her snout in the lapel of my nightgown.

I pressed my ear to the wood and heard a faint sound, as if someone were moving about just outside my bedroom. Then a door shrieked somewhere along the lengthy corridor, parting ever so slowly. My heart pounded, and I realized I was still holding my breath. Piper growled without raising her head from the safety of my garment.

"Shh, shh," I whispered, patting her back. She quieted down, but her shaking persisted.

Creak...creak...creak... Floorboards complained under the weight of footfalls. One slow step after another, they seemed to grow closer. Every nerve in my body screamed for me to move away, to retreat to the far corner of the room. Then the door down the hallway protested again, as if closing.

Mustering my courage, I dropped to my knees and looked through the keyhole. I strained my vision and distinguished a few silhouettes along the walls. I quickly recognized a graceful half-moon console table, a settee, and a long-case clock.

A few seconds passed as I watched the obscure hallway, but there was no movement. After checking the lock, I armed myself with a fire poker and the torch from the nightstand before returning to bed. With my furry friend still in my embrace, I sat against the headboard, unmoving for what seemed an eternity, feeling the loud thumping of Piper's heart, which surely matched mine. The noises of doors opening and closing mingled with footsteps came again. Someone was creeping stealthily about in the night, but who?

I continued to listen, my body rigid. I could hear sounds everywhere now: hissings, mysterious whispers, rustlings up and down the chimney. The noises came from all directions, blending until it was hard to tell them apart. Unable to do much else, Piper and I waited until, little by little, the disturbances subsided, and as the dim light of dawn peeked around the curtains, sleep came to our rescue.

The persistent rapping on the door followed by Mrs. Goswick calling brought me back from slumber. "Miss Addington, I have breakfast."

I blinked to clear the fog, then left the warm bed, threw on my robe, and unfastened the lock. "Good morning, Mrs. Goswick."

She bustled into the room with a tray of food. "Did you sleep well?"

At her question, I remembered the restless night Piper and I had. Was she being polite? Or had she too heard the disturbances? "We had a rough night. There were noises out in the hall. Did you hear Piper barking?"

"Not a sound." She smiled apologetically. "Keep in mind that the first few nights in a new place are always difficult. It'll improve as you grow used to the noises. Old houses are never quiet. If it's not the windows, it's the floorboards, the plumbing leaking somewhere, or the electrical connections acting up. And as if that wasn't enough, now and then a bird gets stuck in the chimney. And let us not forget the wind that sweeps the forest." Her explanation was so quickly and eloquently expressed, I wondered if she'd rehearsed it.

"I see. Yes, it could have been any of those things." Venturing further, I added, "And if I didn't know better, I might add a ghost or two to the list."

"Ghosts?" She laughed. "Oh no. One must be worried about the living, not the dead."

She did not elaborate, so pondering her remark, I poured tea into a cup and strolled to a chair, heavy with weariness. "I shall remember that."

"If it's all right, I'll take the dog down to the kitchen. She might like some breakfast as well."

Piper lay sprawled on the bed with no apparent desire of getting up. She hadn't even made a sound at the newcomer. Mindful of the anxiety she'd experienced in the past hours, I asked, "What do you think, Piper? Are you up for it?" She pricked her ears and yawned. Whoever had been out in the corridor had done a great job of depleting her strength too.

"I'll come back to fix your room midmorning. I have plenty to do downstairs at the moment," Mrs. Goswick said.

"No need for that. I'll take care of it."

"Nonsense. A guest shouldn't burden themselves with such menial chores."

Mother wasn't the only one holding on to old customs. "Please, Mrs. Goswick, you must allow me to do at least this much. Boredom will get the best of me otherwise." I gave her the best pleading expression I could produce.

"All right," she barely agreed, clearly not thrilled with the idea. She then turned to Piper and called, "Come, girl, come now," and hastened from the room.

"Go on. Go," I encouraged. Unenthusiastically, Piper hopped off the bed and trailed lazily behind the housekeeper down the now brightly lit hallway.

Staring into its peacefulness—all entries dormant, all shadows gone, not a single noise nor movement—it was only human to question last night's events and my emotional stability. Having been guided my whole life by my parents to pretend that the otherworldly didn't exist, at times, I did doubt myself. But I didn't believe I had imagined Piper's response. If it was a ghost out in the corridor, it left no doubt it inhabited the house. However, I had to consider an even more disturbing possibility—it could have been someone of flesh and bones wandering about. Mrs. Goswick's previous words echoed in my mind. *"One must be worried about the living, not the dead."*

The feeling of danger was unnerving, but Mrs. Goswick didn't seem criminal. Perhaps she'd meant something else entirely. Recognizing that there wasn't much else I could do about it right now, I headed to the dressing room and readied for the day. After giving my black trousers and burgundy blouse a nod of approval in the mirror, I returned to the bedroom and ambled to the window. Through the glass, I observed the side of the manor and an extensive garden basking in the radiant morning sun. The area was somewhat well-kept. The grass was trimmed, and the plants were clustered in small gardens. The rest of the property was a different scenario, however. The vegetation had crept beyond its bounds, determined to reign, except for where it was suppressed at the edge of the pathways.

From the far corner of the property, I saw Julius pushing a wheelbarrow down the cobblestone trail. Seemingly oblivious to the world around him, he halted in the geranium garden and extracted a long saw from the wheelbarrow. His actions were calculating and exact as he took the saw to a thick branch on a tall tree. With one hand, he held the branch steady; with the other, he pushed the tool in a back-and-forth motion to sever the limb from the tree.

A sudden movement drew my gaze to a bench across from the gardener. A man sat there with arms folded, observing Julius. He smiled, apparently enjoying the other's arduous enterprise. *Who is he? How did I not notice him before?* I leaned closer to the glass, intrigued. There was something odd about him. He shifted on the seat, providing me a better view of his profile and apparel.

My eyes widened, and my jaw dropped. The soldier I had seen in the forest—and again in my dream—was out in the garden. This time, he wore no helmet or rifle. Was he a friend of Julius?

The soldier's expression seemed suddenly mocking as he threw his head back and laughed. I looked over at Julius. He had propped a ladder against the tree and had started up its steps. Under his weight, the structure wobbled menacingly. The soldier, obviously amused, continued to enjoy the spectacle of determination, albeit poor planning.

Julius was almost to the top of the steps when the soldier walked over to the ladder and gave it a vigorous shake. *What on earth?* Even more puzzling was that Julius seemed to take the mocking quite well—so unlike the image I had of him.

Who does this soldier think he is? Indignation surfaced, but something inside me told me to calm down and think it through.

But then, the soldier shook the ladder again, dissipating any desire to remain a silent spectator. I bolted down the staircase and out the front door, and then rushed around the corner of the house and over to the east side. I had no idea what was going on, but I wasn't about to stand by and watch anyone be deliberately harmed. I couldn't imagine Julius's massive frame collapsing onto the ground without considerable injury. I dreaded not reaching him in time and ran haphazardly through the jungle of rose bushes. Their branches were intertwined like fingers clutching each other, preventing my march. But I did not care even when they snagged my shirt, threatening to tear the fabric. I pressed through the thorny path and reached the garden panting, with hands scratched and bleeding.

I could see Julius over the geranium hedge and cried, "Julius, get down! Get down!" Where I had gotten the courage to speak to him like this, I couldn't say, but it must have something to do with the manor and its destabilizing influence. Disregarding my frantic call, he went on sawing at the branch overhead.

I traversed the final stretch around the hedge, my gaze scanning the area expectantly. I wasn't sure if I was relieved or disappointed that there was no trace of the soldier. Only Julius remained, balancing precariously on the battered ladder. I grasped the sides of the steps and repeated, "Julius, come down, please."

With a few sounds of annoyance, he obeyed. Once on solid ground, he towered over me. Sporting a loose pair of blue overalls and a long-sleeve undershirt, he appeared larger than he already was. "What, miss, what?"

"You were about to fall off," I said, though my discontent had more to do with the soldier's bullying than with Julius's carelessness. "You could have broken your leg or something. You mustn't take such risks."

He observed me as if I had lost my mind. "Fall off? No, I wasn't."

"The man who shook the ladder seemed determined that you would."

"What man? There was no one here," he assured me, several emotions flitting across his face.

"You must have seen him." I pointed at the bench. "He was sitting there, laughing at you. He then stood by the ladder. It's impossible that you didn't see him."

Julius contemplated me for an uncomfortably long while, but when he spoke, his answer remained the same. "There was no man here. Can I get back to work now?"

His denial was frustrating, as was the fact that he remained placid, just staring at me. "All right. Saw away." I shook my head in utter disbelief.

Julius turned to the ladder. I huffed and made to leave when he added, "No man—just Ghost. He comes now and then."

I stopped midstride. "Ghost? What do you mean?"

"Just Ghost."

"Who is he?"

"No one." The gardener yanked his attention back to his task, deliberately blocking me out. I was about to press him further but realized he wasn't one to be pressed. I was almost certain that if I did, he would teach me a lesson about unpleasantness.

I started back toward the front lawn, accompanied by my shocking discovery. *Julius can see the otherworldly.* He'd told the plain truth. There had been no other man in the garden—just a ghost. A ghost, he'd said, who came now and then. The way Julius spoke of him, as if shielding his identity, and the way the ghost had interacted with Julius attested to a connection between them.

All Hallows's ghosts did not follow the pattern I was accustomed to. As a child, I had tried more than once to play with ghost children but they had ignored me as if they couldn't see or hear me. Throughout my life, I observed them as if they were a motion picture. The closest I had come to interacting with them was when I tried to help the boy in London during the raid—a dangerous encounter that could have cost my parents' lives and mine.

The possibility of communicating with the supernatural was uncharted territory. It was thrilling, in a way, to maybe come to know their world at last—and absolutely terrifying. I had no idea what that world might be like.

My musings ended when I caught sight of a rider on horseback headed in my direction. Piper emerged from the house and dashed toward the newcomer, barking excitedly. The rider dismounted near the front steps. Wagging her tail, Piper made a lap around Ross as she smelled the bottom of his trousers.

"Hey, Great Dane, how are you today?" He briefly scratched Piper on the head before she ran off across the yard and into the woods.

"Good morning, Captain Stewart."

"Did you already forget to call me Ross? Unlike the Goswick lady, I have no intention of keeping things formal," he joked. "Besides, 'Captain Stewart' coming from you makes me feel like an old man, and I just turned twenty-five."

· "Good morning, Ross." My gaze swept over him. I was flustered, and a bit shocked when I realized that I was appraising his attractiveness—finding it quite appealing. He was dressed in a white short-sleeved T-shirt tucked into his military trousers.

"Ah, much better."

"I did not expect to see you here—and this early."

"Early? I've been up since five." He chuckled. "I hope you aren't disappointed."

I wasn't, but I wasn't about to say so. "Are you looking for the Goswicks?"

"No, I came to see you."

"Me?"

"Yeah, I wanted to make sure you survived the night."

"Why wouldn't I have?" Normally a decent liar given my mother's unbending view on things, the irony almost choked the words in my throat.

He let out a short laugh. "Okay. I knew you would. Just making sure." Taking a step closer, he looked at my hands. "Is that blood? What happened to you?" I could tell by the timbre in his voice that he was truly bothered.

"Nothing. Just a few scratches. I had a little disagreement with the rose bushes."

"Are you serious?"

"Yes, earnestly. I took a shortcut through the garden"—I signaled in its direction—"not realizing how thorny the plants were. Once I was in the maze, I had to fight my way out of it."

He shook his head, apparently relieved. "I get the feeling that once you start something, you won't let go until it's finished." He winked. "I like that."

My face grew hot. I knew my skin had reddened at his words. Whatever he was alluding to, I quickly dismissed it. "It's kind of you to check in on me."

"Nah, I have errands in town, so I figured I might as well swing by."

"Would you like to stay for a cup of tea?"

"Perhaps later. I don't have time now. Besides, I wouldn't want to ruin the Goswicks' morning. I don't think they like me much."

After yesterday's tense encounter, I couldn't argue against his assumption. "Maybe another time, then."

He nodded. "How did my friend Julius behave after I left? Did he stay up all night trudging about?"

An interesting remark. "Why do you say that?"

"He likes to wander in the woods at night."

"I wouldn't know anything about that. He sleeps at the cottage."

"That's good news." He mounted the horse. "I better keep going. The mechanic is waiting for his order." He patted his shirt pocket.

"Thank you for stopping by."

"Don't think too much of it."

"I shall try not to," I answered playfully. I thought of Mother blanching at this rather forward comment, but truly, the need for formality with Captain Stewart had long been abandoned in the woods.

"I'll see you around. Meanwhile, stay away from the roses." He pressed his heels into the horse's side, encouraging it to gallop away.

I retraced my steps along the main path, finding Ross's visit a bit odd. While I was pleased to see him, his conversation with Mrs. Goswick last night about safety told me there was something about All Hallows I didn't know, and which his visit just confirmed. It couldn't be about the supernatural since Ross didn't believe in that.

Oh, All Hallows... I halted to take in its I. Bathed in sunlight, with its cream walls, dark-framed windows, and full-grown pine trees around its perimeter, it portrayed an innocent image—a striking contrast to what I had seen at night. Infused with hope that the inside would be as appealing in daylight, I started my explorations on the main level, musing that perhaps I would come across something about the mysterious Rose and maybe even about the ghost of the soldier—for there must be a reason for his presence at All Hallows.

In addition to a grand entrance hall and sitting room, the main floor housed a good-sized library with hundreds of volumes and a cozy spot for reading; a conservatory that must have been glorious at one time but was now deserted and gloomy; a study with walls covered in wood panels too dark and serious for my sensibilities; a small area designed for social gatherings; a lavatory; and of course, the kitchen. Several corridors connected these rooms in one way or another, making the house a bit of a maze.

In the kitchen, there were cupboards lining the wall, a sink, a prehistoric range, an icebox, a fireplace, and a massive working table in the middle of the space. The floors were stunning. The square stones, filled with a mixture of red, orange, and brown, were the liveliest thing I had seen here so far. They reminded me of the historic floors in one of the halls of Westminster Abbey, which last year had sustained considerable damage when its medieval wooden roof timbers had been set alight by incendiaries. Burning beams and molten lead had fallen on the wooden stalls more than a hundred feet below, and the roof had crashed down into the crossing. I closed my eyes against the tragic memory and whispered a fleeting prayer that the abbey would be spared further bombings.

Done touring the first level, I ascended to the second. With its east and west wings, it was more extensive than I anticipated. It housed as many bedrooms as the architect could possibly fit in the floor plan, so much so that he had accommodated each wing with only one washroom. Most rooms were furnished with a bed, an armoire, and a bedside table; however, one bedroom in each wing was considerably larger than the rest, having a dressing room.

The attic was overrun with all sorts of rubbish and the suffocating smell of mildew. Years of accumulation were threatened by the mold born of a leaky roof. It was a place haunted with unheard voices trapped inside the books scattered about. A place where forgotten pieces of furniture seemed to cry out for help to rid themselves of the rodents inhabiting them and to be restored to their former glory. I finished my tour a bit disappointed, not having found any portraits or personal items on my quest to learn more about Rose and the soldier.

The only thing clear was that the overall theme of All Hallows was neglect. I could almost picture how the manor must have looked in its glory days, filled with light and joy—with life. But the mental image quickly slipped away, replaced by the sudden presentiment that the manor held dark secrets—secrets that imprisoned the manor in a state of misery.

Late morning, Mrs. Goswick intercepted me as I came out of the library. "Miss Addington, General Lewis is here to see you. He's waiting in the sitting room. Let me know if he would like some tea. I prefer not to interrupt the visit."

I was pleasantly surprised by this and nodded as she led me through the winding corridor. He represented a connection to my past, and I had anticipated that it might be a while before he could find time away from his duties to stop by. As I came into the room, I hesitated when I saw the man standing half turned from the fireplace. He looked as if the weight of the world lay upon his shoulders—his back was slightly hunched forward, and what I could see of his face appeared somber.

He was dressed in a brown uniform that reminded me of the one my father kept in his special box from the war. In his early fifties, the general was slim but well built, with olive skin, dark eyes, and thick, black hair.

He looked at me, and while his gaze brightened, I saw a trace of surprise in it. About four years had passed since he had last seen me, and I had changed much during my adolescent years. Straightening his posture, he seemed to gain an inch or two as he said, "Miss Addington, it's a pleasure to see you again." Closing the gap between us, he took my hand and kissed it. No one had ever done this. It felt strangely pleasant.

"General, it's good to see you. It's been too long. Please call me Seraphina."

Letting go of my hand, he wrapped his arm around my shoulders and guided me to the sofa. "Please sit down," he invited. I did. He settled in an armchair. "First of all, Seraphina, I must apologize for yesterday's misunderstanding. Edward's telegram did arrive on time, but I didn't receive it until this morning when I returned from Bristol. So I wanted to come right away to clarify the situation."

"I should be the one apologizing."

"What for?"

"For causing you unnecessary distress. I know that you have enough to deal with at present, but know that my family is most grateful for your generosity."

"Nonsense." He waved a hand in the air. "Let us not forget that I owe Edward a few favors from the old days. He came under my watch during a time when I needed men I could trust, and he is trustworthy. I was a young lieutenant and didn't know what I was doing half the time. I never thought I would live to see something so atrocious again." He spoke with an air of profound sorrow, but then he took a quick breath and shifted right out of it. "Forgive me. I sometimes get carried away. What I wanted to say is that your father was a source of wisdom to rely upon during the wretched war."

"I'm glad to hear that. Indeed, he is a clever man."

"He is as clever as he is stubborn. He and your mother should have come out here with you, but he wouldn't listen to me."

"He has his pride to protect."

"I suppose we all do." He chuckled. "I just wish I were in a better position to help. I fear that placing you in this dilapidated house, with too few comforts, is shameful on my part, but I'm afraid my home is out of the question, overrun with troops as it is."

"Let me assure you that anything is preferable to bombs falling over my head."

"You are not being entirely truthful with me," he said with a smile.

"Honestly, I'm quite comfortable here." I returned the smile.

"How are the Goswicks treating you?"

"Like a daughter. They are very kind."

"They brought me up to speed on your journey. It was a relief to know that one of my men accompanied you through the woods. The forest is beautiful but dangerous. May I recommend you be cautious as you travel about?"

"Is there something I should know?" Was he speaking about the menace the captain and the Goswicks alluded to? Or perhaps of Rose's disappearance?

"Don't be alarmed. Being forewarned is being forearmed. In the past, there have been a few tragedies in the vicinity. But I trust that with our heavy military presence, it will not happen again. Just be cautious."

Sensing he wouldn't expound on his remark, I assured him, "I shall take precaution."

I was about to offer him some tea when he jumped to his feet and briskly informed me, "I'm afraid I must leave. I'm on a tight schedule." He extended his hand to help me stand, and we made our way to the front yard, where a car awaited him. "If you'll permit, I wish to respond to your father's cable with the news of your safe arrival."

"That would be wonderful."

"I'll see to it, then."

"Thank you for your visit."

"If ever you need anything, please don't hesitate to come by or send me a message," he said, turning toward the vehicle. Then, after getting inside, he gave me a friendly wave as the car pulled away. I waved back, reassured that I wasn't alone in this unsettling place.

CHAPTER 5
THE GHOST OF THE WOMAN

In the kitchen, I found Mrs. Goswick industriously slicing a loaf of fresh bread. Without preamble, I went straight to what I had in mind. "General Lewis mentioned the tragedies that have occurred in the past. Is that what you meant when you spoke about safety measures with Captain Stewart?"

"Oh dear, I'm glad you brought that up," she answered, but her voice belied her. "Terrible as this sounds, there have been murders and disappearances in the past—Rose being one of them."

"More than one?"

She nodded. "I pray nothing like that will ever happen again. The locals have adopted the simple rule of not traveling the forest alone at night, especially the women. After twilight, you *must* follow this advice. If you need to be out late, one of us will accompany you."

I almost laughed. Between last night's ghost on the staircase and the one harassing Julius, the house seemed more dangerous than the woods. True, it was only sensible not to roam the forest at night, but now that I was enjoying a taste of freedom away from the rules of my parents, I was reluctant to concede even a little of that. "But, Mrs. Goswick, if the incidents were long ago, it's unlikely anything will happen again."

"That's what we thought every time a woman died."

"They were all women?" I was astounded and deeply intrigued. "How did they die?"

"That's a topic for another day. Suffice it to say that you must be cautious."

"But—"

"No buts, dear. Another time," she said firmly and handed me a stack of plates. "Please take these to the table."

Though I was displeased with her unwillingness to tell me more, I did as I was told. While I prepared the table, the Goswick men stormed into the kitchen through the back entrance. The father wore an old black coat with patches on the elbows, matching the ones sewn on the knees of his trousers—clothing that reflected a life of hardship.

"Good afternoon," greeted Samuel. Julius just gave me a cold look.

"Good afternoon."

Quickly ridding themselves of their coats and hats, they settled into their places at the table. Mrs. Goswick engaged herself in serving a delicious cottage pie with a thick sauce and sweet onion I wouldn't soon forget. The main conversation at the table focused on the destruction last week's wind had caused to the tallest evergreens. Unlike his quietness yesterday, Samuel launched into a full explanation of how to prune the branches that had become partially detached. I feared I would learn more about gardening in this one sitting than I had my entire life.

Julius dug into his pie with the ferocity of a man at war. "I'm pruning the tree in the geranium garden," he said dryly in between bites. "I would be done by now if it weren't for some interruptions." He shot a glance at me. Luckily, his parents didn't inquire about the nature of his delay.

"Good. It needs to be lightened up before the next windstorm," Samuel said, and the discussion rambled on to different trees in need of assistance and how to provide that assistance.

Even as the men carried on with the conversation, they devoured a double portion before I had finished my small serving. Sliding their chairs back harshly against the tile floor, they rose to return to their world outside. While Mrs. Goswick tackled the dirty dishes, I attacked the dust and crumbs on the floor with an old mop, pondering all the while the events of the morning, particularly Julius's earlier declaration.

"Just Ghost. He comes now and then." Not one but two spirits haunted All Hallows. Who were they?

"I think the floor is clean enough, dear." Mrs. Goswick brought my focus back to my work. "You can let go of the mop now. You aren't a kitchen maid."

Propping the mop against the wall, I approached, then backed up against the countertop, and faced her. Perhaps knowing more about the manor and its former inhabitants would help me sort out its ghosts. "Mrs. Goswick..." I started as she submerged another pot in the soapy water. "I feel like an intruder not knowing the history of the house. Would you tell me about Rose and her father?"

As if she had been expecting my request all along, she disclosed, "Rose was an intelligent young woman, full of life and enthusiasm. I loved her like a daughter." There was a mixture of longing and sorrow in her voice. "She created much of the beauty here. She repainted many of the rooms and brought in the cheerful furniture."

"You must have an opinion of what happened to her."

"Just vague ideas, but nothing solid. Her father, Richard, was a humble soul. After the loss of his wife, he dedicated his life to raising Rose. After he passed away, she was never the same, and as the months went by, her emotional state deteriorated. In a way, she walled herself in. I mean that in a literal sense. She spent hours locked in her bedroom." Mrs. Goswick paused as if what she would say next hurt most. "Then, one beautiful spring day, she was simply gone. I knew it before they confirmed it. Her energy, or aura—whatever you want to call it—left a void, a hole, in the house."

"She didn't leave a note, a message, anything?"

"Nothing."

"What about her belongings? Her jewelry? Her clothing?"

"It was all here, intact and in its place. The general organized the largest search party ever seen in the forest. Police officers, soldiers, search dogs, you name it—a host of people who left no stone unturned— but the effort bore no fruit. It was as if the earth itself had swallowed her."

The earth had swallowed her. I shrank at the image of the grave, dark and cold, that formed in my mind. "Do you have a picture of her?"

"The few pictures we had were packed before letting out the house. The general took everything. They might be at the Burley mansion or maybe even in his London flat—if he still has them. You know men. They don't care for things of that sort."

"What did Rose look like?"

Picking up a loofah sponge, she started to scrub an already clean pot. "She was tall, with a graceful figure. She inherited her fair complexion and dark hair from Richard"—her eyes grew moist—"and her blue eyes from her mother, Sarah."

"Sounds like she was a beautiful woman."

"And the most educated one in the forest. She spent most of her time reading, drawing, and composing music. There was a time when she even got into writing riddles. Every morning, I would find a riddle on the kitchen table for me to solve. She was a free and happy soul."

There was a short period in which neither of us spoke. The housekeeper's thoughts probably traveled down the path of years long gone. Mine busily dissected every piece of information that could be relevant to the present.

Interrupting the silence, Mrs. Goswick almost imperceptibly said, "I'll never lose hope that she'll return."

I felt guilty about prying, but it was too late for that. "Why won't you accept the possibility that she's moved on from this world?"

"Because if I lose hope that she'll come back, I will lose hope in everything, and I'll have nothing left."

We were startled when the back door flung open and slammed against the wall. Julius stood on the threshold, a sinister look in his eyes. From his hand hung a decapitated rabbit, its blood dripping on the Italian floor.

"How many times did I tell you not to kill the animals of the forest?" cried his mother.

Ross was right. Julius was a brutal hunter.

Piper was already situated on the rug by the hearth. I quickly changed for the night, and wrapped in the softness of the sheets, I fell into a deep sleep, the exhaustion of the past days finally taking over. But it wasn't to last. Piper's angry growls snapped me to wakefulness.

She stood by the door, which, thankfully, I had locked. Whatever moved on the other side had her in a frenzy. Except for my loud heartbeat and the prickling of my skin, I couldn't move. I sat petrified on the bed, staring at the door through the dying light of the hearth. Piper's escalating anger brought about an eerie feeling of déjà vu. We were experiencing another midnight disturbance.

She dashed back and forth along the door, shoving her snout into the gap at the bottom and snapping in rage. If the door opened, she would launch her attack with all the force her little body could muster, risking that whatever lurked in the hallway would tear her to pieces. After all, she wasn't really a Great Dane.

Gaining a little composure, I pushed the covers off. If Piper would only quiet down for an instant, perhaps I could hear the source of her disruption. But that was a fool's wish. She wouldn't relent unless I picked her up. Determined to retrieve the torch from the nightstand drawer, I swung my legs over the edge of the bed. And at once, like the sound of a shot, from somewhere out in the hallway came a bang so loud I jumped to my feet and stood by the nightstand; my hands shook so terribly I could hardly open the drawer.

An even louder boom reverberated through the corridor as I turned on the torch and moved closer to Piper. I placed the light on the floor, aiming toward the corner of the room to minimize its radiance reflecting under the door. I did not want to attract any attention, though the dog was doing a good job of that already.

When I attempted to grab Piper, she lowered her head, threw her ears back, and nipped at me in her frenzy. I suppressed a cry and brought her into my embrace. "It's all right. It's me. Calm down," I whispered, and though her tiny body trembled, she stopped growling. Balancing between her uncontrolled shaking and my wobbly legs, I kneeled to peek through the keyhole out into the hallway.

Two wall sconces, which I had purposely left on, dimly lit the lengthy corridor. Their pale light reminded me of stories of the will-o'-the-wisp—the strange light that lured people to a watery death in the marshes. Suddenly, a black shape materialized from a bedroom and floated into the hallway—the swift way it moved just inches above the floor affirmed it wasn't human. And the long, flowing dress told me that it was the ghost of a woman. Like the sun rose in the east, I knew it was the woman I had seen leaving the house yesterday.

The spirit crossed the hall and went into another room, the door behind her shutting with a bang—its reverberation impossibly loud as if the whole structure had shaken. Piper wrestled in my arms and uttered a horrifying yowl. "Hush now," I ordered Piper while I pressed my eye to the keyhole once again.

Seconds later, the ghost reappeared, moving violently from room to room, slamming doors, rattling furniture, and making a terrible din. After witnessing Ghost interact with Julius, I was no longer sure whether a spirit could cause physical harm or not. Though it was evident that she had some power over her surroundings, I didn't want to find out the extent of it.

When the woman traveled to yet another room, I realized her trajectory would bring her to the blue room—to me. Terror clenched my insides, and every inhale threatened to crack my ribs as I contemplated a possible encounter.

Will she come into my bedroom and attack us? How in the world can I defend myself and Piper against her? The thoughts circled in my head, not finding an escape.

She surged into the hall once again. Moving slowly, she inched closer and hovered two doors down from mine. Along with her stillness, my breathing halted, waiting for her next move. I wondered if she sensed my presence, my fear. She rotated slightly to face the green room, and after a moment, she entered it. The knot in my throat released, and I took several quick breaths.

This time, she released a long, heartrending cry that seemed to fill time and space, vast and powerful in its reach. I could feel her anguish in my very bones, rendering me helpless. I fell backward onto the floor, fearing that the life in me would wither away. Piper scurried to hide under the bed, whimpering.

Convinced a sudden doom awaited me, I was instantly relieved when, as if heaven-sent, rays of light touched my face. I scrambled from the floor and dashed to the window, where I yanked the drapes open, thankful Julius had fixed them because the fury with which I pulled would have brought the entire rod down. Daylight, faint but healing, flooded the room.

I paused, letting the daylight soothe my fears while I listened for doors slamming or any other noise, but all was quiet. After a time, I looked through the keyhole to find daylight inching its way down the hallway. There were no signs of the woman, just profound silence. The house was at rest.

Utterly exhausted, body and spirit, I called for Piper to come out from under the bed. Still trembling, she obeyed and jumped onto the bed to curl up beside me. In the pale dawn, the entire encounter had the feel of a dream. I closed my eyes, but terrified that the ghost would return, I could not sleep.

At length, I readied for the day, preoccupied with my situation. In London, it had been easy to ignore them and go about my business. Here, I felt endangered body and soul, for after last night, there was no doubt that the ghost of the woman was gaining strength. Or worse yet, my gift was inching further into the otherworldly, uncovering another layer of its sphere.

My mind swung back to the ghost and how she preferred the cover of night. *What does she seek? Could this be Rose?* It was logical since she had a connection to the house. On the other hand, the ghost of the soldier seemed to favor daylight, which meant I was likely to be disturbed at any hour, day or night, a prospect that left me feeling drained. Aggravating matters, they had something in common—they were determined to be heard.

With a feverish mind, I stumbled into the kitchen and grabbed a piece of bread before heading out the back door to the gardens. Not paying attention, I jumped over a patch of uneven stones that long ago must have formed an intricate path. Landing on something unexpected, I gave a shrill cry as pain shot through my ankle. I took a few tentative steps to ascertain that nothing was broken and then turned to see what I'd stepped on. Half hidden in the tall grass lay a dead raven.

The sight of the inert bird summed up my dilemma: death surrounded me—first in London and now here. Unless I did something about it, nothing would change, and I was tired of being acted upon. More so now when they were in the same house. I had to stop running from who I was. I had to embrace it. The only thing I could think to do was to discover the identity of the ghosts and their reasons for haunting the manor. I felt I would be less frightened if I knew who they were. Yet the opposite could also be true. Where I would go from there, I wasn't sure. I would take things one step at a time.

Setting out at a brisk pace, I followed the narrow path at the edge of the woods that led to the village. My first stop was the post office. I needed to send my parents a telegram. Mother was bound to show up in Burley if she didn't hear from me. There would be no mention of ghosts or other disturbing things. I would only convey what they hoped to hear: The people at All Hallows were welcoming and caring, the accommodations more than I'd expected. I had not had another "episode" since leaving London. I was perfectly content. No need to afflict them with the truth. They already had enough to worry about

Next, I was determined to delve deeper into All Hallows's history. I suspected that Mrs. Goswick had withheld information and that there was a connection between Rose's disappearance and the haunts. Hence, the idea was born. I would pay a visit to the graves of the Lewis family. Perhaps the cemetery's keeper would know something about the family.

The ancient church of Burley was a good-sized redbrick building with an impressive tower and Gothic-style doors and windows. The parish's graveyard abutted the west side of the church. In the dappled sunshine, a gentle peacefulness filled the cemetery.

The graves were dispersed throughout the property like pieces in a chess game. Most were old burials, as if death had escaped a generation.

Tragically, the war would change that. Many tombstones were upright slabs with attractive inscriptions paying tribute to their permanent inhabitants. Others were more elaborate, with impressive statues of cherubs guarding them. The north corner of the yard was the subject of much neglect. Many headstones had fallen to the ground, some half broken, some hidden among the overgrown weeds.

Guessing the Lewis family would be in the nicest part of the grounds, I ambled about it, reading the inscriptions. So many lives had come and gone, having spent the days allotted to them—days filled with dreams, love, and laughter. Although, undoubtedly, they had also suffered a great measure of failure and perhaps even hate and despair.

It wasn't long until I located the Lewis' graves. In a secluded spot under the security of two beech trees rested Richard Lewis alongside his beloved wife, Sarah Sandford Lewis. Not much was written on their headstones, just their names and dates—nothing of their character or deeds in life. Beside them was enough space to accommodate a few more graves that had been marked as the Lewis' property. The presentiment that their daughter, Rose Lewis, would soon occupy one of these spots entered my heart and put me on edge. Who would occupy the rest of the designated space?

"Ah, the Lewis family," said someone from behind me. I gave a violent start and whirled around. "Forgive me, I didn't mean to frighten you," he expressed.

At first, I questioned whether the strong voice had come from the small man before me—a man in his fifties with vibrant-green eyes, his silver-lined hair neatly combed back from a widow's peak. Dressed in a black robe, hands intertwined in front of him, he looked like an oversized magpie. His imposing aura made up for what he lacked in stature, for he held my gaze with a boldness that left me uneasy.

"I'm sorry to have frightened you," he reiterated. "I'm Albion Baker, the local vicar."

"It's quite all right. I'm afraid I was caught up in my thoughts." I extended my hand to him, feigning aplomb. "Seraphina Addington. It's a pleasure to make your acquaintance." His grip was firm but cold. I tried to retrieve my hand, but he grasped it a bit tighter before he let go.

"Ah, Miss Addington, I've been made aware of your arrival at All Hallows. Burley is a small town where rumors spread like wildfire."

"Rumors always do." I forced a smile, fighting the unexpected hostility I felt inside. "How long have you been the vicar in Burley?"

"Longer than you have been alive, I'm sure."

"Did you start your service here?"

"In the parish at Lyndhurst over thirty years ago."

Glancing at the gravestones beside us, I stated, "I suppose you knew the Lewis family well, then."

"Richard and Sarah?"

"And Rose, their daughter."

His eyes darkened at the name. For the first time, he averted his gaze and fixed it instead on the Lewis headstones. "I did not know Sarah Lewis. She passed before I came to Burley. And Richard, I knew only briefly, unfortunately. I attended to him in his final hours."

"And Rose?"

"I'm afraid I didn't know her too well either. She attended Sunday services, but after her father's passing, she seldom came anymore."

"Why the change?"

He shrugged with indifference. "It could have been anything."

"Anything, such as..."

"Such as the distance she had to travel to get here. Her sadness about her loss. Grief can isolate a person quite effectively."

"You mean the death of her parents?"

"That and..." His unfinished sentence hung in the air, pricking at me.

"And what?"

"The loss of a lover."

My eyebrows shot up in surprise. "Rose had a lover?"

"Oh..." He hesitated. "Forgive me. It is not in my right to speak about it. You surely understand."

I observed him for a split second and decided he wasn't concerned with propriety. He wanted me to beg for the information. I did want to know, but I wouldn't allow him the pleasure of gaining my interest. "Entirely." I faked a smile. "Besides, I'll hear about it sooner or later. Like you said, it's a small town."

"Yes, yes, you'll find out soon enough. The young folks, especially, like to speak about it. They like to fantasize about lovers, murders, and all kinds of nonsense."

Sly as a fox, he'd conquered my curiosity with those words. "Lovers and murders? What does that have to do with Rose Lewis?"

He sighed as if I had at last forced him to disclose the details—when in reality, his tongue was only too happy to share them. "Oh, well, might as well tell you. You see, Rose was involved with a young man in the vicinity. He went to the Great War, and rumor has it that upon his return, she was no longer interested in him, so he killed her."

"That's horrid." His tale left me dumbstruck. "But then again, it is only a rumor, right?" Mrs. Goswick hadn't said anything about Rose having a romantic relationship.

"Of course, though rumors often bear much truth." He sounded more like a solicitor than a vicar.

"You believe the story to be true?"

"All I'm saying is that it's possible. A young man scarred by the horrors of battle, having held on to the hope of love, coming home to her, if disillusioned, might do something deplorable."

"I suppose it is." My mind turned to Ghost and his unexplained presence at the manor. Was he Rose's lover and murderer? His mocking demeanor flashed through my memory, how he had treated Julius that day in the garden.

"It is said that once a person kills, it's easy to do it again—in war, it is necessary. But after, if not properly handled, it can become a habit," Baker reflected.

A chilling breeze swept over the graveyard, and a bank of clouds blotted out the sun. I shuddered, whether due to my new inquietudes or to the abrupt change in the weather, I wasn't sure.

"Where did this come from?" I gestured to the gloomy sky.

"It's a normal occurrence in the forest. It goes from sunny to stormy without notice."

"I ought to go. It's a long walk back to the manor." I drifted up the narrow spaces between the graves to the center path, Albion Baker alongside me.

Pointing at the church edifice, he informed, "See those windows? They date back to the Victorian restoration. It's a pity the church is planning to replace them. They always find a replacement for everything. I guess that's the sequence of life—one always comes to replace another."

Who did he want to replace? I promptly decided his statements were designed to say something without saying it, almost like a warning.

"Good day, Vicar. Good luck with the windows." Propelled by a feeling of distrust for the man and the angry sky, I half walked, half trotted out of the graveyard.

CHAPTER 6
THE KILLER IN THE WOODS

The wind whistled through the streets of Burley, and the trees swished from side to side, protesting the harshness of the approaching storm. Silently thanking heaven I'd worn trousers, I quickened my steps. A sudden gust blew against me, and mechanically, I folded my arms across my chest for protection.

Hoping to gain some time, once out of town, I took a different footpath bordering the trees. Among the noises of the natural elements, there came a rumbling from behind me. It intensified until it became apparent a small vehicle approached. Soon enough, a motorbike pulled up alongside me.

"Well, well, look who it is," said the rider.

"Good afternoon, Ross," I greeted without stopping.

"What's good about it?" he answered over the hissing wind and the roar of the bike.

I shook my head slightly at his quick-witted response and flung a look at his machine. "Your transportation has improved since last I saw you."

"I borrowed it from a guy in the Fire Service convoy."

"It's a nice bike."

A light but rapidly increasing rain began to fall.

"It hurts less than riding a horse, I can tell you that much." He smirked. "But compared to the motorcycles we have in the States, it's a piece of junk."

With a dismissive wave, I responded, "Welcome to England, Captain."

"Welcome to the New Forest, Seraphina. You're about to get drenched."

I feared he might be right, and if it hadn't been for my pride—he'd have a good laugh if I bolted like a rooster afraid of the rain—I would have made a run for it.

"It's just too bad this thing doesn't have a sidecar, or I could give you a ride."

"Yes, too bad..." I could imagine my mother's hysterics were I to jump into a motorbike's sidecar. All too suddenly, the gusts of air decreased, giving way to a stronger rain. Instinctively, I headed into the trees to shelter under their massive branches.

Following suit, Ross dismounted and parked his bike. "Here, put this on." Taking off his brown leather jacket, he handed it to me.

Since my teeth threatened to start chattering, I was happy to take it. "Thanks. I didn't expect this weather."

"Storms are very sudden around here, and they can go on for days."

I zipped up the jacket. It drowned me, but at least it was warm. "What do you propose we do?"

"Well, at this rate, the water will get through the treetops in no time. One way or another, we'll get soaked. But the longer we wait, the worse the roads will get. And trust me, it's ugly."

"Please, don't wait for me. You have the advantage of the bike," I said.

"Yeah, but All Hallows is on the way to the Burley mansion. Might as well stop by." He cleared his throat. "If you don't mind, of course."

"I don't." On the contrary, the idea made my heart miss a beat—that, he would never know.

"Okay, then. If we ride, we'll get there faster."

"We?"

He nodded emphatically. "Have you ridden on a bike before?"

"No."

"I think you are small enough to fit behind me without major problems." He pointed to the cargo seat on top of the back wheel. Reading the apprehension on my face, he added, "It's a piece of junk, but it's a sturdy piece of junk. It might not be as comfortable as a sidecar, but it will hold both of us for sure."

Feeling a twinge of remorse that Ross was in this situation—he could have been at the mansion by now—I answered, "I think you are right. Let's try it."

He stood momentarily frozen, not camouflaging his shock at my willingness to ride with him. A bolt of lightning illuminated the gloomy fields across from the trees, followed by an ear-splitting boom of thunder, and surprisingly, the rain abated somewhat.

"Here is our chance," I said. "Let's get on with it."

"Okay." Ross reached for his goggles and mounted the motorbike. I climbed on behind him. "We might slip and slide a bit. Just hang on to me and don't panic if we get stuck. Ready?"

"Yes. Wait—do you want your jacket back?"

"No, I can take it." He turned the key in the ignition, and the machine roared to life.

I wrapped my arms around his waist and hid my face in his back.

"Hold on tight."

The bike moved quite slowly at first, but as the minutes passed, we picked up a decent speed considering the conditions. I agreed with Ross and preferred the bike to riding a horse. It was smaller, its movement less impactful on my body. Soon the rain turned into a drizzle, but the breeze was bitter.

"Are you doing okay back there?"

"Yes," I shouted, my face leaving the security of his back for the first time. I looked at the turbulent sky, and again a lightning bolt shot through it, backed by thunder. Without warning, the rain picked up again. I felt sorry for Ross. His jacket and body were doing a great job of stopping the rain for me, but he was soaked.

"Yeah!" he exclaimed. "This is fun!" The motorbike wobbled a bit as the wheels spun through a pool of water. Ross pressed harder on the accelerator. I held my breath until the puddle was defeated and left behind. "What do you think?"

Fun? My friends in London would have thought it fun. But I had always been under my parents' watchful eye, and fun hadn't necessarily been at the forefront of my actions. However, here in the New Forest, I could allow myself to enjoy life a little—to be myself.

"Indeed, it is." I was not only referring to riding the bike, but to my proximity to Ross.

"Do you want to trade spots?"

The laughter that erupted from me did something unexpected. Like dawn after a thick night, it cast the anxiety from my very core. I felt exhilaratingly free. Unable to stop smiling, I lowered my face into the protection of his body, enjoying each second of the ride.

Only too soon, Ross announced, "Look. There it is."

Peeking around his side, I saw All Hallows's outline in the near distance. I held on tighter as we struggled up the muddy road leading to the manor. When the bike stopped on the front lawn, I jumped off and ran to the security of the porch. Ross parked the bike alongside the house. Eagerly, I wrestled with the doorknob, but it wouldn't give.

"Here, let me." Shoving his shoulder against the door, Ross forced it open, and we rushed in. The heat from the fireplace in the sitting room greeted us warmly.

"Thank goodness for Mr. Goswick," I exclaimed, approaching the fire.

"You can say that again." Ross shook himself like a dog on the entrance mat and took off his boots. Wasting no time, he walked to the hearth, poked the fire with the iron stick, and fed it more wood. Long tongues of flame sprung up, luring us closer. Ross pulled his shirt over his head. Reaching for the wastepaper basket, he wrung the water from his shirt into it, laid the shirt on the floor, and then proceeded to unbutton his trousers. Drawing in a sharp breath, I turned away.

"Sorry," he said. "I don't want to catch pneumonia."

"Here, wrap yourself in this." Reaching for a coverlet resting on the armchair, I threw it to him.

He caught it midair. "You could use it more than me."

"I'll change."

"Where are the Goswicks?" Flinging the blanket over his shoulders, he stripped down to his undergarment.

"Mrs. Goswick leaves after luncheon to care for their animals at the cottage. She'll be back before supper."

"And the men?"

"They work out on the property, so I imagine they've gone back to the cottage as well." I headed to the stairs. "I'll be right back."

With the fireplace in my bedroom dormant, it was as cold as a storage cellar, and my damp clothing had me shivering. My numb hands were clumsy, but once I was undressed and wrapped in a towel, I felt better. While my thoughts went back to the bike ride and how exhilarating it had been, I quickly dried off.

What is going on with me? I couldn't get Ross out of my mind and was eager to return to his side.

I dressed in a pair of brown trousers and a red blouse, and then headed downstairs, where I found Ross kneeling on the rug near the heat, his gaze lost in the crackling fire.

"It's still coming down thick." I pushed a chair close to him and slipped down onto it, watching the rain beat against the window.

"What were you doing in town?"

"I sent my parents a telegram, and on my way back, I visited the graveyard. I'm afraid the vicar is a gregarious fellow and rambled on for a while."

Ross shot me a look of disbelief. "You should not walk in the woods alone."

My defensive side kicked in. "Why not? I was told it's all right during the day. And after all, I'm not a child."

"Neither were the others."

"The women who were killed?"

"Yes." Ross shifted to face me.

"That was long ago."

"You don't know the whole story, do you?"

"I suppose not."

Without warning, a deluge of words came out of his mouth. "I don't believe in the hocus-pocus so prevalent among the locals, but this is a different matter. The first to disappear was Rose Lewis. Since then, every five years, like clockwork, there has been a murder or a disappearance.

Some people argue the cases are unrelated, believing the women who disappeared are still alive or that different people committed the murders, but I don't buy it. I think we are dealing with a single killer—one who follows a pattern."

"A hunter of women on a schedule? I thought killers were too unstable to stick to a routine," I observed in a soft tone.

"Not serial killers. It doesn't matter if they are naturally crazy or naturally evil. Perhaps it's a mix of both. What matters is that they are organized—goal oriented. Killing is like a drug to them, and often, they don't get caught until it's too late. Take the case of Eugene Butler, for instance."

"Who?"

"He was an American serial killer who lived alone on a farm in North Dakota in early 1900. When he started to show signs of mental illness, saying that invisible figures were chasing him, he was placed in an asylum, where he died two years before his crimes were discovered. The doctors there liked the guy. They described him as a gallant man who liked to dance—imagine that."

Could he see the otherworldly, or was it something else?

Eagerly, Ross went on. "Two years after Butler's death, the new owner of his property decided to dig a cellar under the house, and that's where they found the skeletons of six young men who'd had their skulls crushed. His crimes were committed over a span of years. Insane or not, the guy took great precautions not to be discovered—and he wasn't."

His words chilled me more than the rain had. "That's a lot of victims…"

"They think Butler lured vagrants to his farm with the promise of work and then killed them."

"Do you think the present killer lures the women to him?"

"Maybe," Ross answered thoughtfully. "That would definitely make it easier for him to plan their deaths."

I reflected, "Much easier for him to kill them if they trust him already." Dreading the answer, I asked the same question I'd asked Mrs. Goswick, and which she'd refused to answer. "How were the women in the forest killed?"

"They were choked to death. Just last week, the police asked the soldiers on patrol to keep an eye out for any suspicious activity. We're approaching the five-year mark."

I left my seat to pace the room. Suddenly, the killer of the woods became very real.

"I didn't mean to scare you," Ross said.

"It's not that. I'm upset I didn't grasp the severity before—but I only knew half the story." Was this the inquietude I'd seen in the Goswicks' eyes all this time? Was this why their daughter was away?

"Don't beat yourself about it. Most people don't want to believe there is a killer on the loose." Ross left the rug and met me by the sofa, the blanket still hugging his shoulders.

"Who do you think the killer is?" I had an inkling he had someone in mind.

"Ugh, the million-dollar question. It could be anyone, really. There are plenty of men in this town who fit the bill."

"That's an evasive answer."

"Okay, among those you are acquainted with, I wouldn't turn my back on either of the Goswick men or the priest."

"The vicar? Goodness gracious! You have a vivid imagination."

"No, I have a sound mind. Those we least expect often are the perpetrators. There is a reason they get away with it."

True, my first impression of the vicar hadn't been awe-inspiring, and the man had lived in town for as long as the killer had been at work. However, considering his religious standing, to think of him as a murderer was disturbing—even after I'd learned of Butler's story. "It just seems farfetched."

"Whoever he is, with the soldiers stationed in the woods, the piece of trash might not show up this time. Just remember that if precautions are taken, you'll be fine."

"That's what the general and Mrs. Goswick said."

"They are right," Ross assured me.

"Is the killer the reason why you stayed with me in the forest until we reached the Goswicks?"

"Part of it."

"And the other part?"

"It's not every day I find a beautiful woman out in the woods."

The affectionate nudge toward him that I'd thus ignored finally conquered me, and I became aware of the man standing in front of me backlit by the flames of the hearth. Until now, I had seen only Ross the soldier, Ross the friend. But now I beheld him in a way I had never seen a man. Ross was handsome, yet his personality was his best feature. Suddenly, the menace of the killer receded to the back of my mind.

Attraction. This is what it is—a burning attraction. I'm falling for him.

Ross's eyes burned into mine, as if saying, "I fancy you as much as you fancy me."

Seraphina, snap out of it, right now! You are making a fool of yourself. The words in my mind could have been my mother's, and they broke the enchantment of the moment. I yanked my gaze from his and returned to my seat. Ross dropped the blanket from his body and reached for his trousers. The temptation to look at him was almost unbearable. I conquered it, though not without difficulty.

"Except for the waistband, they're pretty much dry," he observed.

Squelching what I would have really liked to say, I encouraged, "Quickly, now, before you get sick."

"It wouldn't be bad if I got to take a break from work." His long legs were soon hidden inside his trousers. Reaching for his shirt, he slipped his arms into the sleeves and sat down on the floor to button it. "But...I wouldn't want you to get any ideas." The side of his mouth turned up into a half smile.

A wave of heat that had nothing to do with the fire in the hearth traveled from the soles of my feet to the roots of my hair. Ignoring his remark, I offered, "Would you like some tea?"

"Tea? I don't drink tea."

"What do you mean you don't drink tea? You did at the Goswicks' cottage."

"Just to be polite. How about beer?" he said in a joking tone. "Or better yet, ale?"

"I don't have any kind of beer."

"Coffee?"

"I'm sorry. No coffee either."

"How about hot chocolate? Do you have that?"

"No, that's a luxury nowadays."

"I guess I have no choice but to give your tea a try." He frowned. "Lead the way."

He followed me through the winding, dark corridor and into the large, chilly kitchen. Without the Goswicks, it felt intimidating, unwelcoming.

Ross stopped in front of the old cooker. "This is worse than what we used to have in the mansion."

"The general got a new range?"

"No, we, the Americans, had a Bakerloo newer model brought in before the other monstrosity blew up in our faces."

"Well, this monstrosity seems to work for Mrs. Goswick, who swears by it. Of course, she knows its tricks."

Ross embarked on a thorough inspection, playing with the knobs and burners like a child with a new toy.

"Careful now—if you break something, Mrs. Goswick will have you hanged."

"Where's the kettle? Let's get some water in it," he suggested, subtly getting me out of his way.

Good question. Where is the kettle? And the cups? And the tea bags? I silently admitted I didn't know where anything was. As gracefully as I could, I started to open cupboards in search of the needed items. I tried to look natural but only succeeded in looking more out of place than usual.

Quick to observe, Ross said, "You know this kitchen as well as I know Buckingham Palace."

"If I hadn't had more pressing things to preoccupy myself with, I might know where things are," I muttered. Cupboard after cupboard, I searched until I found the blessed teacups and tea bags. "Where could she have placed the kettle?"

"Right here." Ross opened a lower cupboard and pulled out the kettle.

"How did you know?"

"It's the most practical place—near the stove and the sink."

"You just got lucky, that's all," I said.

"I get lucky a lot."

"Sure you do," I mumbled, holding the kettle under the tap to fill it. After I replaced the lid, Ross took it from me and set it on the burner. I dropped the tea bags into the cups. "Don't let the water boil. It's not good for the herbs."

"Okay." He planted himself in front of the range, eyes glued to the kettle.

"You don't have to stay there."

"Heck, yes, I do. I know how peculiar you people are when it comes to your tea. You'll never forgive me if the water boils."

"Or if it's not hot enough," I taunted. Time passed with the kettle murmuring softly. Ross pressed his hand to the knob. I cautioned, "Not yet. It's not ready."

The captain scowled. I smiled.

Time kept ticking. "It's going to boil!" Ross exclaimed in alarm.

The kettle reached its span of tranquility, and its murmuring turned into a whistle. "All right—now!"

Ross was quick to comply. The kettle's noise died down, and with it his tension.

I laughed. "Now I know where your weakness lies, Captain."

"Yeah, I'll go to war any day, but I'll never make tea again."

I poured the water into the cups and extended the sugar bowl to him, but he barely took any.

"Let's take this out to the sitting room," he suggested. "It's warmer there."

Teacups in hand, we made our way to the coziness of the fireplace. I turned on the lamps, and Ross rekindled the fire before we settled into our chairs. We sat in companionable silence for a few minutes, drinking the tea.

Chamomile tea usually relaxed me, but today my mind kept turning over the strange events of the past few days. "Ironic how I came here to escape death, yet it is everywhere."

Placing his empty cup on the floor, Ross adjusted his chair so his legs touched mine. I didn't object. "Are you homesick?"

"Somewhat, though I imagine my parents are feeling the separation most. I'm an only child—their entire world. Because of that, I'm afraid they'll forever see me as their little girl." I sighed in defeat. "They are overprotective."

"That's not necessarily a bad thing."

"No, unless I want to grow up."

"I think I know what you mean."

Without thinking, I found myself speaking to Ross as if he were an old friend, someone I could trust completely. "Their opinions always took precedence over whatever I thought or felt. They are set in their ways, and new things scare them. And now that I finally have the freedom to do as I please, I realize that taking charge of my life is not as easy as I thought, but it's the only way to become a responsible adult."

"It's like flying. The first time I flew a plane by myself, I felt exactly like that—free to do as I pleased."

"Is that why you joined the air force?"

"Yeah. Ever since I was little, I knew I wanted to fly. I wanted to be free."

"And what did your family think?"

"My mum wasn't sure at first. My brothers are older and have their own families—and are too busy to care much about me."

"And your father?"

"My dad..." Ross said softly. "He went to work one morning while I was still in high school and never came back."

"Like...he vanished?"

"Into thin air."

"I'm sorry. That must have been horrible for you." I would have never guessed he'd gone through something like that. Considering this new information, I could understand better why he had interrogated Mrs. Goswick about Rose in such an insistent manner. He probably could not bear the thought of it.

"It doesn't bother me like it used to. Though I understand how people feel. I know how it is to want to know what happened to your loved one. People need closure."

"That's true in Mrs. Goswick's case. She still longs for Rose's return. She can't let her go."

"She won't until Rose's body is found or by some miracle she comes back."

I wondered if it was the same in his case, but as it was a sensitive subject, I did not ask. Instead, I said, "Do you think Rose could be alive?"

"If she was the only one who'd vanished and there weren't murders in the mix, I might entertain the possibility. But as things stand, I doubt it."

I couldn't argue. The mere idea that she was alive was a false hope. "I'm afraid you might be right."

Ross took my hand into his and leaned forward. My heart raced at his nearness, hammering against my ribs in anticipation. I focused on his lips as he tilted his head to the side to kiss me. But instead of connecting with him, I inhaled a sudden breath as the front door swung open. And like a whirlwind, Mrs. Goswick shot into the house, closely followed by Piper.

Surely, Mrs. Goswick had seen Ross's bike out front, so his presence wasn't much of a surprise. On the other hand, her abrupt entrance was. Ross pushed his chair back from me, and his face colored.

"Good evening," she promptly greeted. "You must excuse my tardiness."

"Good evening, Mrs. Goswick," I responded. Piper dashed to the bricks at the base of the grate and shook herself, water flying in all directions. "Oh, dear, you need a bath." She tried to jump on my lap, but I wouldn't let her. She tried Ross's lap. He welcomed her, his generosity astonishing me.

"Hey, Great Dane, what's the matter? It's just a little rain." He rubbed the Yorkie's back.

Mrs. Goswick called back through the door, "Stop fiddling with the umbrella and come in already."

Julius stepped in, observing us with a bad-tempered expression. He looked quite wild in his long trench coat, windblown and soaked.

"It's good to see you again, Julius," said Ross, rising from his seat with Piper snuggled in his arms.

"Good evening, Captain, Miss Addington," responded Julius curtly.

"Come, now, let's get to the kitchen," the housekeeper said to her son, and to Ross, "Set the dog down. I'll give her a quick wash before preparing supper."

"Thank you, Mrs. Goswick," I said, starting to think that she enjoyed giving Piper baths. "Please, don't stress."

Ross placed Piper on the floor. "Go now. Go get clean."

Muttering something about the weather and bad luck, Julius trailed behind his mother and out of view.

"I should get going. I can't wait to walk back through the swamp," Ross said sarcastically.

"You'll end up worse than Piper, covered in mud."

"Nothing new."

Ross moved to the door and stepped out onto the porch. I followed, staring out into the black night. The rain had changed into a soft drizzle, allowing the lively humming of insects to fill the air.

"You wouldn't happen to want me to stay the night, would you?"

"Not a chance."

"I was afraid you'd say that. Okay, I better be on my way."

"You can leave the bike here until the roads improve."

"Nah, I'll be okay."

My gaze fell to his bare feet. "Do take your shoes."

"Yes, ma'am."

Returning to the entrance hall, he dropped to the floor to lace his boots. Observing a different concern than the roads in his eyes, I inquired, "What is it?"

"His behavior—I find it peculiar."

"Julius's?"

Ross nodded.

"He's always like that—oblivious to the world around him," I reflected.

"No, not that."

"What, then?"

"There are two umbrellas out there." Ross lowered his voice. "Other than her feet, his mother was hardly touched by the rain, yet he was drenched."

"That's true."

"So either he doesn't know how to use an umbrella or he's been out for a while."

"Why would he be out in the storm?"

"That's exactly what I'd like to know."

CHAPTER 7

BURLEY'S DEMONS

Done lacing his boots, Ross got to his feet. "Stay out of trouble."

"I'll do my best."

He contemplated me, and for an instant, I thought he would kiss me. Instead, he said, "I'll see you around, then." Pushing his bike, he went into the night.

Perhaps next time...

I returned to the sitting room and stopped by the side table near the sofa. Curiously, both lamps flickered and then went out. I turned the knob to no effect. I started toward the other lamp when I felt a sudden cold rising from the floor, crawling up my legs.

I couldn't hear it or see it, but I could feel it. I wasn't alone. The tension in my body was heavy and tight, like a coat that didn't fit properly. Instinct drew my gaze toward the staircase, and I inhaled sharply at the sight materializing at the top of the steps. The ghost of the woman, who was not much older than me, stood there in heavy mourning attire—a style that hadn't been seen in England for decades. She looked like she had come straight from the catacombs of Castle Bran, and her presence bore the most malevolent energy I had ever felt— a paralyzing energy that seemed to smother the house as well as me.

Matching the color of her dress, her long black hair was disheveled. The veil that should have covered her face was pulled back, showing she had suffered a wallop. Bruises spread over her high cheekbones, and blood streaked her jaw and chin. With one hand, she clutched the railing. The other was pressed to her stomach. Her gait was slow and weary, as if she were in a trance. I couldn't tell if her feet actually touched the wooden steps or not. Without understanding how, I perceived that there was an endless emptiness in her, a void she desperately wanted to fill but was out of her reach.

Unable to move, I watched the apparition, hoping she would soon be gone. When she was almost to the landing, she made a small movement toward me, and her dark eyes penetrated mine. The anguish I saw in them made my entire frame tremble in terror. What kind of pernicious evil accompanied this ghost?

Her gaze pulled away from mine, and instability gripped me. My vision seemed to grow dark at the edges, as if I were viewing the events from a thousand miles away.

Somewhere in the deepest recesses of my mind, I heard Mrs. Goswick calling, "Miss Addington, are you all right?" A soft hand pressed on my shoulder.

The ghost of the woman passed through the closed door and out into the night.

"Miss Addington," Mrs. Goswick called a bit louder this time.

The instant I focused on her voice, I was back in control of myself, although my knees shook and my mind felt muddled. I looked at her with what must have been terror in my eyes. "Yes...I think so."

"I'm not so sure." She took my hand, helping me to the sofa. "You're pale and trembling. You look as if you might faint."

"I...don't know what came over me." I briefly shut my eyes, and the haunt replayed in my mind. My old intrigue regarding a ghost's ability to harm the living, in part, had just been answered, for I had suffered a shock that made me physically ill.

"I'm afraid you have been going nonstop since you arrived."

"Mrs. Goswick, would you sit with me?"

She contemplated me compassionately. "Well, of course, but supper is ready."

"I'm afraid I've lost my appetite."

"Well then, since I had supper at the cottage, I'll grab my crochet."

She left the room in search of her project, and the dark eyes of the woman appeared in my memory again. What had caused her despair? Could she be Rose? More than the unanswered questions, I dreaded the possibility of falling victim to other haunts, especially if they were as fierce as this one.

Thankfully, the housekeeper came back quickly, and soon we were engaged in discussing her work. She had taken to making hundreds of little hats and gloves for the children of the Jewish refugees. When I expressed interest, she retrieved an extra needle from her basket and put me to work.

"Just this past week, England received another large group of orphans," she noted. "Their state is difficult to believe, and one can do nothing but wish to help."

Mrs. Goswick went on to relate in detail the awful situation of the Jewish people, starting with the rumors about the concentration camps. Her honest opinion was that Germany had launched a false campaign advertising their hospitality to the prisoners when in reality they were treated worse than animals.

The tragedies of others made me reconsider my situation. I felt ashamed to complain. Still, the thought that the woman might return later tonight, when only Piper and I would hear her, made my stomach turn.

Piper's growl started even before the ghost slammed the first door in the corridor.

No, for heaven's sake...not again.

Still groggy, I scooped her up before kneeling to spy through the keyhole. The woman burst from a room with an aura of dark energy, only to pause. For an instant, she stood there brooding, looking about warily. Had she forgotten her path? Or was she considering an alternative route?

Piper whimpered, and I tightened my arms around her. She dug her claws into my skin in protest. "Ouch! What's wrong with you?" Frustrated, I let her loose.

When I looked back, the woman was headed down the hallway and straight toward me, her black dress swirling about like wisps of smoke. She could pass through the door, but would she?

Please don't come any closer... The plea bounced through my head, loud enough that I finally let it out. "Please don't come any closer!"

Her trajectory slowed and then stopped but a few doors from my bedroom. She moved her head from side to side as if assessing her surroundings. *If she doesn't kill me, her unpredictability will.* Beads of sweat broke out on my brow, the blood in my veins heating up like a pot of water. My head started to spin, and for an instant, I thought I would collapse. Piper's fright wasn't any better than mine, for she let out a long, doleful cry from under the bed. Aided by the desire to calm her fear, I found the strength to release myself from the terror possessing me. I was convinced I would hide by the dog, but instead I made it to the window to pull open the drapes.

Faint rays of light traveled through the glass, and the ghostly racket faded as if she found sunlight unbearable. I dropped on the floor by the bed and called to Piper, who had curled into a shaking ball. At once, she came to me, and for the longest time we just stayed there on the hardness of the wood, comforting each other.

When the clock finally hit seven, I dressed and went to the kitchen. Sitting at the table was a woman with long, blond, curly hair and large green eyes. I was baffled, my brain too slow to process her unexpected presence. Was I seeing a real person or a ghost?

"Good morning, Seraphina. I've been dying to meet you," she declared, a smile plastered on her slim face. Bursting from her chair, she stretched her hand out to me. "I'm Caroline Goswick."

"Good morning. It's a pleasure to meet you." Relieved that she wasn't a ghost, I was excited to find someone closer to my age at the manor. Between seeing the dead, being sheltered by my parents, and the war, I hadn't had the chance to make new friends. And adding to my delight, she wore trousers.

"Do have a seat. I'll get you some coffee," she said.

"Coffee? I didn't know Mrs. Goswick had any coffee."

"She doesn't. I brought it from Nottingham." She was quick to prepare a cup for me.

"Your parents must be thrilled to have you home. When did you get in?"

Playing with a lock of her hair, she answered, "Late last night. Father picked me up at the station."

With my drink in hand, I settled in across from her. "Welcome home. I'm glad you are here."

"So am I. I was dreadfully bored at my cousins' house. Their children are lovely, but after a while, they grow tiresome." In a rapid flow of words, she continued to enlighten me about her trip and how, upon hearing of my arrival, she had immediately made up her mind to come home. "And now that you are here, maybe Mum will let us attend the Women's Land Army more often. Until now, she has only let me go occasionally, which is ridiculous, to say the least."

"I can relate, though. Your mum's concern is understandable. The supposed killer in the woods has people on edge."

"True, but staying idle is worse than any threat. I mean, think about it, there is so much we can do—we can plant and pick potatoes, look after the mangolds and sugar-beet harvests. There's also fruit picking and working with the animals—oh, the baby horses and cows are so adorable! Or if you prefer, we can help with forest management." Seeing the blank expression on my face, she explained, "They need assistance with burning brush, sawing, and measuring. And there's always a need for planting more trees."

Still processing the large amount of information, I reflected, "I had no idea there was so much to do."

"Let me tell you this. England's future rests on the shoulders of women as much as it does on men's. They fight the war, but we keep the country alive."

"That's true, indeed."

"Meanwhile, let's not forget to have fun, especially while the soldiers are in town." She smiled mischievously.

Her lively energy was something I hadn't encountered in a while. It was sure to bring me out of the gloom of the past days. I deduced that Caroline was younger than Julius by more than fifteen years, and with her fair complexion, she looked nothing like him. I recalled Mrs. Goswick saying that conceiving a child hadn't come easily for them. "I'm blessed to have the two," she had said. Perhaps her difficulties in bearing children accounted somewhat for the motherly angst that shadowed her. I suspected all mothers entertained a certain degree of concern for the security and success of their children. Still, Mrs. Goswick's conduct attested to something more. Something that, for the time being, evaded me.

One thing was evident: the Goswick children were opposite in every possible way. Julius was reticent and harsh-mannered. Caroline was an outgoing, overtly expressive person. And as such, as soon as breakfast was over, she practically dragged me from the house. A group of women had assembled in town to mend military clothing, and Caroline was eager to involve me in their work.

Under a clear blue sky and accompanied by clean, fresh air, we were in town in no time. The cobblestone road, overlooked by houses and shops huddled together, came alive as people surfaced here and there, ready to get on with their day. As we rushed past the bakery, the smell of fresh pastries reminded me of London's coffee shops. I was surprised by my sudden longing for home and my parents.

Caroline took an abrupt turn and passed through a white gate, and then led us to a gray house at the end of a stone path. Pounding on the door, she explained, "Old people don't hear so well."

"They heard that all right."

A bespectacled, thin, elderly woman greeted us. "*Bonjour, bons amis.* It's good of you to have come."

"Good morning, Mrs. Bisset," said Caroline. I echoed her greeting.

"*S'il vous plaît, entrez.*"

We stepped into a cozy room that served as a combined kitchen and reception area. Two women sat at a square table covered with clothing in need of repair. Caroline briefly introduced me to Mrs. Jones, a sturdy middle-aged woman, and to Mrs. Dixon, a woman with an angelic face and delicate features.

Mrs. Bisset had us working in no time, armed with thimbles, scissors, needles, and thread. Mrs. Dixon placed a stack of military uniforms in front of us. Hoping I remembered the sewing lessons my mother had taught me, I threaded the needle and reached for a shirt.

"So," started Mrs. Jones, "you are staying at All Hallows."

"That's right."

"Have you seen any ghosts yet?" she inquired matter-of-factly, taking me aback.

Was she in earnest, or was she joking? I couldn't tell. Regardless, I knew better than to speak lightly of such matters. I shamefully lied, "No, I'm afraid I haven't yet had the pleasure."

"Just wait. You will," assured Mrs. Jones with a smile.

Caroline said, "I grew up around the manor, and regardless of the rumors, thanks to all the angels in heaven, I have never seen ghosts. Surely it's nothing to be excited about."

"It isn't," Mrs. Bisset echoed. "Those things are better left alone before we become *complètement fou*."

"Yes, yes. Completely crazy. Take Abigail Walton, for example," Mrs. Dixon reasoned. "The poor creature got too carried away by it all. It was her undoing."

"Terrible case, that was," Mrs. Jones agreed, shaking her head in commiseration.

"What happened to Abigail?" I asked for curiosity's sake.

Mrs. Jones seized the opportunity to tell the story before the others could. "Abigail was a young woman from a farm on the outskirts of town. Supposedly, she saw the ancient ghosts of three monks from the Beaulieu Abbey traveling the forest in search of medicinal herbs."

"Oh yes, she claimed they taught her how to use the herbs to heal the sick, and she started to make her own remedies," Mrs. Dixon added.

Throwing a sharp glance at her friend, Mrs. Jones regained control of the conversation. "Abigail said the monks wanted the cruelties done them by Henry the VIII brought to light."

"Meaning when they were thrown out of their churches and all of that?" Caroline asked.

"Yes, yes," Mrs. Jones replied swiftly. "Abigail was going to compile their accounts and publish them."

"Did she?" I inquired.

"She didn't have the chance. Her parents were concerned and had her meet with the vicar."

"Albion Baker?"

"The very same, though he couldn't do much to help. And regrettably, Abigail was sent to an asylum in London."

"She should have seen someone more competent than the vicar," Caroline opined wryly.

"But the most dreadful part of the story," reflected Mrs. Dixon with compassion, "is that poor Abigail took her life not long after."

"That's rather horrid." *Perhaps she detested the confinement because she wasn't mad after all.* My hands started to sweat. I felt exposed, as if they could see right through me and already knew I was acquainted with apparitions. Suddenly, I understood the wisdom in my parents' warnings to keep my supernatural experiences private. "Ouch," I cried out. I had pushed the needle through the fabric harshly, poking my finger with unexpected force. The blood trickled down as I held my hand away from the sewing.

"Are you all right?" Caroline looked at my bleeding finger in horror.

"It's nothing. Just a poke." After the fight with the rose bushes, this really was nothing. Producing a handkerchief from my pocket, I pressed it to my skin.

Possibly propelled by the sight of blood, Mrs. Jones, whose mind seemed to work nonstop, commented, "London is in chaos, isn't it?"

Grateful for the switch of subject, I responded, "I suppose you can say that."

"Well, you were wise to come to the country. Are you related to General Lewis, then?"

"No. He is an old family friend."

"Well, he is well known all over, after all," Mrs. Bisset said.

The irrepressible Mrs. Jones intercepted again. "And terribly busy with the war. Let's just hope he won't have to deal with local drama on top of it all."

My gaze left the needle in my hand and fell on Mrs. Jones. "What kind of local drama?"

"Well, the possibility of another murder, of course. It's been five years," she responded. "Surely you've heard about the killer in the woods?"

"Yes, I'm afraid I have."

"I think the killer is a thing of the past," Mrs. Dixon quickly offered.

"Nonsense. He has been punctual all these years. There is nothing to suggest he will change his routine now," affirmed Mrs. Jones. "He's a cunning monster with the patience of a tiger. He'll strike again soon enough, you'll see."

"It all started with the disappearance of Rose Lewis," reflected Mrs. Bisset, and looking at me, she added, "She lived at All Hallows—*un endroit maudit.*"

"According to the rumors, she was involved with a young soldier. And when he came back from the war, they eloped," Mrs. Jones recalled.

"The rumors also say he killed her and buried her somewhere in All Hallows." Mrs. Bisset confirmed the vicar's tale. "*Son fantôme hante la maison.*"

Caroline shifted uncomfortably in her seat, as did I. *Eloped with the soldier? Killed by the soldier? Buried at the manor?*

"We may never know," lamented Mrs. Dixon.

"Her tragedy was followed by the murder of Beatrice Wilson," said Mrs. Jones. The other women grew instantly quiet, and their gazes fell to their work. Mrs. Jones was quick to move on.

"Then we had Mary Beresford. The poor creature was found in the churchyard," Mrs. Jones recalled. "Can you believe his audacity—to leave a corpse on holy ground?"

Caroline and I looked at each other sympathetically. Though the conversation was enlightening, the small details made it more realistic and grueling. The older women carried on with great interest.

"Remind me who the next victim was," Mrs. Bisset requested.

"It was Aria Lancaster, wasn't it?" Mrs. Dixon replied.

"Daughter of Judge Lancaster from London," Mrs. Jones noted. "Aria and her brother were tenants at All Hallows. Like Rose Lewis, she also vanished. Her parents never lost hope of seeing her again, but I understand they have recently passed away."

"If her brother lived with her, wouldn't he have seen something?" I reasoned.

Again, Mrs. Jones satisfied my curiosity. "Her brother was a scoundrel. Raised with too much money and no accountability, if you know what I mean. He spent most of his time in the local taverns or playing in the pubs in London. Some say he didn't want to be out here, that he was just doing it to please his sister. She was the one fascinated with the idea of being in Burley."

"I remember her quite well. I met her at Sunday service. She was always the first to arrive and last to leave..." Mrs. Dixon observed.

"Oh, *yes*, I remember that," Mrs. Jones emphasized.

"She came across as a well-mannered, devout young woman," added Mrs. Dixon.

"Martha Cavendish became the fifth victim," Mrs. Bissett recalled

"I feel awful saying it, but she was a silly woman who flirted with every man who crossed her way," Mrs. Jones accused. I had the feeling she didn't feel terrible at all. "If you look for trouble, you are sure to find it." She threw a suggestive look at Caroline. The latter colored slightly.

"I remember her death. I had just arrived from France when her body was discovered by a hunter in a secluded part of the woods," informed Mrs. Bisset. "And that was about five years ago."

Intrigued by the obvious omission of the details of Beatrice's death, I asked, "Where was Beatrice found? How did she die?"

Surprisingly, Mrs. Jones averted her eyes, not attempting to answer my question.

Mrs. Dixon spoke. "Beatrice Wilson was my dear niece." Her voice vibrated with sadness.

"Oh, I'm so sorry."

Holding my gaze, Mrs. Dixon further disclosed, "Like the others, Beatrice was strangled."

Now that the sensitive information had been revealed, Mrs. Jones addressed Caroline. "Her body was found near your cottage. Your brother found it, didn't he?"

"He did," Caroline replied.

"He was in love with her, wasn't he?" Mrs. Jones pressed.

"The three of us were good friends," Caroline answered edgily.

Mrs. Jones's leading remarks continued. "But I understand she didn't reciprocate the sentiment."

Caroline shifted abruptly in her seat. The needle in her hand stabbed ferociously at the trousers she worked on as she responded, "It's true. Julius adored her. I have never seen him care for someone like he cared for Beatrice. Her death devastated him. As a matter of fact, Mrs. Jones, I think it still does."

"Well, well," Mrs. Dixon interjected. "Let's hope that whoever the killer is, he is dead already and paying for his deeds in the most severe way possible, wherever his soul has gone—for all the anguish and speculations in the world won't bring back the girls."

Mrs. Bisset moved her head up and down in assent. "We must honor their memory by being *vigilante*."

"Yes. Rose, Beatrice, Mary, Aria, and Martha—each deserves to be remembered," Mrs. Dixon added.

For the first time, the room grew silent. Yes, even Mrs. Jones quieted. Our attention dropped to the work in our hands as we processed all that had been said, dissecting the information and drawing our own conclusions as to the fate of the killer.

The more I contemplated his ruthless personality, the more I understood why people were so frightened of him. The methods he used to kill revealed that he liked to be in control, to feel powerful, to feel the life leaving his victims as they stared helplessly into his eyes. I shuddered at the thought. Worse yet, like Ross had said, he was meticulous and patient. Striking every five years required an immense amount of self-discipline. Yes, he would hunt and kill again.

An unexpected knock at the door brought us out of the confinement of our thoughts.

Mrs. Bisset answered the call. "Oh, Father Baker, what a wonderful surprise!"

"How is the project coming along?" he inquired, advancing into the room. There was a cheerful, collective welcome from the women, excepting me and Caroline.

Caroline dropped the sewing from her hands and stood rigidly her hands fisted. "Thank you for inviting us, ladies," she said. "We ought to go now."

I glanced at her, baffled. I had hoped to help a little longer and perhaps garner additional clues, but her demeanor left no doubt. We were leaving. Leaving the shirt I had just finished mending on the table, I turned to her and, trying to sound natural, said, "We do have a long walk back to the manor."

Caroline marched to the exit, throwing the vicar a look of disfavor as she passed him. I made my good-byes and joined her. Once outside, she paused as if the air had been knocked out of her.

"What's the matter?"

"I can't stand the sight of him," she hissed, starting down the pavement.

"The vicar?"

"Who else?"

"Why?" I asked.

"He's the consummate hypocrite." Her steps increased in velocity as she spoke about Albion Baker.

"How so?"

"Have you met him before?" she inquired.

"Briefly. At the churchyard."

"And?"

"He's an interesting person, but I don't know him."

"Keep it that way. You won't regret it."

"What did he do?" I hustled to follow her down the uneven path. "Tell me."

"The reason why I went away is that I fell in love with an American soldier."

"You did?" Could it have been Ross? "What's his name?" I asked a little too eagerly.

"Why does it matter?" She looked at me sideways. "Wait, you've met one of them, haven't you?" She laughed. "Don't fret. His name is Mark, and he was sent to the north after I left town. My parents didn't approve of our relationship. They were convinced he was just playing with me."

"Was that the case?"

"I don't know." She shrugged. "At any rate, I enjoyed being with him. But after a while, my mother's nitpicking got to me, and guilt pushed me to visit the vicar."

"And he wasn't helpful?"

"Far from it. You know, confessing my shameful deeds was an experience I don't wish to repeat, but even worse was being asked to relate the explicit details. When I realized he was a sick man, vicariously enjoying others' sins, I tried to leave. He stood between me and the exit, telling me to be submissive and to remember he had the power to forgive my sins—if, of course, I rendered something in exchange."

My mouth dropped open, and I expressed my disbelief. "Could you have misread his intentions?"

"Not in a million years. I fled the church as if it were on fire, but not before telling him I would gladly go to hell if need be. You should have seen his face." Caroline let out a triumphant laugh. "He's desperate to find a wife. The problem is that no one wants anything to do with him, so he tries to get whatever he can from vulnerable women."

"I would have never thought him to be so straightforward." I had some other words to best describe him, but civility prevented me from saying them aloud.

"That's a nice way to put it," she said. "Last I spoke to him, he had the audacity to threaten me. He warned me that if I said anything to stain his name, it would be his word against mine, and no one would believe me."

"That's contemptible!"

"Atrocious enough for my parents to insist I go away until the dust settled, though I think they were more concerned about keeping me away from Mark. Whatever it was, in the end, I left to appease them."

"And what about Mark? Do you keep in contact?"

"No. He promised to write, but he never did."

"I'm sorry."

"Don't be. Men are like that. He's probably enjoying himself with someone else."

Her words were cold and calculating. I wondered how many times her heart had been broken. Since her tale reminded me of the soldier who wanted to marry Rose Lewis, I had to ask. "Mrs. Jones mentioned Rose being involved with a soldier, but Mrs. Goswick didn't say anything about him. Was he real or just rumors?"

"Quite real. Mum doesn't speak about it because she didn't think much of him. She thought he was beneath Rose, and even if he survived the war, their relationship wouldn't have lasted."

"Did he survive the war?"

"Some say he did, but Mum thinks otherwise."

"She didn't see him after the war?"

"I don't think so."

I was surprised yet delighted to find a note from General Lewis awaiting me on the kitchen table.

Seraphina,

I regret not having been able to visit you again. You must forgive me. The pressing affairs of the war have kept me away from the New Forest. I do hope you continue to find peace and comfort at All Hallows.

I will be at the Burley mansion for a brief interval later this week. Would you be so kind as to accept an invitation for tea? I would be much obliged if you'd honor me with your presence.

General Lewis

Caroline snatched the note from my hand. Her face lit up as she devoured every word with great satisfaction. "This is wonderful—an invitation for tea at the Burley mansion!"

Mrs. Goswick turned from the range and shot a deadly glance at her daughter, and rightly so. Whenever Caroline heard the mention of the mansion or anything involving soldiers, she showed an inordinate amount of excitement.

"The invitation is for Miss Addington, not you," her mother reprimanded.

"I know, but Seraphina doesn't want to go alone. She would feel awkward. The place is overrun with men." Caroline had a valid argument, though I had the feeling she only cared about it because she wanted to tag along.

"I'll be happy to accompany her," snapped the housekeeper.

"Yes, you can, Mother, if you want to make a fool out of Seraphina in front of the general and his men. We aren't in the 1800s anymore. She doesn't need a chaperone."

Inwardly, I smiled. Caroline didn't like the turn the conversation had taken. I pushed the chair back and stood, ready to make an escape.

"And how would that change if you were to go with her?" Mrs. Goswick attacked again, the patience in her voice diminishing.

"I look like her sister, not her mother," Caroline defended petulantly.

"If you'll excuse me, I have things to attend to." I did not think they heard me or even noticed as I withdrew from the kitchen. Their quarreling went on.

I took myself to the library, the area I enjoyed most in the house. The vast accumulated knowledge within its walls produced a serene atmosphere. Sunshine filtered through the tall windows, lifting my mood. In sharp contrast to the neatness surrounding me, I saw that a group of scattered books lay on the floor as if they had just fallen off the bookcases.

How odd. Mrs. Goswick patrolled the house constantly, and disarray like this wouldn't go unnoticed. Gathering the volumes, I tucked them into the empty spaces between the other books on the shelves. Taking a step back from the robust wooden case, I traced the spines of the volumes with my fingers. *Medicine books.* I skipped to the next shelf.

Music volumes. I wasn't very good at music. I moved on until I found some classics.

Wuthering Heights by Emily Brontë seemed to jump at my fingertips. Moving a chair closer to the window, I slid down into it, eager to start the journey in its pages and escape reality. Soon I was caught up in the tale.

I was at the funeral of Catherine's father when a tumultuous noise from the hall startled me. I left the book on the chair and padded across to the door, carefully pushing it ajar. Julius argued adamantly with someone in the corridor. I remained hidden, straining to hear.

"I…don't know," Julius said. A pause, and then he spoke again. "Leave me in peace. I told you already. I don't know."

My curiosity was piqued. I had to know who Julius's tormenter was, for no matter how hard I tried, I couldn't hear the other voice. Ever so slowly, I pulled the door open enough to slip out into the hall.

Standing in the shadows, I heard Julius say, "No! No! It wasn't me."

With my heart thumping against my ribs, I tiptoed in his direction. I was almost to the bend of the corridor when his voice went quiet. Fearing I would miss the chance to discover who he spoke with, I launched forward. And like hitting a brick wall, I collided with the large frame of the gardener. The crash pushed me backward, and I stumbled before catching my balance.

"Goodness gracious, Julius! Where are you going in such haste?" I scanned the deserted hallway beyond him.

"Sorry, miss. Sorry." He took a few steps and grimaced.

I raised my hand, detaining his march. I'd never seen Julius this flustered before, and it wasn't pleasant. "Who were you speaking with?"

"Excuse me. There's work to do," he grumbled, attempting to go around me.

"Wait." I stepped in his way. "Who was here with you?"

With a stern look, he said, "It's none of your business," and trotted away. I supposed after the incident in the garden, he was tired of my pestering.

Who had he been speaking to? What had they accused Julius of to upset him this much? The desire to find out forced me after him despite his demeanor, but his long legs and nervous energy gave him the advantage. I popped into the kitchen just in time to see him slip through the back door. Mrs. Goswick and Caroline sat at the worktable, peeling a large pile of potatoes.

In passing, I heard Caroline say, "There you are, just in time for tea." Tea was the last thing on my mind.

Once outside, I broke into a run—the notion that the grounds were Julius's kingdom and no one could navigate them better than he pressed at the back of my mind. The truth was that my chances of reaching him were slim unless he allowed it to happen. I implored, "Julius, stop. Just stop!"

He halted for an instant but not long enough for me to reach him. And then his flight resumed. My steps faltered. There was no use in keeping up the chase. His march was designed to go on until I gave up. And I was about to do just that when a sudden change in his course energized me. I had a chance after all. Julius had disappeared into the stable. There was only one entrance to the wooden structure. He had no choice but to face me before coming out.

I was out of breath by the time I came to the entrance. The first thing I heard was the Goswicks' horses neighing from their stalls in a state of distress. As I moved down the center aisle, the source of their angst became apparent.

At the end of the aisle stood Julius with his back to me, waving his arms in the air as he spoke. In front of him was none other than the ghost of the soldier. There was no doubt now that he was a disembodied spirit. Of course, it was him Julius had been arguing with in the corridor. And the ghost, apparently as relentless as I was, had also come after the gardener.

The ghost acknowledged me first. Though we were several yards apart, his gaze fell on mine with such ferocity I paused in my tracks. Most of the spirits I had encountered seemed almost as unaware of me, as if I were the ghost. Even the woman in black hadn't seemed fully conscious of my presence.

Come on, Seraphina, you mustn't be afraid. It's too late for that. I repeated these words while a cold sweat prickled my skin. Mechanically, I proceeded down the aisle, vaguely aware of the horses' increasing restlessness. The ghost's eyes never left mine. In them, I saw fierceness give way to intrigue.

Before losing my wits, I said stoutly, "What's going on in here?"

Julius, a bit startled, turned to face me. The ghost vanished. The horses hushed.

"Who is the ghost? What does he want from you?"

Julius regarded me coolly. "I already told you—he is no one."

"That's not true. Who is he? What does he want from you?" Julius tried to move past me, but I was determined. "Who is he?"

Julius grabbed my arms, and I feared he was ready to teach me that lesson on unpleasantness. He was unpredictable, strong, and in the blink of an eye could break me like a twig. If nothing else, I had to keep a steady voice and project some self-confidence. "Julius, let go of me." Ignoring my petition, he tightened his viselike grip, and I let out a small gasp of pain.

"Ask *him*," Julius suggested in answer to my question. Like a boa constrictor, he squeezed my arms, and then he proceeded to lift me off the ground. I braced for a blow. Instead, he planted me by a stall and out of his way.

He was almost to the gate when my brain registered what he had said. *Ask him.* Ask Ghost. With a controlled voice that contradicted the hammering of my heart against my ribs, I cried out, "I will ask him. But you must tell me where to find him."

Over his shoulder, Julius responded, "At dusk, follow the narrow path between the tall trees. You'll find him by the stream."

I paced the sitting room, a thousand apprehensions preying on my mind. How much did I really want to know about Ghost? Was he Rose's lover and murderer? Would he confess to her killing now that he was dead? Maybe his evil deeds wouldn't allow him to rest, and being in a repentant state, he hoped to find solace by bringing to light what he had done.

My assumptions were rapidly refuted by the facts. What I had witnessed of Julius's ghostly intruder wasn't worthy of repentance. He appeared to enjoy tormenting the gardener and even wanted to harm him. Just today, it seemed the restlessness of the horses in the stable might have been instigated by Ghost to hurt Julius.

If Julius was in harm's way, now that Ghost realized that I could see him, would I become a target too? Even more troublesome was the thought that he might be using the gardener to bring me to him. Perchance, the soldier, having been a murderer in life, still thirsted for violence and blood in death. *What did the vicar say? Oh, yes—once a person kills, it's easy to do it again.*

Throwing a glance at the window, I saw that dusk would soon descend upon the New Forest. In my heart, venturing into the woods at this late hour was against my better judgment and the advice I had promised to heed. I dropped onto the sofa and shut my eyes to calm my overactive imagination. As my mind cleared, I recalled a detail I hadn't yet considered. There had been a certain recognition in the ghost's eyes, as if there were an invisible link between us, bringing us together— although the type of link, whether good or evil, remained to be discovered. I might be going mad, but it felt right. I would go down to the stream and confront him.

I stood to leave, but a loud rap on the door halted my plan. Considering that Mrs. Goswick and Caroline were still at the cottage, with the pressing twilight, I would have to get rid of the visitor quickly. I pulled the door open and, to my dismay, found myself staring into Albion Baker's catlike eyes.

"Good evening, Miss Addington," he said promptly, touching the brim of his large black hat. "I hope I'm not imposing. I was in the vicinity and thought to check in on you." He flashed a wide grin.

"Good evening..." I said, in a colorless voice. Indeed, he was imposing on the little time I had to execute my plan, but how could I explain that? *Sorry, I can't receive you because I'm on my way to meet a dead man.* Even though I would have liked to see his reaction, I refrained, especially after learning about Abigail's fate. Being confined to an asylum for seeing apparitions wasn't appealing.

"May I come in?"

It was amazing how propriety, when firmly implanted, could take control to the point of encumbrance. "Please do."

"You are most kind, Miss Addington." He stepped in, his gaze scanning the grand hall and staircase as he spoke in a longing tone. "Ah, All Hallows and its grandeur. It's been too long since I was last here. It hasn't changed much."

"I suppose it hasn't."

"There are some impressive quarters in the east wing. Is that where you are staying?"

What an odd and intrusive question. "They are impressive indeed."

"The best ones are the yellow, blue, and green rooms, if memory doesn't fail me." He smiled and quickly explained, "I got a tour when I attended to Richard."

Changing the subject, I offered, "May I take your coat and bag?"

"Thank you."

Swiftly removing his black shoulder bag, he lowered it to the floor and handed his overcoat to me. I hung it on the peg by the exit, finding it peculiar when he picked up his bag and kept it with him. Moving to the heart of the sitting room, he settled comfortably on the sofa, crossing his legs.

Caroline's story guaranteed I would take the farthest possible seat. "What brings you to these parts?"

"Oh, nothing much—routine visits to those who aren't able to attend Sunday services." He waved a hand in the air in a pathetic effort to depict humbleness. "Older folks, you understand."

"That's very kind of you. I'm sure they appreciate your visits," I lied. If the parishioners liked him as much as I did, seeing him only at church was best.

"On the other hand, Miss Addington, you look lively and in excellent health. I haven't been informed of your plans to attend Sunday meetings." His voice was filled with a reproach designed to inflict guilt. "You know, it's a matter of formality to notify the clergy of one's intentions to be part of his parish when relocating."

My newfound confidence was instantly rekindled. I hadn't come this far, determined to escape my parents' capriciousness, to succumb to the whims of a stranger. "I'm afraid I haven't decided on the matter yet."

"I can't imagine what would keep you from worshipping."

I gave him a wry smile. "The only thing that keeps me from worshipping is my disposition. You must forgive my bluntness, but I have no intention of being a regular attendant."

His face drained of color as if the devil himself had spoken to him. When he took a brief instant to realign his attack, I knew I had struck a deep chord. "Is there a reason for your religious disdain?" Before I could respond to the assumptions he'd made, he further said, "I mean, the state of your soul is more important than lingering in bed on a Sunday morning."

I was nonplussed. Had he called me slothful or irresponsible? Maybe both. If he only knew my only religious impairment, at present, was him, he would hide under a rock. Sunday or no Sunday, I had no desire of seeing much of the man. Yet here he was, testing my patience.

"I do not dislike religion. I dislike hypocrites—those who profess to be religious yet are far from caring about others. Those who, veiled in sheep's clothing, go about seeking the opportunity to take advantage of their neighbors." As soon as those words left my lips, I knew I had said too much. Being insolent wasn't in my nature, but something about the man had disturbed me, even before Caroline shared her story.

Unable to mask his discontent, he shifted in his chair as his eyes protruded from their sockets and his jaw tightened. Had no one ever been so candid with him? Caroline surely had. For a split second, I feared he would lash out, but to my sheer astonishment, his demeanor transformed radically. A soft expression of—was it compassion?—came over him. His unexpected change reminded me that part of my aversion was founded in gossip.

"I shouldn't have said that. It's been a long day."

He left his seat and neared me. "I can see that. Is something the matter, child?" Squatting down by my chair, he placed a hand on my knee.

At his touch, I realized my previous sympathy had been offered too quickly. I was now filled with a wave of revulsion. My gaze darted to the poker standing by the hearth.

"Being alone in this enormous house must be trying. You must be lonely and frightened half the time." He reached for a strand of my hair and tucked it behind my ear. I wanted to bolt but found myself unable to move. I felt like a bird cornered by a wild cat—if I moved but an inch, he would pounce.

My best weapon was my voice, so I said, "You are mistaken. I'm not afraid or alone." I was both, but he would never know it. "Would you like some tea? Shall I call for Mrs. Goswick? Or Caroline?"

Where these words came from I wasn't sure, but they saved me. At the mention of Caroline, Father Baker's hand left my knee, and like an agile cat, he sprang to his feet. The chair that held me captive instantly released me, and I walked to the fire poker, ready to grab it. Meanwhile, I reached for the domestic cord hanging down the wall by the fireplace.

"No, that won't be necessary. I should be on my way. It's growing late," he quickly said.

I nodded in full agreement and let go of the cord.

Gathering his overcoat, he observed, "I did not know Miss Goswick was employed here."

"She works alongside her mother." I walked to the door and placed my hand on the knob. "We have become good friends. Really good friends."

"I see. Well then, it was a pleasure to visit with you. Give my regards to the Goswick family."

"Rest assured that I will." With a little more energy than I had intended, I pulled on the doorknob. "Good evening."

He secured his hat on his neatly arranged hair. "Good night, Miss Addington."

I slammed the door before the end of his salutation. Thankfully, my bluff about the Goswicks had worked, and hopefully he would catch the hints and realize I was aware of his tactics with women, which should dissuade him from pursuing me. And if that didn't work, my heathen status should. I would not make a good wife for a clergyman.

Taking a moment to make sure he was truly gone, I slipped my coat on, and from the box near the fireplace, I selected a fire poker. Ghost might not be intimidated by it, but he was not the only one I feared in the woods.

CHAPTER 8
THE GHOST OF THE SOLDIER

Ignoring my misgivings, I hastened through the deepening twilight. Had my resolution to be an independent woman taken me to the border of stupidity? And in trying to prove myself, was I running into a trap? The only certainty was that it was too late for regrets. I refused to give my imagination free rein, but I stayed vigilant.

Much farther than I had anticipated, I heard the stream—a solid, inviting sound like the soft but constant melody of chimes dancing in the wind. Before emerging from the concealment of the trees, I stopped briefly to scan the area and adjust my grip on the fire poker. If any mortal lay in wait to cause me harm, I would not go down without a good fight.

Coming into the open space, I felt exposed, but I walked quickly to the edge of the water. The stream overflowed from the recent storm. The moisture and freshness filled my nostrils. It was beautiful here. I could understand why the ghost liked the spot. Would he show? My question was instantly answered when my heart skipped a beat. Several yards from me, tall and still, stood the ghost of the soldier.

He looked downcast, consumed by his thoughts. The fleeting impression that his heart carried a terrible burden overshadowed me. It had become increasingly clear that death wasn't the end to the pain and heartbreaks of this life.

He noticed me at once. Strangely, though I didn't know what to expect, I felt somewhat calm. He approached with a blank expression on his face. I almost laughed at the peculiar situation, but still I gripped my weapon firmly. A radiance surrounded his frame that made it easy for me to distinguish his features in the fading light.

"Good evening, Miss Addington." He had a pleasant voice, like the inviting melody of a piano. His dark-green eyes accentuated his skin in a way I hadn't anticipated. He was strikingly handsome. "It's a pleasure to make your acquaintance."

"I'm not sure I can reciprocate the sentiment."

"Fair enough." He took a step closer, his eyes filled with an intense energy. Under his critical observation, my courage dwindled, and words escaped me. He spoke again, his voice cutting through my insecurities. "Are you afraid?"

Not responding would imply a positive answer. I opted for somewhere in the middle. "Should I be?"

This time his eyes showed incredulity. "Yes, you should."

"Why?"

His laugh was a mixture of amusement and grief. "Well, in case you haven't noticed—I'm dead."

Aware of his confident stance, I reflected, "You knew I would come. How?"

"By the way you looked at me in the stable."

"And how did I look at you?"

"Well, first and foremost, unlike others, you can see and hear me. And instead of trepidation, you contemplated me with much interest."

"Julius can see you too."

"Yes, like you, he's an exception."

"Why did you leave, then?"

"The timing was wrong, but I lingered outside and overheard Julius tell you where to find me."

"You like to eavesdrop on people's conversations?"

"If you must know, I hovered outside the doors to make sure you were safe. Julius can get a bit rattled at times, and when he does, he loses his head."

"That's ironic," I snapped, his apparent act of kindness taking me aback.

"Why?"

"Why?" I gave him a look of incredulity. "Your presence is what rattles him. The poor creature is terrified of you and whatever is going on."

"I wish he were."

"You would be foolish to think he isn't."

His eyebrows knitted in disbelief. "Well then, I must be a fool."

I fortified my attack with another angle. "Don't pretend to be so innocent. I saw you in the garden taunting Julius—making fun of him, trying to make him fall off the ladder. Tell me, what's in it for you? Does picking on others give you pleasure?"

"I'll say, you've got an imagination! You seem to have conjectured a whole lot of things," he retorted. "I was laughing at his stupidity. I told him he was too heavy for the ladder. I couldn't believe he was going up all the way. But as usual, the pigheaded fool didn't listen."

"I'm not sure I believe you."

He shrugged. "That's your choice."

If he was a liar, he was a good one. I had never entertained the possibility of Julius being the problem. "Listen, I don't know who you are or what your intentions might be, but I doubt Julius possesses the wherewithal to deal with you. Why even speak to him?"

"You are not safe here," the ghost said, moving instantly to my side.

"Are you trying to sidetrack me?"

"Shh...listen," he ordered. After a brief silence, I heard it—a small disturbance coming from the trees. "Did you hear that?"

"Yes." The sound came again, closer this time. "Who is there?"

"I don't know. I can see and hear better than mortals, but only to a certain extent."

"Well, I still have this." I raised the fire poker in front of me.

"I admire your grit, but you don't stand a chance against a man with that."

Had he seen how helpless I had been against Julius in the stable?

Even if he was correct, I wouldn't give up easily. "And you're not much of a help. Are you?"

His brow contracted in a displeased gesture. "Depends how you look at it. Listen, what I can do is guide you back to the house. I'll be a second set of eyes in the forest, but you'll have to trust me."

The forest's floor, crunching underfoot, warned us that someone approached. *I should not have come.* Yes, amid the advancing veil of night, I needed his help, for I wasn't even sure in which direction I had come.

"All right."

The footfalls stopped abruptly, and Ghost said, "Someone is watching you from the trees at nine o'clock. He is not alone. I hear his horse nearby."

Nine o'clock...nine o'clock... Suddenly I couldn't think clearly. Where was nine o'clock? Seeing my confusion, the ghost pointed to the spot, but it was too dark for me to make anything out. Wishing for a reasonable explanation, I whispered, "It could be the soldier on patrol."

"He wouldn't behave like this."

"Like what?"

"Like a predator stalking its victim." With a firm tone, he directed, "You must run like your life depends upon it, straight through the trees on your right. Don't look back. I'll do that for you."

I think my life does depend on it.

"Ready?"

I nodded.

"Now, run!"

Like a fawn, I dashed into the vegetation, hoping the woods were more merciful than the rose garden.

"Keep moving. He's coming after you!" the ghost warned, his soft radiance making it easy for me to follow.

The deeper I ran into the woods, the darker and denser it became. Why had the ghost selected this route? In front of me stood a colony of wild shrubs. Branches and twigs stretched across the way, grabbing and scratching, slowing me down. Escalating my agitation in the confusing maze, I lost sight of the ghost. This was much worse than the rose bushes as I was forced to get on with the escape even when I wasn't sure where I was going.

I conquered the shrubbery, but my relief was short lived. I now faced a host of tightly knit trees. And I had no idea where I was and felt completely disoriented, like the time my parents had taken me to the fair as a child and I'd gotten lost inside the mirror tent. Worse yet, I did not know where my pursuer was. Looking madly around me, I stood petrified, afraid to make a move or produce a sound that could become my last.

"No, no! You can't stop. Keep going." The ghost reappeared at my side. "Come on. This way."

The sound of his voice released me from the paralyzing gloom. "Is he close?"

"Yes. Run, Seraphina, run!"

Gasping for breath, I dashed after the ghost. My legs burned from the exertion, and I discarded my overcoat to lighten the weight. Somewhere along the path, I also lost my hat. The only thing I still had was the weapon in my hand.

My ghostly companion disappeared again, though only briefly. When he returned, I understood that he was checking on the progress of my assailant. "He knows the woods well," he said over his shoulder. "But the horse is slowing him down."

The horse. I had forgotten about it. It now made sense why we traveled the densest parts. I did have the advantage, but I worried that my body would not cooperate much longer.

"My legs are burning," I blurted out almost unconsciously.

"Don't think about it. Keep your eyes on me. Keep up."

I forged ahead, but the muscles in my legs had other plans. A sharp pain shot through my thighs, and I tumbled to the ground. My arms were too slow to catch me, and my face hit the ground hard. It hurt, but I contained my scream as best I could.

The ghost cursed and came to my aid. "Get up! Get up!" I made a weak attempt to do so. "Never mind. Scoot back. Scoot back!" he shouted in my face. "Get behind those trees!" He pointed to a small cluster nearby. Half scooting, half crawling, I backed against a tree trunk.

Crouching beside me, he put a finger to his lips, warning me to be quiet, but I couldn't stop gasping for air, so I brought my hand up to cover my mouth and nose. Not even during the air raids had I been so scared. Maybe it was the familiarity of the attacks, the other people sharing my plight, or the warning sirens that had kept the fear at bay. In contrast, this was the killer strangling his victims and discarding their lifeless bodies in places much like this one.

Out of the past, Father's words came to me. *The time to fear will come, but it's not now. Now is the time to fight and to survive.*

The sound of hooves was devilishly close. The ghost turned to his left. There, I saw the animal come to a halt behind a wall of shrubbery. The rider, a bulky black figure, turned his head from side to side, scanning the area with unsettling serenity. Sweat, hot and thick, bathed my face. I pressed my hand tighter against my mouth.

His closeness filled me with a staggering impulse to run, even when I still had the advantage of concealment. And though running was the wrong thing at the moment, I was about to rise from the ground when the ghost walked out and stood in front of the animal, waving his arms up and down while he ordered, "Shoo, now! Go! Get out of here!" The horse neighed in panic and ferociously stamped his hooves. "Go now! Shoo!" Ghost commanded again.

The rider struggled to gain control, yelling at the horse to calm down. His voice was muffled by the animal's thrashing, so I failed to recognize it, though I had the vague impression I had heard it before. Ghost encouraged the horse to flee once again, and the animal took off, carrying the helpless rider away.

"Come on, come on," the ghost urged. "He'll soon regain control and make his way back."

Ghost took point, and I ran behind, yard after yard, until a growing pain in my legs slowed me down. Even so, I kept moving through the trees until the muscles in my calf had had enough, and they turned into a ball. There was no choice but to halt. I pressed my knuckles to my leg to try to loosen the knot.

Ghost was instantly beside me. "What are you doing?"

"I just need a second," I stammered as another spasm of pain assaulted my calf.

"We don't have a second," Ghost hissed. "I hear him. He is coming after you on foot."

I hobbled forward, frustrated that my weakness might mean my death. The ghost must have thought as much, for this time it was he who told me to stop. Facing me, he placed his hands on my shoulders. At once, all my aches were gone, and a sensation like hot water falling over my head and traveling down my entire frame reenergized me.

"Follow me." The ghost turned to lead the way again, the speed with which he dashed ahead incredible. But more stunning was that I kept up with him. I didn't know how, but I was convinced he had transmitted some of his strength to me.

When my feet crossed onto All Hallows's property, I looked back at the woods. It looked back at me darkly. I had defeated evil this time, but it would remain there, awaiting another opportunity to beat me.

"You can't stop until you get to the house!" the ghost warned.

I ran farther from the danger, my companion at my side, and soon we crossed All Hallows's threshold. With shaky fingers, I locked the door, conscious that my breathing was extremely loud.

Moving down the entrance hall, I called, "Mrs. Goswick, Caroline, are you here?" In return, I received an echo followed by thick silence. Standing at the bottom of the staircase, I tried a few more times with the same result.

"Let me check." The ghost vanished to search the house.

I used the opportunity to catch my breath.

"They are gone," Ghost announced, reappearing beside me.

"I wonder why they are not back from the cottage yet." It was so unlike them to deviate from their schedule.

"Listen. Stay here and don't open to anyone. Do you understand me?"

"I do. Where are you going?"

"To follow the rider."

"Did you see his face?" I asked.

"No. He wears a mask."

"You have seen him before?"

"A few times, but he is fast and an expert at disappearing." The ghost moved a step away and then, turning back to me, said, "I'm not sure I should leave you."

"Why? I'll be safe here."

"I don't trust you."

"I won't leave the house. Besides, I still have this." I waved the fire poker at him.

His lips pressed into a tight line, and without another word, he disappeared through the door. The exhaustion from the chase coupled with the emotional turmoil finally overcame me. I dragged myself to the sofa across from the lifeless hearth, allowing the weapon to fall from my grip and onto the floor. Alone with my thoughts, I found it challenging to make sense of what had just occurred. Was the rider the killer? Had he known I would be out there? If it weren't for the ghost's help, what would my fate have been? *Tonight, my name could have been added to the list of murdered women.*

My mind traveled back to the underground in London.

The blast of explosions in the distance wrenched my heart as more and more of our beautiful city was erased. The ceiling shook and the scattered lightbulbs flickered, threatening to collapse on us.

"Look at me, Seraphina," Mother had said as we huddled against the roughness of the wall. "Take a deep breath through your nose—let your chest swell with air like a balloon—then let it out through your mouth."

Mother would have me do the exercise for a few minutes. Amazingly, that simple breathing routine sent a calming message to my brain, dispelling the acute stress. As if I were there in the underground with my dear parents, I breathed in and out, in and out. And it wasn't long until the tension in my chest subsided.

At length, the disembodied soldier stepped back into the house and came to the sitting room. Finding it peculiar that he'd used the doorway, though he really wasn't using it, I inquired, "Do you have to use the door?"

"No, I can come straight through the walls, but I didn't want to frighten you."

"That's thoughtful of you." His mortal mannerisms did abate his spectral presence. "Did you find the rider?"

"No, there was no trace of him. He must have retreated when you reached the clearing."

Surmising he knew of the menace, I asked, "Do you think he is the killer?"

"Of that I have no doubt."

"You said you have seen him before."

"From a distance and at night. I lose him once he enters town." Looking a bit uncomfortable, he sat down in a chair in the corner of the room—a shadowy niche in the vast area that kept him on guard like a rook perched on a lofty branch.

It was then that I noticed the light around his form had dimmed. My apprehension toward him had also lessened. "Are you all right?"

"Shipshape. You?"

"Fine."

"I would have never guessed. You're a frightful sight to behold. Ghastly," he noted.

"In case you haven't noticed, you don't look too great yourself."

The ghost stretched his hands in front of him. "No, I guess not."

"Is there something wrong?"

"Nothing." He shifted in his seat.

"I don't believe you."

For a long, uncomfortable moment, we stared at each other. Here we were, two complete strangers, functioning in two different states and carrying on a conversation that would challenge the sanity of the cleverest people on the planet.

Ghost was thinking as much, for he reflected, "Not every day do I get to behave like a living person—I mean, to just sit here and visit as if I were alive feels extremely out of place."

"Imagine how I feel. Not every day do I converse with a ghost. I didn't even know it was possible—at least not to this degree." I smiled reassuringly, though cautiousness warned me he was still a stranger.

"Well, if I do something dull-witted, don't hold it against me."

The pounding on the door came so unexpectedly it brought us to our feet.

"Don't open it. Let me see who it is first." I nodded but followed him to the entrance. The ghost reached for my arm, and though I couldn't feel the density of his flesh, my skin felt warm where he touched me. He reiterated, "Do not open it," and walked through the wall to the porch.

Pressing my ear against the door, I heard Ghost saying, "What are you doing here?"

"Not speaking to you," Julius retorted.

"Come, now. What do you want?"

The gardener didn't respond. Instead, he slammed his fist against the door again.

Fearing he wouldn't stop until I answered, I called out, asking who it was.

"Julius," he responded. "Father sent me to light the fire."

"Where are your parents? And Caroline?" I leaned against the wall to keep my balance as the exhaustion crept back in.

"At home, helping Sally have her baby. They'll come later."

"Sally the cow?" I faintly remembered Mrs. Goswick saying something about the cow being ready to give birth.

"Yes."

"I'll manage the fire. Go home and help with Sally."

"No. I'll light the hearth for you," he insisted, giving the door a solid pounding that made me jump back. "Let me in."

"She told you to go. Now go," Ghost hissed.

"Please, Julius," I pleaded before the ghost lost his temper. "Go home. I'm going to bed, so I don't need the fire after all."

A pause ensued, and I imagined the men stared each other down, mentally sparring with their eyes. The ghost must have won the match, for I heard Julius's heavy footfalls move away from the house.

Minutes later, Ghost came back, finding me in the same spot.

"Where did you go?"

"I followed Julius. He went back to the cottage."

"You don't suppose it was him out in the woods?"

"It's hard to tell. He was bundled in dark clothing, but his horse was clean and unsaddled. That's the first thing I checked when I went out the first time."

"He could have been riding any horse," I muttered, returning to the sofa. I fell onto it heavily, feeling like I had fallen down the rabbit hole.

"I'm not so sure." Ghost retreated to the same chair in the corner, far from me.

"You act as if I'm going to hurt you," I pointed out. "I don't think that's possible. Is it?" Inwardly, I acknowledged I should be the one who was afraid. I had no idea what he was capable of or what his intentions were.

"No, it isn't."

"Well then, come closer," I encouraged, hiding my disquiet. "Normal people don't sit so far apart."

"All right, don't fuss." He moved to the armchair across from me. "You know, you were brave out there in the woods."

"It was all you. You, Ghost, saved me."

He let out a short laugh. "We haven't introduced ourselves properly. My name is not Ghost, but ladies first. I know your name but nothing else."

I sat a bit taller. "I'm from London. Due to the war and *other* things, my parents wanted me out of there, and General Lewis offered for me to stay here."

His eyes narrowed when he asked, "Are you related to the Lewis family?"

"Not at all. The general and my father served together in the Great War."

"Sensible enough."

"I suppose."

"Do you have siblings?" he asked.

"No, I'm the only child."

"It must have been hard for your parents to send you away."

"Keeping me in London would have been harder."

A wave of sorrow enshrouded his face. "I suppose London has changed since I last saw it."

"When was that?"

"Long ago," he said.

"The air raids have caused quite a bit of damage."

"I hear about it through people's conversations and the news whenever someone has the wireless set on."

"You do move about, don't you?" The notion that, like him, other ghosts roamed our living spaces, often unknown to us, was unsettling, especially considering that not all of them bore honorable intentions.

He shrugged. "There is not much else to do."

"It's your turn. Tell me about you. I still don't know your name."

"My name is Elliott." He pronounced it softly, as if the very sound grieved him. "Officer Elliott Kennard."

"You were at the edge of the woods the day I came to Burley, weren't you?"

"I was."

"It was you who had Piper in a fit, wasn't it?"

"That little overgrown rat. If I were mortal, your beast would have had me killed by the patrolling soldier. She gave away my position in a most tenacious way."

"I can't blame her. She's been through a lot."

"Where is she now?" His gaze searched the area for her.

"Probably at the cottage. Mrs. Goswick spoils her with treats."

"Good, keep her there."

I shook my head in a dissatisfied manner.

He was quick to advise, "Don't take it personally. Your presence, even with the dog, is the best thing that's happened to me since the Great War."

Considering that the Great War had taken place almost three decades ago and it was me he spoke of, I reflected, "How is that a good thing?"

"In my current state, I'm bound to certain limits. I can't go beyond the woods. And to complicate matters, as you know, few can see me, but they take off in haste, as if—" He laughed, illuminating the room with his charm. "As if they have seen a ghost."

"That must be frustrating, but surely you can see their point of view."

"Only too well, but I have to keep trying. So far, the only one I've had to work with is the dimwit."

"Don't call him that. His name is Julius."

"Don't get worked up. If you had endured all I have with *Julius*, you would sympathize with me."

"Well then, enlighten me. Why are you so anxious to communicate with people? Why haven't you moved on to whatever place the..." I hesitated, not wishing to give offense, though I had no idea what the rules of etiquette were when conversing with a ghost.

"The dead," Elliott said for me.

"Yes, where the dead go."

Looking at me with piercing eyes, he assured me, "It's not as easy as you think. You might not understand."

"Give me a try."

CHAPTER 9
OFFICER ELLIOTT KENNARD

"I hail from Ringwood," Elliott disclosed. "Do you know where that is?"

"No."

"It's about six miles west of here as the crow flies. It feels like an eternity since I lived there. I was a lad then…" His eyes wandered to the past as he spoke, to memories clearly mingled with intricate emotions

You still are very young. With his childish face and sweet smile, he couldn't be any older than twenty—yet his soul had lived much longer. "When was then?"

"1915."

I could hold neither my curiosity nor my tongue. "How old were you?"

"Eighteen. You probably weren't alive yet."

"No. I was born after the war, in 1922," I said.

"I moved to Burley to work, and that's where I came across Rose Lewis. Do you know who she is?"

I gave him a practical answer. "General Lewis's first cousin once removed and the owner of this house."

"That's right. I was courting her when I was called to the war. Well, to simplify things, let's just say that when I returned, she was gone. And I've been looking for her ever since."

Elliott's words reminded me of what the vicar had said. *"She was involved with a young man from the vicinity. He went to the Great War, and rumor has it that upon his return, she had fallen out of love with him, so he killed her."*

Was Elliott telling the truth? Like the vicar had said, if Elliott had been madly in love and Rose had rejected him, he could have done the unthinkable in a moment of rage. Furthermore, he could have taken his own life in remorse. Could he be in a state of denial? Could that be why he lingered in the woods?

Trying to answer my questions without revealing my suspicions, I said, "You survived the war but lost Rose. That must have been hard."

"I didn't survive the war. I died in battle. I came back in this spirit form to say good-bye, but I couldn't find Rose or my way out of here." His tone was now sullen. "The only person who can communicate with me, until now, has been Julius, and he refuses to tell me what he knows about Rose. I had almost given up until you came along."

"Me? I don't know anything about All Hallows's past. Apart from the general, I didn't know the Lewis family until I arrived. And just so you know, Julius hates me. He will not tell me any more than he has already told you."

Elliott left his chair and drew near. He sat on the edge of the coffee table, his eyes staring into mine with chilling intensity. "It's not what the mortals can tell you that I'm interested in."

What in the world does he mean by that? My instinct urged me to escape his dominating presence, but I held my ground. "What, then?"

"I'm interested in knowing what the dead have to say." He leaned toward me. "I'm not the only ghost at All Hallows, am I?"

My tongue felt heavy.

"Am I?" Elliott pressed.

"No, you are not."

"How many more are there?"

"Just one I'm aware of."

"Is it a man or a woman? What does it look like?"

His sudden indefatigability to know took me aback. All I could do was to respond as fast as he was asking. "The ghost is a woman. I sometimes see her in the evening on the staircase. She has long black hair, but it's hard to see her. She's shrouded in darkness."

"How old would you say she is?"

"Late teens, early twenties—I'm not sure."

"It must be Rose..." He anxiously ran his fingers through his hair "Is that the only time you have seen her?"

I shook my head. "Before dawn, she haunts the hallway upstairs. I've only seen her through the keyhole in my door, but there is no doubt it's the same ghost."

"What does she do?"

"She rushes down the corridor opening and closing doors in a rage."

"She searches for something."

"I think she finds it in the bedroom two doors down from mine. That's where she usually ends her journey with the most petrifying scream I have ever heard."

"She's definitely a tormented soul—one looking for justice. And maybe revenge." His hands fisted. "I can't believe Rose would have suffered that fate, but that's exactly why I need you to help me."

"Help you with what?"

"You have the ability to communicate with spirits."

"Are you suggesting I speak to the woman?" The idea was beyond terrifying and a supreme absurdity. *Oh, this is not good—when will I learn to control my tongue? I shouldn't have told him any of it.*

"Yes, I need to know if this ghost you speak of is Rose—and if it is, I need to find out what happened to her." The timbre in his voice grew dark, determined. "I have to know."

"Listen, I'm bothered by the drama of this place. That's why I took the risk of reaching out to you, but you are different from the other ghost. She is malevolent—violent. I..."

"You are afraid of her."

I answered with a resounding, "Yes! I would be an idiot if I weren't. Why don't you speak to the ghost yourself?"

"Because I can't. You must do it for me."

I fled the couch to stand by the dead hearth, confused.

In an instant, he stood but inches from me. "I won't leave you alone until you help me."

"I..." What was he trying to accomplish? Torment me like he tormented Julius? The dilemma was that, unlike with humans, I couldn't get a peace warrant against him or throw him out of the house. Indeed, he could make my life a living hell. This, in my frenzy to figure out the mystery of the manor, I had overlooked. Trying to take hold of a situation that was rapidly getting out of hand, I said, "I might consider speaking to her if there is a reasonable explanation. Otherwise, you can haunt me all you like. I won't stay here long."

"Has it ever occurred to you that not knowing everything might be best for you?"

"Not when I'm being threatened by the very person who wants my help." I gave him a look that showed my resolve. "If you want my help, you must tell me why you can't communicate with the dead."

His gaze dropped to the floor as he paced about the room. The seconds that ensued helped me to regroup, but when he spoke, my heart began racing again.

"All right," he conceded. "I'll explain my disadvantage, but I have to warn you that if you don't believe me, I might get angry."

"And you aren't angry already?" My eyebrows shot up questioningly.
"No."

"Go on, then." I moved to the armchair and sat down.

Glowering, he remained on his feet as he proceeded to explain. "In this disembodied state, there are dimensions. First, there are those spirits who, like me, stay behind wishing to find someone or stay with those they love. We do so at a high cost. We live in a space where there is no progress. Few can see or speak to us. We become lonely, and time becomes our prison. Ironically, what moves on with us is our knowledge and emotions. Our feelings of happiness or misery. The essence of who we are—it lives on forever.

"There are a few of these souls scattered throughout the forest, but we don't often see each other—the travel boundaries account for much of that. Then, there is another dimension for the angry spirits who linger to seek revenge for whatever evil was done to them. Or in some cases, there are spirits who can't let go of mortality, refusing to accept that they are dead. They are in shock, not comprehending what's happening to them. These souls live in a state of terror and darkness, blind to all that is good."

I wondered if he really belonged to the first category as he had said. I feared he could fit into the second as well.

He went on. "The dimensions are unbreachable by us. Only humans who have the gift to see beyond mortality can pierce them. Hence, I can't see or speak to those not in my sphere. How this works, I have no idea. All I know is what I've told you."

"I see."

"Now that you know why I need your help, will you speak to her? If she is Rose, she needs to know I came back, and I must find a way to help her escape that awful state." The loving way he spoke of her, combined with the intricacy of his tale, attested to the fact that he might not have had anything to do with her disappearance after all. At any rate, I would learn the truth if I spoke to the ghost of the woman. However, what did he conceal from me? There was something in his eyes that told me he withheld a large piece of the puzzle.

"Give me some time to think about this. She is not friendly and only appears at night. It would be easier to approach her during the day."

"The restless ones operate during the dark hours. It's a representation of their lost and sorrowful state. There is no natural light, no direction, no happiness, no rest for them. There are exceptions, but they are rare." Maybe he did belong to the first category after all.

"Is that why she wears such an atrocious, old-fashioned mourning dress?" The thought of how truly horrendous her state might be was distressing.

"I think so. Now, you do have guts. I'll give you that." Elliott laughed, lightening the mood a little. "When I was mortal, I'd have died of terror if I saw a ghost."

"I still might."

"I won't allow it until *we* discover her identity." He smirked.

"You have no idea what you're asking for."

"Seriously, you'll be all right. Besides, I'll be nearby."

"Is that supposed to make me feel better?" I asked with irony and stole a look at the clock resting on the mantel. It was growing late, and the last thing I needed was for the wandering woman to come down the steps. Elliott would realize that something paranormal had taken place just by looking at me, and no way under heaven did I want to confront her tonight. I needed to retire and quickly. But how did you dismiss a ghost? It wasn't like I could give him a hug and send him out the front door. Or was it? Perhaps a few hints would suffice. "Do you sleep?"

"Not really."

"What do you do at night?"

"I pace the woods, hoping to find the killer. If I can discover his identity, I might learn something about Rose. Whether or not he had something to do with her disappearance, I have to explore all options."

"Well, unlike you, I do sleep."

"Go on, then. Get to bed."

Was he planning to stay in the house? I supposed he could, but it was odd. How many times had he been around without me noticing?

Seeing my vacillation, he explained, "Don't fret. I'll stay down here. If anyone tries to break in, I'll alert you. Unless, of course, you prefer that I leave."

His words were calming. There was an advantage to his friendship. After the chase in the woods, I could use a watcher in the house. Even if he wasn't totally trustworthy, he wouldn't hurt me, at least not until I helped him. And with Piper apparently and shockingly gone for the night, I could use his help. "How would you let me know?"

"I will shake you awake."

"Umm...that's not a good idea."

"Better me than the killer."

I gave him a fake smile. "Good night, Elliott."

"Good night, Seraphina."

I trudged up the stairs, my head reeling. It had been a day filled to the brim with extraordinary new developments. While I walked down the hallway to the blue room, my mind replayed the memories of the women at Mrs. Bisset's house and their long discussion about the victims and killer; Caroline's rancid opinion of Albion Baker; the invitation to tea by the general; Julius's quarrel with Ghost; the vicar's unexpected visit the hunt in the woods and how close I had come to a dreadful fate; and finally, Elliott's tale.

Who was the marauder in the woods? For certain, there had been two men out there this evening. The vicar, with his silver tongue and leering eyes, could have been watching the house after I practically threw him out. He could have followed me into the trees, waiting for the right moment to strike, away from the manor, away from the Goswicks, though I had to admit the rider looked much larger than the vicar.

And there was Julius, whose timing in reaching the manor after I did had been impeccable. Had he been ready to finish what he started in the forest? Perhaps he preferred to kill in the woods, but my escape had infuriated him enough to risk coming after me. Then I had to consider Mr. Goswick. The man was unpredictable. Not even his wife knew where he was half the time. And to make matters worse, he slept under the same roof as I did.

Mrs. Goswick. She hadn't returned yet, and neither had Piper. True, their cow needed them, but it was quite late, and being alone for the night with just ghosts for company wasn't a pleasant thought. Still, I reminded myself that most of it was a baffling mix of absurd conjectures.

I couldn't take one more thing tonight, so I locked my bedroom door. Yet I knew the ghost of the woman wouldn't miss the chance to disrupt my sleep.

CHAPTER 10

THE BURLEY MANSION

It seemed I had barely closed my eyes when the dark woman's tantrums woke me. The crawling on my skin started even before I was fully alert. How much fear could a person experience before fainting? In my case, it seemed the surmounting terror had no limits. Passing out would be a mercy from heaven, but I was not so lucky. The ghost of the woman traveled the semidark hallway, uttering prolonged, high-pitched cries that jolted me inside and out. To complicate matters, I felt vulnerable without Piper.

Through the keyhole and aided by the dim light in the hallway, I saw the fast-moving specter. Instead of her customary visit to each room, she headed straight down the corridor toward me.

Thump, thump, thump. My heartbeat pounded against my chest, matching each of her footsteps. I wanted to bolt away from the door, but I was rooted to the ground.

Thump... She took one more step in my direction. *Thump...* And another one. She was now standing inches from me with just the door between us. A heavy, angered breathing traveled through the wood and then a hiss. Still not able to move, I opened my mouth to scream, but my voice died in my throat.

I saw her move again, this time in the opposite direction as she retraced her steps to the farthest end of the hallway. While she hovered there as if reconsidering her plans, drops of perspiration beaded on my forehead. The notion that her route was different tonight—that it would end in my room instead of in the green one—washed over me. Turning in my direction once again, she launched through the hallway with devilish speed, her arms outstretched in front of her as the bottom of her black dress swirled menacingly through the air. Neither heaven nor hell could now hold me in place. Since dawn was yet to come, I stormed to the light switch in a blur. The bedroom was immediately illuminated by the many bulbs in the chandelier. In a trice, I was hidden behind the far edge of the fireplace.

The doorknob rattled and rattled as the woman tried to break in. Goose bumps covered my body, and I started to shake violently. I feared this was where my heart would have enough and stop working. Even more disturbing, if she could come through the door, why didn't she? Perhaps she thought she still roamed the mortal world. Or was she taunting me? Perhaps it had been the light that disconnected her from my world.

Whatever it was, at last, it was a mercy that she did not come in. As swiftly as her presence had manifested itself, it evaporated—or so I thought as a heavy silence returned. I dropped on the spot, huddling between the wall and the side of the fireplace. I supposed Elliott's tale of not being able to see or hear the dark spirits was true. Otherwise, he would have been drawn to the second floor by the woman's racket.

For all my desire to embrace my gift of seeing the dead, the ghosts of All Hallows and the serial killer were too much for me to deal with at once, especially when Elliott wanted me to speak to this evil specter. The idea of going home started to grow within me. At least the disembodied spirits in London didn't haunt me. And at this point, I would even take the bombs over All Hallows's ghosts. Still trembling and almost in tears, I eventually fell asleep on the cold floor.

When the daylight caressed my face, I rose from the ground with a moan. My body was stiff, my thoughts muddled. As soon as I changed out of my nightgown, I escaped the blue room. The Goswick women were already assembled in the kitchen, preparing for the day.

"Good morning, Miss Addington," said Mrs. Goswick. "I'm sorry we didn't see you before bed last night. Sally had a difficult delivery that went on until one o'clock in the morning. It wasn't until two that Goswick and I finally got to bed."

"Please, Mum, don't remind me. After seeing the poor thing's suffering, I'm seriously reconsidering having children," Caroline said with a sincerity that spoke volumes.

"How is she today?" I asked.

"Thank heavens mother and calf are doing well," the housekeeper responded.

"Wonderful. I'll have to stop by to see the new addition sometime."

"It's adorable," assured Caroline.

Adorable—it reminded me of my little deserter. "Have you seen Piper today?"

"Yes, she came back from the cottage a while ago but went out again," Mrs. Goswick informed.

"She didn't sleep here?"

Avoiding my gaze, she replied, "No, she was dead set on staying with Julius."

"Oh…" That was unexpected. Perhaps Piper preferred Julius to the ghost of the woman. I settled on a chair, dreading the appalling disclosure I needed to make. Since there was no easy way to say it, out it came, straight to my shame. "Last night, before Julius came to light the fire, I walked down to the stream."

Caroline gasped.

Mrs. Goswick's reproachful eyes left the range and found mine. "What possessed you to do such a thing?"

"I don't know," I responded untruthfully.

"The foolishness of youth," retorted the housekeeper, taking a seat by her daughter.

"Perhaps." I hurried on before I lost my courage. "A man on horseback chased me through the woods. I got away because the horse didn't fare well in the denser parts of the trees."

The fright I detected in their eyes matched my own at the memory of the event.

"Miss Addington, I hope you've learned your lesson and will think twice before disregarding the rules again," Mrs. Goswick reprimanded, and rightly so.

"Did you see his face?" Caroline asked.

"It was too dark. All I could tell was that he is a large man."

"We should call the constable," Caroline decided at once. "People need to be aware of the incident."

"We mustn't be hasty. We don't want to incite panic. The rider could have been anyone," Mrs. Goswick opined.

"Incite panic? How can you say that, Mother? Haven't you heard what Seraphina said? He chased her! The killer is on the prowl."

"I'm just saying we mustn't jump to conclusions."

"No," snapped Caroline, "that's the constable's job."

"What time did Julius come by?" Mrs. Goswick inquired abruptly.

"I'm not sure. Sometime after nine. I really don't know."

"Why does that matter?" Caroline interjected.

"It doesn't." Harshly pushing the chair back, the housekeeper stood. "I'll send Julius to inform the constable." For not wanting to cause a panic, she left rather quickly, an air of tension hanging about her.

"I did not mean to upset her, but I had to tell her," I said.

"I'm not sure what's gotten into her—apart from the fact that if it was the killer and he had caught you, you would be dead right now."

If it weren't for Elliott, I would indeed be dead.

"That's not a cheerful thought." I got to my feet. "Oh, and I almost forgot. I'm going to visit the general this morning. Did you talk your mum into accompanying me?"

"I will talk to her again as soon as she comes back."

"I'll be in the library."

I withdrew from the kitchen, having forgotten all about breakfast as my appetite seemed to have left since arriving at All Hallows. I headed to the library, ready to pick up *Wuthering Heights* where I had left off. Crossing the threshold, I was confronted by the very chaos I had previously encountered—books lay scattered across the floor.

This is dreadfully odd...

The only difference was that a few of the volumes had landed open, exposing their stories to all who happened upon them. Convinced that something had forced them from their places, I inspected the shelves but could see no obvious cause. Once again, I rearranged the order of the books, storing the wandering ones in different spots before sinking into a chair with the book in hand.

***

Having won the battle with her mother, Caroline accompanied me to visit General Lewis. The Burley mansion sat in all its splendor against the midmorning sun. The incredible quantity of war machinery stationed on the grounds, including the airplanes on the south fields, was a rude awakening. The intrigue and mysteries currently occupying my time had pushed the reality of the war to the back of my mind.

"Oh my," exclaimed Caroline, calling me to the present. "I hadn't realized how many soldiers are stationed here."

Neither had I until she mentioned it. Feeling their eyes upon us, like hyenas on their prey, I wished Mrs. Goswick had accompanied us, for I did not like being appraised like merchandise on a shelf. She would know how to keep them in line.

The side entrance led to a small reception area. An older man with a round middle section and an exuberant mustache sat at the desk. At least I didn't have to worry about Caroline's flirting while I stated our business here.

"Make yourselves comfortable," advised the soldier, pointing to a row of chairs along the wall. "I'll inform General Lewis."

"Thank you, sir."

Tired from the long walk, I settled next to Caroline. A telephone on the desk caught my attention. All Hallows and its ghosts had made it difficult to check in with my parents on a regular basis. The mansion presented an opportunity to correct my error. I would ask to use their phone.

"What do we have here?" exclaimed a young blond soldier who burst into the room. "What are you ladies in need of?"

"Absolutely nothing," I retorted and, hoping to subdue his interest, added, "General Lewis will see us soon."

The mention of the general was enough to make him check himself before speaking again. "Old Wagner, I suppose, went to fetch him?"

"If you are referring to the soldier who sits on that chair"—I signaled to the spot where the older man had been—"then, yes, he's gone to fetch him."

Caroline, who surprisingly had held her tongue for this long, could contain it no longer. "If you must know—"

"No, he must not," I interjected, fearing that in a matter of seconds she would expose our entire lives to the stranger. Almost imperceptibly, Caroline's gaze found mine before darting back to the man. I was in trouble. She was like a dog with a bone and wasn't going to let it go anytime soon.

Confirming my worries, she spoke again. "Seraphina is here to see the general. I'm not. And I must say I find this house fascinating. It would be a dream come true to peek around. You know, with the history of the place and all..."

I was dumbfounded at her barefaced audacity. *Oh, Earth, please swallow me. This woman has no scruples.* I was at a complete disadvantage. Anything I said would only encourage her to contradict me further.

"I totally understand," he said, his gaze roaming over her appreciatively.

Ugh, of course you do.

"Please, allow me to show you around." He gave her a firm handshake. "Officer David Robertson."

"Caroline Goswick."

Before I could protest, Caroline had left with the soldier. I leaped to my feet, ready to bring her back, only to be stopped at the exit by Wagner calling from behind me. "Sorry about the wait. You aren't leaving, are you?" He looked about, probably wondering where my companion had gone.

I held his gaze, disguising my irritation with a smile. "No, of course not."

Graciously, he didn't inquire about Caroline's absence. "Please, if you would follow me."

The house was a labyrinth. Corridors branched out in every direction, like the roots of a tree. The connecting hallways were disrupted by large open areas inhabited by personnel, where workstations had been set up. The elegant drapes and gigantic paintings on the walls were, at present, the only reminder of the mansion's former glory. We passed the largest room yet—what must have been the ballroom at one time. This vast space now served as the main workspace. It was dotted with desks and small tables overflowing with typing machines, wireless sets, boxes, and various other things. A herd of soldiers in light-brown uniforms dashed about the room, speaking to each other and moving things here and there. Others sat at their workstations, perusing stacks of papers with an air of seriousness.

As Wagner guided me to the north side of the house, the soldiers' presence thinned out until nonexistent. The atmosphere grew quiet. Like a hospital wing of dying patients, it held a solemn reverence. Without warning, Wagner turned into a narrow hall and knocked on a door. When there was no answer, he knocked again and then again.

"The general must have stepped out for a moment. He is expecting you, so go ahead and wait for him," he instructed, allowing me to enter. "I'll find him."

The isolated office was a statement of the general's character. The mass of papers on his desk bespoke leadership and responsibility. The infantry of books stacked against the walls attested to great knowledge and discipline. And the deep serenity, away from the commotion, affirmed its master valued equilibrium and tranquility of mind.

Despite feeling as if I trespassed on hallowed ground, I moved deeper into the room. Like a curious child, I picked up the small frame on the desk—a picture of the general and a radiant woman in a wedding dress. The caption read simply, "Mr. and Mrs. Lewis, 1909." *I'll say, he is a handsome man, but I had no idea. He was breathtaking back then.* As these thoughts crossed my mind, I became uncomfortably aware that I wasn't alone.

Returning the frame to its place, I spun toward a woman who

watched me from a painting on the wall. She had fair skin, brown eyes, and long, honey-colored hair. Her red lips matched the intensity of her dress of the same shade. But what captivated me most was the look in her eyes. It held me in place, hypnotized. She stared from her eternal image with unquenchable suffering.

"I see you have found the treasure of the manor," said General Lewis.

The sudden interruption pulled me away from whatever force existed in the image of the woman. I turned to see the general smiling at me. "It's a remarkable painting," I commented.

"The lady of the house, Mrs. Helen Lewis," he introduced as an intense longing seemed to descend upon him. "It was taken shortly before her passing."

Throwing a glance at the small portrait on the desk, I realized that, indeed, it was the same woman, just a little older. A swift image formed in my mind: The happy couple entering the ballroom; a crowd awaiting them, admiring them as they passed; the general taking his companion to the center of the dance floor; the orchestra playing a soft, inviting melody that inundated every corner of the house and every fiber of my heart. They danced, the love emanating from the general for his wife awe-inspiring.

"Her beauty is stunning, don't you think?" he remarked, pulling me from my reverie.

"Indeed, it is." Feeling out of place, I added, "I didn't mean to pry. Wagner said I could wait for you here."

"Whatever Wagner says is the law. Thank you for waiting." Taking a step closer, he briefly took my hands in his. "It's wonderful to see you again, Seraphina."

"Thank you for inviting me. The mansion is impressive. I had no idea how expansive and busy it is."

"It can get a bit hectic, but we manage. Please, have a seat."

I settled on the visitor's chair. The general sat on the opposite side of the desk. A tap on the door was followed by Wagner, tea tray in hand.

"Thank you, Wagner," said the general.

The older soldier placed the tray on the desk and almost noiselessly left the office. With natural easiness, General Lewis served the drink.

"The reason I wanted to see you is to personally extend an invitation for a social gathering this Sunday evening here at the house. Amid the undesirable things surrounding us, spending time among friends and forgetting about the war, even if it's for a few hours, will be refreshing."

"It's kind of you to invite me..." The mere idea of being among a large crowd, more so if they were strangers, left me uneasy. I did not like being around people that way.

"Is there a problem?"

"No..." Try as I might, after his generosity toward me, I couldn't turn down his invitation. "It sounds lovely. I'll be here."

"If you would like, feel free to bring Miss Goswick along."

"I'll let her know. Actually, she came with me."

"Yes, I saw her out in the garden."

"Oh." I looked down at the cup in my hands and then brought it to my lips. At the thought of Caroline's conduct, my face felt hotter than the tea. "She enjoys the outdoors," I said in a pathetic effort to justify her presence on the grounds.

"Young people often do." He took a sip of tea. "Since the gathering on Sunday will go on late into the evening, I will drive you back to All Hallows."

"I wouldn't want to impose on you."

"After I was injured in battle, your father dragged me seventy-five yards to safety. Hence, young lady, I think I owe him many years of my time."

I couldn't argue with his reasoning. "It's settled, then."

Like the after-supper discussions with my father I missed so much, my time spent visiting with the general slipped away almost imperceptibly. We discussed a variety of interesting topics, from politics to gardening and everything in between. And although he was one step ahead in all subjects, I did my best to sound knowledgeable, though it wasn't easy.

When the general spoke of the days he'd studied in London before the Great War and how much he delighted in learning, I realized it was missing in my life. I glanced at the army of books once again, this time with a tinge of longing.

"Those were some of the best days of my life," he recalled. "Fresh out of school, I met Helen. She made a good man out of me. We had big plans for our future, but the same year that war broke out, she became ill. We saw all the physicians in London, but it wasn't enough." He paused, clearly suppressing his emotions. "She was young and gentle. She died in my arms." He glanced at her painting with moist eyes. He had loved and suffered immeasurably. Returning his gaze to me, he snapped out of the past. "You must forgive me. I see I have shared too much."

"The love you had for each other is exceptional."

Leaving his seat, he stood before the window. "I do take comfort in that." He looked at his wristwatch and noted, "Is it really that late? I apologize, Seraphina. I'm due for a meeting."

"Yes, of course."

With his leadership manners back in full control, he secured a stack of papers under his arm. "If there is anything at all I can help with, please, don't hesitate to ask."

"There is one thing…"

"Ask away."

"I would like to call my parents. May I use your telephone?"

"We have a line for personal affairs. If you wait here a moment, I'll have someone show you the way. You are welcome to use it whenever you'd like."

"I'm much obliged to you."

"I'll see you Sunday." He left with a small bow.

Though I was now alone, I wasn't. Helen Lewis's eyes watched my every move. Her imposing presence dominated the ambiance, and I had the unsettling notion that she had never left her general. He was hers, and she would not allow anyone to have him. Again, my gaze locked with hers. The aura the painting projected was so vivid I wouldn't have been surprised if Helen stepped out of her portrait to chase me away.

The door opened, and I turned from the painting. Captain Ross Stewart stood on the threshold, looking even more attractive than I remembered. His fresh haircut and clean-shaven face immediately reminded me that he had the power to make my heart race. The feeling of safety that accompanied his presence grew closer with his steps.

"Hey, it's you," he exclaimed. His relaxed demeanor reminded me of California's beaches and girls—and I found myself a bit jealous. "It's only been a day, and you couldn't wait to see me."

Keeping up with his sarcasm, I responded, "That's exactly why I'm here."

"How are you, Seraphina?"

"I'm well. And you?"

"Busy training the new pilots. A bunch of them got here yesterday. But seriously, why are you here? The general asked me to show you to the phone, but that's not the reason, is it?"

"No, he wanted to see me."

"What for?"

"To invite me to the social event on Sunday."

"Where?"

"Here, at the mansion," I said.

"Hmm, this is the first I've heard about it."

"Maybe you aren't invited."

"Don't worry, I don't need an invitation. I'll be around."

"I'm not worried at all. May I use the telephone now?"

"Straight to business. I like it. Okay, follow me."

Ross led me through a series of short corridors to the south wing.

"In here." He pointed to a tiny area dressed in a flowery red wallpaper. A man's voice met us as we moved in. A young soldier sat by the table, the receiver to his ear.

"Hey, how much longer?" Ross inquired.

"Easy, Stewart. I'm speaking to my girl. Do you mind?" came the response.

"We'll be back in a few," Ross told him, scowling.

Back in the hallway, I asked, "How often do soldiers call home?"

"Not often. Usually only for emergencies, though I doubt my friend in there has a real excuse for his call."

"Families must dread the calls, then."

"Yep." Ross's face lit up with a new idea. "Listen, I have the feeling he'll be in there for a while. Come with me." Not giving me the chance to say no, he reached for my hand and pulled me down the hall.

"Wait—where are we going?"

"To my quarters."

I yanked my hand free and halted midstride. "To your quarters? Are you allowed to bring girls there?"

"As many as I want." He was poking fun at me. "Come on. It will only take a minute."

"I don't know…" If the general found out, I might as well disappear from the face of the planet. After all he had done for me, breaking his house's rules wasn't wise.

"Okay, okay. We can take longer if you'd like."

"You are an impertinent man, Captain."

"And you take things too seriously, miss. Relax. I might be impertinent, but I'm not stupid. To disrespect the general's ward would be the end of my career."

Finally, something coherent out of his mouth. I contemplated him, still undecided.

"Let's go." Ross grabbed hold of my hand again. We climbed an old set of steep stairs. At the landing, it opened to a completely deserted, narrow corridor. "This part of the manor used to be the servants' wing back in the day. Of course, it now houses the Americans," he said, grinning. We came to a stop halfway down the corridor. "In here." He stepped aside to let me in. His room housed a single bed, chest of drawers, chair, and a side table below the window encasement. On the table sat a Victorian lamp surrounded by a mess of papers and books.

"I see you like to read," I noted, though he did not strike me as the kind. I wondered what else I was underestimating about him.

"You are darn right I do," he bragged, turning the key in the keyhole. "That I'll behave honorably doesn't mean you can be in here. The fewer people who know, the better."

"You lied."

"Mea culpa."

"Why are we here?" I asked.

"Have a seat." He pointed to the bed. I sat on the chair.

"Smart move." Smiling, he opened a drawer of the chest, pulled out a brown box, and handed it to me.

"Thank you...?"

"Go on. Open it." He settled on the bed.

I removed the tape, pulled the top apart, and extracted a small jar. Words failed me.

CHAPTER 11

THE BEGINNING OF SOMETHING

Ross leaned forward, elbows on his knees. He perused my face with an intensity that left me breathless. The overwhelming attraction was uncomfortable but also exhilarating. I dropped my gaze to the tin of cocoa in my hands.

"What do you think?" he asked expectantly.

The gift was a thoughtful one. I hadn't seen a teaspoon of cocoa since food rationing. My mouth watered at the thought of a sweet cup of hot chocolate. "I don't know what to say. This is very kind of you."

"Before you think too much of it, know that my goodness is not entirely altruistic."

"Meaning?"

"I'm hoping you'll share it with me."

"That can be arranged," I said.

"Saturday afternoon? It's my day off."

"Saturday afternoon it is." I returned the tin to the box. "But you must tell me how you got it."

A mischievous gleam came into his eyes. "Let's just say the cook lost a bet."

"What bet?"

He shook his head decisively. "You don't need to know that. Suffice it to say I won the cocoa fair and square."

My brow furrowed, and even though I was curious, my focus fell on the papers scattered across his desk. The corner of a tiny book peeked out from under a newspaper, and I unburied it.

"What is this?"

"Oh no, you don't want to read that," Ross exclaimed, attempting to take it from me.

I lifted my hand, holding him back. "Oh yes, I do." I read the title. *Instructions for American Servicemen in Britain.*

"It's just a bunch of guidelines, that's all." The alteration in his voice told me there was more to it than met the eye.

I opened the booklet to its first page. "Interesting."

With a groan, Ross stretched out on the bed, arms behind his head.

The book offered suggestions on how to behave and treat people during a stay in Britain. I moved to another page—perhaps to one Ross didn't want me to see. I read aloud. "'Almost before you meet the people, you will hear them speaking 'English.' At first, you may not understand what they're talking about, and they may not understand you. The accent will be different from what you are used to, and many of the words will be strange, or apparently wrongly used... Don't make fun of British speech or accents. You sound just as funny to them, but they will be too polite to show it.'"

"You are failing at this, Captain."

"What else is new?" He suppressed a smile.

"Wait, I like this." I continued reading aloud. "'A British woman officer or noncommissioned officer can—and often do—give orders to a male private. The men obey smartly and know it is no shame.'" I flung a triumphant look at him. "I should have joined the army."

"What for? You've already succeeded in keeping me in check."

Ignoring his sarcasm, I finished the paragraph. "'For British women have proved themselves in this way. They stick to their posts near burning ammunition dumps, deliver messages afoot after their motorcycles have been blasted from under them. They have pulled aviators from burning planes. They have died at gun posts, and when they've fallen, some other girl has stepped directly into the position and carried on. There is not a single record in this war of any British woman in uniformed service quitting her post or failing in her duty under fire. Now you understand why British soldiers respect the women in uniform.'"

What started as a casual read turned into a solemn contemplation. The impact the new information had on me was humbling. In the face of other women's willpower to do those things that would frighten even the bravest of men, my pride had suffered a blow. My ability to see the deceased and the way it upset my life seemed minor when compared to the dangers these women faced.

"Hey," called Ross, bringing me out of my self-reflection. "Are you done with that?"

"Not quite." My eyebrows shot up as I read on. "'The British don't know how to make a good cup of coffee. You don't know how to make a good cup of tea. It's an even swap.' I'm afraid this might be true."

He turned on his side, the springs complaining at his movement. "Yeah, the coffee part is true, but you know, there are worse things than that." Propping his upper body on his elbow, he stated, "When I first came to England, I didn't know how much it had been affected by the war. The destruction and the food rationing are pretty bad."

"Yet we somehow make it work."

"The booklet also says that waste means lives. I did not understand that before. America is a producer nation. Britain, on the other hand, depends on imports. And right now, the British seamen are dying as they try to get those convoys through."

"It's not your fault."

"I know, but the injustice of it frustrates me," Ross said.

"It frustrates all of us."

"I guess." He sighed in discontent. "I just wish this country was a little more prepared in certain things."

"Such as?"

Ross left the bed and pointed to the fields through the window. "Such as those planes. They are in really bad shape. I'd never flown a bird in that condition until I got here. We need newer planes, but I don't see it happening anytime soon."

"It sounds like a terrible, unfair challenge for the pilots."

"It is, though we adapt to our circumstances enough to make it through." Ross went on as if speaking to himself. "My first flight here was during a night raid. I wasn't supposed to fly, but so many didn't return. I took a plane that had just landed. There was no time to check the damage or clean the blood that covered the cockpit. The pilot had been shot several times, and as the medical crew pulled him out of the cabin, I jumped in." He looked at me again, raw emotion in his eyes. "As long as the engines ran, we had to fly them. That night as I took off, I was convinced that was it, the end of my life, and suddenly war became real."

"The air strikes made war real for me as well." I swallowed a lump in my throat. When had this conversation moved from flirting to weighty?

"The one thing that keeps me steady is knowing we must protect freedom at all costs."

"The cost is high."

"Extremely. A large percentage of the men I train don't make it back. I avoid developing relationships with them anymore. We all do it. War has a desensitizing effect. In a way it's good. It helps us not to go completely crazy," he said.

"But you don't fly nowadays, do you?"

"Nope, I mostly train and repair the aircraft. But enough of that." Taking my hand, he brought me to stand and was back to his cheerful self. "There is one thing the pamphlet should have mentioned."

His nearness was like a magnet. The closer he was, the closer I wanted him to be. "And what is that?"

"That English women are a temptation impossible to resist." He leaned over, and as he brushed his lips against mine, I took a step back. If I kissed him in the seclusion of his room, things could get out of hand —and I hardly knew the man after all.

I turned the key in the lock and peeked into the corridor. "Do you think your colleague is done with his call?"

"Only one way to find out." He retrieved the cocoa box from the table. "Here, take this."

Silence followed us the entire length of our march through the deserted hallways. I feared my rejection had been a blow to his confidence, but perhaps it was good for him. Perhaps he could use a little humility when it came to women.

"I'll be out here," Ross said, halting outside the telephone room.

I dialed the operator to connect me with London. After a few tries, she put me on hold. When she returned, the news wasn't welcome. 'I'm sorry, miss. The reason we can't connect you is due to last night's bombing. The entire area is without service."

"Until when?" Though air raids were an almost daily occurrence in London, they had never interrupted communication near our home.

"The damage is extensive. With some buildings completely gone, there is no way to know when the lines will be restored."

My limbs went rigid. Had my house been hit? Had my parents reached the bomb shelter in time? I felt numb at the thought of my neighborhood being destroyed—the busy streets; the shops with gigantic window displays; the row houses with balconies full of pots, their flowers cascading to the pavement below; rowdy youth riding their bikes and ringing their bells at anyone in their way—all gone in a heartbeat.

"Miss, are you there? May I connect you to another number?"

"No, thank you." The receiver dropped out of my hands. I had nothing without my parents. I was ashamed that, having been so wrapped up in my dilemma at All Hallows, I'd lost sight of the deadly situation my parents were still in.

Before my mind ran wild, voices in the corridor brought me to gather myself. The pressing matter was to find out if my parents were safe and sound. Meanwhile, I resolved to be brave, like the women in the army and on the farms. And though I was at a loss as to how to proceed with the ghosts' dilemma, the time for fear had passed. I would face the threat head on.

With my plan in place, I swiftly returned to Ross.

"See you later," he said to a soldier who had been conversing with him, and to me, "That was fast."

"I couldn't get through."

"Are you okay?"

If I said too much, I would cry, and that was the last thing I wanted to do in front of him. "Last night's strike disrupted the telephone lines."

"Oh..."

"I ought to find Caroline. We must leave."

"Caroline Goswick?"

"You know her?" I asked.

"Just by name." Something in his demeanor told me her name was known by the entire troop.

"General Lewis mentioned seeing her out on the grounds. She might still be there."

"This way," said Ross.

Taking a side door, we rapidly exited the mansion, surfacing among a bunch of dilapidated aircraft. The war had not been gentle to them. They had seen too much of battle. Worse yet, they seemed destined to certain doom.

"Do you take off from here?"

"Sometimes, but for missions, we usually take off from the airfield in Christchurch."

I recalled Mrs. Goswick saying the aerodrome in Christchurch had become operational about three years ago, causing excitement and anxiety in equal measure to the inhabitants of the New Forest.

"How far is Christchurch from here?"

"About nine miles. A twenty-minute drive," he answered as we hurried through the yard. "Here at the mansion, we mostly do repair work and training. As soon as the aircraft are in decent shape, we send them on their way. After what happened in Pearl Harbor, we keep everything pretty spread out."

The surprise military strike by the Japanese against the naval base at Pearl Harbor in Hawaii had forced the formal entry of the United States into the war. Since the attack had occurred without a declaration of war and without explicit warning, leaving thousands of Americans dead or injured, it was one of the most shocking events of the conflict to date. I thought about the twists and turns of fate. If not for Pearl Harbor, Ross might never have come to England, and I might never have met him.

We neared the last few dormant planes in the field when a soldier suddenly emerged from the inside of a cockpit, cursing. He flung a wrench over the side to the grass below.

"Watch it, man!" Ross shouted.

"This piece of sh—" Upon seeing me, the man stopped midsentence. "Hey, Stewart, what are you up to? Trouble?"

"Just taking a walk," Ross replied.

"A very nice walk," the soldier responded with an appreciative grin.

"Get back to work," Ross said and then pointed to something up ahead. "Hey, look, unless one of the guys grew a mane, that's your friend at the far end of the hedge." Caroline's loose blond hair stuck out over the wall of greenery. Beside her, I saw the spiky blond hair of the soldier she had left with earlier. "Come through here." Ross signaled to a short gate that led to the other side of the wall.

Feeling he had already done enough for me, I said, "Thanks for helping me, Ross. I can manage from here."

He shut the gate behind us and suddenly grasped my hand, pulling me into a cluster of trees. Backing me against a tree trunk, he trapped me between his arms. "Listen, I'll come by All Hallows on Saturday."

"You already told me that."

His warm lips brushed against my ear as he leaned in and asked, "Can I kiss you before you leave?" His persistence combined with the pull I felt toward him made it challenging to refuse. He put his arms around me.

I was about to give in when a voice, firm and loud, rang through the air. "Captain Stewart, I see you've lost no time in befriending Miss Addington," General Lewis noted.

At the sight of his superior, Ross jumped away from me as if he had received an electric shock. Feeling like a helpless fool, I was paralyzed on the spot.

"Sir..."

"Of course," the general said pensively, "you've already met Seraphina. You found her in the woods when she arrived."

"That's correct, sir."

General Lewis smiled coolly. "I trust you helped her to the civilians' telephone?"

"Yes, sir. I did."

"How is your family, Seraphina?"

"I'm afraid I couldn't get through," I responded, still a bit shaken by his sudden appearance.

"The lines are down due to the bombing," Ross explained.

"I see." Glancing at the box in my hands, the general inquired, "What is that?"

"Tea from the shop downtown. I had some extras and thought she might like them," Ross lied.

"Hmm. I didn't think the Americans were into tea," his superior observed. He looked at me, then at Ross, and then back at me. In a calculating tone, he spoke to his soldier. "You may return to your duties. I'll see that Miss Addington finds her way out."

Ross opened his mouth to say something but must have thought better of it. Instead, evidently displeased with the dismissal, he simply walked away.

General Lewis took my arm and laced it through his. "Shall we find your friend?"

"I saw her a moment ago, just up ahead."

As we started down the pebble path bordering the evergreens, I racked my mind for something coherent to say. Nothing came to mind fast enough, for I was painfully conscious that having been caught in Ross's arms and at the brink of kissing spoke for itself. Even more so, I was certain the general knew the box didn't contain tea, and I'd silently corroborated the lie.

General Lewis broke the uncomfortable silence. "I was young like you once, and after all, I have been a military man for quite some time," he said in a soft tone. "Would you permit me to give you a word of advice?"

I was mortified. A word of advice was the last thing I wanted. However, there was no way under heaven I would say so, not if I wanted to salvage some of my pride. "Please do."

"War brings about trying times, especially for those who serve in their youth. They do their best not to show their insecurities, but they are only human. The lads wonder if they'll see their families again. If they'll get to live a full life. They wonder what love feels like.

"At some point, most men in their predicament decide that only today is certain. Hence, they want to live each day to the fullest. Now, Seraphina, forgive my bluntness, but a man's weakness is a woman. Nothing comes even close or is more comforting to a soldier in his trying days than the company of a woman." He looked at me sideways. "Do you understand what I mean?"

Unable to find my voice, I nodded.

"The problem is that their shortsightedness not only affects them but those with whom they interact. For example, many soldiers find relief from their misery in having fun with innocent young women. Now, they are very, very unlikely to return to their post of service either because they die in battle or go home, and that's the end of it. As a man well-informed with the situation on and off the battlefield, I assure you that one of the greatest tragedies of our day is the thousands of heartbroken, single young mothers left behind."

He couldn't have struck a deeper chord. Whatever delusions I had entertained, even if fleetingly, for Ross had been put in their proper place. Looking through the general's lens of judgment, my feelings toward the American soldier coupled with my actions—the ride on his motorbike and my visit to his quarters—filled me with shame. Yet there it was again—the everlasting fight between what society expected of women and what women wanted for themselves. What if Ross was different? What if he was seriously fond of me?

Surely a balance existed to pursue one's happiness without being torn with remorse. Perhaps it was the lack of experience that made me second-guess my actions. And while I tried to acquire it, I would have to be patient—it would take time to sort it all out.

The general continued. "Now, you are a clever young lady. No doubt your parents trust your moral uprightness—otherwise, they would not have sent you here."

Had he just given me praise? No, he was finishing the task of putting sense into my head by reminding me my parents expected me to do the right thing, whatever that might be. All that came from my mouth was, "Thank you, General."

He halted, taking both of my small hands in his large ones, and nodding in Caroline's direction, he asked, "Can I count on you to share our little discussion with your friend? She seems only too eager to please the young men who cross her way. The Goswick family has worked for me for a long time. I would hate to see them suffer." No doubt his speech had been centered on me, but evidently the general knew what had occurred between Caroline and Mark.

"I'll see to it. And rest assured I won't forget what you have said." I sounded pathetic.

"Now, if you'll permit, I'll make a few calls to find out about your parents."

I was a bit taken aback but grateful for the drastic change of subject. "Oh, that's most generous of you, and truly, it's a great relief to me. I wasn't sure how I was going to reach them."

He smiled broadly, and the sweetness and maturity in his gaze warmed my heart somewhat. Had he been one of those soldiers who'd left a trail of broken hearts? No, I was convinced he was a man whose entire heart and loyalty belonged to one girl. Helen had been that blessed woman. She still was.

Our walk resumed. I couldn't wait to reach Caroline and get away from the Burley mansion.

CHAPTER 12

MIND VERSUS HEART

When Caroline and I finally reached All Hallows, I felt like the worst friend on the planet. Though I tried to make peace with myself, the thought that the general would think less of me—or worse—that he'd tell my parents I was pursuing the soldiers made me mad. And I had allowed the awful frustration to burst like a volcano on poor Caroline. As if I had behaved any better than she had, I reproached her for her silliness in leaving with the soldier to explore the mansion. I resented her for abandoning me and, albeit unjustly, in part blamed her for my ending up alone with Ross. I had suffered double humiliation: first, the general had found me being seduced by the captain, and then we'd found Caroline in similar circumstances with Robertson.

Ugh, Seraphina. What an imbecile you are! I couldn't blame others for my actions, but I was guilt-ridden and didn't know how to handle it. More than anything, I was confused and upset with myself. Ross, the war, the ghosts, all of it had left me feeling vexed.

"There are things I need to attend to. I'll be back later," Caroline grumbled. The unspoken message—she did not want to be in my company. Not waiting for an answer, she hurried down the path toward the cottage at a pace that conveyed her irritation.

Piper sat at the front entrance. She raised her ears and wagged her tail as I approached. *At least someone is happy to see me.*

Kneeling, I rubbed her back. "What have you been doing? Hopefully you are smarter than me and have stayed out of trouble."

Piper got to her feet and, as we entered the house, headed straight to the comfort of the sofa. I was in the process of getting rid of my hat and gloves when Mrs. Goswick came in.

"How was your visit to the Burley mansion?"

"An absolute nightmare," I wanted to answer, but instead, I said, "Pleasant. The general invited us to a social gathering on Sunday."

"I see..." she said, sounding intrigued. "Where is Caroline? She did come back with you, of course?"

"She went to the cottage. The outing wore her out."

A shadow of concern crossed the housekeeper's expression. Knowing Caroline best, she probably suspected something like the debacle that had taken place at the mansion. Luckily, she did not launch a full interrogation. Instead, she stated, "General Lewis is a gentleman, isn't he?"

"He is." I dropped onto the sofa beside Piper. "I saw a painting of his late wife. She was beautiful."

"The grief he experienced when he lost her was something I will never forget. He was inconsolable."

"I think he still misses her."

"That's probably why he works so much," she reflected. And throwing me off-balance, as I hadn't thought her much of an intellectual person, she quoted from memory, "'Woman is sacred—the woman one loves is holy... Moral wounds have this peculiarity—they may be hidden, but they never close—always painful, always ready to bleed when touched, they remain fresh and open in the heart.'"

"*The Count of Monte Cristo?*"

"That's right," she said.

"How do you heal a wound like that?"

"Time, I suppose."

"Time..." Considering Elliott's and the general's stories, I wasn't sure how much of a helper time really was. Even after years, both still longed for their lost loves.

"Now, if you'll excuse me," she said. "I really ought to get on with what I was doing in the kitchen." At the doorway, she turned to me and added, "Oh, and the constable will come by later to take your declaration."

The idea of facing the constable was troublesome. I would have to relive the hunt in the woods, being as truthful as possible without mentioning Elliott. Locking my inquietudes somewhere in my memory, I marched to the library in search of some solace. Once again, like the leaves in autumn, several books had fallen off the shelves.

I walked past and slipped down onto a seat by the window, ignoring the urge to pick them up. After all, there was no use—somehow, they would manage to hit the ground again and again—but why? Was someone deliberately doing this? According to Mrs. Goswick, she had never found such disarray. "Someone must be putting them back in a rush, and so they fall off," she had said. And since that someone could only be me, I dropped the subject.

I turned to the tomes as they taunted me from the floor. They contained account upon account of real and imaginary people trapped within their pages, eagerly waiting to tell their stories.

An idea suddenly came into my mind, and I stared at them in awe. Was it possible the house was trying to speak through them? That my initial presentiment that it was a living entity was real? Or could the ghost of the woman be behind the mischievous act? As fast as the thought had come, I rejected it. She was too engrossed in her misery to reach out for help.

As I knelt next to the volumes, my heart stamped against my ribs like a thousand horses trying to reach the end of the track. Cautiously, I examined the first volume—*The History of England*. Not finding anything helpful, I moved on to the next, then the next, until I had inspected them all, not seeing anything out of the ordinary. I slammed the one in my hand against the floor. It fell open.

Two words from its pages caught my interest. *Deeds* and *caressed* had been underlined in a peculiar manner in two different colors. I flipped through the pages of the book to find that no other words had been marked. *How odd.* I went through the rest of the misplaced books and found one word underlined in each, leaving me with *the, day,* and *first*.

In a frenzy, I collected a paper and pencil from the table. Since it would take an eternity to go through all the books on the shelves, I first concentrated on the unit from which these had fallen.

Meticulously, I inspected the books one at a time. There were no words marked on the first dozen I went through. Worried I did this in vain, I picked up a tiny blue book. On its very last page, the word *touch* had been underlined. I wrote it down.

Once I had looked through the very last book in that unit, I randomly inspected various tomes from the other units. Finding no underlined words, I decided to concentrate on what I had discovered so far.

Deeds, caressed, the, day, first, four, green, year, a, hidden, touch, of, safely, times, while, attire, night, by, and, changes, rest, the, remains, theirs, keeping, my.

Captivated, I reread the twenty-six words. What in the world did they mean? While I racked my brain for an answer, the grandfather clock chimed from the corridor. Time moved fast when one did not wish it to. I had to solve this riddle before I was interrupted.

Riddle. That's it. It's a riddle. Mrs. Goswick's remark hit me with astonishing clarity. *"There was a time when she got into writing riddles. Every morning, I would find a riddle on the kitchen table for me to solve."*

Rose, owner of the books and an avid reader, loved riddles. She must have marked the words, but why? Were they important or just one of her games? There was only one way to find out. I had to put the puzzle together and figure out its meaning. I almost laughed at myself. The fact that it sounded so simple meant it was going to be anything but.

I cut out each word and spread them on the reading table. I arranged and rearranged them. *Darn, she was good. There are too many.* I continued working until I had to force myself to close my eyes and take a break. When with fresh eyes I beheld the pieces of paper again, I noticed that *While, Theirs, Keeping,* and *Caressed* were capitalized.

Pushing the articles to the side, and with the four capitalized words as the starting point for the sentences, I played with the rest. At length, I put together an arrangement that felt about right, and when I added the articles, I had a winner.

While the rest change attire four times a year
Theirs remains green
Keeping my deeds safely hidden
Caressed by the first touch of night and day

I had jumped the first hurdle. The second was even more challenging: What did the riddle mean? Did I even have it right? *Goodness gracious, why can't something just come easily in life?* The more I thought about it, the more my head ached.

Piper's whimpering woke me from a deep nap. She stood on her hind legs on the chair by the window, front paws on the glass.

"What is it, girl?"

Piper glanced at me, but her attention was fixated on something in the gardens. I rolled off the bed and joined the dog. Down in the garden, I saw Elliott amble past the rhododendrons. His steps were slow, his shoulders slumped as if he carried an unbearable burden. He looked like an ancient man who had been through countless years of toil, not the eighteen-year-old he once was. He had gone through the refinement of experience and the purging that came with suffering. All he had left was himself.

Poor Elliott. How much longer will he have to hang about with the rhododendrons in the garden? I sympathized with him, but my inkling that he hid something from me kept me on guard. Was he really interested in finding Rose because he loved her? Would it make a difference in his journey if I spoke to the grim woman? The unknowns were many. But the thought of confronting the woman was arguably the worst unknown, for she was filled with so much violence and fury I would almost prefer the killer in the woods over her.

While I reflected on my situation and how to go about it, Mrs. Goswick came to fetch me. The constable had arrived. I made my way downstairs, arranging in my mind the best way to tell the story. Soon I came into the sitting room, and Constable Jones bolted from the sofa to present himself. He was a short, chubby fellow with a beefy face. After the expected formalities were over, he took out his notebook and the interview began.

To wrap up my eventful day, he asked a million questions and wrote down my declaration three times. His inquisitive personality made sense when I learned that he was Mrs. Jones's husband. By morning, the entire region would be aware of every detail I had disclosed, his wife being the first to read and spread my testimony about the chase in the woods. "Many clues are found when the memory is jogged," he said. I hoped he was correct, for my headache was back with a vengeance, and I couldn't think clearly about anything. At last, when I started to repeat myself more than once, the constable decided to leave. Assuring me that if any further questions came up, he would contact me, he left the house, crossing Samuel Goswick at the door.

Having inspected the grounds, Samuel had come to check and reinforce the locks. I imagined most folks in the forest would do the same as the rumors of the killer's presence were on the rise.

"Safety measures," the groundskeeper grumbled, seeing my interest in his work as he moved to a window in the sitting room, screwdriver in hand. While he fidgeted with the encasement, he proceeded to do something I never expected. He gave me some safety tips, and I saw a hint of genuine concern and sympathy in his rough eyes. Yet just like with his wife's, there was something else in them, something that weighed him down. Why did it feel that everyone in my orbit, living and dead, seemed to be hiding something?

Watching the groundskeeper work, I worried that his age, though he was a man of much strength, would play against him if someone broke into the house. I knew what I needed.

"Mr. Goswick, I'd like a gun," I announced in a voice as firm as steel.

His response was a short, uncaring grunt.

"Can you get me one?"

Turning from the glass, he observed me with a blank expression. "What would you be doing with a gun?"

"Defending myself."

He grunted again, a big grunt this time, as if saying, "*That's the last thing we need.*"

"Mr. Goswick," I insisted, "I'm no match for the strength of the killer. And I can't be caged in this house or chaperoned everywhere."

"A gun, miss, is a dangerous weapon. It's not something to be taken lightly."

"I understand that."

Straightforward as he was, he continued. "It's not like you can go shooting around at any little noise, and I don't want to be muddled in a murder."

"If I can't defend myself, then you very well may be."

"If the miss wasn't so set in her ways, she wouldn't go about alone. Then no one would agonize over her safety." Satisfied with his response, he withdrew from the room.

"I still want a gun!" I cried, though likely upon deaf ears. I did get one more of his grunts.

Retrieving the pieces of paper containing the riddle from my pocket, I arranged them on the coffee table. With all the secrets that seemed to surround me, now, more than ever, I was convinced to not trust others with it, not even Elliott. If it was an important clue, it was worth the hassle. I would have to sort it out by myself—and who knew how long that might take? *While the rest change attire four times a year... Theirs remains green... Keeping my deeds safely hidden... Caressed by the first touch of night and day.*

CHAPTER 13
FACING THE UNKNOWN

Morning broke after what felt like an endless night, and I awoke to the sweet song of birds. The ghost of the woman had been punctual in her rounds. As terrible as her appearances were, the reality that only I was aware of her presence was frightfully isolating. Each encounter left me feeling more lonely and empty. I had the fleeting thought that she could somehow absorb the good from my soul, like a parasite eating my flesh from the inside out.

I turned on my side and, with a scream, reached for my blanket and pulled it up to my neck. I was not alone. "For heaven's sake!" I blurted out.

"Good morning." Elliott sat by the fireplace, a smile plastered on his face.

I sat up in bed, still clutching the bedding. "What in the name of goodness is the matter for you to be here?"

"Nothing, I just wanted to say hello, but you seem in a very odd sort of mood today," he observed.

"It might have something to do with the fact that I slept terribly. Piper has taken to staying at the cottage with Julius, and the woman was out and about again. And then I awoke to find a male, well, the ghost of one, installed in my bedroom. Now, can we continue this discussion elsewhere?"

As if ejected from his seat, Elliott moved to the window. "Come to the garden. Someone is coming up." He walked straight through the wall and to the outside world. Good thing he wasn't mortal—he would have fallen one story to his death.

Not a second later, Mrs. Goswick came in with breakfast. I took my time getting dressed and finished the last piece of bread on the tray. Shortly thereafter, I found the ghost of the soldier on the front lawn.

"We need to set some boundaries," I decided.

"Boundaries?"

"Yes, boundaries."

"You can't come into my bedroom as you please."

"But I can." A smile crossed his eyes.

"Let me rephrase that. You shouldn't come into my bedroom uninvited."

"True. I guess having a friend to talk to got me a little carried away. I couldn't wait to see you."

"Don't do it again unless there is a life-threatening situation. Agreed?" Though I felt lousy for reprimanding him, having a place to myself was a must. A place I didn't have to share with either the living or the dead.

"Define 'life-threatening situation,'" he teased.

"Promise me."

"All right. I promise."

We moved farther from the manor, ambling along the line of tall trees.

"Where have you been?"

"Roaming the woods," he said.

"Looking for the rider?"

"Yep. History is a good predictor. He is the same man I've seen before, and he is hunting to kill."

His words made me cringe. "The constable came last night. I told him about the chase in detail."

"What did he think about me?"

"I did not mention you."

"I see—you omitted a few details."

"Just the unimportant ones." I smiled.

"Very amusing." He frowned. "I do hope they discover something though. So far, they have been a bunch of incompetent fools."

"Give them some credit. The killer is a clever man, so clever he might border on lunacy."

"Or he's so mad he might border on cleverness."

My gaze snapped to the ghost. His words carried a measure of truth. "Maybe so."

We came to a large patch of grass, and I sat down and wrapped my arms around my bent legs.

"Have you thought about speaking to the woman?" he asked, kneeling in front of me.

I vacillated, staring into his eyes for a while. Assuming he wasn't guilty of Rose's death, what this encounter could mean seemed to have kindled his hope. I found myself between facing my fears and extinguishing the light that radiated from him like a lamp on the darkest of nights. "I'll leave All Hallows someday, but you need to work this out."

"Does that mean you'll reach out to her?"

"It means I'll try. After all, fools rush in where angels fear to tread."

"Don't fret. I'll be right there with you."

"Thanks." His intentions of helping were noble, but I doubted he could do anything to safeguard me against the evil of the woman.

"You'll never know how much this means to me," Elliott assured me. "Tonight, then?"

"Tonight."

"Do I have permission to come to your room?" He gave me a silly smile.

"You do." I returned his gesture.

"Well, well, what do we have here?" Elliott exclaimed.

I followed his gaze and saw a car rapidly approaching the manor. "Who is that?"

"I see a soldier driving General Lewis."

"How can you see that far?" I stood and dusted the grass from my trousers.

"I can see quite well during the day."

"Well, that's an understatement."

"Come on. I'll walk you back to the house. I haven't seen Lewis for ages."

We hurried back, my mind racing ahead of my legs. Did he bring news about my parents? Was it good news? I hated when my mind jumped to conclusions before I even knew if it had reason to do so.

Elliott noticed my agitation. "You look as if you've seen another ghost. What's the matter?"

"My parents' neighborhood was bombed the other night. I'm not sure what happened to them."

"Oh."

Without warning, Julius shot out from the trees and onto the path ahead of us. By now, I should have been used to his erratic behavior, but he'd startled me again. I never knew where he was or what he would do next.

"Hello, Julius," I called after him.

Julius halted and spun around toward us. I suspected his intentions had been to return my greeting, but at the sight of Elliott, an expression of disapproval formed on his face.

"Heading to the house, aren't you?" said Elliott. "What's the rush, old chap?"

Julius looked at us sideways as we matched our steps with his, and mumbled, "It's time to get some food. I've been out working since dawn."

"Well, you are right on time. Your mum will shovel the goodies out of the larder for the visitors," Elliott mocked.

"Who's at the house?" the gardener inquired.

"Your old friend, General Lewis," Elliott answered.

"Lewis?"

"The very same," Elliot assured him.

Julius stopped. "Nah, I can wait until luncheon. I'll get back to work." His change of plan was actually like the pouncing of a beast. As suddenly as he had appeared, he reversed his course and strode away.

Staring after his rapid departure, I wondered aloud, "What's gotten into him?"

"Who knows?" Elliott answered. "There is always something hidden at All Hallows. Nothing is ever what it seems."

"What do you mean?"

"There must be a reason Julius avoids the authorities. He is not as innocent as you want to believe he is."

"I don't want to believe anything," I defended. "I like giving people the benefit of the doubt."

Elliott groaned. "All right, you do that."

We crossed the garden, and I gave a courteous nod to the soldier who sat in the car, waiting for his superior. He cordially touched the brim of his hat in return. Elliott lingered by the entrance. I rushed inside and found General Lewis near the hearth, engaged with Samuel Goswick in what appeared to be a serious discussion.

"General Lewis, what a pleasant surprise." I extended my hand to him. "I did not expect to see you before Sunday."

"Good morning, Seraphina. I hope it's all right to have come without notice."

"Of course." Under the mask of small talk, I was anxious to know why he was here. "This is your house, after all."

"If you'll excuse me, I have much work to do," the groundskeeper stated.

"Thank you, Samuel," said the general. "I'm counting on you to hold down the fort."

With a reassuring nod, the groundskeeper departed.

"Please do have a seat." I signaled to the sofa as I settled at one end of it.

"I bring you news. I thought to send you a message, but after speaking to the constable, I took the liberty of intruding. He said you had been chased through the woods. I had to see you with my own eyes to make sure you were safe."

Oh good. If he wasn't planning on coming, it's nothing terrible. "You shouldn't have gone to such trouble."

"I was surprised to hear you ventured out alone."

I flushed. After the counsel he had given me about the woods and the reprimand at the Burley mansion, surely this affixed a seal of stupidity upon me, especially when I had visited him and not mentioned the incident. "I'm not sure what came over me that night. I guess the threat of this man didn't seem real."

"I hope it does now."

"Very real indeed." I sheepishly avoided his gaze. "Do you think it's the same killer as before?"

"It's possible. Though it's also possible, hypothetically, of course, that we aren't dealing with the same man. People like to exploit others' fears. If you'll allow me to be frank, after these many years, it's likely that whoever is stirring up all this fear is someone using the murderer's name for a cover-up."

"Still, it might be the same man."

"True, but one has to consider all angles," he said.

"Do you have someone in mind?"

General Lewis chuckled. "I like your forwardness, Seraphina."

"Forgive me. I suppose being a candidate for murder has made me a bit bold."

"Nothing to worry about. It would make me bold too. Now, the most important thing is that you take care of yourself. I spoke with Samuel about the manor's security. He has been working on it already, and he owns a couple of firearms. He won't hesitate to use them if need be."

"He has more than one gun?" My brows contracted in displeasure.

"That's my understanding. Why?"

"Because he won't lend me one. I want to defend myself without depending on others."

"You know men can be protective of their firearms, but I do think you are safe here." After contemplating me briefly, he offered, "If it puts your mind at rest, I can have one of my men guard the house at night."

A gun! A gun will put my mind at ease. True, I didn't know much about firearms and how they worked, but how hard could it be? To my chagrin, both Samuel and General Lewis had dismissed my desire to protect myself. Or at least to feel safer by relying on something other than my strength. What was it with men not wanting to give women firearms? Did they fear losing their manliness? Whatever the reason, it was pathetic.

"That's a generous offer, but like you said, I'm protected here." *After all, the worst that can happen to me is death.*

"If you change your mind, I'll have a guard here as soon as you say the word."

"Thank you, but I don't think it will be necessary."

"Very well—just remember that this is not the first time the Goswicks have dealt with something like this. They are faithful to their duties. They'll make sure you are safe, for they know I will hold them accountable otherwise."

Mrs. Goswick came into the room just then, tea tray in hand. Wondering if she had heard the general's last words, I noticed that the teacups and silverware were an expensive set not normally used. She did know how to properly attend to her employer.

"Excuse the interruption, General. I thought you might like some tea and freshly baked scones."

"If they taste anything like they smell, I'm afraid I'll eat them all," he replied.

"Indeed, they are very good," I affirmed.

The housekeeper engaged herself in serving the guest first.

"Going back to our discussion," General Lewis continued, "while the indoors are safe, the outdoors are a completely different matter. The woods have always been a treacherous place. Any deranged person acquainted with the landscape could become entangled with hunting and killing more than animals."

The cup in Mrs. Goswick's hands dropped, hitting the edge of the table on its way down. Glass shattered everywhere as the hot drink bathed the floor. "Oh my! Forgive my clumsiness," she exclaimed, swiftly bending to gather the scattered pieces.

"Allow me to help you." I joined her on the rug.

"Oh my! What a mess," she sputtered.

"Now, Agatha, don't fret," the general comforted. "There are greater tragedies than the loss of a teacup."

Her hands trembled almost uncontrollably as she placed the last visible piece of glass on the serving dish. "I shall take care of this immediately. I need to collect the mop, and I'll bring you another cup," she said to me.

"Please, don't trouble yourself. It can wait until the general leaves.'

"Yes, there is no rush," the general reaffirmed.

"Very well," Mrs. Goswick responded in a curt voice. Her gaze swept the area one last time before she retreated to the kitchen.

As if nothing had happened, the general tasted his drink. "A little cold but otherwise excellent. I had forgotten what a great cook Agatha is."

"She is marvelous." And not able to wait any longer, I inquired, "Did you say you have news for me?"

"Yes! How silly of me. I should have told you already." He placed his cup on the table. "Your parents have been dislodged by the attacks, but they are well. They have moved to a safe area on the outskirts of London. I got a cable to Edward and received one in return for you." He delved into his pocket and handed me a piece of paper.

"Thank you. I've been worried sick about them. This is such a relief." I could barely contain my excitement as I scanned the black ink on the telegram.

Dearest Seraphina,

Your mother and I are all right and dwelling in one of London's rest centres for now. John has kindly advised us of your favorable circumstances. While most of our earthly possessions are now part of the past, we find reassurance and peace knowing that our family is safe and, the war permitting, we will be reunited in the near future.

We send you our love,

Your father, Edward Addington.

PS. John invited us to join you in the New Forest, but there is a lot to be done here to help other families. Not having small children gives us the ability to succor those who do, and I'm still working at the Royal Mail. I hope you understand.

My heart throbbed in contentment. Though it was apparent that much of our house was gone, my parents were safe and in good spirits.

"General, again, I'm indebted to you. What can I do to show my appreciation?"

"Come to the party on Sunday."

Night had come, and with it the time to fulfill my promise to Elliot. *How in the world did I get myself into this?* Thinking of the task ahead, my stomach turned upside down.

Everyone was abed except for me and Piper, whom I had snatched into my room before she could run off to the cottage. The corridor was semidark, lit by the wall sconces, which were almost as useless as not having them. Thankfully, we wouldn't face the ghost of the woman alone tonight. I had my own soldier to encourage me, but unlike with Ross, I didn't feel quite as safe in his presence.

Elliott was situated on the floor by the hearth, hands twitching in anticipation. I sat on my bed, nervously watching the hands on the clock. Piper lay on the rug, round eyes fixed on the ghost. I couldn't tell whether she liked him, but at least she wasn't growling anymore.

"I will leave the light off," I decided. "It's best we don't disrupt her routine in any way."

"If you say so," Elliott agreed.

It was ironic to think that just hours ago I had been preoccupied with getting a gun for protection. And now I was jumping headfirst into an unknown danger—where not even a gun could help me. Knowing what was to come, it was hard to be enthusiastic. Though I was determined to be brave, my human nature threatened to overrule me. Part of me wished to rise to the challenge with a devil-may-care grin. The other wanted to flee All Hallows kicking and screaming at the thought that I would soon march straight into the woman. What was I supposed to say to her, and how would she react?

Elliott and I sat in silence for what seemed like a long time, like mourners at a funeral with no corpse to weep over. I wondered if my body would soon fill a coffin, were the woman to kill me. Aided by the light of the hearth, at the first sound of a door slamming down the hallway, I jumped from the bed, startled. The woman's ritual had started.

"Are you sure about this?" Elliott whispered.

"I am." I moved to the door before I could think twice.

Piper followed me, her bark soft and deep in her throat, building for an explosion. Though Elliott couldn't see or hear any of it, he trailed close behind.

Slowly, as if the mere action hurt, I pulled the door open and stepped into the penumbras of the corridor. I could hardly believe what I was doing. I supposed that having Elliott as a spectator added to my courage. Or maybe it was just misplaced pride. Neither prevented my body from jerking violently as she exploded from bedroom to bedroom, shutting the doors with a force that shook the entire length of the obscure hallway. The alarming fact was that she wasn't pushing them with her hands. The elements seemed to obey her very thoughts—as if she were a cyclone sweeping everything in its path.

I waited for the black specter to come closer, an icy breeze prickling my skin whenever she crossed the hall. Shuddering at the notion that my bones and flesh might turn into an iceberg at her awareness, I pressed my hand to my heart to hold it in place. It hammered against my ribs, determined to break free. *Stay still—fool or not, I can do this.*

From the corner of my eye, I saw that Elliott stood not too far away. Refocusing, I prepared to intercept the woman before she went into the green room. Unfortunately, I wasn't the only one who had built up some grit. As the woman briefly traveled to another room, Piper threw her ears back and let out the most nerve-racking howl I had ever heard.

"Piper, hush!" Apparently, my command didn't match what she had in mind. Her little body became rigid, and her hair stood on end like a porcupine's quills. Then and there, she lunged at the dark woman who had resurfaced in the middle of the hallway, her nails sliding and scratching on the floorboards. As the dog charged, the woman halted, and so did my heartbeat.

She is going to kill us—she is going to kill us. If I were to run, now was the time, but my body did not respond.

What took place next was a blur. With one swift movement of the woman's head, the dog was lifted off her feet and thrown across the hallway toward me. She hit the wall with a terrible thud and squeal, and then her body lay inert on the floor, an almost inaudible whimpering coming from her. Elliott was quick to kneel beside Piper, but I feared he couldn't do much to help.

"How dare you?" I sputtered with indignation. Torn between anger for what she had done to Piper and fulfilling my plan, my hands turned into fists, and I marched at the ghost as she prepared to move into the green room. I supposed it was good I couldn't punch her, for hearing my little friend's suffering, I would have loved to deal her a few unforgettable blows.

As she slowed her devilish march, I drew in a short breath. Unable to contain the contempt in my voice, I blurted, "Stop right there. Speak to me."

Hovering near a sconce, she turned, and the bravery that brought me to this point fled. I froze. What I saw in her eyes was not of this world but lay hidden, gnashing and twisting with basilisk horror. Even if I wished to, the words were stuck in my throat, and I could not produce another sound. And clearly, she did not wish to speak to me, for she dismissed me at once.

Ever so slightly, she made another movement with her head, and I was airborne, flying backward with a tremendous force. My back slammed against the doorframe, and I was sure my spine was engraved in the wood. I collapsed on the floor, my body huddled in pain, bracing for the next attack. My gaze traveled to my little friend not far from me. She uttered a soul-wrenching whimper of pain. *Piper...*

A sound like the rustling of silk told me that the woman was almost to me. I tried to move, but all I could do was to close my eyes and await the impact. It never came. Instead, the woman entered the green room and produced her final wail. I covered my ears to muffle the shrill sound. It wasn't long until her voice faded, and like every other night, she evanesced as if she never existed.

"Seraphina, are you all right?" Elliott asked in alarm. "Say something." For a moment, everything was blurry. I stared blankly at the ceiling. Elliott dropped beside me. "Can you hear me? Answer me."

"Give me a second." I tried to sit up, but the sharp pain in my back made me reconsider. I rolled onto my side, pressed my hands to the wood, and pushed my upper body off the floor. I stood on shaking legs. Clenching my teeth in exasperation, I flipped the lights on and gathered Piper into my arms, fearing the worst. As soon as I held her, she opened her eyes and started to lick her paws. Noticing that her leg hung limply, I gently touched it. She let out an excruciating shriek.

"Oh, my darling. What has she done to you? I'm so sorry."

Elliott ran his hand over her leg. Piper looked at him and stuck her tongue out as if she wanted to kiss him. "Place her on the bed. Let her rest. She'll be better by morning," he assured me.

"It's morning already." I glanced at the gaps in the curtains. The first rays of sunlight lit the room. I deposited Piper on the bed. Without a sound, she stretched out on the soft mattress and closed her eyes. I lay down beside her.

My friend the ghost stood at the footboard of the bed, waiting patiently.

"I think we've suffered a setback."

Elliott gave a grim chuckle. "A setback? That was a disaster. I should never have asked that of you. I feared it would be a risk, but I was convinced that if it were Rose, she wouldn't hurt you." He looked away regretfully. "Rose or no, she did not spare you. Do forgive me."

"There is nothing to forgive. I had a fairly good idea of what I was getting myself into."

"We can't do this again."

I looked at poor Piper. "No, we can't."

From the deepest chambers of my memory resounded the words: *While the rest change attire four times a year... Theirs remains green... Keeping my deeds safely hidden... Caressed by the first touch of night and day.* Perhaps the riddle, though unknown to Elliott, would be my lighthouse in the raging storm.

CHAPTER 14
ADJUSTING TO CHANGE

I ached all over from the blow I had received, and poor Piper had a slight limp, but I wasn't complaining. We were lucky to have gotten away with just a few bumps and bruises. While I mulled over my ghost problem, I found myself distracted by another issue. Ross hadn't shown yesterday. I had looked forward to his visit despite the general's warning. Caroline's remark about Mark never writing to her came to mind.

Frustrated by my inability to detach my thoughts from the young captain, I dug through the armoire and pulled out my burgundy dress—a fancy piece of clothing I hadn't worn since before the war started. Laying it flat on the bed, I pressed it with the ancient-looking iron filled with coal Mrs. Goswick had graciously prepared for me.

I pulled the dress over my head and fastened the zipper at the back. Not surprisingly, it was looser than ever. After sponging some complexion powder on my face and a bit of rouge on my cheeks, I escaped the mirror, and in an effort to not overstress about tonight, I headed for the library. There was harmony there. No books had fallen off the shelves since I had put the riddle together.

Ruminating on the unsolved message, I retrieved a book out of habit. While anxiously pacing about, I repeatedly rehearsed the riddle aloud.

While the rest change attire four times a year

Theirs remains green
Keeping my deeds safely hidden
Caressed by the first touch of night and day

"What did you say?" inquired Julius from the threshold.

My gaze snapped from the book in my hands to him. "Oh, it's nothing—"

"That was a riddle," he stated.

"Yes…" I stared at him, momentarily unsure what to do.

"Say it again," he encouraged.

"While the rest change attire four times a year, theirs remains green—"

"The conservatory," he said matter-of-factly.

The conservatory. I was stunned. Being the gardener, he had the advantage of seeing it plainly. All this time, it was so simple. Though, while toiling with the idea of evergreens, I hadn't been too far from the truth. "I'll say, Julius. It sounds about right."

"Rose used to challenge me with riddles." He smiled at the memory with a distant, detached expression.

"Did she, now?" I did some mental calculations. He was close to Rose's age. They could have been good friends.

"Mum wants to know if you need anything from the market."

"I don't think so." He turned to leave, and I called, "Wait, Julius. What about the last part of the riddle?"

He simply walked away. I guess he didn't think it fair to free me from my burden so easily. However, his cleverness in deciphering the first two lines was incentive enough for me to push myself to solve the rest. Stubbornly, I rehearsed it until a new idea emerged.

Keeping my deeds safely hidden. Rose had hidden something in the conservatory. In a frenzy, I rushed through the winding corridors to what had once been a lively greenhouse but now lay dormant under a sheet of dust and abandonment. Taking in the many terra-cotta pots scattered on the floor and the cobwebs crawling up the glass walls, I dreaded where her secrets might be hidden. *Please don't be at the bottom of one of the pots. If I dump all the soil on the floor, the Goswicks will hang me.* I carefully paced the area, scanning for something to help me stir the dirt.

Caressed by the first touch of night and day... First touch! The notion came suddenly, like a ray of light. *The east corner!* And then another burst of light. Pots had come and gone. Besides, she must have anticipated that Julius would have found whatever she'd placed inside, for he was always fumbling with them. *It must be on the wall or floor. Those would have remained in place.*

Most of the conservatory was made of glass, so my exploration moved quickly from the walls to the floor. I circled the spot, inspecting it carefully. Observing nothing unusual, I resorted to probing the floor with my feet. When the end of my shoe caught the corner of an uneven stone, I hurried to grab an old shovel from the pile of abandoned tools near the door. Mindful of my nice dress, I applied pressure to the loose end. It was not an easy task, but I doggedly toiled at it and soon had it out of its place.

There in the shadows of the square cavity under a sheet of dirt lay a metal box. Retrieving it from its slumber, I sat it on the floor. My fingers shook in exhilaration as I coaxed the lid open and revealed its treasure— a brown leather-covered book, impatiently longing for someone to bring to light its forgotten days. I opened it to its first page and found that my expectations had been exceeded. The long strokes of carefully written ink read, *Diary of Lady Rose Lewis.* I took in a stabilizing breath. This could very well be the discovery of Rose's fate and the identity of the killer.

Like a guilty thief, I looked around me as I returned the box to its place, followed by the stone, and sealed the hole. After swiftly moving a pot over the spot to conceal the area I'd disturbed, I started toward my bedroom with a million thoughts calling for my attention.

Elliott. The urge to share my discovery with him was almost unbearable, yet I suppressed it. I did not know what I would find in Rose's writings, and perhaps I could spare him unnecessary anguish. Staring at the book in my hands as if I had unearthed a trunk of gold, I made up my mind to go through it first. I would then decide how to proceed.

Locking the door behind me, I washed my hands and settled into the old armchair in the corner of the room. The leather binding glistened in the light of the chandelier. I had heard so much about this Rose that holding something she owned felt surreal. She had been one of those people who left a permanent mark on all she met.

The first third of the diary, although important in her life, contained little of interest to me. She told about her days at All Hallows: her walks in the garden, her horseback rides through the woods, her love of literature, art, and poetry. Her wonderful relationship with her father. The dreadful war, which she described as hard to believe but far removed from her world. Some of her remarks were a poignant reminder of how I had felt when the current war started. No matter where or when, war had the power to throw life into chaos, shake stability, and destroy sanity. One night, we happily went to bed with our future mapped out, only to wake up the next morning to find that our plans had been put on permanent hold, replaced by uncertainty. History repeated itself in ways I couldn't fathom.

A constant theme was that of her longing for her deceased mother. Little mentions here and there of the Goswick family were made, but nothing out of the ordinary. Apparently, she'd gotten on quite well with them, especially Julius. His name appeared more than anyone's. She trusted him.

In one entry, she wrote:

My dear Julius, he is a peculiar creature but as innocent as they come. One of the purest souls to have ever walked on this earth. I can always count on him. It pains me that people don't respect him. He is different from others but brilliant all the same. Irrefutably, he is unlike his father, whose presence has the invisible power of dominating those around him. Mr. Goswick is a simple man, yet a strong one. Short of words but with a set of eyes that pierce others to their very core.

I couldn't have described the groundskeeper any better. I leafed through the pages until I came to the day Rose met Elliott.

A few weeks back, my father insisted I bring some of the family's old tools to the blacksmith for repair. He takes much pride in our "relics," as he calls them, which were handed down throughout the generations. Dutiful as I am, but not without a few complaints, I did.

The blacksmith has a new helper, Elliott—a young man from Ringwood. At first, I didn't think much of him, but soon I found myself returning to the shop whenever I visited town. Visits, which, to my surprise, have increased with alarming frequency. After I had taken just about everything we owned (made of iron, of course) to the blacksmith, Father noticed that something was amiss.

He observed that at this rate, I'd make the blacksmith a rich man and us the poorest folks in the forest. He then ordered me to invite the young man to dine with us so he could meet him.

I did, and since then, our relationship has only flourished. To my relief, Father took an instant liking to Elliott. Last night, under the most beautiful moon in the rose garden, he kissed me for the first time. He is so delicate, so careful. We spoke of marriage, and my heart leaped in anticipation. I would be honored to be Mrs. Rose Kennard. I think about Elliott and our future life together my every waking hour. And when I'm asleep, he is the sole protagonist of my dreams.

Another entry:

My darling brought me a gift today. It was so unexpected and so beautiful it brought tears to my eyes. He gave me a silver necklace. The chain, he said, was his mother's, and the round pendant was made by him at the silversmith. It has a rose engraved in the metal.

The pages that followed were filled with tales of their outings and their love, which seemed to have no end. For a short while, I lost myself in her story, but I was mindful that Rose did not mean for others to intrude, and so I gave their intimacy due privacy. I moved on, looking for the information I hoped to find.

How can this be possible? My heart, like a crystal chalice, has fallen and broken into a million pieces. Elliott has been drafted into the army. I'm so afraid. I reached out to Cousin John to plead Elliott's cause. He tried, but the war is relentless. We have almost run out of men to sacrifice to this senseless carnage. They are now resorting to the young, the old, and even the disabled. All they want are bodies to fill their ranks. The regard for human life is nonexistent.

He left this morning, and my heart went with him. He promised he would come back to me. I'm suffocating in grief. I cry myself to sleep every night, and each new day finds me with a painful lump in my throat. Will I ever see him again? Life is cruel. The only things that keep me going are the love of Father and Elliott's sweet letters.

Father's health is rapidly failing. Two physicians have attended to him. Their verdict: there is not much time.

The odious vicar stopped by to see Father. I avoided him as much as possible. I'm not sure why he took so long in Father's bedroom, but I waited until he was gone before I returned to Father's side.

Father was taken from me last night. He was my anchor in the storm. I'm now adrift.

Elliott's letters stopped. Where are you, darling? You said you'd return to me. I'm waiting for you. Always waiting.

When I heard that the war was officially over, I dared to hope again. But I'm cursed. Cousin John came by this morning to bring the unwelcome news of Elliott's passing during one of the last battles fought. My life ended with his. When I think of a future without him, I see only darkness. I'm frozen inside and out.

A few tears rolled down my cheeks. I tried to keep more from coming, but they overpowered me, streaming down my face unrestricted. She loved him just as much as he loved her. It was now evident that he still loved her with that same intensity. He was still looking for her, determined to keep his promise to return to her, but where was she?

I read through her last entries.

His presence makes me uncomfortable. Since Father's death, he has taken more liberties. His presence is too palpable. Something in me warns me to flee. All Hallows is not safe.

The way he looks at me is sickening. How did I not notice it before?

After this morning's encounter, I'm afraid for my life. As if that is not horrendous enough, I'm convinced that trying to find help would only accelerate the evil coming at me. I have no proof, just my instincts to guide me. I'm alone in this vast forest he knows so well. I must do something soon.

I could have never imagined life would turn out this way. Some things hurt too deeply. Like roots, each day, they continue to dig deeper, to cut through my very bones, trying to find an escape. But there is no relief. Without Elliott, the anguish is eternally housed in my body.

I still wonder how it would have been to be Mrs. Rose Kennard.

I placed the diary on the bed, dumbfounded. Rose had known her life was in danger. She had needed to protect herself, but was she able to do so? Why hadn't she written the name of whoever it was that tormented her? Maybe she had run out of time. Or perhaps she was afraid that if the diary had fallen into the wrong hands and she'd been mistaken, her assumptions would only cause grief. Amid the enigma surrounding Rose, one thing was clear: the killer wasn't Elliott. He'd died in the war.

The ballroom of the Burley mansion felt like an overcrowded theater. The desks and workstations had been removed. A gigantic wireless set played soft music, creating a welcoming atmosphere. Groups of people were dispersed throughout the floor, chatting happily, and judging by their attire, there was a considerable number of military personnel in attendance. Along the back wall, an extensive table offered all sorts of foods and drinks.

Despite the attempt at normalcy, the shadow of war wouldn't leave entirely. Even unseen, its presence was felt. Caroline and I moved deeper into the throng, which seemed to multiply by the second, and I felt claustrophobic, hemmed in by the lack of space.

"There is Robertson," Caroline exclaimed in a lively voice, waving at the blond soldier she had met at the mansion on our previous visit. He beamed at her from across the ballroom. "I must speak to him."

"No, wait, Caroline, don't," I begged uselessly. She had already left me. Using her elbows to push any obstacles out of her way, she swam through the sea of people.

Heaven-sent, a hand pressed against my lower back, followed by a soothing voice. "Seraphina, welcome," greeted General Lewis. In a blue uniform decorated with a few medals, he owned the attention of the older females in attendance.

"Good evening, General."

"I must say, you look beautiful."

"That's kind of you to say."

"Come join us." He motioned for me to gather with his acquaintances and introduced me to Mr. Davis, head of the postal office, and his wife. Next, I met two short gentlemen with thick mustaches and long sideburns who owned the local bank—their names escaped me. And the last couple I already knew: Constable Jones and his wife, whom I had met at Mrs. Bisset's house.

"It's a pleasure to see you again," said Mrs. Jones. "After your rapid departure the other day, I hoped you were all right. But then, of course, I heard about the little incident in the woods."

I'm sure you have. I ignored her leading remark. "I'm doing well, Mrs. Jones. Thank you."

"It must have been such an awful fright." She patted my arm with pretended commiseration.

"So awful I'd rather not think or speak about it."

"Of course, dear, of course." She picked another subject. "And how is Miss Goswick? Is she in attendance tonight?"

"She is."

Mrs. Jones's hawklike eyes swept the ballroom. "Oh yes, there she is. She's found a friend, I see." And taking a longer look, she observed poignantly, "Her white dress is well-fitted to her figure, isn't it?"

Purposely sidetracking her from whatever might escape her lips next, I inquired, "How have you been?" Miraculously, she abandoned her inspection of Caroline and proceeded to recount her marvelous deeds of the past week to all within earshot.

While my mind drifted in the ocean of Mrs. Jones's words, someone rushed past me, their arm brushing against mine. I turned and saw Ross head to the refreshment table, the corner of his lips curled up into a smile. My gaze stayed with him until Mrs. Jones reclaimed my attention.

"What's your opinion?" she asked.

I had no idea what we were discussing. "I…"

"Surely Miss Addington agrees. The need to reinforce security throughout the forest is a pressing concern," General Lewis said, rescuing me.

"Indeed," I echoed. In my peripheral vision I saw Ross watching me. I glanced at the general. He seemed unaware of the soldier's evident interest. For the sake of discretion, I waited a decent amount of time before giving in to Ross's gaze.

He mouthed, "Hello."

My focus came back to my company.

"London is barely holding on," Mr. David said. "The postal service there is having an unprecedented number of letters returned." I could only imagine how busy my poor father was, trying to keep up with work as well as being, at present, homeless.

"You don't say!" exploded Mrs. Jones in horror. The mere idea of missing out on a letter had her upset.

"That's the current reality," Mr. David responded. "Either due to their recipients being dislocated by the bombs or dead, I'm afraid."

The discussion took a sudden turn to the aerial warfare, and one of the bank owners spoke to the general in a hushed tone, acquiring his attention. I used the opportunity to silently slip away. Avoiding eye contact with those in my path, I reached the serving table and started to pour myself a drink. Soon, Ross joined me.

"Hi, Seraphina."

"Hello, Ross."

"Are you enjoying the party?"

"Until now..."

He chuckled. "What is that supposed to mean?"

"Nothing." I gulped down the drink.

"Take it easy, would you? That's powerful stuff."

"I've noticed."

"Do you have a minute?"

"I...should get back to the general."

"I'm sure he'll survive a few minutes without you." He snatched my cup and set it on the table before grabbing my arm and briskly maneuvering me to the French windows that opened out onto the garden. It was farther from the vociferous multitude and more tranquil.

"Listen, I'm sorry I didn't come to see you. Is that why you're giving me the cold shoulder?"

In a large part, it was, but no need for him to know. "Of course not. I just don't want to make a fool of myself in front of the general again."

He brought me closer to him. "Let's take a walk outside."

"Hey, Stewart," called an American soldier. "The general wants you to check in with the night patrol."

"What?" Ross sounded startled.

"Yeah, you heard me," the soldier responded. "And don't worry about the lady. I can keep her company." To me, he said, "Hi, there."

"Okay, O'Reilly. Beat it. I'll be on my way."

With a laugh, the soldier disappeared into the crowd.

"I can't believe this. Wow. The nerve of the man!" His jaw tightened, and his eyes filled with fury.

"Who?"

"Your protector. He wants me out of the way. I'm sure he is aware of every move you've made since you left his side."

"Don't be absurd."

He gave me a distinctive frown. "I have to go. I'll come by tomorrow after three—and don't drink anymore."

Disappointment crushed my heart as he walked away. No matter how much I wanted to convince myself otherwise, I liked the man. I ambled to the table of goodies, where the tray with the chocolate cake lured me in. After a few pieces too many, I made my way around the edge of the crowd.

"There you are," General Lewis called. "I want to show you something." Lacing my arm through his, he guided me away from the noise and into the hallway that led to his office.

The door creaked on its hinges as he pushed it open. He moved to his desk, and I chanced a momentary glance at Helen's painting, instantly regretting it. Her eyes bored into mine with lethal force, as if she wanted me out of here and out of her husband's life.

From a drawer, he pulled an oddly shaped bundle. With a look of satisfaction, he handed it to me. "Take a look at this."

It was heavy. I unwrapped the white cloth and drew in a sharp breath. "Oh my!"

"It's a Webley revolver. A solid weapon, not like the ones we have nowadays," he explained with pride. "Do you know how to shoot a gun?"

"I have a fairly good idea. When I was little, my grandfather owned a gun shop on Lombard Street. He instructed his customers, and I made sure to pay attention."

"That's a good start, but come with me."

We traveled down a narrow hallway and came out on the north side of the mansion. Though it was twilight, the garden lanterns cast a soft glow across the barren yard.

"Do you see those targets?" He pointed to some large wooden boards backed by an ancient wall that long ago must have served as an impressive fence. "Those are shooting targets."

With the gun still in my hands, I reflected, "Is it safe? I don't want to injure anyone by accident."

"No one is allowed in this part of the grounds unless they are practicing." General Lewis stood beside me, ready to guide me through the process. "Relax your elbows. Don't lock your arms. Move your right leg in front. Allow your body to move slightly forward. Remember that your left hand is there to support the weight of the revolver and to strengthen your overall grip." Next thing I knew, there was a loud blast. The sudden force of the bullet startled me. "Well done! Well done! You hit the board for sure."

"The blast was louder than I anticipated." My ears were ringing.

"Come back sometime during the day. Wagner or I will continue the lesson."

"I might take you up on that."

"I hope you do."

"You better take this before I shoot you," I teased, extending the gun to him.

Not reaching for the weapon, he informed, "Helen gifted it to me right before her passing. It's yours now."

As much as I wanted a gun, his words petrified me. I felt I was robbing the lady of the house and that it would not go well with her. "Then I can't accept it."

"Why not?"

"It was Helen's. It must be too meaningful to you."

"It is, but she gave it to me, and I can give it to whomever I please. Besides, I would like to believe that if I had a daughter, Helen would have wanted her to have the extra protection."

The finality in his voice gave me no choice but to say thank you.

"Keep it safe, and may I give you a word of advice?"

"Of course." I started to fear that whenever I saw the man, he would have a word of advice for me.

"Keep this to yourself. The fewer people who know, the better."

───────

I stared out the window and saw Caroline and Piper saunter across the garden. Each passing day, Piper fell more in love with the country, spending most of her time outdoors. In fact, I couldn't bring her in if Julius was out on the grounds. She was obsessed with him, following him everywhere. He returned the attention by rewarding her with treats and playing fetch. Their relationship was a bit startling, for she had grown comfortable with him to the point of not alerting me when he was near, which allowed him the advantage of surprise.

Caroline jerked her head toward the road. Piper barked and began to run back and forth in excitement. Enveloped in a cloud of dust, Ross and another biker neared the house. Concealing my awareness of his arrival, I dashed back to the library, where Caroline had last seen me. Leaving the door wide open, I pulled a random book off the shelf and perched on a chair. My eyes were glued to the printed pages, but my ears strained to hear the noises that would soon come down the hallway.

The front door opened, followed by chattering voices and Piper's little paws pattering down the stone floor. Expecting Caroline to come find me, I flipped the page as if I were reading.

The footfalls were quick and soon crossed the doorway. "I told you I would come," Ross announced.

My plans to stay calm and to keep my emotions in check fell apart as soon as I glanced at him. Dressed in civilian clothing—white button-up shirt with the sleeves rolled up to his elbows, dark trousers, and a black belt secured around his trim waistline—his good looks were a mockery of my self-control. All too abruptly, General Lewis's warnings flew out the window, and marriage seemed scarily appealing.

Drawing near, Ross sat on his haunches beside me. "Either you're shocked I came or too immersed in whatever you're reading," he reflected, reminding me that I should say something.

"Well...you are not necessarily reliable. I didn't think you would come."

"Don't act so disappointed." Taking the book from my hands, he read the title, *Human Anatomy and Physiology*, and flipping it over, he looked at the page I had presumably been studying. A mischievous gleam came into his eyes. Smiling, he inquired, "Are you enjoying yourself?"

I snatched it from him, dreading what he alluded to. When my gaze fell on the bolded chapter title, "Male Anatomy," I wished to be swallowed by the earth beneath my feet, evaporate into thin air, or be adopted by some extraterrestrial being. I didn't care which.

"There is nothing to be ashamed of," Ross mocked, deepening my shame. "I like girls who are well-informed."

I needed to think fast and erase the silly grin from his face. Careful not to show my embarrassment, I shot straight at his ego. "I wanted to make sure I could recognize a real man in case one ever comes my way."

He produced a little laugh but otherwise was left speechless.

I left the chair and tossed the incriminating volume back onto the shelf where it belonged. "Let's have some cocoa. Shall we?"

"After you." He signaled for me to lead him down the silent hallway. "The house is mighty quiet."

"It usually is in the afternoon."

"The housekeeper isn't back yet?"

"Not yet," I said.

"What's happened to the Great Dane? She's mellowed since I last saw her."

"It must be the outdoors. She loves it so much I hardly see her anymore."

"What about her owner? Does country life suit her also?"

"For now."

"That's a good answer," he said.

As expected, the kitchen was deserted. "Have a seat. I'll get the water going."

Ross settled down and watched my every move. I filled the kettle with water and placed it on the burner. "I see you haven't forgotten where the kettle is," he teased.

"Surprising, isn't it?" I teased back.

I went to retrieve the cocoa tin from a cupboard and, unable to suppress the anticipation, eagerly peeled off the seal.

"You haven't had any? Were you waiting to share it with me?"

"If truth be told, no." I smiled. "But you did tell me I had to share it with you." I finished mixing the drink, and the smell hit my nostrils, reminding me of better days. I brought the cups to the table and settled down beside him. "It does smell extraordinarily good."

Ross took a big sip. "It's delicious."

I raised the cup to my lips, and as I tasted the cocoa, I felt as content as if the old days had returned and peace was reinstated. "Indeed, it is."

"I can get you more when it runs out."

"Hmm...are you sure? You lied to the general about it. You aren't supposed to share supplies, are you?"

"I can neither confirm nor deny that."

"Go on, you must tell me."

"I don't think I will."

Angling my body toward him, I took the liberty of making him uncomfortable. "What would it take to persuade you?"

Maybe he couldn't believe what I had just said, but he choked on the drink.

Making a conscious effort to keep up the charade, I patted his back. "Are you all right? Was it too hot for you?"

In a wheezing voice, he replied, "You have no idea."

Doubting he had the cocoa in mind, I suppressed a laugh. "Answer my first question."

Reaching for a serviette, he wiped the chocolate from his face. His brown eyes fell on me with an intensity that told me I was in trouble. Whatever he was about to say, I would handle it accordingly.

"Kiss me," he challenged.

My heart stopped beating, but my mind was made up. I would annihilate all memories of the California girls from his remembrance. *One punch, Seraphina. Make it count.* I stood up next to him. He sat up a little taller and stared at me with wide eyes. Bending slightly from my waist, I placed my hands on his shoulders and kissed him with a potency that, doubtless, would bring the best of warriors to their knees. When I let go, he stared at me, stupefied. It took all my acting skills to pretend I hadn't been affected. My only regret was not having done it sooner. This kiss was no comparison to the few I had experienced in my teen years. Those kisses had been a fun, but this one I hoped to repeat.

"Your request has been fulfilled. Now, it's your turn to fulfill mine. Why did you lie to the general about the contents of the box? Did you get in trouble for giving it to me?"

Finding his voice, he straightened and answered, "You are right. We aren't allowed to give away supplies. General Lewis still doesn't know what it was, but he did get ahold of me to make sure I understood the rules."

"Just a reprimand, then?"

"That and a warning."

"I'm sorry."

"I'm not. For that kiss, I would do it all over again."

"I'm flattered," I responded, pretending indifference.

"He has taken the role of being your protector very seriously."

"He doesn't want to disappoint my father, that's all."

"I can understand that. In the army, we don't form many relationships, but when we do, we make sure we stay loyal to them."

"Out of grief can good things be born."

"And disobedience." He grinned.

I shook my head, dismissing his comment. "I'm surprised Caroline hasn't barged in." I played innocent since he didn't know I had seen the other rider.

"She is talking to Robertson. I brought him with me," he announced casually.

I gulped down the cocoa in my mouth before I choked on it. "You brought Robertson?" It hadn't occurred to me that his companion could be Robertson, which meant trouble. Caroline was topsy-turvy for him.

"I thought your friend would like to see him."

"Indeed, she would. But her parents won't like it much." I glanced at my wristwatch and sprang from the chair. "Mrs. Goswick must not find them together. You have to leave."

"Leave?" His eyebrows furrowed. "Listen, I was hoping you'd come with me. There is something I want to show you."

"What would that be?"

"I'm not telling you. You have to see it."

"Where?"

"Out in the woods."

"I suppose I could..." Rapidly trying to concoct a plan, I ordered, "Bring your bikes to the back. I'll grab Caroline and meet you there. If we are lucky, Mrs. Goswick won't see Robertson."

We found Caroline and Robertson getting cozy on the sofa, but like a farmer chasing the fox from the chicken coop, I shooed him out the front door with Ross. Caroline and I came out to the grounds through the kitchen door.

"Caroline, you really should be more careful."

"Don't be overbearing. I'm old enough to know my place."

Mindful of her parents, I required, "Still, promise me you won't do anything you might regret."

"Don't fret. I promise, though you should be more worried about yourself."

"And why is that?"

"Come on, Seraphina. I'm not blind. The way you look at Stewart is alarming. You've fallen for him quite badly."

Her words hit a nerve. "Nonsense. I'm very much in control."

"I might be a country girl, but believe me, I know what I'm doing," Caroline said with an air of self-assurance. "Do you?"

Her simple observation gave me a start. *Did* I know what I was doing? Did I trust myself to do the right thing? I couldn't answer those questions truthfully. I hadn't yet come to terms with my growing affection for this man I barely knew.

Ross and Robertson turned the corner of the manor, pushing their bikes across the pebble path. With their arrival, Caroline's question remained unanswered but vivid in my mind.

The four of us walked into the woods and out of sight.

CHAPTER 15

FALLING IN LOVE

Since the men didn't want to push the motorbikes through the thick trees, they were left hidden not far from the manor. Sometime after that, Robertson and Caroline managed to evade us. When I noticed their disappearance, I looked around anxiously.

"Robertson is not a bad guy." Ross advised, "Relax."

Influenced by General Lewis's warnings, I spoke for Caroline as well as myself. "Soldiers come and go. I don't want to see Caroline's heart broken."

"That's what love is."

"What?"

"A risk. It's allowing someone to enter your heart and maybe break it."

His frankness was stunning. Had his heart been torn to pieces, or had he broken the heart of someone else? Maybe both. "You sound like an expert."

"Yep."

If there had been a lucky girl, who was she, and did he still love her? Whoever she was, I was instantly envious.

Ross interrupted my growing interest in his love affairs by saying, "Hey, don't look so...how do you people say it? Oh yeah, *dreadful*." He half smiled. "I've been wounded before, but my heart is healed and ready to be broken again."

"Is that so?"

"Absolutely."

He took my hand, and we moved through the woods until we came to a high point that overlooked a drop of about five feet into a clearing. In the distance, an abandoned runway stretched under the clear sky. A small aircraft lay inactive on it.

"Can you make it down there?" Ross asked, staring at the steep drop.

"The plane. Is that what you want to show me?"

"That's exactly right."

"I can make it. Just don't let go of my hand."

His grip tightened. We half walked, half slid down the slope and onto firm ground. As we neared the aircraft, far from us, a pillbox rose under the cover of thick bindweed. It was half buried in the ground and mostly hidden from aerial view. The concrete dug-in guard post was equipped with loopholes through which defenders could fire weapons.

"How many runways are there in the woods?" I asked.

Ross shrugged. "I'm not sure, but quite a few. Most were built during the last war, along with the pillboxes. Only a few are still operable."

Ross's strides lengthened, and I hurried to keep up as we waded through the wild grass and across the clearing. As we neared our target, I realized it was much larger than I'd previously thought.

Why is he so excited about this particular plane?

As if reading my thoughts, when we at last stood next to it, he informed, "This is a Hawker Hurricane aircraft—the best night intruder in Britain. The Luftwaffe can't even see it coming."

"What is it doing here?"

"When the yard at the mansion is full, we land the planes in other places until we can bring them in for repairs."

Its battered, bullet-riddled body was a pitiful sight. "It looks quite old."

"It's not more than five years old. It's seen many raids, that's all." In a flash, Ross climbed the fragile ladder on the side and opened the cockpit. Before I knew it, he was sitting inside.

"Come on, Seraphina." He offered his hand to me. "Come take a look."

"Is this all right?"

"I wouldn't invite you if it wasn't."

"I'm not so sure about that," I mumbled, climbing up the ladder.

Ross reached for my waist and pulled me onto his lap. The closeness was awkward, but I had never thought that awkward could feel so good. He closed the cockpit and wrapped an arm around me, and then lifted his right hand so I could see what he held between his fingers—a silver key. He inserted it in the panel, and the engine roared to life. "Don't be nervous, okay?"

"Wait, what are you doing?"

"Relax. We won't take off. We'll stay on the ground."

"You are lying!" I panicked. The machine wasn't fit to fly.

Ross chuckled, confirming my fears. The plane accelerated faster than I could organize my thoughts. My stomach turned and twisted as the airplane's wheels left the track, momentarily touching down with a forceful thump. I gasped as Ross kept me in place so my head wouldn't bang against the cockpit roof.

"Ross, you are insane. Stop!" I knew my words were in vain.

The wheels left the ground again, and this time we stayed airborne.

"Welcome to the skies, Your Highness," Ross said proudly.

"We should go back down."

"We will, but you have to enjoy the flight first. When will you ever have the chance to see the New Forest from the sky again?"

"If we crash and die, it won't matter."

He laughed. "I love your optimism."

"Worse yet," I continued, sounding like my mother, "you could get in lots of trouble." Despite Ross's confidence, something in me warned that one couldn't keep secrets from General Lewis. One way or another, he would hear about this. After my behavior at the mansion, I knew my reputation was already smeared. But for Ross, this adventure could be detrimental to his career.

"Nah, I have permission to test-fly these planes anywhere in the forest."

"Except that we aren't test-flying it," I said.

"As far as I'm concerned, we are."

"And you usually do it with a civilian on board?"

"No, but I won't say a word. Will you?"

"I'll think about it." With a sigh, I settled into my circumstances, for regardless of what I said, it was too late now. We were airborne, and I couldn't let the beauty of the woods below us go unnoticed.

"When I'm up here, I feel like the sky has no end and, like life, is full of possibilities," Ross said.

"It's magnificent, and the forest looks so different." The treetops formed a green mantle that spread out in all directions. From this point of view, the woods looked innocuous.

Words became unnecessary as we enjoyed the peacefulness of the flight and being together. Resting the back of my head against Ross's chest, I reflected on the contentment I felt.

It had never occurred to me that my heart could, at times, know better than reason. This had been my struggle since I'd left London. Flying over the forest with a man who made my heart race every time he was near, a man whose eyes and smile I couldn't stop thinking about, was worth the risk. Eventually the war would end, and who knew? Maybe Ross and I could make a life together. The thought of going to sleep and waking up in his arms filled me with longing.

I turned my head so I could see his face. He lowered his lips until they touched mine, and I wished that time would stop right here, the moment lasting forever. His lips were sense-numbing—the connection effectively disarming me.

The sound of metal grinding against metal brought us apart. Ross groaned, and I cringed. It came again, shaking the cockpit. I realized that it originated from somewhere within the carcass of the plane.

"What in the world?" Ross blurted. "We are dropping altitude fast."

I clutched his knees. I couldn't speak. My stomach dropped, matching the rapid descent of the plane. How could we have gone from total bliss to chaos so fast?

After fidgeting with the buttons, Ross punched the navigation board. "Wake up, you piece of junk!" He wrestled with the yoke and somehow was able to give the plane some direction. "Okay, we'll do this the hard way. See that field up ahead? We'll bring it down there."

"We are not going to make it."

"Yes, we are."

I didn't know much about flying, but anyone with a little intelligence could tell we were coming in too fast, and the clearing wasn't big enough. We would crash into the edge of the forest. Knowing that if I didn't say it now, I might never have the chance, I cried out, "If we don't make it, know that I have thoroughly enjoyed your company."

"No way under heaven are we going to die. Brace for impact."

My body went stiff. My voice dried in my throat. In the blink of an eye, the plane struck the ground with brutal force, bouncing on and off the deserted field.

"Almost there, almost there," Ross kept saying.

With devilish speed and my heart beating mercilessly against my ribs, we were headed toward the trees. Ross gripped the yoke tighter, his knuckles white with the strength being exerted.

I found my voice, which vibrated in terror as I exclaimed, "Ross! The trees! The trees!"

"I see them! Come on...come on... Stop!"

I closed my eyes. Ross swore in exasperation. The almost surreal drop in velocity came all at once, and with great suddenness, Ross managed to turn the aircraft before we hit the barrier of trees head on. Simultaneously, an uproarious sound accompanied by another shake of the plane brought a scream from my throat.

"Easy, easy. We are okay," Ross assured me as the machine finally came to a rest.

"What was that?"

"The Hawker just lost its tail to a tree."

"Goodness gracious!" I flung a look to the ground but couldn't see any detached parts. "This is not good."

"Are you okay?" Ross asked, his face drained of all color.

"I'm going to have an awful headache. Other than that, I don't feel much else."

"Good." Swiftly bouncing back from the shock, he moved my hair away from my face and kissed my cheek. "Let's go before it blows up."

At his remark, I jolted.

"Easy. It's not likely," he quickly said.

"But possible?"

He nodded. "Just in case, hurry. Let's go."

We got out of the plane and ran a safe distance away from the crash. I looked around me, perceiving that I had no idea where we had landed or where this spot might be in the forest. "Where are we?"

"Somewhere on the other side of Burley. If we cut through the trees, we might reach the manor in an hour."

"That long?"

"Yeah. Are you sure you are okay?"

"I'm all right—just worried about the Goswicks. They will be furious. I should've been back already."

"I wish I had your problem." He laughed nervously. "When the general finds out about this, he is going to execute me."

"I'm sorry it ended like this."

"With me being executed?"

"No, I mean the crash."

Ross stopped midstride and pulled me into him. "I'm not. I'll never forget how it felt to fly with you." Smiling, he clarified, "Before taking the dip." He lowered his head, and his lips met mine. The fervency with which I responded affirmed I wasn't about to give him up.

"I can do this all night," he said, "but I need to get back and take care of this mess."

"And I have to face the Goswicks, which I'm starting to think may be worse than being executed."

"You might have a point there."

It was a long walk back to All Hallows, and much of it was spent in silence—a silence that spoke of preoccupation. Ross was surely consumed with the repercussions of the accident while I thought about the way his closeness made me feel. Elliott and Rose came to my mind. She had loved him with such devotion. I couldn't fathom how she must have suffered when she heard the news of Elliott's passing. Her diary offered at least a possibility that she might not be dead. But again, if she were alive, where was she? The idea that she was still around struck me so forcefully and felt so right I did not question it.

"Listen, Ross, I know you are busy, but may I ask a favor?"

"If it's within my reach, ask away."

"I can't stop thinking about General Lewis's cousin."

"Rose?"

"Yes, I think she might be alive."

"I hate to rain on your parade, but I think she's dead," Ross opined in his straightforward manner.

"I've been doing a little digging, and from what I have gathered, I think she wanted to disappear and leave no trace, no history."

"Ah, you've been hanging out with the old Goswick woman too much," he joked.

"Truly, Ross. I'm serious about this."

"Okay, okay. But why are you telling me this?"

"Surely you know someone in the Intelligence Service. Yes?"

He shot a startled look at me. "Maybe."

"I've heard they can dig up information on pretty much anyone Is that true?"

"Maybe."

"I would like to know if there is anything, anything at all, out there about Rose Lewis."

"Wouldn't the general be better suited to the task? I mean, the man is in a high place."

"Yes, but no. When she went missing, he failed to find her. And since I have no real reason to ask such a thing of him, I wouldn't dare."

"I don't blame you. The man is intimidating."

"Is that a yes?"

"It's a definite maybe."

"Ask them to search for..." From the deepest chambers of my memory, a line from Rose's diary surfaced clearly. *I still wonder how it would have been to be Mrs. Rose Kennard.* "Rose Kennard."

"Kennard? Why?"

"Please, Ross, don't ask. Trust me. Rose Kennard. Yes?"

"Whatever you say, but you have to give me a bit more than a name. Do you have a date?"

"She was born in 1898."

"Okay. I'll see what I can do, but I can't promise anything."

"That's good enough. Thank you."

After a lengthy apology to the Goswicks, I hurried to the staircase. I was tired yet excited to lie down and revisit the good memories of the day, but before I could place my foot on the bottom step, a black figure engulfed me. Like a windstorm, it circled me four times, keeping me in place until I screamed. Immediately, it stopped, taking the shape of Elliott.

Elliott laughed. "You look white as a sheet."

"For goodness' sake! You scared the life out of me!"

"Sorry, I was just having a little fun."

"You call that fun?"

"Yes."

"I can't believe you."

"Well, I couldn't believe you either when you left with that good-for-nothing American." He leaned against the banister, folding his arms as if awaiting an explanation.

"Were you spying on me?"

"Depends how you look at it."

I grimaced.

"Don't get edgy. Whatever your captain and you did, I missed it. I just saw you head into the woods."

Concealing how relieved I was that he hadn't seen how intimate Ross and I had grown, I informed him, "Well, I'm glad you are here. I've been wanting to see you."

"Because...?"

"I found Rose's diary." He stared at me as if he had not heard me. I reiterated, "Elliott, I found her diary. It was hidden in the conservatory. Would you like to read it?"

"I would, and if possible, at this very instant," he answered in a startlingly calm manner.

"Come with me. It's in my room."

"In the conservatory... All this time, and I had no idea," he murmured, trailing behind me up the flight of steps and down the hallway.

He lingered just outside my door, rubbing his hands anxiously until I invited, "Come in." After turning the lock, I hurried to retrieve the diary from the almost empty suitcase stored in the dressing room. Returning to Elliott, I sat on the edge of the bed and patted the spot beside me for him to join me.

He sat with an expression of disbelief and astonishment. I opened Rose's writing to the first page, preparing to read it.

"If you don't mind," Elliott said. "I can read. All I need you to do is to turn the pages for me. Can you do that?"

"Certainly."

Elliott's eyes followed Rose's writing, and he gave a little nod when he was ready for me to turn the page. Unlike me, he read all of them, especially those detailing the moments they'd spent together and her feelings for him. Now and then I observed the different emotions that crossed his face as he traveled through Rose's days. Awareness, disbelief, anger, remorse, love, and tenderness rose and died away, but the latter two were the strongest. Those tested by time had endured.

Elliott read the last sentence in the journal, and I placed it on the bed. I wondered what was going through his mind. Had he picked up a hidden clue about her disappearance? Perhaps something about the identity of the man who had frightened her? Or was he simply immersed in those days now long gone?

If silence had a name at that instant, it would be "harrowing." My heart swelled with tenderness as I contemplated him. His unstable emotions were easily discerned. His eyes were sad, his jaw tight, his hands fisted. I pressed my lips together and forced myself to remain quiet. He needed time to process his feelings.

Minutes later, as if Elliott had been abruptly released from a coiled position, he sprang from the bed. "Where is she? Why have I failed to find her? Why?" His eyes demanded an answer from me.

"I don't think you have failed. Finding the diary is a step in the right direction."

Moving back and forth across the room, he sputtered, "I don't see how this is helpful. On the contrary, it tortures me." His voice was filled with grief. "I miss her."

There was no doubt in me now that they had loved each other fervently. He was beyond desperate to find her, and I was in too deep to abandon ship. All Hallows's mysteries had to be solved.

"Don't forget that half a loaf is better than none." I briefly explained how I found the diary and went on to say, "Listen, I'm not sure what force was behind the diary's discovery, but it wasn't a coincidence."

"Some force as in someone's interference?"

"No." I walked to the darkened window and pulled the drapes together. "You know, even when the curtains provide privacy, I feel that I'm never alone in this house. It's strange, but sometimes I think the house itself is a ghost."

Elliott's eyes narrowed. "Well, there are plenty of tales of restless houses."

"It might be tired and want to rid itself of…"

Elliot finished my sentence, "Of its ghosts. If you ask me, it should do a better job. The diary hasn't told us anything."

"On the contrary, I think it has. Rose was one step ahead of whoever she was afraid of. This tells me she had time to protect herself, to leave without a trace. Elliott, there is a good chance she is alive."

"But why did she not write the name of the prowler?"

"Maybe she was afraid she was wrong. Maybe by the time her suspicions became certain, it was too late to write it down."

"She could have gone anywhere—France, London, Belgium —anywhere."

"It's not going to be easy."

"Easy? It's impossible."

"No, it's not. There is more information available nowadays. The Secret Service can help. If we can get to them, they might bring up something useful."

Elliott looked at me as if I had just said the stupidest thing he had ever heard. "You speak of the Secret Service as if they were a newspaper agency. Have you forgotten they are the highest level of security in our country and might be a bit busy with the war? What makes you think they'd even consider a request from you?"

"Well, no, not from me."

"Who, then?"

"Someone closer to them." I said.

"General Lewis?"

"No, Ross."

"The American idiot? No way." Elliott laughed mockingly.

"Why do you have to call people names?"

"I don't call everyone names, just those who've earned them."

"That's enough." I left the bed and, placing my hands on my hips, took a strong stance. "Why are you jealous of Ross?"

"Blimey, Seraphina! I don't know, but it might have something to do with the fact that he is alive and I'm not. He can be with the girl he fancies, and I can't."

"Don't be daft, Elliott. Get ahold of yourself. Like it or not, Ross is the best—and maybe the only—option we have."

"All right. I'll try anything to find Rose." Though Elliott's tone was harsh, he sighed in resignation.

"Good." I smiled. "I've already asked him."

"I knew I shouldn't trust you," he retorted.

"And while we wait to see if he gets any leads, we need to figure out a way to speak to the woman. Even if she is not Rose, she might know something helpful."

"You want another wallop?" His eyebrows rose questioningly.

"No, but I won't let her get the best of me so easily."

"I must say I admire your courage—or stupidity—not sure which it is."

"Thanks, Elliott, but if she isn't Rose, who do you think she is?"

"No idea. This manor is ancient. She could be anyone who has lived here in the past centuries."

CHAPTER 16

THE OTHERWORLDLY

I was already awake when the new day arrived. In fact, I had been awake most of the night. Briefly after I'd fallen asleep, a nightmare had haunted me. In it, I dreamed of dying in the airplane crash. My bewildered ghost returned to All Hallows to roam its halls forever. I saw myself traveling the upstairs hallway in anger at having lost my life and awoke with a scream to find that, instead of me, it was the woman who traversed the corridor. She'd ended her journey in the green room, lingering there with unusually long wailings. Her shrill voice cut through the air like a blade, stabbing every inch of my body and tearing apart my emotions.

The nightmare had to end, but how? Neither she nor Elliott would be at peace until their plight was solved, and hence, neither would I. A new, startling thought formed: if any living person had an idea of how the world of the dead interacted with ours, it might be the vicar. But the idea of speaking to him made me uneasy. After readying for the day, I left my room and went out to the gardens in search of my ghost friend.

I found him in the rhododendrons. My plan astonished him more than it had me. "I'll say, Seraphina—the vicar? The encounter with the woman must have affected your sanity."

"I'll say, Elliott," I mocked. "No, it did not."

"For all we know, Baker might have the killer lodged in the church." Elliott slumped onto a wooden bench. "Or worse, he could be the killer.

I've seen him roaming the woods countless times. Heavens only knows what he does, but he goes about with an air of troublemaking."

"True, but that doesn't mean he is the assassin."

"All should be considered guilty until proved otherwise."

"It's the other way around," I corrected. "All are considered innocent until proved guilty."

"Not in my book."

I waved my hand, discarding his opinion. "Listen, we don't have many options here. We need to figure out how to speak to the ghost of the woman."

"All right, but you must know that if something happens to you, I could never forgive myself—so make sure that it doesn't."

"Trust me, I'm in no haste to get hurt again. I'm just hoping to find a safer way to speak to her. It might be our only chance to find out who she is, and if we are lucky, she might know who the assassin is."

"All of that sounds marvelous—if you don't get killed in the process." He ran his fingers anxiously through his hair. "The last thing I need is for you to come back in spirit form."

"I'll do my best not to." I gave him a derisive smile. "I ought to go."

"To the church?"

"Where else?"

"Why don't you send him a message to come here?"

"I want to go about it in a subtle way, and inviting him here would be more suspicious. Besides, since he is actively hunting for a wife, I don't want him to get the wrong impression."

"You have a point." Elliott scratched his head. "Then bring Lewis's gun with you."

"You didn't miss that, did you?"

"No. Bring it with you."

"I shall be fine."

"You are afraid to use it," Elliott challenged.

"I'm not, but I should be. I'm more likely to shoot myself than any assailant."

"Well then, bring Caroline with you. She'll have no problem shooting him."

"Believe me, I wouldn't mind having her reinforcement, but her presence would only complicate matters."

"All right. Have it your way," he said, but his fatherly warnings continued. "Just don't get too close to him. Remember that I can't go into town."

"Don't worry. I'll take care of myself." I stretched my hand out to touch his. It was strange not being able to feel his flesh, yet a soothing energy entered my body whenever I encountered his intangible form.

"Yeah, that's exactly what I worry about. You seem to always have a difficult voyage."

"Thanks, Elliott."

"I'll be watching for you from the far end of the woods."

———

I wandered openly through the churchyard, waiting to be noticed. Albion Baker was bound to come out as soon as he became aware of my presence. Remembering his audacious advances at the manor, I hoped he had learned his lesson and would exercise restraint this time.

Compared to the London cemeteries, the graveyard here was small. To the local folks, this was a positive attribute. The deceased were quickly located without their loved ones having to comb through thousands of graves. In my case, the size of the place presented a challenge. There was a limit to how many times I could read the same headstones before becoming mentally unhinged. I flinched at the idea that my mind would store all these names, replaying them forever in my memory.

The temptation to knock on the vicar's door grew unbearable. But instead of inching closer to the fox's lair, safety called for patience, and I left the church grounds. He might not be home, after all.

The town of Burley exuded a surreal sense of calmness. The shops were quiet, some with their curtains drawn or displaying a Closed sign on their doors. Others, though open, were dark inside. Few people walked down the narrow sidewalks, keeping to themselves, their gazes distant.

I stepped inside the tea shop. The sound of the doorbell, a sharp, irritable noise, announced my entrance like a swarm of African wasps. The man behind the counter sat close to the wireless set, unmoved, utterly sucked into the seriousness that came from the speaker. Since he made no attempt to greet me, I browsed the merchandise, picking up boxes of tea and putting them back down. Meanwhile, I strained to listen to the news without success. The broadcast's signal wasn't clear, the announcer's voice was gruff, and he spoke too fast.

I sauntered closer to the counter before the attendant finally offered, "May I help you?" turning down the volume on the box.

I brought a package of tea to the counter. "I'll take this."

"You are lucky, young lady. This is the very last Earl Grey I have. And with the latest events, heaven knows when we'll get more."

I knew then that something had occurred with the war. "What's happened?"

He looked at me, incredulous. "You haven't heard?"

"Heard what?"

"Our air campaign against Germany has taken a turn for the worse. Very few pilots returned from last night's raids. Our poor lads are being shot from the sky like ducks in hunting season," the man lamented. "And every time a setback like this occurs, production and distribution slow down. Terrible for business."

I could imagine life without Earl Grey tea. What I couldn't envisage was how horrendous this must be for the families of the lost pilots. Furthermore, we were losing to the enemy on all fronts. Our greatest hope had been placed in air battle. Without it, I wasn't sure what we had left. My awareness zeroed in on a closer repercussion. *Ross...* With the loss of so many, he would soon be up in the air.

Being at the mercy of things we couldn't control was maddening. With urgency, I fumbled in my pocket for the money to finalize the purchase. "Thank you, sir."

I came back to the churchyard faster than anticipated. Time was pressing, and not just for Elliott. I mechanically paced about the graves. My mind fought the possibility of losing Ross to the war, of seeing his name on a headstone. Or worse yet, of never having a final resting place for him. Most pilots were not recovered.

Forcing myself to focus on the task at hand, I started my pacing at the edge of the cemetery once again. A beautiful marble grave caught my eye, its beauty standing out from the others. It rested peacefully by a beech tree in a secluded spot. How had I missed it before? If I hadn't known better, I would say it had just been built.

I leaned over and ran my hand across the rectangular stone, brushing off the layer of fresh leaves. Its intricately carved inscription read:

Lady Helen Lewis 1888–1914
Your memory will forever live in the wind that fills the New Forest

I shivered as a cool breeze blew across my bare arms and then bent to read the inscription again. The words were simple, nonetheless poignant and soul-reaching. I would have taken longer to ponder on the writing were it not for a quick movement from behind me that brought me to whirl around on my heels.

The vicar stood with an exuberant smile plastered on his face. This was the second time he had sneaked up on me. He could have easily knocked me out. Even a gun would have done no good. Keenly mindful of my folly, I folded my arms, my fingers clutching my biceps.

"Good afternoon, Father," I said, managing a faint smile. Now that we were face-to-face, I had to stay focused on my purpose for being here.

"Miss Addington, what an unexpected surprise."

"I came to the tea shop." I pointed to the sack lying on the ground near Helen's tomb. "I took a shortcut through the churchyard, but I got distracted reading the names on the graves."

"This one is magnificent, isn't it?" He motioned to Helen's tomb. "It's the finest one on the grounds."

"Such a terrible story. No one should die so young."

"But many do."

Channeling the conversation, I asked, "Father, where do our spirits go when we die?"

He took a step closer. I feared he would say, "Would you like to find out?" Instead, he said, "According to the holy writ, the souls of the righteous move on to a state of happiness in paradise."

"And the souls of the wicked?"

"That, my dear child, is more of a mystery," he answered elusively.

"Why do you say that? People say they go to hell."

"Strong words...strong words..." he said.

"You don't believe in hell?"

"Oh no, I do."

"What, then?"

"I don't picture it as common belief portrays it." He took another step forward.

"And how is that?" Not breaking eye contact with him, I reached for the sack of tea, cautiously increasing the gap between us.

"You know, a place of fire and burning."

"How do you see it, then?"

"As a place where people are lost in their unfulfilled expectations," he answered.

"Do you think that place is among us? I mean, on this earth?"

This time, I was the one to startle him. Stuffing his hands inside the pockets of his robe, he hesitated. And when he did respond, he did so with another question. "Why do you ask?"

"We are in Burley, home of folktales, ghosts, and witches. Many in town claim to have seen an apparition at some point."

"That's true."

The day grew dark as the sun hid behind the silhouette of the vicar. How in the world could it be so low on the horizon already? A sense of urgency accosted me. I asked point-blank, "Have you ever seen one? A ghost, I mean." To loosen his tongue, I added, "I imagine the graveyard is no stranger to their haunts."

"Miss Addington, you are brave to be speaking so freely about the supernatural, especially in this setting and at this hour."

I started to doubt he would ever tell me something useful. "I'm not afraid of it. Are you?"

"No, I'm not." Tugging at the collar of his robe, he cleared his throat.

"If it satisfies your curiosity, then yes, these grounds house more than just dead bodies."

"You have seen them, then," I clarified. "Did they speak to you?"

"Holy Peter, James, and John. What is this fascination with the otherworldly? Inquisitiveness can be dangerous. Perhaps you would do well to be on your way."

Was this a threat? Even if it was, I had to be bold. With a firm determination in my voice, I said, "Not until you tell me if you have ever interacted with them."

Unlike any other time when he would have been eager to divulge information, with obvious dissatisfaction, he started, "My first autumn here, after visiting the sick, I often returned home at night. The first time I saw them, there was a large group dressed in black clustered about the tombs. The second night, I arrived even later in the evening, and they were closer to the path. The third night, even later than the previous one, they planted themselves in my way, as if the advanced hour empowered them. They followed me to the door of the parish, some insulting and cursing me, some laughing at me."

Indeed, this was an appalling revelation. The vicar saw the dead as well. I wasn't sure I liked having anything in common with him, but I pressed for more information. "Did they ever come inside the church?"

"No, they can't go inside a holy place." He flung his hands in the air as if thanking heaven. "And I soon realized they only operate under the cover of night, so to avoid confrontation, I made sure to come home before dusk, which is why you should get going."

Brushing his words aside, I let my curiosity lead. "Abigail Walton saw ghosts as well, didn't she?"

His eyebrows knitted together in surprise. "I see you've been unburying Burley's stories."

"Did she?"

"She did."

"And you tried to help her?"

"Without success," he confessed.

"What went wrong?"

"Her ability, or perhaps her unwillingness, to get rid of them."

"Meaning?"

"It got to the point to where she was doing their bidding without question. They told her to do things, and she did them. At least that's what she claimed. As you can imagine, it was an alarming situation. I did my best to help her see their evil intent but in the end, she wouldn't listen. And of course, when the fires started, there was nothing else to be done. She was confined to an asylum."

"Fires?" *Wow, this town truly is full of surprises.*

"She took to burning the forest."

"That's rather dreadful."

"If she would have heeded my instructions, she would have been all right."

"How did you know what to do?"

Reluctance distorted his features. His mouth twitched as he responded, "Much research."

I knew then that he harbored a troubling secret. "Research? You mean books."

"Yes."

"What kind of books?"

"Old, forgotten books locked in the church for ages."

I needed to get my hands on those volumes. "They sound fascinating."

"Indeed, they are."

"All Hallows has a decent collection of reading material, but nothing as old. Do you think I could borrow them?"

"Oh no," he said with a short laugh. "They do not leave the church, and they are for the eyes of clergymen only."

"I could bring them back by morning," I proposed, pitifully begging for the chance.

"That will never happen." The tone in his voice left no room for me to argue.

I gave a silent groan of defeat, and in consequence of the lateness of the hour, I was forced to relinquish my endeavor. Perhaps he would be more approachable another time. "I ought to get back, then. Good night,

Father Baker." Cautiously, I backed away before turning to skip around the graves.

His voice cut through the air like a tempting demon. "Unless, of course, you'd like a cup of tea."

"I'm sorry...?"

"You can browse a volume if you'd accept a cup of tea."

Did he literally mean a cup of tea? Or something else?

Not wanting to sound desperate, I responded, "Umm, it is late..."

"I can have tea ready in no time."

"Well..." I said, cringing. "I suppose I can spare a few minutes."

"It's more than enough. This way. Follow me." He maneuvered through the tombs like an agile feline.

As I watched the hem of his robe swirl with his every step, the wheels in my mind turned frantically. I should have brought the gun. No, I needed an unexpected weapon. One I could use easily. I saw a rock the size of a fist near a half-broken headstone. Falling a few steps behind him, I picked up the rock and deposited it inside the sack with the tea box.

We turned the corner of the redbrick church, and the atmosphere grew unnaturally quiet. The vicar pressed his hand to the doorknob, and the door to his private quarters parted with a screeching sound from its unoiled hinges. I couldn't help but feel I was entering a mausoleum, cold and gloomy, with a hundred invisible eyes watching me. We traveled through a long hallway to the kitchen—a tiny affair housing a prehistoric range, a basin filled with dirty dishes, and a square table adorned by two chairs. I sat on the seat backing the wall, noticing at once that the window was covered with a thick fabric no one, not even remotely, could see through. I gripped the sack on my lap, making sure the rock was still there.

While he opened the tap to fill the kettle, I proposed, "If you don't mind, I would love to read while you prepare tea."

I got the impression that he did mind. He did not like being told what to do, especially not in his domain. Nonetheless, he acquiesced. "Very well." He pulled a large coffee tin from a cupboard and extracted a thick book from within. Not in a million years would I have guessed to look in there. "This is the only one handy. The others would take a little longer to retrieve." Opening it to the first page, he laid it on the table for my examination.

"Thank you."

The volume looked ancient, the pages worn and fragile. The vicar returned to his previous task, and I engaged in reading as fast as I could, though some of the text had faded and was impossible to decipher.

I glanced at the chapter headings, hoping to quickly spot something useful. "Angels of Light," "Demons and Their Realms." No, not this. "Herb Potions," "Blood Potions," "Spells and Their Secrets." What kind of book was this? I was about to look at the cover when a heading caught my eye. "The Fight of Humans against the Unseen." The introduction disclosed: "There is nothing more dreadful than fighting against that which we cannot comprehend." Nothing new there.

I turned the page and scanned the paragraphs, all the while keeping the fox in the corner of my eye. "Habitable dwellings infested with spirits trapped in the mortal dimension will do all in their power to purge themselves. Hence, they might use different conduits to attract those who are gifted to hear their cries." Perhaps this section would confirm my suspicions about the falling books in the library, but no matter. I had no time.

I flipped through a few more pages: "Afflicting Dreams," "Visions and Their Implications," "A Threshold in Time." Nothing seemed applicable. On the contrary, the more I read, the more dissatisfied I became.

The vicar came to the table and extended a cup of scalding tea. I hadn't even heard the hissing of the kettle, but the steam rising from the cup and the dark-colored water testified he had overboiled it.

"I hope you like it. I cultivate the herbs myself in the garden out back."

"Thank you." *The garden out back*? I translated his words into cemetery dirt, corpses, bones, putridity. No, I wouldn't be drinking any of it. "I'll let it cool a little."

He moved his chair closer to mine. "I see you are enjoying the book."

"Is there a section about encountering ghosts?"

"Umm...no, not in this one. If you would like, we can go to the cellar to look for the other books."

His words, coupled with the image of a cold room half buried underground such as were the local cellars, caused the hair on my arms to bristle. "This one is fine." My gaze returned to the book. I turned the aged pages quietly, pleading for a hint about communicating with tormented spirits. To my regret, I soon ran out of pages to look through.

"I see you are done," he said expectantly.

"Not yet." I moved a few pages back and then a few more. The chapter titled "A Threshold in Time" jumped out at me.

In rare instances, when the spirits haunting a place are... The next part was so faded I couldn't read it. *The house might facilitate a merging point for the living and the dead.*

"A merging point?" I muttered. Could this be what I sought?

"What was that?" he asked, touching my arm.

"It says here that a house might facilitate a merging point between the world of the living and the dead. Is that true?"

"Oh, well, I wouldn't mess with that."

"Why not?" I pressed, suspecting he already had. "Please, tell me."

"You see, a merging point is created by a ritual, a ceremony where one summons the dead to communicate with them. It's a treacherous deed, where we are at the mercy of whatever responds to our invitation."

"It sounds like witchcraft." I did not need to summon the ghost of the woman. I just needed to claim her attention long enough to have a coherent discussion. "What if, hypothetically, I wanted to speak to a spirit I already see?"

"Hypothetically, if it's a dark spirit, it's not a good idea." The vicar turned the page for me and said, "Read here."

I read on. *Trying to commune with lost souls is not only unwise but extremely dangerous. Such an attempt could result in injury and even death.* I should have read this before confronting the woman, though, admittedly, the point was obvious.

"Have I ever told you about my good situation in this post of service?" he asked suddenly.

I looked up at him, my mind still on the information in the script. "No, no. You haven't mentioned it."

"Would you like to hear about it?" His hand drew closer to mine and I grasped the book harder.

Hoping to gain more time with the volume, I said, "By all means."

He launched into a thorough explanation of his duties along with his income, not to mention his ability to support a family. Yet while he advertised himself as the most desirable suitor in the New Forest, I could focus only on the book.

"Miss Addington, wouldn't you agree that whoever is the lucky woman to be my wife will have a life of ease?"

"Umm...I suppose..." My mind turned to Elliott. He'd concealed something from me, and perhaps this was my chance to figure it out. "What do you know about regular ghosts?"

The expression on his face screamed of my lack of interest in his personal life. Howbeit, he answered me. "You mean those who are a bit more pleasant?"

"Yes."

"Not much. One of the other volumes speaks about it. Would you like to get it now?"

What was it with him and the cellar? Deliberately overlooking his invitation, I insisted, "What do you know about them?"

"All I know is that instead of staying around causing trouble, they move on."

He reached for my hand, his strong grip indicating he had no intention of letting go. But I had no intention of allowing him to touch me. With one rough pull, I freed myself from his bony fingers. Pushing the chair back with a terrible screech, I stood and closed the book. The inscription on the cover shocked me. My gaze ran over it again, not believing what I saw: *What Lies Beneath Witchcraft*. He should not have had this book. They had been banned from the church long ago. In fact, they had been burned—along with those who used them.

Beholding my reaction, he quickly collected the volume, threw it in the coffee tin, and returned it to the cupboard. "Let me assure you that this volume is not in violation of the regulations. On the contrary, I'm allowed to have it in case I have to deal with something abnormal—as was the case with Miss Walton. Now, what I'm not allowed to do is share it with patrons. I trust in your total discretion."

It was stunning how rapidly he had turned the tables, but I was in no position to argue with him. "I shall remember that. Thank you." I spun toward the hallway, but he pulled me back by my arm. Jerking free, I tightened my fingers on the bag in my hand.

"Don't leave just yet." He shot a glance at the cup on the table. "You haven't even touched your tea."

"It's late. The Goswicks expect me."

"I insist." He took hold of my arm again.

"I'm leaving." I tried to free myself from his clutch to no avail. "Please let go of me."

"I insist you stay a little longer." His eyes gleamed like those of a wildcat ready to strike.

"Let go of me!" I readied myself to fling the sack at him. *At the count of three. One, two, three.* As I was about to land a blow, a booming sound came from the end of the corridor. Instantly, he released me. I couldn't deny I was a bit disappointed at the interference, for I would have loved to take the wind out of his sails.

"Who might that be at this hour?" he said edgily.

An angel of God sent to save me.

I practically ran through the hallway and opened the door. A hunched elderly man stared at me with wide eyes. "Excuse me, sir." I pushed past him into the night.

CHAPTER 17

THE DECEPTION OF SIGHT

Accompanied by the failure of my risky visit to the fox and the urgency of night pressing upon me, I dashed into the woods. I was emotionally disturbed, having been thrown into disorder by the complete waste of time that had only added to my otherworldly lack of understanding. It seemed every time I made a step in the right direction, I was pushed back two. Why even try?

In this foggy state of mind, I selected the route most sheltered by vegetation, the fastest path through the woods.

"Miss Addington, is that you?" a familiar voice called, or did my mind play tricks on me? It came again, louder this time. "Miss, stop. It's me, Samuel Goswick!"

My first impulse was to keep moving, but the voice did sound familiar. Cautiously, I slowed until my legs ceased all movement. "Mr. Goswick?" Adjusting my vision to the silhouette nearing me, I saw that, indeed, it was the groundskeeper. "What are you doing here?"

"I should be the one asking you." His voice held an edge of anger.

"I'm afraid the night caught me by surprise."

The groundskeeper emitted one of his disapproving grunts, which I sensed was meant to say, "You should know better than this." Aloud, he said, "Out here, the night brings nothing good with it. Let's be on our way." Taking point, he headed down a different path.

Questioning his decision would be unwise, so like a prisoner taken to the dungeon, I marched beside him, knowing the journey would be anything but cheerful.

When the silence stretched on too long, I offered, "My intention was to return before twilight."

"Hell is filled with good intentions."

"That's a bit harsh."

"Not as harsh as a killer might be. You can't run from the devil, Miss Addington. He will find you." This he said in an unemotional and practical way, stirring some echo or recollection in me. What he had said meant more than I understood, but for now, it would remain like that.

I hustled to keep up with my guide. His large frame blocked much of the path, making it almost impossible for me to see more than a couple of yards ahead. Hence, at the flash of something scurrying across the forest floor in front of me, I gave a startled jump. The groundskeeper, unmoved, kept his steady march. Getting a better look at the barely visible shaggy tail of the squirrel who now climbed a tree, I laughed, only revealing my unsettledness.

But then Samuel commanded in alarm, "Stand behind me," and wasting no time, he picked up a good-sized stick from the ground. While I had been preoccupied with the squirrel, my companion, accustomed to the forest noises, had been alerted to something more ominous.

Swiftly directing me to the barrier of shrubs, he signaled for me to remain in place as he moved some distance away. Huddled behind a sequoia, his motionless figure melded with the growing obscurity until he became part of it. His dexterity and agility I could have never anticipated.

Wildly trying to discover the source of the groundskeeper's distress, I focused on the blackened silhouettes of the woods. The large, immobile shapes were quiet—too quiet. Even the evening insects had gone still, as if holding their breath in the face of the impending menace. When my gaze traveled to the groundskeeper, the darkened spot seemed lighter. Was he still there? I couldn't tell. I scanned the area but could barely distinguish one thing from another.

An almost imperceptible disturbance, like light footsteps carefully touching the fallen leaves nearby, brought a chill to the back of my neck. It was déjà vu. I felt the killer zeroing in on me just like he had the other night, but this time Elliott wasn't here to help me. And try as I might, I was losing the advantage of sight to the encroaching night.

My attention returned to the spot where I had last seen Samuel, and to my horror, I saw a tall figure, weapon in hand, stepping closer to him. Despite the groundskeeper's patience and knowledge of the woods, the element of surprise favored the newcomer.

"Drop your weapon and stand slowly," the man ordered.

I saw the groundskeeper's outline rise from his hiding place.

The newcomer again instructed, "Hands up in the air. Turn around." I knew that voice.

"Easy. It's just me, Samuel Goswick."

Revolver still aimed at the groundskeeper, the man demanded, "What are you doing out here? I could have shot you."

"I came looking for Miss Addington. If you don't mind, Captain Stewart, lower your gun."

Ross? A wave of relief swept over me, and I could breathe again.

Ross did not change his stance. "Miss Addington? Where is she?"

"I'm here." I joined them. Ross gave me a stiff nod. "Mr. Goswick found me on my way back from town."

"Good thing he did." I had the feeling Ross would have loved to lecture me. Instead, he lowered his gun and said, "I've been on someone's tracks since dusk. He's evaded me like I was a schoolboy."

"That's hard to believe," Samuel grumbled, probably annoyed at having been held at gunpoint.

"Not really," Ross disagreed. "He is thoroughly acquainted with the area."

"Can we go now?" asked the groundskeeper, not disguising his irritation.

"I'll walk with you to the edge of the trees," Ross decided.

Samuel set the pace, which was almost too fast for me. The march allowed no time for words, the tension between the men almost palpable. If the suspect Ross had been pursuing was the killer, I was lucky the groundskeeper had found me first. What was I doing? I didn't know anymore.

Ross did not leave us where he said he would. And when he didn't, Mr. Goswick increased his lead, reaching the manor before we did. Once at the door, Ross took my hands in his and pleaded, "Promise me you will stay in the house."

"You have my word."

"I have to hurry back. Good night, Seraphina."

I entered the house, knowing one storm was behind and another—Mrs. Goswick—gathered ahead. I braced for a well-deserved reprimand, but the chaotic scene unfolding in the sitting room caught me off guard. Mrs. Goswick paced the area like a caged animal. Near the sofa stood the Goswick men, quarreling. A glance at Julius told me his feathers had been badly ruffled. He was unquestionably discomposed.

At my appearance, the three fell as silent as the grave. It was then that I saw Elliott standing by the hearth. I wasn't looking forward to telling him of my failure. At the same time, I felt out of sorts with him. He had not been waiting in the forest like he said he would.

In my defense, I could argue that the day's events had taken a toll on me, for I addressed Elliott. "Where have you been? I didn't see you in the woods."

"We have been right here, where we are supposed to be," snapped Mrs. Goswick.

Julius threw a nasty look at Elliott, reminding me that his parents could not see the ghost standing behind them.

"Oh...I..." I shut my mouth. Mother had always said silence was a virtue. It was about time I tried it.

"Miss Addington, I'm fully aware that we don't have a blood claim on you, but you must know that we feel a great responsibility toward you," Mrs. Goswick said. "At least the other day, thanks to Caroline, we knew you were out with the American soldier, but we didn't expect the incident to be a recurrent one."

Samuel produced a grunt that reaffirmed his wife's words. I lowered my gaze to the floor, abashed.

"Responsibility is not something to be taken lightly," Julius echoed, glowering at me. "The killer is in the woods."

His mother eyed him coldly and quickly reprimanded, "Keep your peace, Julius," though Julius had probably only expressed the truth. But how did he know the killer was hunting in the forest? Addressing me, she continued. "You left without a word. I can't describe the feelings that possessed us when evening came, and you were nowhere to be found." She drew in a sharp breath.

Again, words failed me. "I…"

"Thank heavens old Goswick found you," the housekeeper rapidly continued, pressing a hand to her heart. "At his age, he doesn't venture so far into the woods this late anymore."

At his age? If I hadn't seen him maneuvering through the woods like an avid hunter, I might worry about his age. There certainly seemed nothing feeble about him.

"I'm afraid my apology is insufficient, but it's all I can offer."

"That's not enough," Julius snapped. "The distress could have given Mum heart failure."

"It will not happen again."

A snort of skepticism came from Samuel.

"It will not," I reiterated.

Samuel stomped to the doorway, addressing his wife and son, "We came upon Captain Stewart. He said he was tracking someone. He walked us home." That confirmed he hadn't told them before I got to the house. "We must be extra vigilant tonight."

"Did he, now?" Elliott's eyebrows shot up.

Samuel went on. "I believe Miss Addington has grasped the importance of minding the rules and will handle her future outings accordingly. There is no need to discuss this further." He gave Julius a nod to follow him. "Let's head to the cottage and check on Caroline." The men slipped out the front door.

Doing her best to disguise her irritable mood, the housekeeper offered, "Supper is ready if you would like to eat."

"I'll eat later if it's all right. I need to unwind first."

"Don't we all?" She looked at me as if saying that no one needed to unwind more than she did—thanks to me. "I'll leave the food on the range, but I'll retire after tidying the kitchen." She headed down the corridor wearily.

I squandered no time in turning to Elliott. Mirroring his pose, I placed my hands on my hips and returned his stern gaze. "You. Where in the world have you been? The killer might have been in the woods. Well, at least that's what Ross said."

"You've been with Stewart again? I thought you were going to see Baker."

"I saw both."

"Why did you take so long in town? Don't you know better? Even if it wasn't the killer, you shouldn't have been out there so late."

I went on to explain my delay due to not finding the vicar the first time I went to the churchyard, my visit to the tea shop, and subsequent return to the church. "And that's why I came back so late."

"That was a stupid thing to do," Elliott sputtered, referring to my visit to the vicar's quarters.

"Don't speak to me as if I were a child—I'm trying my best to help. In case you haven't noticed, I'm still alive," I reprimanded. "Besides, I've had enough scolding from the Goswicks."

"Did it sink in?"

"It did. Can we move on now? And answer my question. Where were you?"

"I went to the other end of the forest. That thickheaded Julius was mumbling a whole bunch of rubbish about the killer being there. I went as far as Blackfield in vain."

"He did? You did?"

"Yes, Seraphina, he did, and I did."

"But how did Julius know about the killer, or whoever he was, being in the woods?"

"Heaven only knows."

"He must have seen something," I reflected. "What were they arguing about when I came in?"

"I got here seconds before you did. All I heard was their frustration with your lack of consideration." He smirked.

"I'll never be able to please everyone."

"We have the opposite problem with Julius. He delights in wreaking havoc with those around him."

"He is hard to read, but I think he does care." I had sudden empathy for Julius. It wasn't easy seeing the dead. Perhaps some of his strangeness came from the frustrations that ability caused. Heaven knew my encounters with the dead hadn't exactly made me the paragon of stability.

"Do you realize he might have lied to get me out of the way?" Elliot said in an accusatory tone.

"I find that hard to believe."

"I'll say! You turn more naïve with each passing day. There are too many coincidences to let him off the hook that easily."

"I don't know..." I exhaled in frustration. "There are things pressing at the back of my mind, but I can't quite place them."

"Keep trying." Elliott produced a mocking smile. "Hopefully, they'll come sooner rather than later."

"Enough with the sarcasm."

"All right, don't get agitated." He moved to his favorite chair and sat down. "Tell me, did Baker say anything useful?"

"I don't think so, but you might have a different take. All I know is that whatever we come up with, we must find a solution on how to handle the ghost of the woman. I can't live with her hanging over my head any longer." Night was here, and soon she would have the chance to torture me yet again.

CHAPTER 18

REACHING BEYOND

Elliott gave a very prolonged whistle. "Who would have thought? The little devil is cunning indeed." He was more astonished that the vicar kept a book on witchcraft than the information it contained. "Well, he's right about not messing with a merging point. Who knows what might enter this world if we did?"

I shivered. "Don't even say that." The ghost of the woman was sinister enough without entertaining the possibility of worse things.

Elliott left his seat, running his hand through his hair nonstop as he did when nervous. "Wait, Seraphina. That's confusing. Tell me again what Baker said about his encounter with the spirits in the churchyard."

"He said they grew bolder in their approach with each day that passed."

"But each time he came across them, it was later in the evening."

"That's correct."

"There was something else he said, something about how they function."

"Yes, there was…" I closed my eyes, facilitating the memory. "He said some spirits operate in darkness, so he avoided coming back after dusk. What are you getting at?"

"Listen, the book said it's foolish to try to reach a distraught ghost, right?"

I was utterly confused. What did one thing have to do with the other? "Yes, we already know that."

"All right, so what does this information mean to us?"

"By all means, Elliott, enlighten me."

"Taking into consideration that darkness empowers them and that it's not wise to confront them in their frenzied state, what works for and against us when you see the woman?"

"Well...in the upstairs hallway, she is totally present but full of rage."

"Go on."

"On the staircase, she is more tranquil but distant, disconnected from this world." I paused to analyze what I had just said. My breathing accelerated as the answer to our problem sounded too simple and terrifying to be true. "It can't be the solution..."

"But it is." Elliott settled on the arm of the sofa, an expression of certainty on his face. "You need to meet her when she's coming down the stairs, but for her to pay attention, we must create the perfect environment."

"A dark one." I rested the back of my head against the sofa, not believing what we were saying.

"We must kill all the lights." A smile touched the corners of Elliott's mouth and spread to his eyes. "I have a better feeling this time. I think it will work."

Before cowardice overpowered me, I rose to my feet. And though there were no guarantees her disposition wouldn't turn vicious at the alteration of her surroundings, sanity had left me long ago, and there was only one way to proceed. "Well then, let's try it. If we are lucky or cursed," I reasoned, not knowing which of the two was more appropriate, "she might come down soon. It's about the time when I have seen her before."

With the unsaid doubts floating in our minds, Elliot placed a hand on my shoulder and said, "Are you positive you want to do this? It's risky."

"Do you have a better idea?"

Elliott shook his head.

"Hopefully, Mrs. Goswick has gone to bed. After this evening, I'm afraid if she finds me roaming in the dark, she will have that heart attack Julius spoke of."

"I'll let you know if she does. I'll hear her footfalls long before she comes in." He moved about, anxiously rubbing his hands. "It's hard to believe this might work...after so long. It's hard to believe."

I could only imagine the emotions running through Elliott. For years, he had waited for this chance to contact the woman he loved.

"It will," I said, willing it to be true. "Now, calm yourself. You are not helping my nerves."

"Sorry. I'll behave."

I extinguished all the lights, already feeling the hair on my arms bristle. Elliott moved into the corner of the foyer while I stood at the base of the staircase. The only light shining was that of the moon streaming through the window above the entry. It felt like an eternity just standing there, waiting in the shadows. However, when the familiar iciness invaded me, I felt it had come too soon.

The faint light in the space was diminished as a stratum of dark clouds obscured the moon. My imagination ran wild. The embers in the fireplace in the sitting room came to life, glowing with a deep red that mirrored the eyes of the woman who now appeared above me. In a single flash, her sunken eyes and the halo of utter wretchedness that accompanied her struck me. The thought of running to the light switch was so overpowering I moved my head a fraction of an inch in its direction.

Instead of giving in to my fears, however, I called out, "Elliott? Elliott?" Without taking my eyes off the apparition, I saw Elliott move into my peripheral vision. "She's coming down now."

With one hand extended, she took the first step down the staircase, her pale fingers gripping the banister. The closer she came, the more my limbs became rigid and my lungs emptied of oxygen. I was being smothered by her energy, sinking deeper into a frozen lake.

"Don't look into her eyes," Elliott urged, briefly touching my hand. "It might be more bearable that way." Warmth surged through my hand, and in feeling his nearness, the coldness soon relinquished its hold on me.

I took a hesitant step up the staircase and was astonished when I took another, followed by another, and suddenly I had intercepted her halfway through her descent. With one step separating us, I stood there trembling. The clouds must have moved, for the moonlight coming through the glass brightened. My gaze traced the black lines of the woman's form, and despite my intention to avoid her gaze as she went right through me, I caught a glimpse of her eyes—eyes that for a second turned from red to blue. I flipped around to face her, immediately aware that something had changed.

In a flash, though I knew my physical body remained on the stairway, I had passed into a different dimension, surrounded by nothing but shades of gray mixed with endless night. The woman must have felt the disruption in her descent, for she halted but a few steps away. Her jet-black hair melted with the umbral plane, and she watched me from the shadows. She looked haggard, worn out, the vestiges of blood on her jaw more pronounced.

It seemed foolish that the fear of death would accompany me into the world of the undead, but with newfound clarity, I knew that the most intimate part of me, the essence of life housed in my body, was exposed and vulnerable. The words of the vicar came to mind with unwelcome forwardness—hell was a place where people were lost in their own unfulfilled expectations. And in that instant, I knew that the longings of the dead posed a terrible threat to the living. These lost souls would try to extract precious memories and energy from mortals in an attempt to heal what they had lost. I would have to proceed with extreme caution.

I asked quietly, "Rose? My name is Seraphina Addington. I came to speak with you about Elliott. He's waiting—"

"Do you know where the snowdrops are?" Her voice sounded like an echo, weak and distant. As if having traveled through an eternity of time and space, it had just reached All Hallows.

Snowdrops? She was delusional. I was not inclined to prove myself an idiot, but how did I respond to that? In that moment, I wished Elliott could hear her. Surely, he would know how to parley with another ghost.

"No, I don't think so."

Her eyes flashed red as she spoke. "I'd hoped for you to live a little longer. It's a pity you had to cut it short—"

"Wait!" I cried out. "You don't understand. I'm here on behalf of someone who loves you."

"Who?"

"Elliott Kennard."

The woman grew still.

"Is that name familiar to you?" I asked.

"No, no, it isn't...but the devil was already there, hidden in his flesh..." Like the unveiling of a blood moon, her eyes gleamed at me once more.

A sense of disheartenment came over me. How was I going to learn the truth from her? She teetered at the edge of violence, still far away, by my estimate, from the precipice of her tragedy. I descended until only one step separated us, and trying to awaken her memory, I said, "Did you not love Elliott? Do you not remember what love is?"

"Do not speak to me of love!" she hissed, and with a violent jerk of her head, I was instantly thrown backward. My spine hit the wooden steps harshly, and for a moment, my vision went blurry, my head spinning. Was this a reminder of what she was capable of? It was nothing compared to what she had done to me in the hallway.

"Seraphina, are you all right?" Elliott's voice came from somewhere in the background.

"I'm fine...I'm fine." I rose, holding the railing for balance. Apparently satisfied with the setback she had given me, the woman turned to leave. I had to think fast. "Wait!" I exclaimed. "Do you know where we are?"

She cocked her head slightly to one side. "No."

"We are in Burley. To be exact, right now we are in All Hallows manor."

"All Hallows..." she repeated, retreating to the bottom of the steps. "All Hallows..."

"Yes, and I'm here escaping the war."

"The war? The war is over."

The war is far from being over. She speaks of the Great War. Oh my, she could indeed be Rose. "Please tell me your name."

"I don't have a name. It was taken from me along with everything else."

I started to realize how obscure her comprehension had become. Trapped in a world without light, she couldn't reason outside the trauma of her tragedy. I tried another angle. "Why are you so sad?"

"She was full of life."

"Who?"

"The girl I once was—a girl filled with dreams and love who believed the world was good and evil did not exist. She had fresh wings and was ready to take flight, but he came, tore her heart out, and clipped her wings. She bled to death inside and out."

I held my breath, hoping she would continue, and she did.

"Oh, yes. It was her twenty-second birthday. Do you know how I know that?"

"No."

"I remember the cake. Twenty-two candles. And there was only one thing on her mind—the man she loved. Even though their love was hidden from the world, he was everything to her. She dreamed with his touch... with his love..." Her voice drifted away as if she still longed for those things.

"What happened then?"

She looked toward the top of the staircase. "She entered the room she wished she never had..." Her voice stuttered. "It was the beautiful green bedroom. The bed was covered with an embroidered quilt. Hearing noises from the garden below, she pulled back the drapes to peek out at the lawn." The expressions that contorted her features assured me this memory was the most excruciating. "Yes, he was here, and as she turned to go downstairs, her foot caught on the floor.

"It was a satchel, his satchel. He had left it during one of his visits and had forgotten about it. She flattened it against her chest, thinking of him. She slipped her fingers inside the outer pocket. Curious, she extracted a folded piece of paper.

"As she read the letter, her heart rejected the idea her mind formed. No, it couldn't be. It just couldn't. There had to be an explanation for such a coincidence.

"But how could it not be? His name was written on it. He was the intended recipient. In it, she described their relationship as having been bliss but of her not picturing a future for them. Yet it wasn't the end of the infamous letter that alarmed her but the beginning. She had penned it a few days before she was murdered."

"Who had?"

"Why, Mary, of course."

Mary?

"She dropped the bag along with her preposterous suspicions, fixed the draperies to their former state, hurried down the hallway, and ran down these steps into his arms.

"She reveled in the smell of his clothing, which spoke of masculinity and strength. It was easy, so easy, enveloped in his embrace, to forget the absurdities that had crossed her mind but minutes before.

"He swept her off her feet, carried her up the stairs, and asked, 'Which room?' The answer came naturally. 'The green one,' she said. Ever so gentle, as was his custom, he placed her on the bed. As he started to unlace her shoes, her gaze unavoidably shifted to the hem of the curtains. Her memory went back to the paper.

"'Darling,' she said, signaling toward the bag. 'I read the letter in your satchel.' He glanced at the drapes, and his face contorted with recognition. She knew then that things weren't as she wanted to believe.

"'So you did,' he replied.

"'No one knew about your relationship with Mary, just like no one knows about ours,' she pressed him.

"'It's just a paper. Nothing else," he assured her, then unbuttoned his shirt and tried to kiss her, but his enchantment failed. 'Let's not ruin our time with impulsive jealousy. That was long ago. Don't fuss over it.'

"'It's far from jealousy. I remember the night Mary died quite well, for it was cold and foggy. No one was out on the streets. I saw you two behind the church as I waited for Father to come out of the bank. The next morning, her body was found in the churchyard. Of course, I thought nothing of it until now.' He was swift to silence her. 'Don't speak nonsense. It wasn't me. Like you said, it was a gloomy night. You have mistaken me for someone else...you simply got things messed up.'

"Certainty backed her words as she said, 'No way under heaven would I have mistaken you for another man. It was you.'

"Now acknowledging that the mantle protecting him had been torn apart, exposing his true self, he groaned in exasperation.

"'You killed her! You killed her!' she choked out, staring at him in anguished perplexity. The fact that she might be in mortal danger wasn't as awful as learning that he was a monster. She felt the stab of betrayal and deception in every bone of her body.

"He said, 'I'd hoped for you to live a little longer. You are a passionate woman, and I'd started to enjoy being with you. It's a pity you had to cut it short.'

"'Please, don't hurt me,' she begged in vain. The thirst for blood was in his eyes. Her heart raced, and she made a run for the door, but he was an expert hunter. No prey escaped his claws. With a force that left her numb, the back of his hand struck her face, and she crumpled to the floor. Fast as a lion, he lunged at her. The hands that once had been so delicate on her skin were now like iron around her neck."

The woman fell silent but extended her hands into the air as if asking heaven why this had happened to her. Then a heart-wrenching cry tore from her soul.

"Please," I said frantically. "He's not here anymore. He can't hurt you again."

My pleading reclaimed her focus just enough for her to respond, "He's always here. Every night, I live it all over again in that wretched room." When she finally referred to herself in first person, I knew something in her brain had awoken.

"Who is he? Who is this man you loved?"

She shook her head violently. "I don't know. I don't know. I can't see his face anymore. It's all black—his name, his memory."

"Please try to remember."

"I see nothing. My head spins. I can't breathe, but I'm alive. I'm here, and I'm there, but it doesn't make sense. Wait...there is a tree. It's different from the rest. It smells lovely. The oxygen is gone from my lungs. Blackness takes me, and I am lost and forgotten." Agony struck her again, and looking down at her dress, she cried,

"No, no! It's going to get ruined by the dirt. Please have pity on me."

I descended the final steps and stood right in front of her. "It's all right. I'm your friend. No one will hurt you now." Trying to ease the transition and keep the conversation going, I turned her attention to Mary. "Tell me, do you remember Mary's family name?"

At that, she responded eagerly, "Mary Beresford."

"Mary Beresford..." The young lady who had been slain in 1928. My legs faltered. My vision became cloudy. The woman started to fade away.

No, no. She can't go. I need to know her name.

"Please tell me your name. Please," I implored, fearing that I might not have another chance to interact with her.

She took one last look at me and, like dew under the morning sun, evaporated. There was a knot in my throat. I couldn't swallow, couldn't breathe. I was angry at my defeat. An icy gust of air hit my chest, and suddenly she reappeared. She launched at me, her black hair and dress moving freely in the air. Her face was whiter and her cheekbones more prominent as she went straight through my body.

Her voice echoed in my ears like the sound of a million drums. "My name is Aria Lancaster."

CHAPTER 19

THE BEGINNING OF THE END

Returning to the land of the living was like breaching the surface of a frozen lake. I drew in a sharp breath and dropped to the bottom step. Beside me, Elliott hovered with the fragility of a distraught parent.

"I was terrified you wouldn't come back."

"That makes two of us." I inhaled and exhaled deeply, calling life back into my limbs and clarity to my mind.

"It's all right. It's over," Elliott soothed.

A while went by before I fully transitioned to the domain of the living. Elliott's arm around my shoulders might have had something to do with my rapid improvement. "I could never have anticipated what just happened. I mean, my physical self never left this environment, yet I interacted with her in another sphere." I held Elliott's gaze. "I wish it was easier to explain."

"I think I have a pretty good idea." He smiled.

"Were you able to hear any of it?"

"Most of what you said. Nothing of what she said."

"You didn't see her either?"

"No. You could have been playing me the whole time, and I would never know."

"She's not Rose."

"I heard you say the name of Mary Beresford. Is that who she is?"

"No. She is Aria Lancaster."

"Aria? She went missing and was never found."

"I'm afraid we just found her."

"Was she murdered?"

"Yes."

"Who is the killer?"

"She couldn't remember." I shook my head, displeased. "Her mind has obscured his name."

"Just our luck." Elliott cursed in disbelief.

"But she did say a lot." I rose from the step. "Come on, let's move to the sofa before I become a permanent part of the stairs."

"That's a dreadful thought."

I stumbled across the hall, adjusting to the present reality. As was his custom, Elliott settled on a chair. I opted for the softness of the old couch. I leaned back and closed my eyes. Before the experience became hazy in my mind, I rehearsed it. Elliott listened with infinite patience and immense interest. I rambled on, sometimes jumping forward, sometimes backtracking, as the details came back to me.

"And that is pretty much it...I think." I heaved a sigh of relief now that he knew her story.

"All right, we know she isn't Rose but Aria Lancaster. We also know Mary was murdered by the same man. And we don't know who that man is, apart from him owning a satchel, which is not very helpful since just about the entire population around here has one."

While Elliott was caught in the specifics of her tale, I was overwhelmed by her condition. "I can't shake off Aria's awful state. If she is ever going to find peace, whoever did this to her must pay for it."

"That's one part of her healing process."

"And the other?"

"Aria will not fully rest until her body is recovered. As things stand, recovering it might prove more helpful to her than finding her assassin. She could be given a proper burial, and her family would have a place to visit her. She might find more peace in that."

I nodded. "It's a start, but easier said than done. It's been more than a decade, has it not?"

"About nine years."

"Good memory."

"I lived through those events. I felt so useless at not having seen anything. Of course, someone reported seeing her in Breamore the day before, so most of the efforts to locate her, including mine, were in that vicinity." A dark shadow crossed Elliott's eyes, and he reflected, "More than once, guided by misinformation, I left the area when the killer wasn't anywhere else but here."

"It could be coincidence," I reasoned. He threw a look of displeasure at me. "All right, going back to Aria. Apart from the murderer, she is the only one who knows where her body is. And I don't think that getting the information from either of the two is feasible."

Elliott's brow knitted. "No, sounds like she was trying to convey the very things her innermost part has blocked from her memory. Tell me the last part of what she told you again—a bit slower this time."

I quoted her word for word, stunned I recalled it so clearly. "'I see blackness. My head spins. I can't breathe, but I'm breathing. I'm here, and I'm there, but it doesn't make sense. Wait...there is a tree It's different from the rest. It smells lovely. The oxygen is gone from my lungs. Blackness takes me, and I'm lost and forgotten.'"

"And you say I have a good memory?" Elliott grinned. "Is that it?'

"I think so..."

"That's not good enough. Seraphina, you must be certain. Did she say anything else? Anything at all?"

I closed my eyes again, forcing myself to retrieve the information. She said, "'No, no! It's going to get ruined by the dirt. Please have pity on me.'"

Elliott left his seat and, rubbing his chin, moved about the room. Silence had the power to calm many a situation, helping provide new ideas and solutions to riddles. I hoped this wasn't an exception. Throughout the quietness that ensued, I could tell Elliott's brain worked at hyperspeed.

"I got it, or I'm pretty close to it," he whispered more to himself than to me.

"Whatever you've come up with is more than what I've sorted out.'

"It might be disturbing. Are you sure you want to hear it?"

"Don't be daft. Go on."

"It's obvious Aria's corpse is hidden in All Hallows, and that's why she lingers here."

"You don't mean here, inside the house, do you?" The house was filled with forgotten nooks and crannies, and heaven only knew what they could be concealing.

"No, in the yard. My best guess is that she died in the house and witnessed her burial through her spiritual eyes."

"It sounds most plausible, and it would explain why she said, 'I can't breathe, but I'm breathing. I'm here, and I'm there, but it doesn't make sense.' Yes, he must have strangled her to death in the green room. That would explain why her suffering reaches a tipping point in there. She mourns the loss of what could have been, the loss of her life."

"And unless I'm terribly mistaken, she told you the exact spot where her body lies."

"The tree," I promptly said. "She mentioned a tree that has a lovely smell. If our assumptions are correct, her grave must be closer, rather than farther, from the house, for it would have been risky for him to carry her too far without being seen. But why bother to bury her in the first place? He didn't bury the others."

"Maybe she meant more to him. Maybe people had seen them together?"

"Hmm, I'm not sure, but whatever it was, the dilemma is that All Hallows's is populated with trees. How on earth are we ever to find the right one?"

"I don't think *we* can, but the gardener might be able to."

"Julius?"

"He's worked these grounds for years. If anybody knows every plant, tree, and crevice in the yard, it's Julius. At any rate, what other option do we have?"

His reasoning was sound. Julius could help us. But would he?

"I suppose you are right, but I doubt very much he'll want to help."

"You'll have to rope him in slowly—he'll grow distrustful if you don't," Elliott reasoned.

"Maybe I can ask him about things that interest him—things in his comfort zone."

"He is a master of the outdoors," Elliott said.

"Yes, that's it. I'll start by asking him to teach me about the forest. He might say something useful without even knowing it."

Elliott smiled. "No one will be the wiser."

A thump came from outside the window, jarring me. Elliott placed a finger to his lips, motioning for me to keep quiet. He moved to the wall and went through it to the side yard. I neared the window and could hear quarreling, but it was too distant to make out who spoke. Even though I would have liked to run out there, Elliott might be able to learn more without my interference. Logic kept me inside, anxiously awaiting his return. When he finally crossed the wall into the sitting room, he looked disturbed.

"What happened? Who was out there?"

"Our friend Julius slipped on the mud and fell against the window."

"Was he listening to us?"

"What else?"

"Ugh, if he heard our plan, he'll never help me."

"Let's hope he didn't."

"You know, all he may need is some attention. No one is sincerely friendly to him."

"That no one is friendly to him may be his greatest weapon."

If being elated about searching for a corpse was a disturbing idea, I was in deep trouble. The thought of finally bringing Aria's soul to rest made my heart leap with gladness. Last night, she'd performed her midnight round as if I hadn't ever spoken to her, still trapped in her world of despair. I had hoped our conversation would temper the horror she seemed to experience, but she left Piper and me as drained as our first encounter.

Considering all that had taken place, I was more convinced that Rose's mystery and the ghosts at All Hallows were somehow interrelated, even if it was through the killer. I hoped that whatever information I discovered shed light on everything.

With a host of ideas in my mind, I left the warmth of the bed. Piper emerged from under the covers and jumped to the floor. Lazily, she pattered across the room and straight to the door, undoubtedly regretting not having spent the night at the cottage.

"Ready to leave me again? Very well. Go on. Go play outside." I let her out, and she dawdled down the hallway. Simultaneously, the housekeeper trotted in my direction, waving a white envelope in her hand.

"This message just came for you." She handed it to me, and with the speed of someone who had been unpleasantly disrupted from her duties, she hustled away.

I stood against the doorframe and slid my finger across the envelope's seal to extract the note.

Hey there, sorry I couldn't stop by, but I'm a bit tied up at the moment. My buddies in London didn't find much. There are no records of a Rose Lewis or Rose Kennard. If they can't find anything, believe me, no one can.

I looked up from the paper to the quiet corridor. The piercing eyes in the paintings hanging on the walls seemed to mock my failure. If only they could speak—what tales would they share? Was Rose buried somewhere in All Hallows's yard after all? Perhaps in searching for Aria's body, I might come across hers.

Annoyed by the disappointing news, I continued reading.

They did say a variant came up, but it's a long shot. There is a woman, Rosalynn Kennard, who started working at the Regency Sanitorium in south London right after the Great War. She was twenty-five years old.

Rose would have been about twenty-one then. But of course, if she did not want to be found, she could have changed her vital information.

Ross's message continued.

She was from Lancashire, but my friends weren't able to verify that. There
are no records for a Rosalynn Kennard in that area before the Great War.
She stills works at the same sanitorium. I hope this helps.

See you soon, Ross

This possibility was the craziest I had considered, but at this point, all
was grist to the mill. I couldn't wait to tell Elliott.

"Here come the Goswicks," Elliott said as we conversed near the house.
Caroline came down the front path, followed by her brother.

"This is my chance to speak to Julius."

"Good luck with that."

"Elliott, I'm sorry the note didn't bring better news."

"It's not totally disheartening. It could be Rose." Elliott marched
toward the back of the manor.

My interaction with Caroline was brief. She was late to help her
mother, and not wanting to cross the housekeeper, she didn't linger. But
before leaving me in Julius's company, she whispered in my ear, "I have a
date this evening." She mouthed the word *Robertson.*

Julius, who had been kicking pebbles from the path with the end of
his boot, looked up at me. "Excuse me," he said, ready to flee.

"No, no—wait a minute. I would like your help."

"Help with what?"

"I'd like to spend more time gardening, but I don't know much about
it. Last night, I read a book about the flora of the New Forest. I had no
idea how ancient these woods are. The book says there are many rare
species of plants and trees. I suppose you know most of them."

"I'd like to believe so." With unsteady hands, he adjusted the satchel
on his shoulder.

"Would you consider giving me a tour? I imagine there are hundreds
of interesting things to see."

When he didn't reply immediately, I braced for a negative answer, but then he said, "All right." I suppose his answer startled me more than mine had startled Ross when I'd agreed to ride his bike with him.

"Do you have time this morning?" From my pocket, I pulled a notebook and pencil. "I mean, I'm ready whenever you are."

"The miss is serious about this," he observed, looking at my supplies.

"Yes, I'll write down some names so I can look them up later."

"I was going to prune the roses, but I suppose I can do that this afternoon," he conceded.

They could definitely use some pruning.

The tour took off near the house, and from there, it expanded into the woods as far as Julius was willing to go. All the while, I kept my eyes peeled for anywhere a body might have been buried nine years ago.

The gardens came first.

"These are wild gladioluses," Julius introduced. "This is the only place in Great Britain they grow naturally. You can spot them in some gardens, but they like to grow at the edge of pastures." The way he spoke about nature was remarkable, as if she had been his childhood best friend. "And these are called orchids. These here are common orchids, and the ones farther back are peacock orchids."

"How pretty. Do they grow any taller?"

"No, that's about as high as they get." As we passed a small pond hidden among the wild grass, he pointed to a patch of plants with white flowers and asked, "Do you know what those are?"

"I don't."

"Their name is coral necklace."

I wrote it on my paper. "They are exquisite."

"They get their name from how the flowers string themselves along the plant." Carefully, he knelt in the soil and pointed out the arrangement. "See, it looks like a necklace made of coral." I watched as his rough hands selected a flower and then, with a gentleness I had never seen from him, plucked it free. To my surprise, he extended it to me.

"Thank you. It's beautiful." I stored the flower in my pocket. "And these?" I had seen them all over the place. They were tall plants with purple flowers akin to the bluebell.

"They are foxglove. In Latin, they are known as *Digitalis purpurea*."

We were out of the gardens now and into the trees. Nature reigned here with its many shades of greens and fresh smell of pine. As the tour progressed, I realized how intelligent Julius was and how much he enjoyed being outdoors. No doubt, this was his area of expertise, and he excelled in it. I also got the impression he had carefully built his personality to not have to deal with people—the fewer people who liked him, the less he had to worry about them liking him. It was brilliant. Like Elliott had said, it was an advantage to the gardener that people disliked him.

Julius's bulky frame moved farther up the path. I hurried after him, and the sweet aroma rising from the edge of the path filled my nostrils. "What are these?" I pointed at a group of plants with longs stems shooting up in all directions, exhibiting an array of tiny white flowers.

"They are common gorse."

"They smell like coconut."

"They grow all over."

Seizing the opportunity, I asked, "Is there a tree that produces a strong aroma? I mean, one you could smell just walking by?"

"Not around here."

"In other parts of the grounds?"

"No, you can find those in town. People plant them because their flowers are attractive and smell good. The vicar has a good variety of them in his back garden."

"Does he, now?"

Julius nodded and turned to another tree. But as he spoke about the eagle oak and how it was named in 1810 when a New Forest keeper shot and killed a sea eagle from its branches, my curiosity fell to a gigantic, isolated tree up ahead.

"What about that one?" I asked.

"That's called the knighthood oak. It's the largest oak in the forest. About five hundred years old."

"It's amazing." The tree wasn't pretty, really, but it was gigantic. "How big would you say its trunk is?"

Julius thought for a moment. "Not sure the exact measurement, but I would say about seven meters at the base." For the life of me, I had no idea how he could calculate it so easily.

He could have gone on with the tour for the rest of the day, but the information so far had been useless for my purposes. He went on to describe something about the fertile soil in the New Forest and the planting seasons. I spaced most of what he said, but when he paused, I swiftly inquired, "So if you were to plant a tree, considering the roughness of the soil in some areas, where would you dig if you had to get it done fast?"

"In the garden by the house. It's always moist."

Another useless answer. While it would be easier to plant a tree there, it wouldn't be a good spot to bury a body. It was in plain sight, and it would be too obvious that the dirt had been disturbed. Even if the body was heavy to carry, the killer had to be clever enough to go a little farther.

"What about out here? In the woods?"

He looked at me sideways. "Why would you want to do something like that? There are plenty of trees in the woods."

His answer made too much sense to refute it without causing suspicion. "I suppose you are right."

Julius turned in the direction of the house. "It's past lunchtime. We better head back."

I presumed the pruning of the roses was at the back of his mind. He did not like to alter his schedule, and that he had postponed it until this afternoon was a stretch already.

"Thank you, Julius. I enjoyed the outing. Hopefully, we can do it again soon," I said earnestly. Apart from the disillusion of not getting closer to finding a grave, I had truly enjoyed his knowledge of the forest. The New Forest had a lot to offer, and so did Julius.

"You're welcome."

Mrs. Goswick had prepared spinach soup and chicken pie. Even though it smelled wonderful, I wasn't hungry. Grabbing a fresh roll with strawberry jam, I sat on the lawn out back, mulling over the various puzzle pieces—although my optimism had taken a complete turn since this morning.

"How did the outing with Julius go?" Elliott popped in from the side garden and dropped down beside me.

"As good as you can imagine. I'm afraid it just dawned on me how vast the grounds really are. And as if that wasn't enough, I got a taste of trying to fish information from Julius." Finding Aria's body had never seemed more discouraging.

"Oh, so you empathize with me now?"

"I'm starting to. At this rate, it will take years before we learn anything from Julius."

"I don't have years," Elliott mumbled, playing with a blade of grass.

"What do you mean?"

"Nothing...nothing." He quickly averted his eyes from mine.

Maybe it was the exhaustion I felt, but I needed him to come clean with me. I couldn't keep this up otherwise. Facing him, I said sincerely, "After this morning's fiasco, I made up my mind."

"About what?"

"I must go to London to meet Rosalynn. If she is Rose, we might be able to solve this conundrum once and for all."

"Wouldn't that be wonderful?" Elliott said with a soft laugh.

"Believe me, I'm fully aware that it would be easier for a camel to go through the eye of a needle than for me to show up out of the blue, discover her real identity, and bring her back here—if she even is Rose."

"Yeah, that might be a bit problematic."

"Most likely, I'll make a complete fool of myself, but before venturing into it, I want to know what you are hiding from me. When you told me your story and about the separation of the ghosts, you left something unsaid. I want to know the whole truth."

"I'm not sure what you are speaking of."

I angled my body toward him and with much earnestness said, "After what we have been through, the least I deserve is to know everything—good and not so good."

He looked down, pondering my remark.

"Elliott, you must tell me."

"It's better that you don't know."

"Why is that?"

"I don't want you to worry. I don't want anything to cloud your judgment while you help me."

"Seriously? In case you haven't noticed, my judgment is already clouded," I sputtered in disbelief. "I hardly eat or sleep anymore. I'm constantly on edge. I can't trust anyone. I simply can't go on like this. I need to know who you really are—your whole story."

"All right, all right. I get the message." Rubbing his forehead nervously, he started, "My parents died when I was little. My older brother and his wife raised me. But as I grew older and the war broke out, I became a burden to them. Money and food were in short supply, much like they are now.

"And another problem was that I was born with a deformity in my right shoulder that impedes the normal use of my arm. Well, it did when I was alive." He smiled, lifting his arm in the air. "What I mean is that I couldn't move it rapidly or hold much weight with it. It was just there, sort of useless. Because of this, I failed my examinations for active duty and was given clearance to stay home."

"Stay home? Wait—I thought you went to war."

He raised a hand in warning. "Let me finish."

"Sorry, go on."

"When I turned eighteen, I came to Burley to work for a blacksmith. There weren't many able men around, and he was glad to hire me even with my bad arm. Since his sons were in the service, he took me under his wing and allowed me to work at my own pace. Believe it or not, I became a great asset to him. He wouldn't let me use the forge, but I did just about everything else. I kept the shop's records, cleaned the tools, swept the floors, and even helped his wife cook meals.

"While working there, I met Rose. She was refined, beautiful, and full of life. I fell madly in love with her. We would wander the woods for hours, dreaming about a future together. When our legs tired from walking, we would lie in the wild grass in the fields. I spent my time trying to kiss her. She spent her time trying to educate me on literature." Elliott laughed. It was a sad, hollow sound. "She loved to discuss the stories she read at length. You know all those books in the library? She read them all. And whenever she couldn't put a book down, she brought it on our date, and we read it together."

"What did the Goswicks think?"

"Not much, I guess. We saw each other out in the woods most of the time. The parents were too wrapped up in their own problems to meddle in the lives of their employers. Julius hated me, but that's not new. He did come across us quite often—imagine his face the first time he saw me as a ghost." He chuckled amusingly. "But then life took an awful turn. I received the infamous telegram summoning me to active service."

"How is that possible?" I was terribly confused. "When I read about it in Rose's journal, it seemed normal, for she didn't write about your arm."

"No, to her I was perfect. She reprimanded me if I ever mentioned my disability."

"But you weren't qualified to serve."

"I wasn't, but I was called." He groaned. "I met Rose down by the stream and gave her the cable, although she'd already read it in my eyes. Feeling helpless, we wept bitterly in each other's arms. Our dreams, our hopes, and our ability to decide for ourselves had suddenly been taken from us.

"However, my dear Rose wasn't ready to accept it just like that. She insisted we discuss the matter with Lewis. He was a lieutenant then, but still, he had some connections. She was convinced a mistake had been made. After all, I could barely hold a rifle steady. I was ashamed of myself, ashamed that I couldn't defend our country, but even more so that I wouldn't be a proper husband."

"Why do you say that? That's not true."

"I say it because I knew that if someone attacked Rose, I wouldn't be of much help. They would drop me without effort. You know, it's ironic, but I used to be jealous of Julius. He was young and strong. I feared he could provide Rose more security than I could."

That explains part of your dislike for poor Julius.

"I didn't agree with Rose, but I did accompany her to visit Lewis. One look at my arm and he was as shocked as we were that I had been called. He tried to persuade some of his influential friends to annul the call to no avail, for the war had escalated to taking anybody who had air in their lungs.

"To make matters worse, as you read in her journal, Rose's father, Richard, was not well. His health had been deteriorating for some time. Rose didn't want to admit it, but we both knew he was near the end of his fight. She would be left to fend for herself. Yet I had to go.

"I reported to headquarters in London soon after. Lewis arranged for me to be stationed in northern England, hoping I would remain there until the end of my service. But as fate would have it, a month later, I was called to the Western Front.

"How I managed to survive as long as I did defies understanding. When rumors of an armistice started to circulate, I began to believe I might return to Rose, but my unit ended up with a group of French soldiers entangled in the Meuse-Argonne offensive.

"It was November 11, 1918. We were ordered to attack German positions until eleven o'clock in the morning. We were behind a large American group and had advanced quite some distance into the enemy's territory. The men—a figure of speech, really, for most of us were lads—started to relax as the enemy appeared to retreat, only to realize we had been fooled. Hand grenades rained down on us before we were attacked at close range. The last thing I saw was a landscape of dead men surrounding me. Funny how in striving to stay alive I hadn't paid attention to the carnage until the moment I took a bullet.

"I felt a blast, and then there was nothing but blackness, yet I rose from the ground quite rapidly. I walked around the clouds of dust, frantically searching for other survivors. I walked past the mangled bodies, one by one. It was then I noticed soldiers moving about with an incredible speed, weeping. I wasn't sure what was taking place. Their uniforms were clean, and the men weren't injured. I knew it couldn't be a rescue team because there were none. I looked down at my clothes, and to my horror, I was as clean as they were. It didn't make sense. I had been in combat for hours, and I had been shot.

"The other soldiers moved about in a frenzy, searching for someone or something among the dead." Elliott looked down, struggling to control his emotions. Those terrible events had reshaped his character as well as his destiny. My heart was heavy, and tears filled my eyes.

When Elliott spoke again, his voice shook. "It took me a while to figure out that they were looking for their remains to confirm that they were dead. To realize this was more dreadful than walking into the ambush, for then we could still fight for our lives. It didn't take me long to find my body among the debris. My mortal life had ended, and I profoundly mourned the loss of my life, just like my comrades mourned theirs. On top of that, the uncertainty of what lay ahead and not having a future with Rose crushed me.

"At length, the confusion settled. Our commander, John Harris, who had also died in the attack, gathered us. He explained that we had to move on, for we had wasted too much time already. Apparently, it had been many days since the ambush—days that felt like hours dwindling between worlds until we came to accept our new condition. And at that point, I understood the boundaries governing this sphere.

"I knew I had only one day to say my good-byes to those I loved. If I didn't return to the group within that time frame, I would be confined to the place where my heart was until I exhausted my energy, which could take a very long time. And then, if I didn't fulfill my mission for having lingered, I wouldn't be with those I love in the hereafter.

"My frame of mind was such that I failed to understand the severity of my situation. Perhaps I simply didn't care. My thoughts were foggy, confused. All I wanted was to see Rose one last time. Foolishly, I thought things would be the same, that I could interact with her the way I had when I was alive.

"As Harris's subordinate, I still needed his permission to leave, which he granted. After assuring him I would return on time, I instantly found myself at the edge of the New Forest. I made haste to All Hallows, only to find it deserted. My initial belief, since Rose's possessions were all here, was that she had gone to town."

The knot in my throat and the pressure in my heart were so intense now that tears freely rolled down my cheeks. I said softly, "So...you waited."

"I did. Days turned into weeks, weeks into months, and months into years."

"I'm so sorry."

His voice quieted as he went on. "Soon I discovered the depth of my predicament. After the initial twenty-four hours, I became confined to All Hallows and couldn't go beyond the edge of the woods. I couldn't visit any of the towns. I could only move in the forested areas."

"Because your heart is here, where you left Rose," I whispered.

"That's right."

"Do you ever regret not having returned to Harris?"

The strength in his voice revealed the surety of his answer. "No. I promised Rose I would return, and I can't move on without making good on my promise. Besides, it's a bit too late for regrets. If I don't find her, I might not ever see her again—not here, not there, not anywhere. It's part of the price I must pay."

"That's rather horrid. I certainly understand now why you must find her." If he failed, the cost of his quest was the ultimate price that could be asked. "But what if, wherever she escaped to, she passed away in peace?"

"Then I suppose I've lost her already, but she wouldn't have died so young unless she was murdered," Elliott reasoned. "You know, realizing that I couldn't see the grieving spirits was the worst. I dreaded the possibility that something terrible had happened to her and that her spirit was trapped in this house without hope, and there was nothing I could do to help her."

"At least we know she isn't the woman haunting the house, and I don't see any other ghosts nearby."

"That's good, I guess." His gaze found the grass. "I'll never give up. I have to find her."

"But if you did see her..." Feeling a bit muddled, I paused to analyze his words. "Wouldn't you still be trapped here?"

"Only until my energy is gone. If Rose were here, I would spend my energy communicating with her, though I don't really know how much energy or time I have."

"You don't?"

"No, it's just like when you are alive. You don't know when you are going to die."

Another thought surfaced, and I said, "Elliott, it's very probable that Rose wouldn't be able to see you."

"I know. In that case, I suppose I would spend my energy being near her, hoping she could feel my presence. Either way, my purpose for having lingered would be fulfilled. And we would have the chance of being together once she moved on."

Making sure I understood him correctly, I queried, "Whenever you interact with someone, or try to, you are burning energy. Wearing it out."

He nodded affirmatively. "That's why I get so frustrated with the simpleminded—" He caught and corrected himself. "With Julius. I'm convinced he knows something about Rose's whereabouts and plays dumb while I grow dimmer. But that energy is minuscule compared to the amount I spend when—" He paused as if thinking better of what he had almost said. "Never mind. There you have it." Sliding closer to me, he placed his intangible hand on mine. "Now you know the whole truth of my journey."

"Thank you for trusting me, Elliott," I said. "I can only imagine how difficult this is for you."

Elliott's gaze held mine with a strength I hadn't thought possible. His eyes radiated the pure, all-encompassing love he felt for Rose. It was as if he communicated this directly to my soul. It was a love that burned through the very fibers of his being, a love that illuminated his existence. I understood then why he hadn't moved on. He was nothing without her.

"Wow," I muttered. "Did you do that to me?"

"No. Sometimes the veil between worlds becomes thin, and if our feelings align, you can step into this sphere and feel what I feel."

"That's incredible and much better than stepping into Aria's realm." I got to my feet, the feelings still fresh in me. "Now, more than ever, I know we have to explore the possibility of Rosalynn Kennard being Rose. Finding Aria's body might bring us closer to discovering the assassin's identity, but it might not bring us closer to finding Rose."

"Unless the body we dig up isn't Aria's," Elliott said softly.

CHAPTER 20
ROSALYNN KENNARD

With Elliott's eternity hanging by a thread and tired of profitless speculation, I was on my way to London. The lie of visiting my parents had satisfied the Goswicks, though they couldn't understand the shortness of my trip. "Such a hassle to spend just one day in London. Why not stay a little longer?" Mrs. Goswick had asked. I had to refresh her memory. Being in a safe house, my parents were in no position to entertain me.

After a long night of listening to Aria's cries, I'd started the day low on energy. As the locomotive pulled away from Brockenhurst, vivid memories of my escape from London resurfaced. So much had changed in my life since that bleak day when my parents had said good-bye to me from the platform of King's Cross station. It had not been easy for them to let me go, but love had a way of doing that—of letting things go for the greater good.

My eyelids closed with heaviness as I revisited the memories: the blue sky; beholding the beauty and life of the forest as the cab driver spoke of the ponies, the soldiers, and the war; Piper and I crossing the dreary field; the ghost of the soldier spying on us; Captain Stewart with his quick wit and captivating smile; the Goswicks, Julius, and the Lewis's ancestors looking down at me from their eternal posts on the walls; the ghost of Aria haunting my every hour; walking into the stable and holding Elliott's gaze for the first time; Rose Lewis and her poignant writing; the killer in the woods...

"Miss, wake up. This is the final stop." The guard shook my shoulder, pulling me from a peaceful sleep. I collected my handbag and was soon among the last few passengers to descend the train.

The weather in London was gloomy, the sky marked by a covering of gray clouds—I'd expected as much. What I had not anticipated were the solemn faces traveling about the streets. Though Londoners weren't necessarily known as the friendliest of people, their rushed, distrustful demeanor had grown considerably.

The repercussions of the aerial warfare were heart-wrenching. Debris covered just about every surface. The damaged buildings were still standing, but dark and empty. There were many Closed signs on shop doors, more so than Open ones. The surviving structures had their windows darkened with blackout curtains to make it difficult for enemy bombers to see the city. And so, for once, the darkness kept us safe.

Did my home block look like this now? It must have been heartbreaking for my parents to witness the destruction of our neighborhood and all that was familiar. I could now appreciate the sacrifice they had made to send me to safety. I missed them.

With renewed resolve, I located the spot the man at the train station had drawn on the map and tackled the twelve-block walk.

The Regency Sanitorium was a wide structure, three floors high, and had apparently been spared from the bombs. A redbrick wall with an iron fence perched atop it guarded the front, a tall gate in the middle of the property the only interruption in the barrier.

My courage dwindled at the prospect of not finding the woman Elliott loved. However, Elliott's forthcoming fate subjugated my fears and pushed me onward. I rang the bell. It couldn't have been more than a few seconds before a slender woman with blond hair down to her shoulders responded. She wore a thick pair of spectacles and a mountain of red lipstick.

"Can I help you?"

"I'm looking for Rosalynn Kennard. I understand she works here."

The woman inspected me suspiciously. "Are you an acquaintance or family member?"

Interesting question. Would she like me better if I said family? I took the risk. "We are cousins."

Adjusting her spectacles, she invited, "Step in, please."

"Thank you...Miss?"

"Thornton. Follow me."

If she walked any faster, I would have to break into a run to keep up. Evidently, in her line of work, agility was indispensable. We traveled down a white corridor devoid of personality. No decorations hung on its walls. Soon, she stopped at the third door before the end of the hall. Stepping aside, she signaled for me to go in.

"Have a seat. I'll inform the secretary that you're here. She'll help you find your *cousin*." Her tone implied her disbelief at the professed family connection. Likely she thought me to be one of the abundant scoundrels who, due to the circumstances, popped up to swindle unsuspecting *relatives*.

I frowned and then smiled. She could believe whatever she chose, for she would never guess the real reason I wanted to see Rosalynn.

Daylight filtered through the large window on the back wall of the tiny room, highlighting a row of filing cabinets to the right of the desk. I settled on the visitors' chair, and soon, an older woman with chestnut hair and a stern face entered. "I'm Mrs. Brown. Don't bother to stand. What brings you here, Miss...?"

"Seraphina Addington. I'd like to see Rosalynn Kennard."

"As surely you understand, our nurses are quite busy, and very rarely do we allow visitors without a prior appointment."

"I didn't know that, Mrs. Brown, or I would have set one up." Appealing to her sympathy, I went on to say, "I've traveled from the New Forest. It's a long way from here. All I'm asking for is a few minutes with her. Please." Considering that if Rosalynn were Rose and that somehow I would drag her back with me to Burley, "a few minutes" was a big lie. But Elliott, the man already dead, was at present more urgent than the convalescents under Rosalynn's care.

With a look of displeasure, Mrs. Brown moved to the filing cabinet and searched the folders starting with the letter *K*. She pulled one with the last name Kennard written on it and took a good look at the information contained therein. Satisfied with whatever she'd read, she returned it to its place. "Miss Kennard works on the third floor. I'll have her come down."

Thank heavens. That had been easy enough.

Reaching for the telephone, Mrs. Brown dialed a number. A brief conversation ensued, and she hung up. From what I could make of it, the news wasn't good. "Miss Addington, I'm sorry, but Miss Kennard has been ill. She was supposed to resume work today, but her maid let us know she needs a few more days of rest. I'm not sure when we'll see her again."

Should I order or beg her to give me Rosalynn's address? I opted for begging. "I could not forgive myself if I didn't have the chance to see her, especially if she isn't feeling well. I know your protocol might be unbendable, but considering the circumstances, could you share her address?"

Her gaze snapped at me as if I had poked her with a needle. "As her relative, you should already have her address or know someone in the family who does," she fired. "I'm afraid I cannot disclose personal information without permission."

Desperate, I suggested, "Does she have a telephone at home? Could you ring her and ask for her permission?"

"I'm afraid she does not," Mrs. Brown croaked. "Now, if you'll excuse me. I have much to attend to."

"Wait—may I leave a note for when she returns?"

"You may do that." After giving me another look of distrust, she handed me a piece of paper and a pen.

Miss Kennard,

We are distant cousins. Well, I'm Elliott Kennard's second cousin. I have important news to convey to you. I would be much obliged if you contacted me as soon as you receive the present.

Sincerely,

Seraphina Addington

All Hallows, Burley, The New Forest

Hoping it would reach its intended reader at some point, I extended the paper to Mrs. Brown. "Thank you for your time."

She nodded, and I withdrew from the office.

My heart matched the heaviness in my legs as I trailed down the bleak corridor. My gaze veered left, and I found a short niche housing a metal bench so inconspicuously placed I had missed it before. Automatically, my feet took me there. I sat down, feeling demoralized and overcome by adversity. I wanted to cry, but the tears wouldn't come, for deep within me, the undefeatable optimism of the human spirit refused to let me give up. There had to be something else I could do, but my brain seemed to be in lock-down. I couldn't think.

Seconds later, the sharp clack of heels came to life and intensified until the owner of the shoes walked right past the niche I sat in, unaware of me.

Mrs. Brown. That woman is in serious need of therapy—lacks human emotions. Particularly compassion. Yet I couldn't blame her. To handle the amount of distress required by her job without losing her mind, she had to be emotionally detached.

As the click-clack of her heels died away, the silence returned and grew thick. The idea came fast. I leaped to my feet and stealthily walked back to her office. My heart hammered against my ribs, warning me that what I was doing was wrong. It was too late. I did not care. I pulled the Kennard folder out of the cabinet, retrieved the page marked "personal records," folded it, and buried it inside my handbag.

―――――

The cab took me to a small cottage with a thatched roof just outside the city boundaries. Behind the white picket fence that enclosed the property lived a well-kept garden with plants of all shapes and colors. There was harmony here—harmony of a life quietly but productively spent. A life that rejoiced in beauty and goodness.

Recalling Mrs. Goswick's description of Rose, I made my way across the stone-paved walk to the front door. Anxiously, I tapped on it. It parted, and a short, gray-haired woman with a wrinkled face stared at me. "May I help you?

I took a confident approach, speaking as if I knew the woman I was looking for. "Is Rosalynn in?"

She observed me in a curious way, as if trying to remember if she knew me. Was she Rosalynn? If she was, then, unquestionably, she wasn't Rose.

"I'm sorry, miss. Who do I have the pleasure of speaking with?" Her critical examination tested my confidence. "And why are you interested in Miss Kennard?"

The cab ride had given me time to analyze possible scenarios and build a quick defense in case of failure. "Forgive me. My name is Seraphina Addington. I'm a cousin of Elliott Kennard. He is related to Rosalynn." I had decided that if Rosalynn wasn't Rose, I would offer the misunderstanding as a mistake due to the shared surname. "I stopped by the Regency Sanitorium, and they said she had the day off, so I determined I must come by to give her this." From my bag, I extracted Rose's diary. It was my best shot at having her confide in me her real identity. "See, I hail from the New Forest, and I'm not sure when I'll make another trip to London."

The woman's demeanor instantly relaxed. I wasn't sure what she thought of the book, but having something tangible to deliver was apparently enough for her. "Welcome, then, Miss Addington. I'm Miss Kennard's maid, Dorothy. You mustn't take my scrutiny the wrong way. You know, these days, with the war and shortage of money, when someone is sick, the crows are the first in line."

"I totally understand," I said, and playing innocent, I added, "Has Rosalynn fallen ill?" Knowingly inconveniencing her would come across as uncaring.

"Oh, miss, indeed she has. But with proper care, she'll be up and about in no time."

"That's good to hear."

"Please, come in." She ushered me into the sitting area.

A stone fireplace on the far wall dominated the pale room. Though the space was small, it was well furnished, with an orange sofa and two matching armchairs. It was simple but elegant. A few oil paintings on the walls called for my inspection.

"These are magnificent."

"Aren't they something? Miss Kennard painted them herself. She has mastered the art quite well."

"Indeed." I stopped in front of one that spoke a thousand words. It portrayed a couple walking hand in hand in the forest. The man was tall and had a broad smile. The woman wore a long yellow dress that contrasted with her long dark hair. Was it the New Forest? Was it a depiction of Elliott and Rose? "Who are these people?" I pointed to the painting.

"Oh, that I wouldn't know. Miss Kennard likes to paint in the park, so it could be anyone who happened to be there that day."

"It looks more like a forest than a park, wouldn't you say?"

"Miss Kennard likes to put her own spin on things."

I smiled.

"Would you like some tea while you wait? It might take Miss Kennard a moment or two before she can see you."

"No, thank you."

"Very well. I'll let her know you are here."

I spent the time I had alone examining the scenes in the paintings. I even took the liberty of unhooking the one with the couple from its spot. I flipped it over, hoping for a name or an inscription of the place. There was none.

When Dorothy returned, her face bore signs of distress. "I'm sorry, but Miss Kennard does not feel like receiving company today. She's asked that you leave your information. She'll reach out to you once her health allows it."

No! Elliott's anguish flashed through my mind, and my resolution was cemented. I couldn't go back to him empty-handed and crestfallen. I would not leave until I saw Rosalynn. If I had to push Dorothy out of the way and search every room for the woman, so be it. But before I took drastic measures, I had to try one last thing. "Would you please try again? Tell her I have her diary and will only give it to her in person."

"She really isn't feeling well," the maid advocated on her employer's behalf. "Come back another day, please."

I assembled my next words carefully, presenting them in a gentle voice. "I totally understand, Dorothy." A wave of relief crossed her face—until I spoke again. "The dilemma is that I probably won't be back for months. In this diary"—I held it high and shook it softly—"there are many intimate details. It would be a pity if it fell into the wrong hands." Despite my efforts to come across as a caring relative, I sounded like a blackmailer. But what was I to do? Nothing now, for there it was—the last jab. My heartbeat quickened, dreading that Dorothy would throw me out or, worse yet, call the police. Yet I clung to the small hope that she might plead my cause.

Dorothy's gaze lingered on me for the longest, most uncomfortable while. Not giving her the advantage of sensing my uneasiness, I matched her challenging gaze. I was stunned when she said, "I will convey your message—this one time."

With an air of exasperation, the maid marched back to the sick woman. This time, it took her longer to come back. The taunting ticktock of the clock on the mantelpiece had me on edge. Had Dorothy exited the house from the back door and gone to fetch the police? Knowing my luck, the odds were high.

My worries were somewhat dispelled when I heard footfalls heading my way. Would Rose cross the threshold? Would my desperate search at last come to an end? I held my breath.

To my disappointment, it wasn't Rosalynn who appeared but her maid. "She'll receive you in her bedroom."

"I'm much obliged to you." I exhaled in relief.

"One more thing."

"Do tell me."

"Miss Kennard asked me to warn you that her sickness is contagious. Do you want to proceed?"

There was no decision to be made. "I do."

"Follow me, then."

We traveled down a short corridor, ending our route in front of a brown door. Dorothy opened it and gestured for me to go in. Hearing the door shut behind me, I stepped into a bright room. Its west-facing window allowed the late-afternoon sun to invade the space with radiance and warmth. A woman sat in a rocking chair, a blanket over her long legs, staring out to the garden through the glass. Her dark hair, weaved with a few strands of white, was in an updo. Her skin was pale and thin, signs of her frailty. Despite her condition, her poise spoke of years of refinement and discipline. Rosalynn Kennard, though older, could very well be Rose.

Rosalynn did not look at me. I crossed the room, taking the liberty of pulling a chair closer to her. "Miss Kennard, my name is Seraphina Addington. I'm a tenant at All Hallows in Burley." At the mention of All Hallows, she turned her head a fraction of an inch.

In a soft voice, she said, "Miss Addington, by being here, you are putting your life at risk. The sanitorium where I work treats infectious diseases such as tuberculosis."

The awareness of the sickness sharpened my observation. It was only reasonable that Rosalynn sat in the warmth of the sunshine spilling in through the glass. The bottles of disinfectant and other medicines now fell into place. I beheld the colorful coverlet, and as my gaze dropped to its hem, I saw a sputum mug poking out from beneath the bed.

Calling me back from my brief assessment, Rosalynn added, "You are welcome to leave if you would like."

"Not until you know why I have come." Since she did not respond, I tactfully started to tell my tale. "This might sound confusing, but please hear me out. At All Hallows, hidden in the conservatory, I found this." I waved the diary in front of me. Rosalynn still did not look. "It's the diary of Rose Lewis. She lived at All Hallows until her sudden disappearance in 1918."

Hopeful that she would add something to the story, I paused. She did not.

I went on. "Through her writings, I've reckoned Rose fled the manor in fear of her life. Her fears were well placed. After her disappearance, four young women suffered a terrible fate. You may have heard about them through the newspapers. You can imagine how all of this has impacted the groundskeepers of the manor, the Goswicks. They still grieve Rose's disappearance." Rosalynn threw a glance my way. "Mrs. Goswick is the most affected. She loves Rose as her daughter. Even after all these years, the wound is still fresh."

"Why are you telling me this?"

"Because I believe you are Rose Lewis."

"Me!" she exclaimed, jolting a little. "I'm sorry to disappoint you, but I'm not. What in the world led you to conjecture such a thing?"

"A friend in the army gave me your information. Your history of employment matches the date of Rose's disappearance, and interesting enough, he didn't find any traces of Rosalynn Kennard in her supposed town of origin. Of course, there is also your surname."

"Kennard? What about it?"

"Rose was deeply in love with a young man named Elliott Kennard. In this diary, she wondered what it would have been like to be Mrs. Rose Kennard. He, you see, was a distant cousin of mine." I looked away, ashamed of the lie. "Sadly, he died in the Great War, and they were never reunited."

"Oh yes, the same story repeated over and over. Do you know how many men die each month in the sanitorium, calling for their sweethearts? Too many to count." She sighed. "Miss Addington, I wish I could be of help, but I'm not the woman you seek. But even if I were, you troubled yourself to bring me an old diary?" She was sharp. She knew there was something else.

My lying skills came to my rescue once again, though this time I could mix the lies with some truth. "I came in possession of a few letters sent to Rose by Elliott in the days preceding his death. If I were her, I would most definitely like to read them." Rose's diary had left no doubt about her love for Elliott and the emptiness of having lost him. It was only natural that Rose would want to know about his final days, his final thoughts and feelings.

"Sounds like this is a matter demanding careful consideration and application, Miss Addington. Surely you don't want to convey such private information to the wrong person," Rosalynn counseled, making me feel quite the imbecile. "I wish you the best of luck in finding Miss Lewis." Her tone was so definite that doubt crept in. Stubbornness could be blinding, and I had been obstinate. To help Elliott, I had wanted her to be Rose so terribly I hadn't been willing to accept an ending that wasn't a happy one.

At a total loss, I stood, diary in hand. "Forgive me for disturbing you. I hope you will recover soon."

"A few more days of peace and rest, that's all."

I proceeded to the door, and turning to face her, my lips trembled as I blurted out, "Tell me, Miss Kennard, do you believe in ghosts?"

In an almost scary, abrupt way, she held my gaze. Her blue eyes were crystal clear, like the serene glow of the sea. "Why do you ask?"

"The ghost of Elliott roams the halls of All Hallows in search of Rose Lewis. I'm afraid his soul will spend eternity trapped in loneliness... looking for her."

I stepped into the corridor. *Well, that was that. She most definitely thinks me insane now.*

"Miss Addington," Rosalynn called.

"Yes?" I moved back, stopping at the threshold.

"I truly do hope you find Rose," she said, compassion vibrating in her voice.

Yes, most definitely insane.

I left Rosalynn's house in haste, my thoughts in disarray. I walked down the pavement in search of a cab, angry at myself. How could I have failed? It seemed that no matter what I did for my ghostly friend, nothing worked. It was as if All Hallows lay under an unbreakable curse.

Adding to my helplessness, I'd missed the train back home by minutes. I purchased tickets for an alternative route. I traveled to Winchester, caught the train to Brockenhurst station, and grabbed a cab to Burley, which thankfully wasn't Mr. Craven's. This driver, braver than Craven, dropped me off not far from the manor. All in all, I reached Burley before I would have had I waited for the direct line.

As I entered the manor's property at the crack of dawn, it was curious to acknowledge that being there felt right. Though my parents were in London, I belonged here. I was home. And while my failures were many, my resolution to help Aria and Elliott remained a priority. My mother once said you never knew how powerful a woman was until you challenged her strength. I was starting to understand what she meant.

Relieved to have missed Aria's rackety ritual, I lay on my bed, Rose's diary in hand, and fell asleep.

I was glad to escape the lies I'd told the Goswicks to cover for my trip to London. I just hoped they would never meet my parents and inquire about my visit.

"She denied being Rose," I informed Elliott as we sat on the back land under gray skies.

"Did you believe her?"

"One part of me did, the other not so much."

"She didn't give you any hints?"

"Nothing. I even mentioned Mrs. Goswick's suffering over Rose's disappearance. She didn't budge."

"Tell me—what does she look like?" Elliott asked with anticipation.

A brief description of the woman, her maid, and her tiny house were enough to satisfy his curiosity. "Her general features do match that of Rose's," I said, "though older. But Rosalynn is a detached, withdrawn woman."

"Rose could never be like that. It's not her," Elliott concluded.

"Well, if she is Rose, she is a prolific actress. There were times I thought there was recognition and remembrance of All Hallows in her, but mostly she was uninterested and bothered by my intrusion."

"I'm sorry you went through all that trouble for nothing. As much as I don't want to admit it, she is probably dead and buried who knows where. I'm such an idiot. All these years and I still hold on to hope. Who am I fooling?" He jumped to his feet. "What else could I have done?"

"Please, Elliot, we mustn't allow despair to stop us now. Not all is lost." I tried to comfort him as much as myself, though we were running out of ideas. "Finding Aria's body might offer some clues."

"I don't think so, unless, of course, we find Rose's corpse too. But then again, you said it yourself before you left. This yard is like looking for a needle in a haystack." Elliott's face grew dark, the anguish that filled it difficult to witness. He tried to speak but couldn't. He thrashed away and vanished from view, leaving me with an aching heart.

Where are you, Rose? There must be some clue, some way to find you. Heavens, what am I missing?

While I tried to recall whatever eluded me, Piper pranced through the kitchen door and joined me on the grass. "Well, missy, it's nice of you to spend some time with me." I softly stroked her back. She yawned and closed her eyes, but her contentment wasn't to last. Soon she was on her legs, quietly heading to the trees. I had seen her do this before around the same hour, but it wasn't until now that I thought anything of it.

"Piper, where are you going? Come back here right now. Piper!" She went on as if I didn't exist. "Where are you going?" I started after her, trying to coax her to come back, but she evidently had a purpose.

She headed into uncharted territory. This part of the woods, as far as I knew, led to nowhere. It was just thick verdure. There were no connections to roads or towns, no paths or marked areas, so much so that no one traveled this way. The only familiarity was the chirping of the birds sitting in the lofty branches and the rustle of animals rooting in the underbrush.

Without a care in the world, Piper went down a steep drop. I contemplated the sudden descent, uncertain of being able to find my way back if I kept going. Yet as Piper forged ahead, I followed with a sigh. Once I got to the bottom of the hill, I found myself in a more compacted area. Even the sunshine struggled to penetrate the treetops. And suddenly, as if I had gone deaf, I became aware of an unnatural silence. No animal life of any kind, not even the birds, could be heard, as if this were a forbidden part of the woods for them.

Nevertheless, Piper was here, and she went straight through a wall of thick vines to completely vanish from view. The stillness was so disconcerting I didn't dare interrupt it by calling her. I just walked through the wall of greenery and immediately realized I had crossed a threshold into someone's space.

I stood inside a hut made of interweaving vines and thick shrubs. The terrible stench of rotting flesh hit my nose at once, and my stomach heaved in revulsion. I was going to be sick. I needed to flee, yet the scene was so astounding it paralyzed me. Hanging from the green walls were the pelts of all kinds of creatures. Some must have been skinned fairly recently. My attention fell to the ground to find an ax and a muddy shovel propped against a pile of old blankets. *Leave, leave now!* The voice inside me urged. *This is not good...*

Piper jumped up to what once had been a chair and comfortably curled up her tiny body. "No, you can't stay here. Come on." As I reached down to grab her, my gaze fell upon a wooden box on the ground beside her. There were all sorts of odd items in it, including a satchel.

Leave! The voice now screamed in my head.

I threw my hand into the box, trashing about its content; old magazines, tools, gloves, and a satchel. *How can this be? He was wearing his satchel earlier this morning.* Having already deduced who the owner of this horrific hideout was, the obvious stared me in the face—he owned more than one shoulder sack.

Then, at the bottom of the box, I saw an item that jolted me to my very bones. With shaking fingers, I pulled it out. The necklace was old, with a delicate rose engraved on its pendant. The hands that had carved it had done so with much love and devotion, for after decades, it remained beautifully well defined. *Rose's necklace.* Quailing at what this could mean, I finally heeded the warning in my head to flee the deadly entrapment.

"Come on, Piper—let's go." She looked at me with heavy eyelids. "Come on," I pressed, making the attempt to pick her up. She flashed her teeth and growled at me. "Fine, have it your way."

I swam through the barrier of vines as if they were cobras slithering around me, franticly pushing them out of my way. I burst to the other side only to crash against Julius's gigantic figure.

"What are you doing here?" he demanded at once.

I stared at him, unable to speak. Why did he have Rose's necklace? Why did he keep this horrendous hideout in the woods?

His voice grew louder. "Who told you about this place? That idiot Ghost told you, didn't he? All this time he's been sneaking, spying on me, and he finally found it."

The thought of involving Elliott in this—when there existed enough animosity between the men already—loosened my tongue. "No, it wasn't him," I defended. "I was looking for Piper and stumbled upon it."

He stepped closer, his body overshadowing me. "You shouldn't be here—no one should ever come here. This is my place. Do you understand? Mine." His irritation rose rapidly, along with my heartbeat as his dark eyes filled with rage.

"I'm sorry. It won't happen again." Acting as if he were a dog ready to bite, I maintained eye contact as I tried to sidle around him.

He was quick. Too quick. He grabbed my wrist and through clenched teeth asked, "What do you have in your hand? What are you stealing from me?"

I shook my head. "Nothing. I have nothing."

"Open your hand!" He squeezed my wrist harder.

"What in the name of all the bloody demons in hell do you think you are doing?" Elliott shouted, hurrying to my side. "Let her go!"

"Open your hand!" ordered Julius. He tightened his hand around my wrist until my fingers fell open.

"That's mine," Julius said. "You cannot take it."

I closed my hand again, unwilling to let him have it.

"No," Elliott said, astonished. "No, that's not yours, you bloody coward. That belonged to Rose. I gave it to her." And then he went ballistic. "What did you do to her? Where is she? You know where she is! Tell me!"

The developing uproar summoned Piper from the hut. Seeing my struggle with Julius, she barked at him, running back and forth from the gardener to the ghost. Julius squeezed my hand so hard I dropped the necklace to the ground. He picked it up and then released me. My wrist burned.

"It's all right, Piper. I'm all right," I soothed as her barking didn't help matters.

She barked a few more times before going back inside the hideout.

Elliott followed Piper through the curtain of vines only to come right back out. "You are a sick man, Julius," he blurted out, convinced now more than ever that the gardener was responsible for more hideous crimes than the killing of animals. "What did you do to Rose?"

"I know nothing about Rose. I loved her," was Julius's only line of defense.

"You don't hurt people you love," Elliott accused. "Unless, of course, you are a sick man!"

"Elliott, calm down, please," I begged.

Far from being calm, the ghost yelled, "Tell me what you know. You know something about Rose. Tell me!"

Again, Piper emerged from the vines and took Julius's side, barking angrily at Elliott.

"I know nothing!" Julius shouted back.

"Move, Seraphina," Elliott commanded, launching himself at the gardener.

Elliott's passed through Julius's body with brutal force, making Julius stumble back. A fierce wind rose, causing the tree branches to whistle like a whip slashing the back of a mule. Simultaneously, the debris on the ground formed into a whirlwind that encompassed Julius as Elliott circled him repeatedly. With a squeal, Piper again ran for the safety of the hut.

The whirlwind around the gardener gained strength while he desperately punched at the air. Once again, the ghost passed right through him. Julius lost his footing and hit the ground.

I screamed at Elliott, "You stop right now!" But he ignored me, readying himself to do who knew what next. "Julius, are you all right?" I yelled over the noise of the flying elements still under Elliott's control. "Julius, answer me!"

Julius didn't respond to my call. Instead, his body started to writhe on the ground like a snake on fire. Fighting the tornado, I took a step closer and saw the dread on his face. Julius knew as much as I did that Elliott wouldn't let him go. I had to say something, however untruthful and hurtful, to stop him before it was too late.

I screamed at Elliott, "You lied to me all this time! After Rose was done writing in her journal, you came back and she saw you, didn't she?

But she didn't love you anymore. You grew angry and lost control, just like now. You killed her after all, didn't you?"

Elliott's frenzy immediately ceased. The elements returned to their natural state. And it seemed to me that the ghost's light was nonexistent now. He was enshrouded in darkness. "Don't you ever accuse me of doing such a thing!" he warned angrily.

"If you hurt Julius again, you'll have to hurt me too." I dashed to kneel beside the gardener. "Please leave."

"He'll kill you like he killed Rose!"

"I'm more afraid of you than him," I sputtered. "Look at you. You have turned into a demon."

The violent way in which Elliott moved testified that he was having the most difficult time restraining himself. For a moment, I doubted he would retreat, even when I was directly in the line of fire. Yet pointing his finger at the gardener, he threatened, "I'll get to you, Julius. Sooner or later, I will." And with a mouth full of cursing, he fled through the vegetation.

"Julius, are you all right?" Though the disturbing scene in the hut and the necklace didn't speak well of him, they weren't evidence of murder. And at any rate, even if Julius was the killer, taking his life wasn't an option nor the solution. "Are you hurt?"

His words came out slowly, painfully. "I did not hurt Rose."

"Oh, Julius..."

With a little difficulty, he rose from the ground. I stood beside him, fearing that he would pass out. His face was colorless, and his hands kept opening and closing into fists.

With broken words he said, "Rose was my friend. She didn't like to hunt, but I taught her how to make shoes from deerskin. She never chastised me for hunting." He glanced at the vines.

Doing my best to not add to his anxiety, I said in a soft voice, "Is that why you hide your collection out here? You fear the reaction of your parents?"

"Yes."

"I didn't mean to cause this confrontation," I said. "I'm sorry."

"Sooner or later it was going to happen."

In an even softer voice, I inquired, "How did you get Rose's necklace?"

"She gave it to me."

Did I believe him? It didn't matter. I had to keep him calm and engaged. "Did she say why?"

"No."

"Julius, all that Elliott wants is to find Rose. Do you know where she is?"

"No."

"Do you know what happened to her?"

"No."

"Julius, too many women have lost their lives. No one knows these woods like you do. You must have seen or heard something. Please, you can trust me."

A light of awareness crossed Julius's eyes, and he said, "You weren't really interested in learning about the forest. You were using me. What are you hoping to find?"

The time to prevaricate had passed. I responded frankly, "A body. That's what I'm hoping to find."

"Whose body?"

"Aria Lancaster's." My words gave him a nasty jolt. The little color that had returned to his face vanished again. "Was she your friend too?"

He evaded my question by responding with another. "What makes you think she's buried in the woods?"

Perhaps, if he was guilty, the possibility of Aria sharing information with me would put pressure on him, and he would help me find the body to cover his back. "I saw her ghost in the house. She told me."

"I don't believe you."

"Why? Both of us see Elliott. I see her as well." She appeared inside the house at night, so most likely he had never seen her. Or had he? "Have you seen her?"

He opened his mouth to say something but instead took off back up the hill, his boots crashing through the leaves on the forest floor like a plow.

Undressing for the night, I checked the pockets of my trousers before putting them away. From one I extracted the flower Julius had given me. I had forgotten all about it. I slipped into my nightgown and, admiring the white coral necklace in my hand, lay on my bed with a terrible ache in my feet. The awful scene at Julius's hut replayed in my mind, adding to the anger I felt toward both Julius and Elliott. Elliott was hotheaded, and though I could understand to a certain extent his exasperation, he had ruined a good opportunity to get information from Julius, for I had the inkling that if approached differently, the gardener might have been a bit more compliant, considering we could expose the secret of his hideout. Julius, of course, was naturally obstinate and responded to hostility by shutting down.

He hadn't shown for supper, which was a relief for me. I couldn't imagine facing him so soon after the altercation. His parents weren't too concerned about it, but the mood was somber. After dinner, Mrs. Goswick rinsed the plates and handed them to me. I dried them and one by one stacked them back in the cupboard. Caroline busied herself with mopping the floor where the men's boots had left their tracks.

"With your trip to London, I forgot to ask you about your outing in the woods with Julius the other morning," the housekeeper said. "How was it?"

"Very enlightening. Julius is a polymath when it comes to the forest. I am stunned by the number of species he knows."

"And I'm sure you have only seen a little bit," Caroline observed, looking up from the mop. "My brother loves to speak about it. I don't know how he remembers it all."

"Since he learned to walk, I haven't been able to keep him indoors," Mrs. Goswick recalled. "He likes to see how things grow and expand."

And he likes to kill things as well. "I took some notes."

"Oh, he must have been flattered," Caroline said.

"Did he show you the knightwood oak?" his mother inquired. "It's his favorite tree."

It took me a moment to remember which one was the knightwood.

Caroline reminded me. "You can't have forgotten it. It's the biggest oak in the forest. It's gigantic."

"Oh, yes, of course." It was the isolated tree that had drawn my curiosity. "It's impressive, indeed."

"Did he tell you it's also called the Queen of the Forest?" Mrs. Goswick asked.

"No, I don't think he did."

"Remember, Mum," Caroline noted, "he used to call Aria the Queen of the Forest." And addressing me, she said, "Aria Lancaster, you know?"

"Yes, I remember." *How could I forget?* "Why did he call her the Queen of the Forest?"

"She was from London and loved the latest fashions. Julius thought she dressed like a queen, so he nicknamed her accordingly." Caroline laughed. "I thought she dressed like a peacock."

"Oh, he didn't like it when you said so," Mrs. Goswick reminded her daughter.

The knightwood oak was the oldest, largest tree in the forest—the Queen of the Forest. Julius had been anxious to bring up every species, but he had ignored the knightwood oak until I had asked him about it. Why? It should have been among the first he showed me.

That moment popped into my mind, and it all came back to me with astonishing clarity. While he spoke of some other tree, I had walked up the narrow trail and, oh, the smell. It was so sweet...coconut.

I sat bolt upright in bed. *For heaven's sake!* Aria spoke of a tree different from the rest and of a lovely smell, but perhaps the smell had come from the flowers nearby and not from the tree.

If he had killed Aria, that's where he would have buried her, under the shade of the Queen of the Forest. That's why he didn't bring attention to it. *No, it can't be. It's too easy.*

There was only one way to find out.

CHAPTER 21
THE QUEEN OF THE FOREST

The night was endless. There were sporadic rain showers, and the wind battered the windows nonstop. And Aria, oh, Aria—while I no longer feared her as much, I still couldn't trust her. I had no doubt she had power to harm and wouldn't hesitate to use that power. Furthermore, her screaming and door slamming made it hard to sleep. When dawn finally arrived, I had had enough time to ponder how to proceed. I had to do this alone, for Elliott couldn't physically help me, and besides, I was still upset with him. And after my vicious accusations, he probably didn't want to see me either.

Julius didn't show for breakfast, missing two meals in a row. Mrs. Goswick explained that he was under the weather and would spend the day at the cottage. I wondered how much Elliott's attack had to do with it. I used the unexpected news to my advantage and soon took to the grounds with more confidence. The gardener wouldn't come upon me and sabotage my plans.

I selected a shovel from the garden shed and, with Piper at my heels, crossed the front yard. About midway, Piper took off in the cottage's direction, leaving me to fend for myself.

I came to the main path and halted at the sight of a motorbike heading in my direction. I recognized Ross from miles away: the daring way he drove his bike, the absence of a helmet, his perfect form. Why were women such fools when it came to good-looking fellows? Ugh, I would never come up with a satisfying answer. At least this time I had a good reason for wanting to see him. A thank-you for the information he had acquired on my behalf was in order.

With a final roar, Ross's bike came to a stop, leaving a trail of dust behind him. The wind had done a number on his hair. He ran his fingers through it, bringing it back to its natural shape. "Good morning." He flashed a wide smile.

"To what do I owe the privilege of your visit, Captain?"

"A few things."

"Such as?"

He dismounted the bike and parked it off the path. "Such as this." He planted a kiss on my lips, one I was sure to never forget.

"Is that it?"

"You want more?" He smirked.

Though I should have been used to it by now, I let out a short laugh at his cavalier ways. "No, I wasn't referring to that." He stepped closer. I placed a hand on his chest, holding him back. "Let me clarify. What else brings you here besides wanting to kiss me?"

His lively expression became somber. "I wanted to check on you. I've been worried about you since the other night."

So much had happened since the night he'd found me in the woods with Samuel that I didn't know how I was. Aloud, I said, "I'm well," as my conscience smote me a little for not having thought much about him. I suppose I regarded him as a capable, well-trained man who could take care of his own problems—I'd no need to worry about him. In my defense, the past days had been a whirlwind of consuming events— stepping into Aria's realm; learning about Elliott's true state; the fiasco in London with Rosalynn; the discovery of Julius's hut and the ensuing confrontation—I could hardly spare time for my personal affairs until All Hallows's secrets were brought to light. Still, it was important to let Ross know that I cared about him.

"How are you? What did the general say about the plane crash? I wanted to ask you about it the other night, but there was no time."

"Nothing much yet, which is worrisome. The man is like a storm delayed. Once unleashed, its wrath will be fierce."

"He is a reasonable man," I said wistfully. "He won't be too harsh."

"I don't know about that. He hasn't earned his reputation by being lenient. But speaking of something more cheerful," he said. "Why were you so late coming back from town? You're the last person I expected to see in the woods."

"I stopped by the churchyard on my way back. The vicar came out, and you know how he can be so..."

"Overbearing."

"I shall call it communicative."

"The day I found you before the storm, you were also coming from the church," Ross said with a tone of curiosity.

"It's the fastest way out of town, that's all," I half lied.

"And the priest seems to be out there all the time."

"He must be bored locked up in that place all by himself. The thing is that our conversation was lengthy, and before I knew it, the day had gone. I came upon Mr. Goswick at the edge of the forest."

"That corroborates his story," Ross said.

"Whose story?"

"The priest's."

"You spoke to him?" I asked.

"I caught him in the woods."

"The same night?"

"Yeah, after our encounter."

"Seriously? What was he doing out there? I left him at the church."

"He said he felt uneasy about your safety, so he came after you. I sent him back to the parish. He was happy to comply, kind of contradicting his concern, wouldn't you say?"

"Once in the woods, he might have lost his bravado." It seemed unlike the vicar to have come after me. I would never have considered him as brave or caring. Even less so when he avoided crossing the churchyard at night. Perhaps I had misjudged him.

"Possibly." Ross's eyes narrowed as he ruminated. "That night was surreal. Seldom do we have people in the woods after dusk. Everyone who shouldn't have been there was there."

"Including me. I was at the wrong place at the wrong time," I said with a sigh.

"Did you see anyone else out there?"

"No, but you did." I held his gaze inquiringly.

"Whoever was hiding in the woods was an expert in the area. He eluded me easily." A puzzled look crossed his face. "Was Julius at the house when you got back?"

"Yes, along with his mother. Caroline was already at the cottage.'

"Is she still seeing Robertson?"

I nodded.

"Hmm, I wonder..."

"You think Robertson might have been out in the woods?" I inquired, the possibility not having occurred to me before.

"It wouldn't surprise me if he has been sneaking out to see her when he shouldn't be."

"It's most possible, but before I forget, thank you for the information you sent me about Rosalynn."

"Oh yeah, that's another reason I came. To make sure you got it."

"I did. I went to London and saw her. She is not Rose Lewis, but it was worth a try."

"You went to London?"

"It was a day trip. Rather fast."

"Sorry, it didn't turn out. I'll have my buddies look again. I'll let you know if they find something else."

"Thank you. Anything at all, even if it seems insignificant, could be helpful. Now, why else are you here?"

"Well..." A mischievous look clouded his eyes. "I went to town to pick up some parts, but the guy hasn't come back from London yet, so I took a detour in this direction."

I laughed. "So that's the real reason you came—to kill time."

"No, the real reason is because I wanted to see you."

I was thrilled he had come but afraid that whenever I saw him, it would be the last time. "Ross, I heard about the air raids. Will you be asked to fly?"

He shrugged as if not concerned, but I saw of flicker of worry in his eyes. "I might, but for now I am of more use fixing the planes. We don't have enough hands to keep up with it. Just this morning, six of them came back almost unsalvageable."

"What are you going to do?"

"Salvage them." Ross's gaze traveled to the shovel I had dropped on the grass. "What are you doing with that?"

"Digging."

"Digging what?"

It occurred to me that I couldn't trust anyone—except for the American. If I enlisted his help, my task would go much faster. "A body."

Ross threw his head back and laughed. I watched him in earnestness.

"You are joking, right?"

"Maybe." I wasn't sure what he'd think if I told him the truth. After all, it was a conjuncture based on Elliott's and my interpretation. I had no proof to back my suspicions—and mentioning the supernatural was out of the question. But even, if I convinced him that there might be a corpse in the yard, he might want to involve the police. And their presence would alert the killer that I was on his tracks—until I had solid evidence, that couldn't happen. "Well, most likely it's not a body, but there is something there. Maybe a hidden treasure? These woods are ancient, and who knows what we might find. The thing is that Piper is infatuated with the spot. Sniffing and scratching the surface with determination. She's never done that before."

"A bone?"

"She wouldn't be so excited for just a bone."

"A whole collection of bones?" he teased, not knowing how correct he might be.

"What is the likelihood of that?" I said playfully.

"Wait—are you are going to do it alone?"

"Julius is out of sorts today."

"Where is this project taking place?"

"About five minutes from here."

"In the woods?"

"Yes."

"Let me get this clear." His eyebrows shot up in disbelief. "You are going into the woods by yourself with a shovel."

"It's going to bother me until I check it out. Besides, I have nothing else to do."

He glanced at his wristwatch and scratched his head. "Do you have another shovel?"

"Are you going to help me?" I gave him a sweet smile.

"I think you are crazy, and that's the only reason I'll come with you."

"That's good enough."

After leaving his bike in the stable, we picked up another shovel and made our way to the majestic Queen of the Forest.

"Where exactly do you want to start?" Ross looked about the immense area.

"I'm not sure. Piper kind of goes around the whole tree."

"Where is the Great Dane when you need her?"

"She has her own schedule."

He gave me a look that said it all. We would be here forever, wasting our time. Thankfully, he didn't say it. Instead, he whistled softly as he meticulously paced the area around the tree. I followed suit, trying to find an odd spot on the otherwise insignificant space.

I noticed Ross searching farther and farther away from the tree. Seconds, then minutes went by, and the immensity and insanity of my plan started to sink in. *It's been too long. Anything that might have been has probably been erased by time.*

While I wrestled with my doubts, I reflected, "I shouldn't have dragged you into this. There is probably nothing here."

"Don't flatter yourself. I came of my own free will and choice."

"I'm happy you accept the responsibility."

He made another lap around the tree and, suddenly halting, announced, "Here, this is the spot."

I dashed to him. "How do you know?"

"Look, what do you see different?"

After a careful examination, I concluded, "The plants?"

"Yep. They are different from the rest, which wouldn't be strange if it wasn't for the fact that there are no others of their kind in sight. It's an isolated patch. Things don't grow like that in the wild."

"You think they were brought here," I said.

"That's right."

Inspecting the plants closer, I remembered. "Julius told me their names. There are some of them in the front garden. They are called peacock orchids." The irony was that Caroline had called Aria a peacock. The hair in my arms stood on end at the thought.

Ross inserted the shovel in the dirt among the orchids, but instead of sinking into the soft soil, it produced a sharp sound. He kneeled to peak beneath the greenery. "Wow, look at this." I knelt by him. He picked up a few pebbles. "This is gravel."

Nothing had to be said. Both of us instantly engaged in clearing the plants to reveal an area covered with the small pebbles.

"It's about one yard by two—the size of...a grave," Ross reasoned.

"It can't be a grave," I said, masking how shocked and delighted I was to have found a probable makeshift tomb. "No one would get away with it."

"Why not? We're far from the house. The area could have been well-prepped beforehand."

"That's true." Though I had dreamed about this moment, it felt surreal.

"This is going to be a bit harder than I expected." Surprisingly, Ross sounded excited. "Let's get going."

Once we broke through the gravel, the soil was soft. Either because Ross was on a tight schedule or he couldn't wait to find something, it didn't matter, but he brought up ten shovelfuls of dirt at the same time I managed five. One scoop after another, we worked in silence, watching the hole grow in size. My heartbeat became uncomfortably loud, and it had nothing to do with the manual labor. With each shovelful of dirt taken from the spot, I was closer to either succeeding or failing miserably. I silently prayed for the former.

"Blimey, Seraphina, tell him to put some muscle behind it!" Elliott exclaimed with a laugh from near the excavation site. "At this rate, you'll never find anything."

"For goodness' sake!" I cried out, startled.

"What's the matter?" asked Ross, instantly alert.

I was quick to make up an excuse. "Something brushed my foot, that's all."

Ross looked at me with concern. "Why don't you take a break?"

"Don't mind if I do." Dropping the shovel, I walked over to Elliott, who now lounged against a tree. I strategically positioned myself so Ross couldn't see my face or hear my voice. In a hushed tone, I taunted, "Would you like to help? Maybe you can try screaming in Ross's face like you did Julius's, and he might work faster. No, wait, why don't you bring up the dirt with your supernatural powers and make the task easier for all of us?"

"Listen, I'm sorry I lost my temper."

"I'm afraid sorry doesn't cut it."

"Don't ask me to leave. You know that this is important to me.'

Even though he had scared the living daylights out of me at Julius's hut, the sorrowful expression in his eyes softened the edge of my anger. "Stay, then, but don't interfere."

"Why are you digging here?"

"I'll tell you later."

Back to his usual self, Elliott said sarcastically, "I'm impressed with your helper. What have you offered him in exchange?"

"Don't be daft. He isn't getting anything out of it. And so you know, I was about to apologize for the things I said to you yesterday, but you've somehow made me reconsider."

"Don't fret. I don't need an apology."

"Good. Stop interrupting, then, and we'll get done faster."

I returned to Ross's side and stabbed the blade into the dirt, eager to achieve success. Ross had rid himself of his long-sleeved military shirt, displaying a white sleeveless undershirt. I took an admiring glance at his impressive physique.

"This has got to be the craziest thing I have ever done," Ross blurted.

"I doubt it…"

Leaning on the shovel for a quick rest, he chuckled. "What about you? Is this the craziest thing you have done?"

"Umm..." Speaking to ghosts was at the top of the list, but that I wouldn't share. "Probably."

"Did I hear hesitation in your answer?"

"No, I'm in earnest."

"You are a good liar, Seraphina."

"I'll take that as praise, Captain."

The sound of his shovel slicing through the soil resumed. One shovelful after another, he worked steadily and efficiently. Soon, his end of the excavation was about three feet deep. Mine was much shallower.

"Look, look!" Ross cried out. A piece of something like fabric poked through the clumps of dirt. He pulled on it. It came up a few inches, but it was only part of a larger piece still underground. "It's red."

"It's some type of cloth." *A dress, perhaps?*

Carefully, Ross dug around it until we saw what at first looked like brownish-white pieces of marble. With the aid of a stick, he brushed off some of the dirt. "Holy smokes! Bones! Human bones—it's a hand!" He jumped out of the hole, scarcely believing what he saw. "Come on, Seraphina, get out of there."

"No, wait," I objected. "We need to bring it up."

"Heck, no. That's a body, no doubt." His face turned white as the realization hit him. "We shouldn't tamper with it. If we do, we might destroy the evidence. I'll stay here. You get the constable—so much for joking about it."

He was painfully correct. Like it or not, I would have to endure the tedious process of a police investigation. "All right..." I hesitantly answered as Julius's sudden illness, not to mention his knowledge of the woods, came to mind. He could take out Ross in a heartbeat, especially when Ross wasn't carrying a gun.

Seeing that my words contradicted my actions, Ross asked a bit edgily, "Are you going or not?"

"I'm not so sure I should leave you here by yourself."

"Whyever not?"

"What if someone is not happy about this and knocks seven bells out of you?"

"Not a chance, but in that case, would you rather I go and you stay?"

I glowered at him. "No, we can both go."

"I'm not about to leave this place unguarded. Now, do me a favor. Stop wasting time and go."

For hours, All Hallows was in turmoil. Since London had jurisdiction over Burley, the constable placed guards over the grave until Scotland Yard arrived, which was surprisingly fast due to their presence in the vicinity attending a theft case. Led by Inspector Wilson, a tall man with a large nose, they were swift to set up a work perimeter around the grave.

Recalling what Ross had told Constable Jones, I smiled. "Yes, Piper was the one to bring our attention to the area."

"We need to speak to Piper, then," the constable had determined.

"Piper is a dog," Ross informed, laughing.

After explaining his involvement in finding the body, Ross kissed my cheek and left to pick up the replacement parts he needed for his planes. Having been informed of the new developments, Mr. and Mrs. Goswick appeared at the scene, a grim expression on their faces.

"You have been busy," said Samuel to me.

"Piper and I have too much time on our hands," I offered, playing down my involvement.

"Oh, Samuel," lamented the housekeeper, taking hold of her husband's arm as two men passed them, excavation tools in hand.

"This was a bad idea. We better go back to the house," Samuel decided, attempting to pull her after him.

"No, I want to be here." She folded her arms and rooted herself to the spot.

As the authorities started the extraction, a harrowing feeling arose in me. *Agony...raw physical and mental suffering that had stretched through time and worlds. She is here.*

My gaze jumped to the shadows among the trees. There stood the ghost of the woman in her black attire, silent and still, like an ancient statue. Her aura seemed to expand across the site like a dark cloud. And though the workers couldn't see the specter, she watched them with piercing eyes as they worked against the encroaching twilight. For her to be here, this had to be significant in her journey—so significant it had called her out of her circle of nothingness, for I doubt she had ever been spotted in daylight. This had to be her remains.

Contemplating Aria's lugubrious stance, I wondered what crossed her thoughts. Did she think about the killer carrying her along the path by the gorse flowers? Did the coconut-like scent come to her memory or the way he must have dropped her body into the darkness? The poignancy of the scene washed over me. My heart went out to her.

"Look at this," observed one of the men clearing the remains. "She was wrapped in a blanket of some sort." With much care, they retrieved the loose, decaying pieces.

Mrs. Goswick saw the cloth and produced a sound of alarm, as if she recognized it. Her husband tightened his arms around her, and in his customary manner, he said, "It will be all right, Agatha."

Seconds later, another man informed, "We are ready." A third man retrieved a large piece of cotton duck fabric from a nearby toolbox. "Careful, now. Slide it in slowly, all the way under her. Let's try to bring her up all at once."

I inched inconspicuously closer to the tomb. When no one objected, I came even closer. One glance at the cadaver and I regretted having done so. I would never forget the image. In the vestiges of a red dress, the corpse lay on her back. Long, shriveled strands of what had once been her beautiful hair caressed her bare skull. Where once there was flesh and blood, there was now a framework of bones, her dark, hollow eyes a never-ending abyss. Her hands were intertwined on top of her midsection and there, wrapped around her wrist, was a golden bracelet.

Aria moved to the edge of the excavation, and as she observed the corpse, her hands shook violently. The intensity in her eyes diminished, giving way to a new awareness. She pressed her hand to her pocket as if trying to extract something, but her hand came out empty. I took a few preventative steps back, fearing she would lash out at any moment.

"One, two, three," said the man in charge, and four of them pulled on the sheet to lift the corpse from the makeshift tomb.

Aria's attention returned to her dead body. For a split second, I thought I saw the scales of darkness fall from her eyes. There was a passing recognition in them and then a dim light—perhaps it was the rekindling of hope in her soul.

Her remains were carefully placed on a stretcher and carried to a waiting vehicle. Throughout the process of sifting through the dirt and surrounding area for items to be used as evidence and carefully retrieving her skeleton, the owner of the body stood nearby, witnessing it all. Now, Aria somberly walked behind the group carrying her mortal tabernacle, her head bowed. As I watched, I felt that a part of my heart went with her. No human being deserved to die and be buried the way she had. It was an abhorrent, far-reaching act of evil.

"If I had to guess, I would say the body belongs to Rose Lewis, missing heiress of All Hallows," opined Inspector Wilson.

"Could be, but we'll know for sure soon enough," Constable Jones responded.

Knowing that until Aria was identified, she wouldn't be properly buried, I asked, "What do you mean by soon enough?"

"A week or two," the constable answered in a dry tone.

"That long?" It was too long to wait, for Aria and for me.

Looking me straight in the eye, he responded, "The corpse waited for many years. It can wait a little longer, don't you think?"

No, I didn't think so. "Rose isn't the only woman who went missing in this area. Aria Lancaster, I understand, was a tenant here. She disappeared more recently than Miss Lewis."

The inspector took out his pocketbook. "What was that name again?"

"Aria Lancaster."

"Jones, do you know about her?"

"Yes, we have her file back at the station."

"I think it's time to pull it out," Wilson said.

"As soon as we get back," Jones replied.

"Aria...or Rose..." The murmur came from Mrs. Goswick, who had been mightily quiet until now. She turned into the consolation of her husband's embrace and sobbed softly.

"Don't cry, Agatha." At his words, she sobbed harder.

To the Goswicks, the inspector said, "We'll be back in the morning to meet with your son." He gave them a curious look before jotting down a few final lines in his tiny book. "Make sure he is here."

Julius isn't at the cottage? If he wasn't feeling well, where did he go?

"Until tomorrow," Samuel responded.

Two policemen were charged with the task of guarding the site. The rest of us, one by one, started to disperse. I strolled behind the Goswicks until I caught a glimpse of Elliott hiding in the penumbra of the trees. I slowed my steps until I was far enough from the couple ahead of me.

"Are you all right?" Elliott asked.

"None of this has sunk in yet."

"Who do you think it is?"

"It's Aria, all right. She stood by and watched the entire thing."

"Out here?" Elliott's eyes widened.

"Just a few feet away from her remains."

"The past must be coming back to her. And now that her body has been discovered, it has a strong pull. It calls for her. Hopefully her memories will be restored, and she'll remember who the killer is."

"Hopefully, but who knows how long the whole thing will take to unravel?"

"Well, for now, I believe she'll go wherever her body goes," Elliott said.

"Why?"

"She needs to know where her final resting spot is. There is closure in that. Then she will be able to move on...unless she wants revenge."

"I wouldn't blame her if she did. And speaking of blame, have you seen Julius? The police said he wasn't at the cottage."

"No, he isn't. I checked twice."

"Did you check his hut?"

"Not there either."

"Where could he have gone?" I wondered.

"Far from the police. This is not looking good for the Goswick men.

There is no way they didn't know about this. The Scotland Yard chaps are clever. They'll get to the bottom of this in no time."

I didn't want to listen to Elliott anymore. He made too much sense. However, despite Julius's strange behavior, I refused to believe he was a murderer. I guess Rose and Aria had thought as much, for both seemed to have trusted him, yet both were gone.

It had been an exhausting day of dealing with Scotland Yard. They had taken new statements from everyone at the house—everyone except Julius, who was nowhere to be found. Thankfully, General Lewis came by in the afternoon and ended some of the police's unnecessary pestering, vouching for the gardener's good character. He assured them they would be the first ones to know when Julius returned.

At last, the day was spent, and the commotion had settled. The house was unusually tranquil. The ghost of Aria did not resume her nightly routine. Elliott must have been correct, and she must have gone wherever her body had been taken, leaving All Hallows, for the first time in years, to the solitude of night.

In spite of the peaceful ambiance, I couldn't sleep. Throughout the long hours of stillness, my mind was plagued with thoughts and images of Julius's hut, Rose's necklace, Elliott's grievance, and, of course, Aria's remains coming out of the earth. The possibility of the killer being someone with whom I was acquainted had never seemed so real. Nevertheless, now that there was an open investigation and a new cadaver as evidence, I could breathe easier. Whoever the killer was, if he were still around, he would stay out of the spotlight as much as possible. I closed my eyes, thankful that things were finally moving in the right direction. Eventually, the stillness of the night absorbed me, and I fell into a much-needed slumber.

The plane flies higher and higher, reaching a dangerous altitude and speed. The pilot struggles quite uselessly to shake off the enemy at his tail. He takes a deep breath, knowing this is it—his last flight, his last moments alive.

The Nazi plane levels with his and unleashes a round of bullets. Constrained by the immediate damage, the British plane spirals downward. The pilot takes off his helmet. He cannot breathe, and seeing his face, I scream at him not to give up.

"It's okay, Seraphina. It's my time," Ross says.

"No! Stay with me!"

"I'll be with you always."

The plane crashes to the ground and explodes into a million pieces.

I opened my eyes, startled and disoriented, caught between the crash of the plane in my dream and the rapid tapping on the door.

Mrs. Goswick's alarmed voice called, "Miss Addington, are you awake? I need to speak to you."

She called again, heightening my awareness. I headed to the door with my eyes half shut, noticing that the day was young. I turned the key in the lock, and she pressed into the room like a cyclone.

"Good morning, miss. Captain Stewart wants to see you. I told him to come back later, but he insists on seeing you right away."

"Wait, what? Ross? What time is it?"

"Six o'clock. The audacity of the man—I'd barely started the day when he called."

Six o'clock. Did she say six o'clock? "I'll be down as soon as I dress."

"I'll let him know." Mrs. Goswick withdrew from the bedroom bearing the same irritation she'd entered it with. I had never seen her in such a disheveled state for something so insignificant, but I suppose the latest developments had a great influence upon her emotions.

Dashing into the dressing room, I splashed cold water on my face. If Ross couldn't wait to speak to me, something must have happened. Whatever it was, my heart told me I wouldn't like it. Almost unconsciously, I changed out of my nightgown and rushed through the hallway and down the staircase.

"Ross."

He stood in the sitting room, staring at the dead hearth. His full brown uniform spoke of change. Meeting me by the sofa, he took my cold hands into his warm ones. "I'm sorry. I know it's super early, but I had to come." He looked pale, and there were lines of weariness under his eyes. I had never seen him like this.

"Are you ready to dig up more bodies?" I teased.

He gave me a weak smile. "I wish that were the case."

"What's the matter? Did the general chastise you for crashing the plane?"

"As far as that goes, I had to help with kitchen duties."

"Not your forte. You look overworked."

"Yeah, you should try it sometime," he joked.

"Amusing as that sounds, you aren't here just to tell me that."

It was obvious he wanted to speak but was having trouble. Instead, with a sadness in his eyes, he leaned close and allowed his lips to fall upon mine. He wrapped his arms around my waist as I intertwined my fingers at the back of his neck. The minutes that followed were too short. When he stepped away, I yearned for him to be close again.

Perceiving his intensifying sadness, I encouraged, "Whatever it is, don't have pity on me. I can take it."

"I...don't know how to say this."

"Please, tell me."

Ross inhaled and exhaled deeply, releasing some of the tension. "I'm leaving for London."

"London? Why?"

"The Royal Air Force has requested pilots. Last week was carnage for our men. We lost too many." He paused, and my heartbeat seemed to do the same, awaiting the rest of the information. "I've been assigned to lead a squadron."

His words sounded like a death sentence. "You are going to lead an air raid?"

Ross nodded. "I wanted to see you before I left. My train leaves in two hours. I'm going with three others."

"I can't believe it." Had my dream been a portent of things to come?

"Me neither, but it was always a probability."

For the longest moment, we just stood there contemplating each other, dreading to say what crossed our minds, dreading to say good-bye. Tears welled up behind my eyes and threatened to surface. I studied his strong features and kind eyes to engrave the memory in my soul forever. I did not ever want to forget him. Ross embraced me. I threw my arms around him, feeling his warmth envelop me.

He lowered his forehead to touch mine and whispered, "Please stay safe. Remember that the killer is still out there, so don't do anything stupid. I'll come back to you, I promise." His words were like an echo from the past.

A profound pain seized my heart. Was this how Rose felt when Elliott made the same promise? I never imagined I'd have to deal with the same heartrending reality. My eyes betrayed me. Tears ran down my cheeks unrestrained.

I felt lost without Ross. I could have never anticipated I would miss him this much. And even when it had only been hours since his departure, the hole his absence left in my heart taught me a simple truth: I loved him. My feelings for him weren't a fleeting fancy. They were an intense and deep affection, binding me to him. The possibility of not seeing him again was bitter. Why hadn't I realized how much I loved him before he left? He shouldn't have gone to war without knowing how I truly felt about him.

Keep breathing. Keep moving, Seraphina. All this time at All Hallows, as the ghost of the woman had harassed me, I'd held on to the knowledge that the darkest hour was just before dawn—and it had saved me from her grip every night. Ironically, now that she was gone, dawn had come, but it had never been so dark.

CHAPTER 22

DEATH RETURNS TO ALL HALLOWS

A soft, pleasant afternoon breeze swept through the garden. I lingered on the wooden bench for the longest time, my thoughts with Ross. So much had taken place since Mr. Craven had left me and Piper at the edge of the field. So much that when Elliott was suddenly beside me, it felt as natural as daylight.

"I understand how you feel, Seraphina."

"I never thought it would come to this."

"Many do return, you know," Elliott soothed.

I smiled sadly. Though his words were designed to offer consolation, the dogfights took the lives of more than half of our pilots. Ross's departure had left me feeling unbalanced. He had been a solid anchor since the day I'd come to All Hallows.

"I'm not sure where to go from here," I confessed.

"Me neither." Elliott scooted closer and placed an arm around my shoulders. "It's just you and me now." His closeness had never felt so comforting.

"Something good will come from Aria's investigation. Don't give up hope just yet." Though I intended well, my words sounded empty. All this time, my ghost friend and I had encouraged each other onward. But I feared we both knew the end of our quest was near.

"I'll do my best," Elliott responded.

"Have you seen Julius today?"

"No, no sign of him. But I did see someone else sneaking around Aria's grave."

"Who?"

"Albion Baker," Elliott informed.

"Are you sure?"

"Of course I'm sure. The man is unmistakable. I followed him here."

"He came to the manor?"

"No, just close enough to get a good look. If you ask me, I think he was casing the house."

"He is probably dying to find out more about the discovery, but after the way our last meeting ended, he might not dare to visit."

Elliott laughed. "He might be more afraid of you than of the dead."

"Let's keep it that way."

Elliott got to his feet. "Listen, Seraphina, while we wait for the police to do their work, I'll spend more time at the stream."

"Why?"

"I need time to sort things out. I need to consider a future without Rose."

Would that be my fate as well? Would I need to consider a future without Ross?

"Please don't go too far. Like you said, it's just you and me now."

The day had passed in an unusually uneventful manner, and I felt Elliott and I were in a suspended state, just waiting for news. Late into the night, my mind finally quieted down, and my body fell into slumber, but the stillness wasn't to last. Deep within my altered consciousness, I heard a voice calling. It was distant, and I dismissed it until an intense vibration, as if I had touched an electrical cord, jolted me.

"Wake up! Seraphina. Wake up now!"

I forced my eyes open, not sure if it was real or a dream. The bedroom was lit by the moonlight coming through the windows. It was a bright moon with a clear light that chased most of the shadows away. I propped myself on one elbow and stared at the figure sitting beside me, his hand on my arm.

"Elliott? What are you doing here?"

"Listen," he said in an urgent voice. "Where is the gun the general gave you?"

"The gun?" Had I heard him correctly? I had to be dreaming.

"Is it here in the room?"

"Yes...it is." My head whirled, and I lowered it to the pillow. My eyelids closed. Elliott shocked me again, and this time I felt as if I had been hit by lightning. Like a steeple set ablaze, I shot from the bed.

"It's not a dream. It's not a dream," I mumbled to myself, shaking off the drowsiness of sleep.

"Listen, you must act quickly. The killer is downstairs." Elliott spoke so close to me, his face almost touched mine.

"Wait, what?" I looked at him in confusion.

In a rapid string of words, Elliott said, "He entered the Goswicks' bedroom last I saw him. He'll be up here in no time."

"The Goswicks..."

"Quick, prop the pillows as if they were you."

Instantly, I became the soldier, following his orders without question.

"There, that's good," Elliott approved as I covered the pillows with the coverlet, and without respite, he ordered again, "Now, for heaven's sake, get the gun."

I pulled the nightstand drawer open and fumbled for the gun. Once I had it, he instructed me to hide behind the door, closer to the corner of the room.

"Is it loaded?"

"It is."

"Good. Now, don't speak. He can hear you, but not me. You have the advantage of being aware and ready. Don't give it away."

When I opened my mouth to do exactly what he told me not to, Elliott placed a finger on my lips. Before he could shock me again, I pressed my lips into a tight line.

He continued. "Trust me. You'll be all right. But you must do as I tell you. He is incredibly skilled. I tried to give him a welcoming fright, but he either doesn't see me or he ignored me. And no, I did not see his face. It's covered. The only thing I'm sure of is that he's here to kill you."

I flinched at my dearest friend's words. Death had entered the manor once again, and I felt its chill running down my spine. Knowing that I was trapped in the bedroom and that once he came in I had no way to escape, my natural inclination was to flee. But the windows were too high. I would break every bone in my body if I jumped. The only escape was through the hallway leading to the staircase. I would run straight into him.

Elliott, keenly aware of my predicament, had developed a plan. "He'll search for you. He'll force the door open. Once he walks in, shoot him."

I had never shot anyone, and now that the moment was upon me, I wasn't sure if I could bring myself to do it. It seemed too final a thing, the repercussions too severe.

Seeing my apprehension, Elliott affirmed, "If you don't neutralize him, you'll be dead before you know it. This is not a game. Let him near the bed, then shoot him and bolt to the front door. Then get on to the Goswick's cottage, to Caroline."

I produced a small movement of assent with my head, and I wondered if Julius would also be at the cottage.

Elliott's instructions continued. "Don't let the discharge of the gun take you by surprise. Remember that it will shake and deafen you briefly. But it must not paralyze you. You shoot and run—you shoot and run."

He made it sound easy. I had never wished he were alive more than I did now. Even with his lame arm, I had no doubt he would manage better than me. I tightened my hands around the weapon. I could do this. I had to.

"Don't move a muscle. I'll check where he is."

Elliott went right through the wall and out into the hallway. Now that it was just me, I started to shiver, making it difficult to concentrate. The pounding of my heart and my breathing were so loud that, try as I might, they were the only things I could hear. And thank heaven Piper was at the cottage. I could never have done this with her barking and giving me away.

Elliott materialized next to me. "He is coming up the stairs. Now stay focused."

The doorknob rattled softly.

"He is picking the lock." Elliott stated the obvious.

My breathing accelerated as the doorknob slowly turned, and the door parted almost imperceptibly. If I had been asleep, I would not have heard it.

He is coming in—he is coming in.

Placing his hand on my shoulder, my friend stated, "You can do this. Relax."

As Elliott had anticipated, the assassin—a tall man dressed in black from head to toe, from what I could tell—moved swiftly to the bed.

I lifted my arms, aiming at him, and though it was clear I had to carry on with the plan, my conscience shrank at killing another human being. Elliott stood behind me. He wrapped his arms around mine, guiding my aim at the target. "Now, shoot," he ordered calmly.

I pressed the trigger on the ancient gun. As the bullet flashed out, its force undid the steadiness of my hands. In the confined space, the noise rang in my ears like the blast of the bombs falling on London. If the killer groaned in pain, I did not hear it. He turned toward me, his hands clenching his left side. I'd hit him, but not where I'd intended.

Elliott, who could think clearer than me, cried out, "Run, Seraphina! Run!"

I made it out of the room, the killer on my heels. He was a hunter, and I was his quarry, but his injury allowed me an advantage. I bolted like a racehorse, the people from the paintings watching my flight down the semi-lit corridor. I had to reach the stairs, which had never seemed so distant.

Almost there.... Instinctively, I slowed upon reaching the edge of the steps to avoid tumbling down them—I immediately knew it was the wrong choice.

My delay was enough for the assassin to clutch my arm and pull me back. He flung me against the wall and away from the steps with inhuman force. The back of my head and my spine hit the solid surface, disorienting me. My knees buckled. I plunged to the floor, and so did the gun. The killer kicked it out of reach.

"Seraphina, get up. Fight!" Elliott commanded, kneeling beside me.

I looked up at the menacing figure standing in my path. His overpowering presence instilled a sudden awareness in me. He would wait for me to make the next move before striking again, for he toyed with his victims. He wounded them and found pleasure in their fear.

Elliott took a firm stance in front of the killer, yelling threats and even swinging at him. If he were mortal, his punches would have shattered the man's nose and maybe even held him back momentarily. But whatever efforts the ghost made against him, they were all in vain.

It's up to you, Seraphina. Make it count, I encouraged myself. With that terrifying notion, I pressed my hands against the floor and raised my lower body. Simultaneously, I kicked his left shin with one solid blow, assuring the wave of pain climbed his leg to the bullet wound. With a painful shriek, he fell against the opposite wall. His brief distraction granted me renewed energy. Despite the awful throbbing at the back of my skull, I made for the staircase.

Elliott shouted, "Don't stop! Get out of the house and into the open! It'll be dawn soon." His voice was so loud I wondered if he was screaming in my ear. "I'll go for help."

Help? The probability of Elliott finding help was almost nonexistent. Even if Julius was back, after the assault in the woods, he wouldn't listen to Elliott. I had a feeling my friend simply didn't want to see me die.

One, two, three... I had never noticed how many steps there were until now. *Four...*

My assailant pressed a hand against my back, shoving me down the staircase.

Everything was a blur. I was airborne for a minute, and then my body hit the wooden steps, whirling and tumbling in syncopation with the scream in my throat. I landed at the base of the stairs and managed to crawl a few feet before I fell onto my back. And for an instant, I lost any notion of where and who I was.

When the black silhouette straddled my body, it all came back with terrifying lucidity. He sat below my torso, his legs pinning my arms to the floor. I struggled to move, but my strength was no match for his. He carefully brought the back of his hand to caress my face—a gesture of evil pleasure.

"Why are you doing this?" I asked in a muffled voice, struggling uselessly to get a good look at him in the darkness of the foyer. "Who are you?" He would not answer. His hands tightened around my neck. This was it—the very moment Aria and the other girls had lived through. My turn had come too rapidly.

Incongruously, now that death was imminent, my desire to live flared, my mind quickening. With tremendous effort, I allowed my muscles to relax. My whole body softened, producing a similar effect on my assailant—his strength lessened as well. Seizing this small window of opportunity, I summoned all the energy left within me and freed my arms from beneath his legs. Then I reached for his head, arms, legs, anything I could grab to tear him apart. I punched, scratched, pulled—but it wasn't enough.

His hands constricted like a snake around my neck. A dry, searing pain filled my throat. I gasped for air. I was choking, drowning. I dug my fingers into his eyes but without force. He flinched but did not let go. He squeezed one last time, and my arms dropped to my sides. My body gave a small, quick movement as I let out a final breath.

In the flip of a switch, my spirit form stood beside the terrible scene of my murder. I felt no discomfort, no scorching in my throat, no aches in my arms or legs. The killer was still on top of my body, observing my stillness, assuring himself that I was gone—and I was. I was dead.

What was time? Nothing but a memory. For in this other dimension, it moved at a slower pace. I was aware of my life as never before. I clearly remembered the smallest things, the ones almost impossible for most humans to recall—even my days as an infant and child.

More poignantly, I now comprehended much of what Elliott had said about this dimension. Unthinkably but completely in balance with this sphere was my knowledge of its laws and boundaries. Petrifying as it was, my life had been taken. In my heart, I had always wanted to bring the assassin to justice, and that sentiment hadn't changed with death. On the contrary, having suffered death by his hands, it was cemented within me. It was a chain that bound me to earth. The desires of my heart had determined my fate.

I would now be the ghost who roamed the halls of All Hallows, waiting for justice. What had the vicar said so long ago? Oh yes—*"I guess that's the sequence of life. One always comes to replace another."*

My failure was a burden I would carry for ages. I had failed Elliott, Rose, Aria, and Ross. My heart shrank at the thought that if Ross returned from his mission, he would not find me. Perhaps my body would never be recovered. Excruciatingly, I realized that the worst agony would come if, as with Elliott, people couldn't interact with me. Especially Ross. A deep sorrow enshrouded me to think of what could have been and now would never be. I now understood my ghost friend only too well.

Refocusing, I determined that if my spirit self and mind were all I had left, I'd better safeguard them. I wouldn't let tragedy fill me with despair and take me into the shadows like it had Aria. My concentration returned to the assailant. He still sat on top of my lifeless form, making sure the breath of life had left me for good.

"Seraphina—what in the name of..." Elliott's voice trailed off.

I ran into his arms. Now that we both were in spirit form, embracing him felt as natural as if we were mortal. "Forgive me. I tried. I swear I tried."

"No, you can't be dead," said Elliott in disbelief. "You're too young. There is much you need to experience in life."

I looked up at him. Being in the same spiritual plane, I was able to see that his light shone from within. At once, I understood how the light signified the attributes he had developed in mortality—among them humility, perseverance, and unadulterated love. Yes, he was one I could trust and follow in this other life, even if he lost his temper on occasion.

"Elliott, I now understand how things work. I'll be stuck here in between worlds. My heart's desire to bring the killer to justice traps me to the earth."

"No...no..." murmured Elliott. "There is a little time left."

"I hope you can forgive me, for I will never forgive myself for failing you," I said.

"Don't talk nonsense. Everything will be all right. I'm the one who failed you, but not this time."

Letting go of me, he marched toward my inert form. At the same time, the assassin, seemingly satisfied with his success, walked away from it. Stunning me, Elliott entered my corpse, and I felt a pull, like from a giant magnet. Without a choice, I gravitated to my body, peacefully merging with it. At once, oxygen filled my lungs, bringing life back to me. Body and spirit had been reunited. I gasped for more air, coughing and choking as I sat up, feeling the awful ache and heaviness of mortality returning.

The killer's attention snapped toward me, and he swore in disbelief, surely receiving a greater shock than I had. How could I possibly be alive? I had died. He had made sure of it.

Elliott... I looked around at the fading shadows of the foyer. With slumped shoulders and a slow step, as if he had been shot a thousand times, the ghost ambled toward the sitting room.

The assailant started back toward me. I was in no shape to fight him. I scooted away on the hard stone floor like a mouse cornered by a cat, and I shrieked as he stooped over me with outstretched arms. My vision became hazy, and it traveled beyond his frame. A large figure overshadowed him. The newcomer swung something in the air and hit the killer on the back of the head, causing him to collapse like a bag of lead. In sheer relief and amazement, I rubbed my eyes to make sure I could see clearly.

"You all right?" asked the voice of my savior.

"Julius?" I muttered, finding it difficult to speak. I reached up to feel the skin on my neck, fearing it would fall off, it throbbed so painfully.

Allowing the shovel in his hand to fall to his side, Julius reached for my arms as I struggled to my feet, swaying and clutching at him for support.

"You are all right," Julius asserted.

"Yes," I responded in a hoarse voice.

"Good." He flipped on the light.

Our eyes flew to the unconscious man sprawled at our feet. No doubt the same question ran through both our minds: who was this evil being who had caused such profound damage to the living and dead? In the light, I could see that his mask consisted of thick bandages wrapped around his face, like the ones used at the hospital but black. They were topped by a wool hat of the same color. The bandages not only hid his face but also distorted the shape of his head. A clever disguise.

Julius and I looked at each other and nodded. He knelt beside the still form and unceremoniously started to unwrap his face. With each layer that came off, I thought of his victims and the suffering he had inflicted. Soon his face would be exposed, and he would be held accountable for the lives he had taken.

As I saw his chin, then his nose, and finally his eyes, I was rendered speechless. For a moment, everything I knew as reality was shaken. Nothing made sense, and I felt utterly lost. *Why, General Lewis? Why?*

Julius stood and threw a look in the direction of the shovel. But whatever he had in mind was interrupted by the frostiness that suddenly filled the foyer. Together, we turned toward the staircase. Enveloped in a cloud of terror, the ghost of Aria Lancaster descended the steps in her full mourning attire, a veil covering her face. Unlike at any other time, she proceeded with purpose and apparent recognition.

Bringing with her an immobilizing force, she stood between Julius and me and stared at the man on the floor. Aria's veil, like a leaf in a soft breeze, swung back, revealing her face. I glanced at Julius. His snow-white, stony face revealed that he had not seen this specter before.

I wanted to reassure Julius, but I couldn't move or speak, and I had the feeling Julius wasn't faring any better. Whatever the ghost had in mind, we would not be allowed to interfere.

Aria made a small movement with her head, and the general's eyes snapped open. Arm outstretched, she neared him, and to my horror, his body started to rise from the floor until it was suspended in midair. The woman's gaze dug into the general's, and his body convulsed as if trying to break free of her spell. Perspiration ran down his forehead, and his countenance registered an agonizing dread. I reckoned the man had experienced fear in war, but I had the notion that not much could have terrified him to this extent.

"And so, here we are again," Aria said to him. "Pretty close to where we left off, isn't it? Well, no. Last time, I was alive, and now I am dead. Let's make things even, shall we? Since I can't come back to life, you'll have to die." Aria raised her hand, and he gave a violent jerk. "What is it, darling? Do you have something to say?" I couldn't be sure, but I suspected each word she spoke pierced his heart like a blade, causing him physical suffering.

His voice, slow and broken, said at last, "Don't do this."

"The unmerciful asking for mercy." Aria laughed, a damning sound. "You seduced me and stole my innocence and my heart. And as if that wasn't enough, you took my life. I loved you. For all the eternities, I'll regret having done so." She moved her head up and down slowly. Each time it did, his body slammed against the wall.

I felt an enormous pressure building inside me. I wanted to scream. I wanted to stop this madness, even if he deserved it, but I simply couldn't move. She was going to tear him apart right in front of our eyes.

The general was thrown again, and this time he stayed there, pinned on the plastered surface, just inches off the floor. "Good-bye, my darling," Aria said venomously as the general's head smacked the wall with terrifying force and blood dripped from his mouth.

As I braced for the end of the merciless attack, I glanced at Julius and noticed the room growing lighter. Daylight moved in, like a peaceful river flooding the area. Aria sighed deeply and turned her back on the assassin. Immediately, his body slid down the wall, and for the second time in the early dawn, he collapsed onto the floor. The woman beheld Julius for an instant, and a smile crossed her face. She then moved to the door and walked out of the house. Julius and I were instantly released from her power. I stared after Aria, wondering if daylight had tamed her or if she had chosen to let John Lewis live.

The man moaned, his body a mangled heap on the floor. Yet Julius and I, though able to move freely now, remained still, processing what we had just witnessed. Once the initial shock wore off, thoughts of the Goswicks compelled me to action.

"Julius—your parents—we need to check on them," I croaked.

Julius stared at me, shock lingered in him.

"Watch him." I glanced at the general. "I'll be back."

I stumbled through the hallway leading to their quarters, praying they had been spared. Flinging the door open, I found that Samuel lay on the ground near the footboard. His wife was on the bed, facedown, her hands tied behind her back. A long strip of silk had been placed over her mouth and fastened at the back of her head, preventing her from speaking.

"Mrs. Goswick, please don't move. I'll have you untied in no time." I worked as fast as I could, all the while offering a silent prayer that they were alive.

"Oh, Miss Addington, you are all right. You are all right!" She took my face into her hands, clearly having a hard time believing I was well. "What happened to the intruder?"

"Julius knocked him unconscious."

"Oh, my Julius. How is he?"

"He is fine. Everything is fine."

"Oh, the old man!" Terror struck her as she moved to her husband. "He hit Samuel in the head with a blunt object." Dropping beside her husband, she called out, "Samuel, Samuel, wake up, dear. Wake up." He produced a few grunts, and his eyelids parted. "Oh, dear. How are you feeling? Speak to me."

"Stop the fuss, woman. You are giving me a headache," he groaned.

"Thank heaven. He is as good as always," Mrs. Goswick reassured.

"We need to call for a doctor and the police," I decided at once. "You take care of him, and I'll fetch Caroline from the cottage."

As I turned to leave, the housekeeper's words struck me. A blunt object? "Mrs. Goswick, what type of blunt object?"

"I'm not sure. It might have been a gun."

Goodness gracious! A gun. He would kill Julius.

I returned to the foyer to find it deserted.

NO, NO, NO— Where are they? I scanned the area in a frenzy.

The men were gone, but how? Why? The front door was still open, and I hurried outside. The rising sun shone in its full splendor. Against its light, I saw Julius pulling the unconscious, half-dead man toward the trees. *Where in the world is he going?*

They were quite far already. Ignoring the pain in my body, I clenched my teeth and dashed across the lawn. It was not long before Julius's destination became clear. He was heading to the Queen of the Forest.

Closing the gap between us, I shouted, "Julius, stop!" My throat smarted.

Things were happening too swiftly for me to come up with a plan. All I knew was that I needed to deescalate the situation so the general could be brought to justice, instead of Julius dying in prison for killing him. When the Queen of the Forest came into view, I pushed my legs to go faster.

The gardener halted next to Aria's empty grave and thrust the killer over the edge. Then, with his bare hands, he started to push the dirt in on top of him.

Panting, I fell beside Julius at last. "Please, stop. He is not worth it."

With rage in his eyes, he addressed the man being buried alive. "You killed Rose. She was my friend. You killed Aria. She was my friend."

"Please, Julius, you are not like him."

"He killed my love. He killed Beatrice. She was beautiful and good." Julius picked up a rock of considerable size and threw it at the general. The latter produced a shrill cry. "Bloody coward. You framed me."

"Julius, what are you saying?"

"He killed Aria and left her in my hut. The police needed a scapegoat, and who better than me? I had already found Beatrice's body, and they considered me a suspect. I had to do something." His large eyes were filled with remorse, and he shook his head. "I shouldn't have. I shouldn't have."

Staggered, I reflected, "You panicked and buried her..." As if what he had done wasn't horrid enough, he had lived with the secret for so long. Aria had been so flummoxed by her death that not only had she forgotten who'd taken her life but also who had buried her.

"And there hasn't been a single day since that I haven't thought about her. I found her. He left her there like an animal. I tried to bring her back, but she was cold—too cold."

Hoping to placate him, I said, "I'm so sorry, Julius. You didn't deserve to go through that."

"See this?" Julius pointed at the scars on his face. "Long ago, I chased him into the woods, and he fought like the coward he is. When I was about to undress his face, he cut mine with a blade, but he couldn't fool me. I knew it was him all along."

I could only imagine the general being chased by Julius—the hunter being hunted by a mightier hunter. It must have led to a desire to destroy the gardener by framing him with the murders. And unjustly, every time Julius looked in the mirror, he had been reminded of the killer and his victims.

The anger in the gardener's eyes increased, and grabbing another handful of rocks, he flung them at the man in the grave.

"Julius," I called, shaking his arm. "I know the girls were your friends, but am I not your friend too?"

"And he almost killed you."

"But you saved me. Think about it. Dying right now is too good for him. He must suffer the humiliation of a trial and hang for his crimes. Aria spared his life. You must do the same." I got to my feet and extended my hand to him. "Come on, Julius, get up. Take my hand."

The internal struggle was evident. Julius's gaze held mine and then traveled to the man in the grave. His hands turned into fists.

"Julius—take my hand," I said again.

After several moments, his rough hand grasped mine. Along with his physical assent came immense inner strength. Like a phoenix rising from the ashes, Julius had subdued his ire and shown mercy to a man who had given his victims none. Then I did something I would have never dreamed of when I'd first met Julius. I embraced him. The security of his arms disarmed me, and the severity of all that had taken place found me broken. Tears welled up and fell from my eyes. Julius produced a few convulsive gasps, and like an innocent child, he sobbed.

We had suffered much. In more than one way, we understood each other. Not only had we both agonized over the killer, but also our burden of seeing the otherworldly united us. I suspected that knowing of each other's gifts brought a measure of peace to his soul as it did to mine. We weren't alone on this strange path.

At length, our sobbing diminished, and a soft moan from the grave drew our attention. Julius's hands turned to fists. Keeping him under control, I reiterated, "He will hang. It's the best punishment for him."

"Hang, yes, he will hang, all right," agreed Julius. No doubt, if he could, he would hang the general from the Queen of the Forest at that instant. The idea wasn't totally repugnant, but it wasn't to be.

"We need to get him back to the manor," I decided.

Immediately, Julius jumped into the grave and brought the wounded man to the level ground, wasting no time sticking the end of his boot into the general's injured hip. Blood seeped through his clothing and he shrieked in pain, writhing on the ground like the miserable worm he was. His eyelids blinked open, and his gaze pierced mine like a dagger.

In a broken voice, he said, "I knew you would be my undoing."

"All this time you pretended to be a friend," I sputtered, "and went as far as giving me the gun."

"And you shot me with it. I didn't think you capable of it."

"That's where you went wrong."

"Why did you kill those girls?" Julius kicked him again. "Miserable coward!"

"Women like to play games until it's too much for men to bear but I did love her..." Did I detect an actual hint of remorse?

"Who are you speaking of?"

"Five years—that was the time allotted Helen and me," he choked. "But her memory endured through the suffering of others."

Helen? Like a window opening to let the light in, clarity filled my mind. *Your memory will forever live in the wind that fills the New Forest.* The answer had been there all along, engraved in Helen's headstone. The wind carried the news, the memories, and the stories of the forest. Every time the forest wept for a new victim, it remembered all those who had suffered the same fate. *She also passed away young... Could it be?*

Her piercing eyes from the portrait came into my memory. She hadn't been trying to chase me away from her husband but from the monster he had become. She had tried to warn me, and in the end, her gun had been the beginning of his fall.

As the conviction settled in me, I said matter-of-factly, "You killed Helen. She was your first victim, wasn't she?"

"He did?" Julius threw me a startled look.

The general smiled sardonically—a gesture that confirmed my suspicions and attested that he might never confess to his crime. "Life is unfair," he said evasively. "One must bring to pass their own justice. Women mock men, but I spared others the same fate by letting them go to war."

"What are you saying?" I asked.

Julius was quicker to understand the intriguing words. "He speaks of Ghost. He sent Ghost to war to die," Julius reasoned.

I reflected aloud, "Rose and Elliott came to you for help, not knowing that you were behind the infamous call."

"Elliott. I'd forgotten all about that peasant. He lasted longer than I expected. We'll see how long this other one lasts."

"This other one? You are speaking of Ross." The realization hit me like a thousand bricks falling on my head. The maliciousness of this man was almost too much for me to take in. "As a mechanic, he was more valuable here than up in the air, but just like you did to Elliott, you sent Ross to die," I sputtered with indignation. "How could you?"

He answered with another question, "How can you be alive? I saw you die." His eyes bored into mine, and I saw a darkness in them I had not noticed before. He wasn't the only inhabitant of his body. Some devilish influence cohabitated within him.

"When you hang for your crimes, you'll understand a few things about life and death. And I hope the last thing you remember is your failure to kill me."

Coughing up a little blood, with great effort, he turned to his side while managing to keep up his rant. "Stewart saved you that night in the forest. If he hadn't been tracking me, I would have killed you. What a pity. His life might have been spared if he hadn't interfered. The meddling fool captured your heart before I even had the chance."

"My heart?" So there it was—he'd allured his victims by enamoring them. "You never had a chance in the first place. Let's go," I said to Julius. "We've heard enough from this piece of rubbish. Take him back to the house and make sure to drag him across the worst terrain possible."

With a broad smile, Julius took hold of the general's ankles. However, the latter wasn't ready to give up just yet, and with the training of years, his hand moved to the holster on his hip. With the rapid turn of events, I had forgotten all about the gun.

"No!" I screamed.

Julius dropped the general's legs and swooped down upon him. One strong tug was enough to disarm the latter, but not enough to calm Julius's nerves. His fist struck the general in the face. He then secured the weapon at his waist and grabbed the ankles of the now-unconscious killer to resume his walk back to the manor.

John Lewis was taken into custody. Considering the high standing he held in society, this was sure to make headlines for weeks to come. Oh, my poor father. Mother would torture him until the day she died for having entrusted me to the killer's hands. I would send them a telegram as soon as I could. For now, we weren't to leave the house until Inspector Wilson arrived.

At present, the events of the past few hours had the disorienting hallucinatory effect of a dream. Mr. Goswick peacefully rested in his quarters after being seen by the doctor. He had suffered a concussion but nothing time and ice wouldn't heal. Julius and Caroline took to the gardens. I sat with Mrs. Goswick in the kitchen, feeling sick to my stomach. The doctor had medicated my bodily injuries, but there was nothing he could do about the hurt in my heart. Assimilating that General Lewis was the killer was beyond appalling—my family had trusted the man since I can remember. Furthermore, the general's brutal attack and the fact that he sent Elliott and Ross to die was a fresh wound. A wound that I feared would take quite some time to heal.

Noticing how the housekeeper's hands shook as she drank her tea, I assumed she felt much like me, tired and vulnerable. She tried to speak, but no sound came out. Instead, she broke into a deep sob, releasing a wave of emotion.

Patting her arm, I offered, "Mrs. Goswick, it's been horrid, but I think we'll be just fine."

She pulled a handkerchief from her dress pocket and pressed it to her eyes. I had the feeling that rather than wiping her eyes dry, she wished to conceal them from me.

In between sniffs, she started, "All these years, I have lived in terrible fear...of the awful possibility that the killer was my own son."

Her confession left me dumbfounded and ashamed all the same. I had been among those guilty of second-guessing Julius. But a mother doubting her son—I couldn't envisage what that must have felt like. Though I felt she was about to tell me.

She crumpled the handkerchief in her hand, held my gaze, and poured out her soul. "My poor Julius has the noblest heart. I never doubted that. But something doesn't function quite properly in his brain. In the back of our minds, his father and I have worried nonstop that he might have committed those awful killings without thoroughly understanding what he did. Whenever he went hunting and returned with a dead animal, I withered with trepidation. I couldn't stop thinking he was capable of killing but not capable of distinguishing between human and animal life.

"You see, I had grown so unhinged I forbid him to hunt. But then I dreaded the possibility that in having done so, instead of fixing the problem, I'd made it worse."

Now, I understood Julius's words about Rose not censuring him for hunting. Rose saw it as a harmless and natural part of him, and she had been correct. And his hut...maybe someday he would tell his mother about it, for I had an inkling his father already knew.

After harshly blowing her nose in the handkerchief, the housekeeper continued. "His behavior and lack of emotion left too much to the imagination, and the imagination, if not kept in check, can be treacherous, though he always maintained he had nothing to do with the murders. Of course, when Aria vanished and Samuel found the fresh patch of flowers by the Queen of the Forest, we looked the other way. We did nothing to challenge Julius's work. And when the police searched the property, we covered for him." New tears welled up in her eyes and rolled down her cheeks. "Oh, the nightmares that possessed me during those nights...the image of my poor Julius hanging...the image of poor Aria dying. And now I was sure the old sins had come back to haunt us."

"Mrs. Goswick, we now know with surety who the killer is. And as far as I'm concerned, General Lewis murdered and buried Aria," I affirmed. "In the woods, Julius explained that he found her body and buried it because he was afraid of being framed. The general didn't refute it, and I don't see any harm in keeping the details of her burial to ourselves." I could only imagine the general's shock when Aria's body didn't turn up.

"You have a good heart, Seraphina, thank you. As awful as the past hours have been, you have no idea what a relief it is to finally know the entire truth." This was the first time she had called me by my first name. "You know, society is not forgiving when it comes to those who are different. All these years, we've worried ourselves sick that if Julius was innocent, he would be blamed for crimes he didn't commit. It seems our worries were well-placed.

"Still, the worst of it all, which I will regret as long as I live, is not having believed Julius when he told us the killer was General Lewis. At the time, it seemed farfetched, and defaming someone's name such as the general's would have come with a terrible penalty.

"Even if Julius was correct, he did not have the ability to explain it, to make a case of it. He had no proof. People would have scorned him, for it was his word over the general's. The falsehood of social status, indeed, is the stumbling block of humanity. Feeling that we had no choice, we made our son swear to never speak of it again." Her stability faltered, and she broke down crying again. "We bound him with a terrible burden."

Not in a million years could I have foreseen all the angles of their torment. Trapped in a life of fear must have felt like they were dead. Those times when they had seemed high-strung when it came to their son made perfect sense now. The mystery surrounding them had been clear as daylight, but I had failed to see it for what it was.

"You mustn't torture yourself anymore. Julius's deeds speak for his character. If it hadn't been for his intervention, I would be dead. He saved my life. And not only that, he spared the life of the general. If Julius had really wanted to kill him, he had ample opportunity to do so, but that's not who Julius is."

Her face lit up. "You have no idea how relieved I feel that, from now on, things will be how they should have always been, with my Julius free of unnecessary worries. My Julius is good. He is reserved, but his feelings run deep."

And how deep we might never know, for indeed, he is a reserved man.

CHAPTER 23
BALANCE OF LIFE

It was almost noon. Seeing that peace of mind had come to Mrs. Goswick at last, I set out to find Elliott. The last time I'd seen him, his spirit had collided with my dead body, and he had stumbled to the sitting room. I'd lost track of him during the ordeal that followed.

My breath caught when I saw him on the sofa. He lay on his back, his light dim. I knelt alongside him, placing my tangible hand on his intangible one. I could tell something was rapidly changing in him and I intuitively knew it wasn't good.

"I've been looking for you." I gave him a warm smile.

"We defeated him," Elliott muttered.

"You saw who he is?"

"I did. He sent me to war, didn't he?"

"I'm afraid so."

"At last, he'll get what he deserves."

I pressed my hand to the skin on my neck. It still hurt. "You must know I'm indebted to you for all you did and for fetching Julius."

"Don't mention it. I took a huge risk not knowing if he was back, but what else could I have done?"

"You did the right thing." The curiosity arose, and I asked, "But how did you know the killer wasn't Julius?"

"Julius would have never attacked his parents—his allegiance to them is unshakable."

"Indeed, he is loyal to his family and friends—too bad you two didn't get along," I teased.

"Yes, too bad." He smiled faintly, and after contemplating me for an instant, he said, "This is it, Seraphina. I'm leaving."

"Leaving where?"

"Wherever the wind takes me. It is time for me to let go of All Hallows—to let go of my quest."

"You are speaking rubbish, and I don't like rubbish."

"The energy needed for my spirit body to be here has been exhausted. I'm being drawn to whatever place I belong," he explained as his light went a shade darker.

"I thought you had more time..." Refusing to accept reality, my mind scrambled to find a solution only to hit a wall of awareness. The memory of my spirit returning to mortal life flooded over me. "When you merged with my body and brought me back to life...you exhausted your energy... you gave yourself up."

"Please respect my decision. You do not have my permission to be crestfallen about it. I wanted to do it, and after the fiasco with Julius the other day, I was weak already."

"I was right. The day the killer chased me in the woods and I was about to give up, you transferred some of your energy to me. You saved me then too."

"I shall never forget you, Seraphina Addington. You have done the unimaginable for me."

"Nothing compares to what you've done for me."

"Nonsense. When you came here, I was in a bad place. Life was dark and without hope. You found me and brought happiness back to my spirit. You even confronted the ghost of the woman. I'll never forget how frightened you were." He chuckled sadly. "And so you know, there wasn't any other time in my ghost life I was more grateful to be a spirit than when you wielded the gun. Your aim is atrocious."

I laughed, a mixture of love and sadness. "I appreciate your honesty, and I need to be honest as well. When I came to All Hallows, I was also in a dark place. My parents sent me here because they believed the escalating casualties were driving me mad and because I could see spirits. Before the war, I saw a few apparitions, but it was easy to brush them aside. When the air raids started, disembodied people were everywhere, roaming the streets, lost in grief. There was so much I couldn't understand, and though I never really said it aloud, they frightened me to the point I wondered if I was losing my mind. All of that changed when we became friends. Now I know that the ability to see beyond mortal eyes is not a curse but a gift. You helped me understand a whole new world. You helped me to make peace with myself."

"I'm very happy to hear that," he answered. "It's been good."

What would happen to him after he moved on? I rejected the notion that he would be alone forever. That reality was too cruel. Elliott's only sin had been to love too deeply, for in the end, he had given up his time here to save me. Our first encounter flashed through my recollection.

"Are you afraid?"

"Should I be?"

"Yes, you should be."

"Why?"

"Well, in case you haven't noticed—I'm dead."

A ghost—my friend—my rescuer from more than just death.

In agony, I pleaded, "Please forgive me. I should have found Rose."

"There is nothing to forgive. I'm tired. Never thought I could be. but I am." As he spoke, to my horror, his legs started to vanish. With every second that passed, a bit more of them was erased until I couldn't see them. His arms went next.

"Please don't go," I begged and placed my hand on his shoulder, but unlike in the past, I couldn't feel anything. No warmth, no electric current, nothing. "Please stay with me."

"It's my time. There is peace in that."

I held his gaze for what I feared was the last time, realizing that something of his own strength to fight had ebbed away. His beautiful green eyes pierced mine with a depth that told me we loved each other, and our connection would never end. Somehow, someday, I would see him again. "Elliott, I love you." Tears filled my eyes.

"A part of me stays with you. It will guide you to find me someday. And I do hope that good-for-nothing American makes his way back in one piece." He smiled the sweet smile I had come to love.

The eraser ran its final stroke. My ghost friend was gone, leaving me in a state of dismal emptiness. Still on my knees, I ran my hand over the spot where Elliott had been. How would I live without him? I hid my face in my hands, and my head dropped to the sofa as I wept.

It couldn't have been more than a few seconds later when the front door burst open, snatching me from my disconsolation. Brilliant light filled the grand hall, spilling into the sitting room, and with it came an overpowering wave of serenity. It was as if the earth itself stood still for just that moment in time. I shielded my eyes against the blinding luminosity and stood, allowing my vision to adjust to the change. Emerging from the effulgent light, the ghost of a woman crossed the threshold and advanced toward me.

She was tall and graceful and wore a cream-colored dress. Her black hair flowed to her waist in perfect harmony with the beauty of her fair skin and blue eyes. Each step she took was filled with self-confidence— with the conviction of one who had fought life and won. One who was here to command and be obeyed.

Although this woman was younger and bore no signs of aging, the resemblance was undeniable. "Rosalynn...?"

Halting at the end of the sofa, she responded, "I am Rose Lewis. I'm sorry I deceived you when you visited me."

"Rose...?"

"Yes, Rose. Pretending not to be myself when you came to London was a hard thing. I must say you are a diligent woman."

She beheld the spot where Elliott had been with a tenderness only profound love could produce. As if by magic, lines started to form there, one after another—like the strokes of the pencil—and little by little, the picture was restored to its former state. I was rendered speechless as Elliott reappeared. His eyes connected with Rose's, and the love I saw in them spoke of an unbreakable bond and a calm sense of belonging. At last, the anguish of the many years of waiting, of wandering and wondering, were cast away. They were finally home, as if they had never left. Elliott left the couch to embrace his love. They fell in each other's arms, and the light that engulfed them shone like a million diamonds under sunlight.

Elliott said, "I can't believe this is happening—I can't believe you are here."

"Neither can I—what took you so long?" Rose smiled brightly.

Elliott cupped Rose's face in his hands and looked into her eyes. "I love you, Rose."

Their lips met in a passionate display of affection, leaving no doubt that love in the hereafter was something to look forward to.

When they stepped apart, Rose looked about and observed, "All Hallows—I have missed this place and all the memories."

My thoughts spun in perplexity. "How can you be dead? You were recovering...and, Elliott, you are back. How?"

Rose answered first. "I wasn't recovering. I was moving on. Working with the convalescents taught me how to cope with the disease, but when I found out it had infiltrated my lungs, I knew I had lost the battle. All I wanted was to die in my home, away from the suffering of the sanitorium.

"You know, working at a place where death is a constant visitor, I was bound to see ghosts now and then. Hence, your mention of the ghost at All Hallows brought me here as soon as I died. Once I crossed onto the property, the knowledge of what Elliott was going through came to me."

"Her energy," Elliott explained, "working through the love we have for each other, reached me and pulled me back before I had completely left."

"You have no idea how long and dreary these past years have been, not knowing if I would ever see Elliott again. When I first moved to London, the thing that kept me going was helping the soldiers recover and return to their families. Every time I dressed someone's wound, helped them to walk again, or simply stayed with them as they took their last breath, I thought of Elliott and wondered how it would have been to spend my life with him. And now, thanks to you, I don't have to wonder anymore." She looked at him with overwhelming affection. "And for that, I'm forever grateful to you. Thank you."

"I don't think thank you will ever be enough, but for what it's worth," Elliott reiterated, "a million times, thank you."

"It was my pleasure."

"Dealing with me was a pleasure?" Elliott joked.

"Sometimes more than others," I joked back. "Rose, may I ask you something?"

"Anything."

"John Lewis was apprehended this morning after he tried to kill me. Everything points to him being the killer of the woods. Was it him you suspected?"

"Yes. In the months preceding his wife's passing, I saw alarming bruises on her. She became quieter and more withdrawn, and at times she seemed terrified of him. She did have some type of skin disease, but I doubt that was the cause of death. Her last Christmas party at the mansion, I overheard the maids saying John had beaten Helen, believing she'd had an affair with the footman. But trust me, it was all in his head. She was a good woman.

"The circumstances of her death were suspicious, but since the war had broken out and he was on active duty, there was never an investigation. His dark side had grown stronger by the end of the war. And after I'd lost my father, he frightened me more than I could bear. I was afraid to even write his name in my diary, and when I looked in the mirror and saw the same dread I had seen in Helen's eyes, I knew I had to leave. I feared he would come after me, and if I refused him, he would harm me."

"Even when you were his cousin…" I reflected.

"Family or not, the man's evil made no distinctions. I had to disappear."

"I can understand that," I said, starting to understand the sacrifice both Rose and Elliott had made. My suspicion appeared to have been well-placed. Helen had been the general's first victim. Perhaps his jealousy had been the beginning of his lunacy and the carnage of war had only fed his impulse to kill.

"And there is much I need to bring you up to speed on," Elliott told Rose.

"But tell me, what now?" I interrupted.

"We move on together. I have a feeling our destination is going to be paradise, indeed." Brimming with happiness, Elliott wrapped an arm around Rose's shoulders.

"Good-bye, Miss Addington," Rose said.

"Good luck to both of you."

With bright smiles, they left the house just like mortals would, through the open door. The afternoon light inundated the foyer, but it was nothing compared to the Kennards' radiance. I ambled to the window, processing our visit and their departure. The developing scene outside brought fresh tears to my eyes.

Elliott, Rose, and Julius formed a triangle in the garden. I could tell their reunion was a joyous one filled with apologies, clarifications, and affection. Rose's return brought healing to the men's relationship. When the ghosts were ready to depart, Rose hugged Julius, and Elliott patted his shoulder.

The happy couple sauntered into the woods and evaporated amid the greenery of the trees, reminding me of the painting in Rosalynn's house. Julius stared after them for the longest time. He would miss them as much as I would, for their ineffable love story would live on in our memories forever.

There were days when it was challenging to believe everything that had taken place, days when believing that all of it had been a product of my imagination, especially Ross's departure, made things easier to cope with. Nonetheless, the passage of time has an interesting way of diluting memory, of muffling grief. I feared the day Ross's face would vanish from my recollection. I thought about him daily, reconstructing his features in my mind, not allowing the memory of him to fade.

The inquest had come and gone. Aria's brother had come down from London. He'd identified the items found with her, and the medical examiner had done his work. In the pocket of her dress, they'd found the vestiges of a piece of paper, utterly obliterated, of course. I surmised it was what Aria had been looking for when she'd fumbled with her pocket as her remains were disinterred. After she had read Mary's letter, she hadn't put it back in his satchel but had kept it. If only Julius had searched her pocket before burying her. Stuck between the bones of her hand, they had found a button. Not an ordinary one, but one fallen from the uniform of a high-ranking official. Sadly, the gardener had missed that as well.

Interestingly, it wasn't the abundant evidence incriminating John Lewis that convicted him of his crimes. It was his willful confession, which included the murder of Helen. Long ago, Mrs. Goswick had quoted from *The Count of Monte Cristo*, describing the general's inner torture all too well: *The woman one loves is holy....moral wounds...they remain fresh and open in the heart.*

I couldn't help but feel pity for him as he sat in the inquest, lost in thought, lost in time. Evidently, his heavy conscience did not want to go on fighting for his life. He seemed relieved to be done, as was the entire forest. In a matter of weeks, he would hang.

Knowing how calculating he was, I wasn't surprised to hear that he'd drafted a last will and testament, allocating his assets to different entities. What did surprise me was that he left the manor "to the woman who brought him to justice and peace to All Hallows."

He also left an exorbitant amount of money to the Goswicks, with the contingency that they work at the manor as long as I required their services. The Goswicks made it clear that even without the financial aid, they wouldn't let me fend for myself. And with Caroline's announcement of her engagement to Robertson, her parents were only the more delighted to keep me around.

The accommodations were good, but the gifts stirred conflicting sentiments in me. I couldn't decide if John Lewis was honestly remorseful for his actions and this was his way of showing it or if it was his way of keeping a grip on our lives, even after he was gone. Maybe time would help me sort it out.

Meanwhile, Rose's maid, Dorothy, had reached out to the Goswicks to deliver a package her employer had left for them. Rose had written a lengthy letter to the groundskeepers. There were also copies of the anonymous letters she'd sent throughout the years to Scotland Yard, accusing General Lewis of murdering the young women in the New Forest. If only they had taken the tips seriously, perhaps he would have been caught sooner. She also left her current diary, along with a request for her remains to be laid to rest alongside her parents in the Burley cemetery.

I took the liberty of asking Dorothy for one of Rose's paintings—the one of the couple in the woods. It now hung in the entrance hall of All Hallows, reminding visitors of its true owner, Lady Rose Lewis. To me, it was a vivid reminder of Elliott and Rose and of true love.

I also attended the proper funeral of Aria in London. The bright morning sun illuminated the graveyard. There was an almost palpable calmness in the air. As Caroline and I neared the burial site, I saw Aria in a beautiful red dress, standing among the small group. The darkness was gone. She was a beautiful woman with the light of hope shining in her countenance. Being among her brother and friends, though they could not see her, she radiated happiness. Her soul was free at last.

When the reverend ended the ceremony, the people respectfully dispersed. Aria lingered for a moment, and finding my gaze she mouthed, "Thank you." She then followed those she knew out of the cemetery. It was the last time I saw her.

Taking advantage of this trip, I also visited my parents. Our reunion provided them the opportunity to see how much I'd grown since I left London. It proved that despite the horrendous events, their sacrifice had been worth it. I did try to convince them to join me in Burley, but they were determined to stay in London and rebuild our home there.

Days after, Vicar Baker came to visit. As we spoke in the garden, he took my hand without permission and assured me that if I accepted him as a close friend, I would never have to fear anything. His power and influence, he said, were enough to protect me.

"Thank you for your concern, but I'm afraid I must ask you to leave," I said, hoping to extricate myself from his unwelcome proposition.

"Surely you don't mean that." He took a step closer.

"I do. Please leave."

"You know, you could even borrow the old books from the cellar."

"I'm not interested in them anymore."

Grasping my arm, he pulled me into him harshly and, lowering his head to mine, tried to kiss me. Pressing both of my hands to his chest, I gave him a push that sent him flying backward. Before he could recover, I beat a hasty retreat to the house. When I felt his grip on my shoulder, I wanted to scream in anger. I fisted my hand as I turned, but before I could take a swing at him, Julius had him by the scruff of his neck.

"You heard Seraphina. She told you to leave. And unless you want me to drag you to the church, you'd better start walking." Julius snorted.

By now, the entire forest knew the story of Julius hauling General Lewis across the yard to the excavation site and back, which meant no one dared cross Julius Goswick.

"There is no need for that," the vicar responded, looking up at the gardener. "I'll be on my way."

"If you ever bother Seraphina again, or any woman in town, I'll bury you in a grave so deep they'll never find you," Julius warned, throwing him to the ground. And I feared he wasn't bluffing.

"Good day, Father Baker," I said as I watched him scamper down the path. In a way, I wished Julius would have given him a few blows, but perhaps that was reserved for a future time.

From the gardens, I beheld the ancient structure against the descending sun. Finally, All Hallows was at rest. No ghosts haunted her. No secrets kept her a prisoner. She was free, and there had been a radical change. Where there were shadows, there was now light. Where there was heaviness of spirit and despair, there was now joy.

All Hallows was a testimony that we fear the unknown because we don't know how to deal with it. The things we called supernatural, I have come to understand, were merely things natural about which the laws were not yet understood. Through the darkness of hardship and uncertainty, I found a happiness that was lived over and over again in memory. In confronting my fear of mingling with the dead, my weakness became a strength, one that blessed me as much as it did those who had passed on.

Piper, who had returned to sleep at the manor, barked in excitement, drawing my attention to the main path. A man with a limp, his right arm in a sling, moved slowly in my direction. Instead of running to greet the newcomer, my furry friend bolted toward the house.

I took a long look at the man. Was he a ghost? I quailed at the prospect, for I had dreaded this very moment ever since he'd left. They said history repeated itself, and awake or asleep, I feared that, in my case, it would be true. The nearer he came, the more convinced I was of his identity. If he was an apparition, how could I face him? This couldn't be our last good-bye, no, not like this.

When he was but a few yards from me, my body went cold, my mind blank.

"I had to see you before I leave," Ross said.

I couldn't react. I couldn't speak.

"My airplane was shot down during our fourth air raid. I spent a while at the hospital..." He paused and looked at me in a curious way. "Seraphina, are you okay?" Then he closed the distance between us, cupped my face in his hands, and kissed me.

A surge of oxygen filled my lungs at his touch. He was made of flesh and bones. He wasn't dead. He was very much alive.

As I embraced him and felt his warmth, my entire being was filled with contentment. At last, I was in perfect harmony with life itself. "Ross...I thought I'd lost you."

He chuckled nervously, sharing my feelings. Indeed, it was hard to believe he had survived. "No, you aren't that lucky." Holding me a little tighter, he informed, "I heard about what went down after I left. I was desperate to see you."

"General Lewis had London recruit you. He wanted you out of the way."

"I suspected as much, but I'm a tough bird to kill."

Seeing his body shake a bit, I signaled to a bench. "Let's sit."

We settled on the stone bench near a patch of azaleas.

"Do you remember the night in the forest when you found me with Samuel?"

"How can I ever forget?"

"You saved my life that night. The general must have found out I had gone to town, for he was hunting me. And getting Samuel out of the equation wouldn't have been a problem for him. On the contrary, he could have framed him for my murder." I recoiled at the thought.

Ross swore in anger. "He is a clever old devil. His skills are those of someone who has survived many battles. Not many of us can compete with that. The ease with which he moved in the woods should have convinced me of his identity, but it seemed so impossible." Incredulous, he reflected, "So farfetched yet so true."

If only he knew how right he was. The Goswicks had traveled the same road of disbelief and helplessness against a man whose standing in society was too lofty to be touched.

Deciding that the monster of the general had had enough of our time, I rewound our conversation. "Wait, did you say you are leaving?"

In a disheartened tone, he answered, "I've been released from active duty. There is something wrong with my hip. I'll fly back to the States to have it looked at."

Was I supposed to be happy or sad? My heart was pulled in two different directions at once. I was sad he would leave but happy that he was alive. "When do you go?"

"They said soon, whatever that means. But so you know, I plan to spend the rest of my time here, with you."

"I'd like that. Ross, there is something I need to tell you. Something that I should have told you before you left."

"What is that?"

"I love you."

His face lit up at my words. "Well, finally—I thought you would never say it. And so you know, I love *you*." Lifting my chin with one finger, he raised my eyes to meet his. "Come with me. Come to the States."

The thought of going to the States had never entered my mind. So far from home. I smiled. "Someday, I just might."

"What can I do to convince you?"

"Come back for me."

Leaning into me, he pressed his lips against mine and whispered, "You know, I just might."

Thank you for reading! Did you enjoy? Please add your review because nothing helps an author more and encourages readers to take a chance on a book than a review.

And don't miss more from Marcia Armandi coming soon! Until then read SORROW'S POINT, by City Owl Author, Danielle DeVor. Turn the page for a sneak peek!

Also be sure to sign up for the City Owl Press newsletter to receive notice of all book releases!

SNEAK PEEK OF SORROW'S POINT
BY DANIELLE DEVOR

It all started with a phone call. To a lot of people, a phone call is a mundane thing, an everyday occurrence that, for the most part, has no bearing on your everyday life. But this phone call, it was something else entirely.

Here I was, sleeping in my bed, warm, relaxed, and then the phone rang. I looked at the clock—three a.m., the true witching hour. I blinked the sleep from my eyes and groaned. The phone rang again. *Are you kidding me?* I picked up the phone.

"Jimmy?" the voice asked.

I wiped my hand over my face to try to wake up. *Who in the Hell is this?* I sat up, pushing the covers off my legs. I turned and dangled them over the side of the bed. It hit me then. I recognized this voice. It was the voice of my past; someone I hadn't heard from in years. This voice, after all this time, seemed somehow unchanged. "Will."

I heard him breathing into the phone. He sounded distressed.

"I'm sorry for calling so late," he said.

Why he was apologizing, I wasn't sure. The deed had already been done. I'd be lucky to get back to sleep at all.

I heard him cough. "It's about Lucy," he said.

Now, I was confused, and honestly kind of irritated. He was calling, waking me up, for someone I didn't even know. "Lucy who?"

"Lucy ... my daughter."

I felt like someone had sucked all the air out of my lungs with a shop-vac. At one time, Will and I had been great friends. I didn't even know he was married, but then, maybe he wasn't. "I ... I didn't know you had a daughter, Will."

"Ah Hell." I heard what sounded like him hitting the steering wheel with his hand. "Shit. Has it been that long?"

I rolled my eyes. *Yes, you idiot, it's been years.* "Yes, it's been that long."

I heard him blow his nose. "Well," he said. "I have a question."

"Okay."

"My daughter needs help, and I don't know what to do."

I wiped my eyes with the back of my hand, trying to wake up. "What's going on, Will?"

He took a deep breath.

"Do you still believe?" he asked.

My eyebrows wrinkled together. They always did when I got confused about something. My mother used to comment on it all the time. It irritated the Hell out of me. But with Will, he wasn't making any sense. "What are you talking about?"

"God. I'm talking about God."

Now it was my turn for a breath. I hadn't been asked that question for a long time. Ten years at least. "Yes, I still believe."

Again, I could hear him take a breath. "Can I meet you somewhere?"

I sat up straighter. "Now?"

"Please, Jimmy. I know this is a lot to ask, but please."

I rolled my head backwards towards the ceiling. I allowed my breath to escape, and my shoulders slumped. My chance at sleep was totally gone. "Where are you?"

"Sitting in your driveway."

I jumped up and pulled back the curtain next to the bed. Sure enough, there he was sitting in my driveway in what looked to be a green Toyota 4Runner that had seen better days. I waved, let the curtain fall and hung up the phone.

It was damn creepy, and I didn't like it. Something was wrong about this whole situation. Least of all, someone I hadn't talked to in over ten years randomly showing up at my house in the middle of the night.

I dropped my phone on my bed. "Dammit." Bed looked good right now, going downstairs didn't. I left my bedroom, stumbling slightly. When I got downstairs, I turned on the hallway light and opened the door. He was standing there, blonde hair mussed, face white, hands shaking. What the Hell had happened to him?

"Come in," I said.

He shuffled in and turned left, walking right into my living room. He narrowly avoided my pile of books and sat down in my old brown recliner. I shuffled my feet on the brown shag carpet then I sat opposite him on the sofa.

"I'm scared, Jimmy," he said.

I shook my head. "I'm not trying to be mean, but what's that got to do with me?"

He sat forward in the chair and looked me in the eyes. "I need a priest."

I sighed. I should have known. "Okay. But I'm not a priest, Will "

His eyes looked haunted, by what, I had no idea, but it was unsettling to see him this unhinged. "I know," he said. "But *they* won't listen to me, and Lucy needs one."

I paused. This was just too weird. "Why do you think Lucy needs a priest?"

Will wiggled out of his coat and laid it on the floor beside the recliner. His arms were scratched so badly, it looked like he'd recently tangled with a lion.

· "See what she did to me?" he asked. His eyes had taken on a crazed look. "Lucy needs a priest. She's possessed."

I sat back. You don't randomly hear someone talk about possession every day. "Why do you say that?"

He looked at me, his face suddenly very serious. "Because she is."

Only I would get someone off their rocker looking for an exorcist at three-o-clock in the morning. For the person to be someone I knew made it all the more strange. "Are you sure? Have you thought about taking her to a psychiatrist?"

His hands clenched the armrests of the chair so hard that his knuckles turned white. His face turned red, and his eyes seemed to bulge from their sockets. "She was in a fucking hospital for two weeks!"

He jumped out of the chair and began pacing across my floor. "They could do nothing for her, and they wouldn't after she almost gouged out a nurse's eye."

This wasn't normal. "How old is Lucy?"

He stopped his pacing. "Six."

I looked up at him. "You're telling me a six-year-old almost gouged out a nurse's eye?"

"Yes." He sat back down in the recliner.

"Will, that could be a bunch of things—"

"We haven't talked about the cat."

The more I heard, the more I wondered if it was Will who needed the psychiatrist.

He stared at me, but more so, he stared through me, lost in his thoughts.

I didn't know what to do. Even when I was a priest, I never had anything like this happen. It was going to be a long night.

#

My name is Jimmy Holiday. According to my mother, we're related to Doc Holiday, but honestly, I doubt it. For one, no one in my family has amounted to much. My father was an alcoholic, a nice drunk he was, but a drunk nonetheless. My mother, an alcoholic as well, is a different animal entirely from my father. Even though she's always been a housewife, and content to be so, she has these grandiose ideas. Let's put it this way, she could give Hyacinth Bucket from the British comedy *Keeping Up Appearances* a few lessons.

In a roundabout way, that's how I ended up becoming a priest. Church was the one place I felt relaxed. My mother was always bickering at my father about this or that. Sometimes, I wonder if she drove him to drink, but I knew better. There was a darker story beneath all of that.

It's not that I feel scarred by my childhood or anything; it's just that I know our childhoods play a part in how we turn out.

But I digress. I took solace in church. It always felt like a safe place to me, and one day when I was fourteen, Father O'Malley asked if I'd thought about becoming a priest. All it took was that one question and I was hooked. As soon as I graduated from high school, I entered the seminary and that was that.

I was fine until I finished and continued "going out amongst the people." That was when I met Tabby.

She didn't go to the church I was assigned. In fact, she didn't go to church at all. I would see her, long red hair blowing in the wind, walking past my church each day. Finally, one day I could bear it no longer and spoke to her. From that first word, I was done for. The church no longer held me. It was the beginning of the end.

I fell for her fast. Ironically, we didn't even have a physical relationship at that point. A parishioner noticed I was spending a lot of time with a pretty young lady. I guess she figured that since Tabby was pretty and I was young, they needed to say something. Unfortunately, what they thought was going on and what was actually going on wasn't the same thing. I hadn't turned my back on my vows then, but the parishioner extensively used poetic license and contacted my superiors. I was brought in for an interview. Needless to say, that interview did not go well. I was pissed—not only at the little old biddy who lied, but at my superiors for believing her instead of me. They wanted me to change dioceses and get away from Tabby as fast as possible. I had had enough. If they weren't going to believe me, then why was I a priest? When I refused to stop seeing Tabby and refused to move, they defrocked me.

I moved into an apartment, enrolled in college and worked part time at the library. I had a Hell of a debt to pay off. When you leave the church — whether you are kicked out or you quit, you have to pay the church back for your education. Tabby and I tried to stick together, but between my schedule and hers, it just wasn't working. Eventually, Tabby and I parted ways. I got a degree in Graphic Design, began working professionally, and minus my irritation about the past, I've been pretty happy ever since. Until the three a.m. phone call that is.

#

I got up from the couch and went into the kitchen. It was too damn late, and I needed some caffeine. My kitchen was a galley style that hadn't been updated since the seventies, but I liked it. Green refrigerators rock, no matter what anyone else tries to tell me.

I pulled out the coffee maker and got it started. Then I went back into the living room. Will hadn't changed positions.

Suddenly, he whipped his head around and looked at me. "Can we turn on some more lights?"

I didn't ask. The way my hallway was situated with my living room, the hallway light provided enough light for me to see perfectly fine. I couldn't read in the light, but it wasn't uncomfortably dark – at least not to me. Maybe the darkness he felt was creeping up on him. I walked across the living room and turned on the lamp.

"I can't stand the dark," he said.

I walked back over to the sofa and sat down.

"I know you think I'm crazy ..."

Yeah, he seemed crazy all right, but I wasn't about to tell him about it. "You seem scared."

He nodded. "I feel safe here."

I sighed. I had no idea if I could do anything to help him. "Will, I need to know what's going on."

He took a deep breath. "I wish I'd never gone to Sorrow's Point."

Don't stop now. Keep reading with your copy of SORROW'S POINT, by City Owl Author, Danielle DeVor.

Don't miss more from Marcia Armandi coming soon. Until then, discover SORROW'S POINT, by City Owl Author, Danielle DeVor!

A defrocked priest offers to help an old friend with a sick daughter, but he has no idea what truly awaits him in this story of supernatural horror.

The Blackmoor residence rests upon the outskirts of town with a history of magic, mayhem, and death, Jimmy Holiday must decide if the young girl, Lucy, is only ill, or if the haunting of the house and her apparent possession are real.

After the house appears to affect him as well with colors of magic dancing before his eyes, rooms warded by a witch, and a ring of power in his voice, Jimmy is met by a transient who tells him he has "the Mark."

Whatever being "marked" means, Jimmy doesn't care. All he wants to do is help Lucy. But helping Lucy means performing the one thing he swore he would never do: an exorcism.

Will he survive long enough to save the child—and his soul?

Please sign up for the City Owl Press newsletter for chances to win special subscriber-only contests and giveaways as well as receiving information on upcoming releases and special excerpts.

All reviews are **welcome** and **appreciated**. Please consider leaving one on your favorite social media and book buying sites.

Escape Your World. Get Lost in Ours! City Owl Press at www.cityowlpress.com.

ACKNOWLEDGMENTS

My deepest gratitude goes to my husband, Chad. Thank you for supporting me through the ups and downs of the writing process. I couldn't have done it without your love and fair criticism.

My heartfelt appreciation goes to my forefront editor, Zach A. Smith, who endured countless revisions. Thank you for your blunt advice and steady patience. I am a better writer because of you.

My special thanks to Lisa Green, who requested the manuscript within hours of submission and pitched it to the acquisition team. Thank you for your hard work and priceless advice in bringing *The Ghosts of Lewis Manor* to publication.

Last, but not least, a huge thanks to the entire team at City Owl Press for believing in me as an author. It is my pleasure to work with such fantastic people.

ABOUT THE AUTHOR

MARCIA ARMANDI was born and raised in Argentina. She is a soccer fanatic and loves listening to tango. Marcia studied International Family History Research and Writing. After decades of compiling personal histories, she has developed a profound gratitude for the strength that can be found in families. So it is that through her fiction, Marcia explores the meaning of love and loyalty in times of fear, war, and finally, death.

Marcia is the award-winning novelist of the Shadows of Time duology: *Awaken, Shadows of a Forgotten Past* and *Alive, Shadows of a Living Past*, which topped Amazon's bestseller list for time travel romance in the United States, Australia, and Canada.

facebook.com/awaken.marciamaidana

twitter.com/MarciaVMaidana

instagram.com/awakenmaidana

ABOUT THE PUBLISHER

City Owl Press is a cutting edge indie publishing company, bringing the world of romance and speculative fiction to discerning readers.

Escape Your World. Get Lost in Ours!

www.cityowlpress.com

facebook.com/CityOwlPress

twitter.com/cityowlpress

instagram.com/cityowlbooks

pinterest.com/cityowlpress

tiktok.com/@cityowlpress

www.ingramcontent.com/pod-product-compliance
Lightning Source LLC
Chambersburg PA
CBHW022220010726
47493CB00002B/541